WITNESS TO DEATH

"Get a shot, Andy. Use your 1200-millimeter lens," John said.

The sea was clogged with coho, perch, largemouth bass, desiccated kelps, burned sea grasses, upended and lifeless squid . . . a great rotting of flesh for miles around.

As the chopper swung low, skimming a mere two hundred feet above the water, Andy unsnapped the guideline. He needed freedom to maneuver into his pack for the change of lens. This was going to be a video like nobody had ever seen.

The light was infernal, even through John's goggles.

Suddenly, two other choppers appeared out of nowhere. No radio contact. The choppers approached on either side, unmarked. The pilot waved them off.

"What's happening?" John shouted.

The choppers came in closer. They were within striking distance. The pilot screamed and threw the craft into a vertical rise to escape disaster. Andy, still unsnapped, was thrown out of the hatch. He clawed at the door, but the force was overwhelming, the light blinding . . . The chopper was still soaring upward and slanting away. Against cold steel, at breakneck speed, Andy didn't have a prayer . . .

FATAL EXPOSURE

MICHAEL TOBIAS

POCKET BOOKS

New York   London   Toronto   Sydney   Tokyo   Singapore

The following novel is a work of total fiction. No attempt whatsoever was made by the author to draw any comparison or likeness to any person, living or deceased; to any institution, university, government agency, small business, private contractor, or corporation. Any such perceived likeness is purely coincidental. As a work of science fiction, all events described herein are purely fanciful.

An *Original* Publication of POCKET BOOKS

POCKET BOOKS, a division of Simon & Schuster
1230 Avenue of the Americas, New York, NY 10020

ISBN: 0-671-72572-6

First Pocket Books printing April 1991

10 9 8 7 6 5 4 3 2 1

POCKET and colophon are registered trademarks of
Simon & Schuster.

Printed in the U.S.A.

For my beloved parents,
William and Betty Tobias

"There is no death. Only a change of worlds."

—Chief Seattle, 1874

CHAPTER 1

NOVEMBER, 1986
Gerlache Straits, Antarctica

They left in the early morning, intending to return by noon. The two men traveled light, decked out in Ralph Lauren cottonwares, a single rucksack between them. Their faces covered with zinc glacier cream, they moved through the choppy water, avoiding fast-moving ice, trying to remember to keep their heads down. The leader of their expedition, Dr. Donald Willard—who remained on the ship—had repeatedly warned everyone about the sun. "Keep your faces down low," he'd reminded the two unenthusiastic men.

The other members of the team stayed inside the *Amundsen*, a polar-class vessel that combined Norwegian rusticity, teak paneling, and old-fashioned bidets with ultramodern navigational equipment. The ship's thermometer showed an unheard-of 76 degrees outside and the reflections off the snow and water were adding to the polar heat. For a continent more accustomed to below-zero weather, such temperatures were freakish.

The two scientists—Shiguru and Pascal—continued toward shore in an inflated rubber Zodiac raft in order to climb up onto the ice shelf and check out an apparently inoperative Dobson spectrophotometer. This portable device, which sat upon a stand mounted on the ice, recorded wavelengths for various molecules in the cold surroundings. Its reason for being in this particular stretch of Antarctica's western peninsula was its unsurpassed capability of measuring the existing ozone. The spectrophotometer literally counted the density of ozone molecules in a vertical column of air stretching from the ground to the top of the atmosphere, some twelve miles above.

There were other such devices scattered about the peninsula. Once the data was recovered, it was compared with a second *opinion,* obtained from the NIMBUS 7 weather satellite that glided over the planet relaying a variety of signals to scientists on every continent.

The process of analysis and corroboration of the two sets of readings took time—as much as two weeks. But for Dr. Donald Willard there weren't two weeks to spare. He had to be certain. Fears had been triggered. Something seemed wrong. The data from the previous test was just too bizarre —unprecedented, in fact. It *had* to be bogus, but the NIMBUS data had not come in yet to corroborate that suspicion, which merely gathered more and more strength in Willard's mind, raising a host of queasy doubts beneath a layer of oppressive Antarctic heat. Hopefully, the reading that Shiguru and Pascal had gone to take would clarify matters. Willard waited impatiently. It would take his colleagues a few hours to complete their task and get back to the ship.

Reaching the shore, Shiguru and Pascal killed the outboard motor and drifted to the one ice-free region before them, a rocky terrain punctuated by small cliffs that served as a nesting site for a large penguin colony. There was a commotion there. A frantic hoopla in the middle of the colony had stirred the entire assemblage of screeching birds.

"It's the heat!" the Japanese scientist said to his companion, staring at the obvious agitation that engulfed the hundreds of restless creatures. Shiguru, trained in the natural sciences, knew that when the temperature soared above 40 degrees, the Antarctic penguin was in trouble. Given the extreme insulation afforded by the bird's thick plumage and subdermal fat, it could quickly expire. He had only heard of this happening once, in a zoo in Africa where the power—and with it the air conditioners—went out, the ice melted, and the penguins perished rapidly.

"They're shitting on one another," Shiguru said to his partner, Pascal, a French atmospheric chemist. He then relayed the same information back to the ship, speaking clearly into his hand-held walkie-talkie.

Willard was listening while seated in the *Amundsen's* computer room. He then heard Pascal relate with an odd note of bemusement, "We're being attacked." The sound of human shuffling, a cacophony of the telltale penguin gutturals were usurped by subsequent silence. The radio must have gone dead, Willard thought. He paused warily, nervous, his head half-cocked, trying to divine what was going on.

"Shiguru? Pascal?" Willard called, talking forcefully into the radio patch. But now he heard only static. The sun's rays could do that to the signal, he reasoned, looking out the porthole at the blinding light. Then he went to the mess hall for a Snickers bar and some coffee.

By midnight, after repeated efforts to reach the men, it was clear to Willard and the rest of the crew on board the ship that the two scientists were in trouble. This had not happened before and the crew was anxious to test its mettle. A rescue party consisting of Willard and three scientist-cum-engineers skilled in crevasse rescue reached the shoreline. The temperature had now fallen below zero and snow-laced wind made it feel much colder. The southern lights, known as the aurora australis, illuminated the hundreds of nesting birds as the four moon-suited scientists skulked across the guano-saturated slopes.

Probing the dark rocky exterior, Willard made out a precarious scene. Many of the penguins had engaged in aggressive feather picking and stood, some of them, haggard and bereft of the down that defined their survival. Some seemed to be dry vomiting. One baby, separated from its mother, looking forlorn, stumbled toward Willard, trying to find shelter against the scientist's thickly clad leg. Willard reached down to touch the bird, which promptly defecated on his hand and stared up at the giant with an imploring look.

Scattered, bleached bones permeated the hillock of nests. Even the nests themselves were haphazard, lacking the orderly construction, the neat array of stones for which this particular species of penguin, the Adelie, were noted. This rookery was in trouble, Willard thought. Nearby, however, Willard noted that other animals appeared more content.

"Stay clear of them mothers!" one of the scientists said as they skirted a piece of beach on which a harem of southern elephant seals lay supine. The seals' late-night assertions— snorts and yawns—suggested the peace and seeming evolutionary lethargy that had prevailed for several million years, Willard thought.

A male, probably weighing four thousand pounds, mounted a female, roaring and snarling, slapping blubber against blubber, then fell back down, spinning around to ward off a younger male that had ventured too close. Willard had seen this behavior before, but there was something else here. Willard couldn't be certain, but he wanted to find out. He cautiously approached the harem.

As Willard crept closer, one of his three companions, Faron, growled, "You piss him off and he'll whip into you like lightning. Cut a man right in half, Donald! Sure as shit!"

But Willard kept moving forward. A grim notion began to register in his mind. At thirty feet he had no doubt. Unless his senses had abandoned him altogether, several of the females were newly dead. But Willard didn't have the time to investigate. He turned back to join the group.

As they climbed over the last of the talus, heading directly for the glacier, Willard thought about what he'd just witnessed. He'd read enough about Antarctic wildlife to realize that something very odd was happening. Life flourished on the fringes of Antarctica. Tens of millions of penguins, seals, three-hundred-year-old adult lichens, graceful pintados and albatross, hundreds of species of colorful fish, squid, whales, krill—a veritable cornucopia—mingled in the water and along the narrow rock-free corridors between the ice and the sea. At least that was the legendary Antarctica.

Willard gathered his strength, fighting off the biting cold that penetrated two parkas and thick woolies, and continued to climb. He couldn't stop seeing that shivering, doomed baby penguin that had looked him right in the eye, shat, puked, and cried out.

By 1:30 A.M. the moon had risen above the sea line. Smooth, bloated icebergs, half-sunken monsters of cobalt large enough to receive a 747, now turned pale and white beneath the varicolored night. The rescuers could see the twinkling of lights two miles out in the middle of the straits where their 186-foot Norwegian polar-class research vessel waited.

Willard's team had been down along the western peninsula for a month now, following up on the astonishing ozone test results of a group of British atmospheric physicists stationed at Halley Bay, one thousand miles away across the Antarctic peninsula. For three years the British observations had yielded measurements suggesting that the ozone layer had somehow shriveled to a fraction of an inch. Scientists back at the space center in Maryland had reevaluated years of satellite data, at first incredulous, then kicked themselves for having written a cutoff point into their computer programs where ozone data was no longer presumed to be reliable and thereby programmed to be discounted by the computer itself. But such data was no anomaly. And the records were still there on the magnetic discs to be deciphered. The National Space Bureau (NSB) had underestimated the presence of chlorine in the polar stratosphere.

"I'd like to be off the ice before sunrise," Willard said, climbing up an aluminum ladder that had been placed against the abrupt labyrinth of glacial seracs, high towers of ice. Everyone else followed him up the ladder, and proceeded across the flat surface of ice. This was the way to the Dobson device. The glacier reared up from the moss-thick terminus that fell in rocky steps down to the water's edge. Suddenly a large brown skua dive-bombed the party from off the ice.

"Gotta be a nest nearby," Faron said, striking out at the eight-foot-wide bird with an ax. Its eaglelike beak struck repeatedly at him.

"You fucking bird!" Faron screamed, thrusting the metallic pick back and forth. The skua normally went after baby penguins and lived in small, solitary nests out in the open along lichen-infested plateaus of rock. Usually the skua only attacked when it was intruded upon. But this particular bird was determined to strike.

"That's it!" Faron screamed, and plunged his ice ax through the creature's neck. "Bull's-eye!"

"Jesus, Faron. You shouldn't of," Metzen called out.

"Yeah?" Faron said, disgusted.

The bird continued to scream and quake, its blood spurting onto the moonlit ice. As Faron scraped his ax clean with his boot, Willard noticed that its eyes were bloody and half closed.

Faron kept on mumbling how "it was him or us," while the party continued on across the ice. From above the first band of hundred-foot-tall seracs, the horizon broke upon them beneath a star-flooded night. Willard took in the gaseous firmament with its colors stretching out from one galaxy to the next. Not the most athletic of the team, he carefully stood higher.

Within an hour the party reached the monitoring station, a metallic congestion of devices partially protected beneath polyurethene, taking up a few square yards. Willard opened the main hatch of the Dobson machine, saw that the data printed out on a small sheet attached to a sensitive stylus had not been retrieved. He set about to do so while the others looked for Shiguru or Pascal. From where the party stood, it looked as if they were probing the moon's surface.

"You guys!" Jack Henessey said, speaking up through the cold. "I think I smell a trail." He kneeled twenty feet away from Willard and the others, examining tracks.

Henessey, an Antarctic buff who could repair nearly any ship's engine or navigate an ice-choked narrows, proved equally indispensable on shore. He moved surefooted across the hard surface, kneeling every so often to follow a track of blood. He was way ahead of the others, who were hard-pressed to keep up with him.

After some time, Henessey reached a point on the undeviating glacial plateau, stopped, and called out, "Are you all right?" He was looking down at something. Willard would never forget the silence that followed. Everyone stood standing back from Henessey, waiting, as the silence built upon itself. "Shiguru? Pascal?" Henessey called out. When there was no response Henessey shouted for help. The rest of the men raced toward him as he hammered in ice screws at the top of what turned out to be a deep cavern in the ice.

Peering down into the total darkness, the headlights on the tops of their helmets illuminated the void but could not offset the darkness or frigid finality: a glacial wound opened tonight could be as easily closed tomorrow. A single length of rope, tied off to a well-placed ax, hung in the depths. The rope was taut, frozen into the groove as a result of the weight that still held it in place. The two scientists were down there.

Henessey quickly tied off the end of his own doubled rope with two locking carabiners, then lowered the eleven-millimeter Perlon rope through a waist harness, which he quickly affixed to himself. The rappel rope was run through another two carabiners, which in turn snapped into the eyelets of two ice screws. Faron belayed Henessey down. He steadied himself by sitting with his boots propped against two downward-driven axes a few feet away from the lip of the crevasse.

"What do you see?" Faron shouted down to Henessey.

"Just hold me, Faron! Willard, Metzen, shine your lights! Here, more . . . there, right, right there. Now hold it."

Henessey saw the hanging bodies. A wave of shudders descended his spine like freezing snow crystals that had gotten under his clothes.

"Shit," Metzen mumbled, loud enough for the others to hear.

"What is it?" Willard called down.

"Them."

"Are they alive?"

"Just hold me. Faron, hold me tight!"

Henessey tried to turn the frozen bodies around. The two scientists had clung together, caught and twisted at the end of their rope, and now faced the ice, where their skin was stuck to the frozen wall. Though there was little room to swing an ax, Henessey chipped away at the tomb that held them. He knew they were dead. The temperature in the crevasse was a deep freeze and these men were unprepared, dressed only in ludicrous cottons.

Henessey turned Shiguru's body around.

The Belgian-born Metzen, a physicist at CAPER, the Swiss Center for Atomic Particle Research, shrank back from the edge, terrified, as Henessey groaned. Willard stood his ground. "What do you see, Jack? . . . Jack!"

"They're dead," Henessey cried.

"Well, let's get 'em out!" Willard shouted. "Jack!"

"There's something . . ." Henessey mumbled from the crevasse.

"What?" Willard hollered. He held on to Faron, his arms wrapped around the bulky man's waist.

"I'm losing my grip!" Faron said, his voice cracking.

"Metzen!" Willard called out. "Don't let him go!"

The two of them began to pull on the rope so that Faron could retake his handhold, but still it was no good. Henessey apparently had freaked out and was not moving.

"Go down after him!" Faron shouted at Metzen, who was in a better position to get down there fast and help Henessey.

"I can't," Metzen said. He was afraid to give up his place, afraid to acknowledge what was happening. Everything about his person rebelled at the idea of going down in there.

"I'll do it," Willard said. "What do I do?"

"You ever rappel?" Faron asked.

"No," Willard admitted.

"Forget it." Faron shook his head, took a deep breath, then began a reorganization. "Here, hold this!" Faron changed positions, turning over the belay rope to Willard, who assumed Faron's spot, his feet positioned against the axes. Faron took the second belay line, tied a figure-eight knot, and snapped the loop into the carabiners on the same ice screws off which Henessey hung. He then wrapped the rope around his waist, twisted it between his legs, and descended over the edge into the crevasse.

As Faron was lowered into the crevasse, he saw Henessey beneath him. One hundred feet down. "Jack, come on, man!" the stout-chested Faron urged. He spat a build-up of green phleghm against the ice wall, wanting to see how green it was—a measure of his continuing bronchitis. Finally suspended at the same level as the others, Faron pulled one of the corpses toward him. Turning it around to face him, Faron gasped.

"Oh, fuckin' shit. . . . Jesus, Willard!"

"What, goddamnit! What?" the cry came from above. Metzen sat frozen, legs akimbo around Willard's waist. Willard, in turn, clung to the ice ax that held the rappel rope. Both men's butts were frozen. The gape before them had swallowed four men. And not another sound was coming out.

"It was the bird, Willard. The fucking bird!" Faron screamed, as he stared crazily at both Shiguru and Pascal, who had lost their eyes. What was left of the corneas and retinas bulged outward, purple, flooded with frozen mucus and puss, like exploded boils. He puked into the aquamarine gape beneath him, where he dangled over a damnation that Henessey now declared, wanting the hell out.

"The same bird must have attacked them! I hate birds!" Faron went on maniacally.

Henessey and Faron used jumars—metal ascenders—to get back up the rope. The urgency of their retreat made this manner of ascent a facile one. Back out on the ice, they rigged a makeshift pulley system to haul up the bodies. Shiguru was small, lean, the product of a traditional Kyoto macrobiotic diet. But Pascal was a giant, bon viveur, built like Falstaff. The combined weight was too much.

"Oh, no!"

"Grab it!"

Willard caught a glimpse of Pascal's hideously deformed face—the burnt and ruptured eyeballs—before the pulley mechanism caved in. The ice screws ripped out without a sound. The first ax snapped into lethal trajectory after them, the steely sharp pick adze catching Metzen's cheek.

"Get it!" Faron hollered.

Henessey dove for the second ax just as it was pulled from its placement. But he didn't reach it in time. The bodies hovered for an instant, then disappeared back into the crevasse, crunching and mingling in the odd collision of flesh against ice, as Faron tried futilely to secure the fast unfurling ropes.

"Don't do it!" Henessey panicked, his hands raised in a futile effort to prevent Faron's error.

There was a scream. Willard watched the slow-motion horror escalate. The rope caught hold of Faron's fist, which frantically clung to the lazy, open hank. With the force of several hundred pounds at free-fall velocity, the hank plunged after the bodies. Faron vanished, his wrist mangled, his big body pulled down into the crevasse.

Henessey counted the seconds, as the scream and then the faraway, clashing thuds vanished. It was over quickly. Then there was silence.

"Oh, my God . . . twelve seconds!"

"Help me!" Metzen cried. The ice ax had gashed his face. Blood seeped from his wounds onto the ice.

"Faron!" Willard screamed.

"Forget it," Henessey mumbled. "There's no way."

Willard turned to Metzen, who was hunched over in a frantic self-saving huddle, blood pouring from his face.

"In your pack, Henessey. There's an antiseptic cloth. Get it. Hurry." Willard was on top of things.

They grappled for pads, cloth—anything that could be used to stop the bleeding. Metzen's jaw was shattered. His teeth, tongue, lips were partially eviscerated. Willard injected him with a syringe filled with morphine. Already the sun was coming up. Willard knew they had to get out. Metzen tried to murmur something. But it was unintelligible. Only Metzen himself knew, even from the horror of his pain, that he was allergic to morphine. Willard and Henessey prepared to start back.

"Janson, can you hear me?" Willard said into his walkie-talkie. But there was only static. Willard cursed as he remembered that their walkie-talkies had been breaking down for weeks.

For several hours Willard and Henessey made their way back toward the ocean, and then the ship, dragging the unconscious Metzen on a makeshift toboggan. By five in the morning Metzen was barely breathing. They carried him a bit further, then agreed to leave him near the rookery, fearing that the journey in the Zodiac, across choppy water, might kill him. They'd have to come back for him.

The birds were deathly still. They had no more energy left to fight. And just as Pascal had seen, there was shit everywhere—not consistent hang-together green shit, the stuff of gunpowder, but loose stools.

The two men passed the elephant seals. There, beneath what had been an orgy of flesh, lay the remains of a great male—a carcass of sorts—partially eaten, partially eroded.

Henessey and Willard untied the Zodiac, careful not to slip on the smooth rocks into the water. They maneuvered back out into the straits. The current was fast and the Mercury 900 horsepower engine was not up to fighting the southern seas convergence waters. Not now.

From the bridge of the *Amundsen,* Janson, the captain, and the others saw the approaching raft. "Alert them!" the captain said.

Janson sounded the ship's horn, which trumpeted with a bellowing echo. Static on the walkie-talkies was broken. The captain could see the Zodiac as he spoke to Willard through his hand device.

"The waves are traveling twenty knots. We'll pick you up downstream. Over. And where is everybody?"

As the raft headed back toward the ship, Willard stared out, meditating on the sun, which was already up. Its spectacular striae bolstered a sea of light. Every cornice, each pointed nunatak and wall of granite shone to the first light of dawn. Cream-colored glaciers, the freshest air on earth—this was the original goodness of creation, the stuff man was made to breathe. Light to see by. Illimitable distance to get lost in. Water as sweet as water gets. Salt, glacial run-off, mineral, elemental. If only he were in a frame of mind to savor it. Willard knew that one could drink the ocean water in Antarctica because of all the melting fresh water from the ice. He leaned over, cupped his hand, and took a sip. The water was freezing. He got splashed in the face. The boat was fighting now to keep a course that would intersect that of the approaching *Amundsen*.

Finally, the two vessels met. A ladder was tossed overboard and Willard and Henessey struggled to climb it. The night had been long. Their muscles were wrecked. Back on board, Willard recounted for the captain and crew what had happened. Henessey had a slightly different version of things. There was enough confusion, anger, and frustration between the two men to warrant, in the captain's estimation, a time-out. No call was placed anywhere, no kin notifications—not yet. They all knew that Metzen was first on their agenda.

"You're not going back," the captain said.

"We're going. We left him, we'll get him."

"Forget this macho crap. Henessey, you're no good to anyone at the moment. Take Willard's lead. Get some sleep."

The men departed for their bunks. Later, after a shower, Willard sat before a computer in the ship's study, tapping into data from McMurdo Base, comparing graphs to those of previous science forays on the southern continent. The SBUV, or Solar Backscatter Ultraviolet, and TOMS, the Total Ozone Mapping Spectrometer, were two instruments up in orbit on NIMBUS 7 since 1978. The McMurdo scientists were, at that moment, busily testing other devices, other scenarios—chlorine dioxide, nitric oxides, sun spots. But none of it yet added up. Willard went back to his berth, bunked down, and lay awake mulling over what had happened—or what was happening.

Several hours later, another team departed to get Metzen. Janson, the captain, the expedition doctor, and two available subordinates, Higgins and Naess, reached shore quickly, having unleashed the larger landing craft from the *Amundsen*. They were not about to take any chances.

"There," Janson said, as they approached the penguins on foot. It was nearly noon.

"Holy Christ . . ." Higgins cried out. The men ran to Metzen, screaming at the birds that had festered around him in a mad eating frenzy.

The men tried everything to get the birds away—kicking them, throwing rocks, stabbing them with their axes. Unafraid, the birds counterattacked. Janson was startled to see that dozens of the larger Adelie, the three-foot darlings of zoos, had turned into cannibals, monsters. The captain realized that the birds were starving to death.

The doctor checked Metzen's pulse. It was cold. All of the men looked at one another. The doctor shook his head.

"He's dead," the captain declared, keeping several birds at bay with an ice ax. "Let's get him back."

By the time they got Metzen away from the rookery, he was covered in blood and penguin feathers. His eyes and fingers were gone. His nose was half eaten.

Many hours later, revived with food and liquid, Willard took careful notes off the computer on the bridge—Lat.S, 62.28.83, Long.W, 56.28.23. GMT 12.50.55. Speed 20.2. Drift 7. The ship's doctor made his report and by nightfall the remaining members of Donald Willard's expedition met in the ship's lounge to discuss their situation.

"You want to be the one to tell next of kin the birds did it? And you think they're going to believe it?" The doctor looked skeptical.

"Well, of course they're going to believe it. Why wouldn't they believe it?" Willard demanded.

The men looked at one another, hit by the senselessness of it. "Maybe you're right," Henessey aired.

"Get serious, gentlemen," the captain said. "Tens of thousands of tourists come down here every summer. When did you last hear of death by penguin?"

The Norwegian first mate, Naess, passed around a warm bottle of red Chianti.

"Whatever it was that set those birds off, others better well know about it," Willard said. "And there was the burn."

"What are you talking about?" Henessey interjected, feeling he had missed something in their discussion.

"There was indeed a burn. I'd concur with that," the doctor seconded.

"What the hell are you two talkin' about?" Henessey said defensively.

"Metzen's iris was blown away—what little the birds missed. He may have stared at the sun too long. You want to go into the infirmary and check, be my guest. I already did." The doctor sipped his glass of wine.

Willard continued. "I saw it in Pascal's face. Now, I'm no doctor, but I know what I saw. If a bird had done that, how do you explain Shiguru's and Pascal's ability to set up a rappel and get down into the crevasse?"

"You guys work it out. But I want a decision by tonight," the captain said, getting up from the table.

The rest of the crew grew silent, staring down at their glasses of wine, looking out portholes. Finally Willard broke the gloomy silence. "I guess that concludes this vacation, gentlemen. There's no more science to be gotten down here—not now. I say we make for the Drake Passage and head back to Punta Arenas. In fifty hours we'll be in a real bed."

The men seemed to agree. The key scientists had been narrowed down to one. This was Willard's expedition. It would be his legacy.

That night, Willard was sitting on the bridge next to the captain when both men noticed an intense splotch of reddish color on the open seas.

"You smell something?" the captain asked him.

"I got a cold. I can't smell anything."

Janson had just come on to the bridge, joined the captain and Willard, and immediately pointed. "Whales!" he declared. "A whole pod. Shit, dozens of 'em."

"What are they?" Willard asked.

"Grays, I think."

But there was something else, something that encircled the whales and fanned out for acres of ocean. The captain brought the *Amundsen* in closer to the fomentation as the

14

vermilion blob passed a nearby iceberg, then encompassed their ship.

"Now I smell it," Willard confessed. "Jesus." He held his shirt up to his mouth and nose. It was a horrible stench.

Henessey was up at the bow of the ship at this time, covering his nose and mouth with a towel. Suddenly he identified the surrounding surge of red. "Krill!" he shouted. A mile of krill. And they weren't moving. The whales passed through them, their enormous mouths wide open, devouring the dead. Hundreds of thousands of two-inch-long shrimplike crustacea in every swallow. Henessey could see the milky-white exoskeletons where the white flesh had withered. Entire clusters of floating bones which the whales fed upon indiscriminately.

From the bridge the captain looked on. "Well, I never saw anything like it, and I've been coming down this way for ten years."

Willard left the bridge for his cabin. He felt sick. The other men retired to their cabins to sit it out, or hovered over toilets, for the smell had the same unpleasant effect as diesel. With sea swells reaching fifty feet, the ship plunged repeatedly into legendary Drake trenches, then came back up at crazy, near-toppling angles. Willard threw up. His eyes hurt. He had a migraine.

CHAPTER 2

APRIL, SEVERAL YEARS LATER
Seattle, Washington

Willard picked his fingernails, chewing on the cuticles with the relish of nervous energy that had no other place to go on a Friday night. He rested against the arm of his cold steel wheelchair to which he was both master and slave. Willard had sores on his behind from the worn-out padding.

Beyond the array of magnetic tape drums and softly glowing work stations sat the night guard, Stan, his vodka in a brown paper bag resting in his lap. He was watching a British game show, "Smart Ass," with his legs propped up against the desk. He coughed up a touch of blood in his raucous laughter. Cleaning off his lower lip with a kerchief, he examined the rag, which was stained from a full day's bleeding.

Stan had been a guard since the first computer was installed twenty-five years before. Willard figured Stan saw his wife, whose name was Dapple, for all of an hour or two a day. She had been a nurse at All City hospital most of her adult life, according to Stan. When Stan came home from the college around six every morning, Dapple would have his breakfast ready. A tough and practical woman, she would dip toast in milk and hand-feed the old drunk. Then she'd be out the door at 7:30. Willard didn't know Dapple, but he knew about nurses. He also knew that Stan and his wife lived somewhere in Northgate, near 105th. He had cause to hate that part of Seattle. It's where the crash happened that had changed his life.

It had been raining, and when the sound of screeching tires and smashing lights abated—days, weeks, months later—he was too broken, too weary to curse the nurses any longer or the sobering turn his life had taken. Between sobs that rose up from lost cisterns of himself and hours spent looking at a picture of his wife he kept near at hand in the hospital, Donald Willard made a slow recovery into his repainted world. The accident happened two years after he'd returned from Antarctica. His spine had been crushed like the ice in a snow cone. Everyone attended Mardi's funeral but him. He remained in obstinate traction for an entire winter.

And then the chair. Every move, each inch had to be negotiated—further reminders that he was permanently ruined. There could be no will to stand. His brain had no counterstrategy, no alternative wiring. Torque at 55 miles an hour, balding radials, a persistent downpour. Pullman cowboys with two old mares in the trailer. This was no matter of destiny. Willard was simply out of business.

Helen Frankenthaler's *Burnt Norton* and Francis Bacon's *Study of a Baboon* brought him back into focus. Something clicked with respect to these two paintings by artists he knew nothing about. No previous exposure. A fortunate, formidable fluke. Forty square feet of dark hills and a sliver of blue, probably a lake, probably Frankenthaler's hope. And Bacon's captive animal, rearing back, the bars surrounding it. Black and blood red, checkerboarded. Pained, in a horrific gesture of final nightmare. There was his own look there.

The juxtaposition of tragedy and new birth worked for the physicist. A miniature world of expression had opened up vistas to which, even in a wheelchair, a scientist like Donald Willard had total access. In their sand and oil and thinned-down colors, these two canvasses afforded Willard a new-found passion, the first since his wife had died. He took up painting.

Other provocations reshaped his flagging career as well—

like the story of a young girl who gained national attention when she wrote a letter to a major manufacturer of chlorofluorocarbons (CFC's). Willard had clipped the story. He was a filing addict. She alleged that her cat, Wayward, was going to die from Freon. She stirred up a great controversy in her town. The manufacturer, Samuel something, caved in. The industry trembled.

Thinking mostly of the little girl and her cat, Willard— new to his wheelchair—managed to testify before a subcommittee in Washington on the unambiguous data in his possession linking CFC's to destruction of the ozone layer above the earth. Even with what little good it did, his testimony left Willard exhausted and subject to attack by industry lobbyists who would stop at nothing to counter his outlandish claims. But Willard was vindicated at the conferences in Vienna, Athens, and Kyoto, where evidence mounted for what Willard and dozens of other scientists had been arguing all along—that the problem was pronounced and the chemical oligarchy was to blame.

Finally, in Montreal, a so-called Protocol agreement among fifty-six nations was reached. Its goal was to reduce CFC consumption and production 50 percent by 1999. The British delegate conceded a comprehensive plan. And then Du Pont's chairman also conceded, following the heckling of the Senate Committee on the Environment and Public Works. This was a radical departure. Civil fines were imposed for CFC violators in Oregon and Vermont.

Of course, such small triumphs were not only too late, in Willard's opinion, but were additionally mired by allowances for even more CFC's throughout the Third World. Neither India nor China signed the agreement. To make matters worse, neither methylchloroform nor carbon tetrachloride were touched by any of the new legislation, two chemicals equally as damaging to the ozone layer as chlorofluorocarbons.

Then, in 1990, delegates from ninety-three nations met in London at the invitation of Margaret Thatcher and hammered out a more comprehensive modification of the Montreal Protocol, an accord that was hailed as a "giant step for mankind." This time, Western powers offered $240 million to the developing world to assist them in curtailing CFC's. The many countries pledged to be rid of most ozone-damaging chemicals by the year 2000. Methylchloroform, carbon tetrachloride, were added to the list of pernicious chemicals to be phased out. But there were countless loopholes in the lionized treaty, dozens of other chemicals that harmed the ozone layer and received little or no attention. Car air conditioners, which used the highly damaging CFC-12, were not regulated. HCFC-22, used in home air conditioning systems and foam hamburger cartons, also escaped regulation. While Willard and the rest of the scientific and engineering communities had long been aware of CFC substitutes, such as helium for a coolant, industry was largely sluggish. There was little that anyone could do to fully assure compliance with the new standards among private corporations abroad. Willard knew that the last decade of the twentieth century would see an escalation of chemical adulterants in the environment, chemicals that were out of control; a runaway effect that no amount of legislation could curtail in time.

"Smart ass!" the TV crowd cheered, as a buzzer clanged and the applause reached a crescendo. A roseate little bugger, maybe ten, hair in his eyes, wiseacre, peevish and calculating, ratted on his fuck-happy, drug-deranged parentage. The Brioni-clad host, turning to the show's on-board shrink for a look of deeply shared commiseration, affectionately patted the ungainly youngster on his head.

"Oh, boy!" Stan shouted, shaking his head at the television. Stan rendered his own commentary from his desk, on the other side of the ten-inch glass wall that separated him from Willard. Seventy-five feet apart, they couldn't see one another.

In the back, Willard asked Burt, his assistant technician, to change tapes. Burt couldn't quite stomach Willard—"the cripple"—bossing him around, but that was his job. Burt was thirty-eight, going nowhere, a long-haired slob, in Willard's estimation—more of a hindrance. He made $6.25 an hour. Willard, who took home $31,000 a year, for which he had no teaching responsibilities, only research, didn't know how the man survived. And didn't care. Burt was a prick and deserved his poverty, Willard reasoned. There was a vindictiveness here, to be sure. Ever since the accident, Burt had gotten stuck on cripple and seeing-eye dog jokes. Willard hated him. An outsider wouldn't want to stay here long—with its weird vibes, incessant hum, perpetually chilled air, and dimmed, fluorescent lights. The data stored in these claustrophobic surroundings made little sense to anyone other than Willard. And tonight he himself was in a blind. Tapping his pencil against his rather large forehead, he slumped back.

He cued in BERING STRAIGHT, POLAR VECTOR MAXIMA on the keyboard for correlation confidence. A ream of data from previous hours suggested southward movement.

"Tape fifteen, Burt. Burt?"

But Burt had zoned out with his headset on. Annoyed, Willard went to change the tape himself. He knew he couldn't get up the one step, but at least Burt would see him and realize he wasn't doing his job.

"Tough life, huh, Donald?" Burt said, removing his headset around his neck. "What tape was that?"

They glared at one another. Willard's chest pounded silently. This was one of the worst parts of it and he didn't have the clout in his department to insist on a new person. He'd been at the College of Washington for ten years, but never on a tenure track. This was the terrible price of delaying a Ph.D. for more field work; not having the power, this night, to can that fuckface Burt.

Stan came back from a good long pee. He opened up the brown paper bag, unwrapped the newspaper, pulled forth a toothpick with its fancy yellow streamer, and took an enormous bite out of the egg-salad sandwich. He turned his attention back to the TV. "Good evening. This is Charles Fields for a KCBD News Brief. A naturally occurring poison. Tonight that's what investigators are claiming may have caused the mysterious death of dozens of whales off the coast of British Columbia. The poison travels up the food chain and has been associated in past years with several mass dolphin kills. We'll have pictures at eleven."

At the KCBD TV station in downtown Seattle, Fields put down his notes. "Okay, camera two, turn yourself off."

"G'night guys."

It was a shift change at KCBD, Seattle's number two independent. Thirty-year-old Fields, a two-year migrant from a station in Miami, with a cheesy pretty-boy smile, golden locks, and cold blue eyes, wet down his forehead in the loo. He returned to the set with a script just handed him by an intern.

"You proof this?"

"Brevetoxin. That's how she pronounced it."

"You orderin' out, get me a pizza. Shrimp. Red pepper. No garlic or onions. And a Heineken."

Wobbly ass, tight enought at twenty. Soon, Fields thought. She was eminently beddable. Five days on the job. He was confident that she was impressed by him. He was feeling victorious. Maybe tonight. He sprawled out in the production lounge, looked over the notes, and measured his coming success.

"Smart Ass" was over. Stan wandered back to Willard's work area for company.

"How she doin' tonight, Capt'n?" he said, lingering over Willard's shoulder as he continued to stare at the gas plasma reds and greens of his Compaq. The little thing was tied solidly to tens of thousands of megabyte power, an "elegant" mainframe system conjured up in cooperation with NOB, NSB, and Fujitsu.

"It's very odd," Willard responded, talking mostly to himself, out loud.

"Oh?" Stan aired with a show of interest. He hadn't had much to drink yet, and his senses were still about him. After midnight, when Willard was sure to be gone, Stan would freely indulge in spirits. That had been the routine for years.

Willard scrolled up, retracing the exodus of figures

through a maze of data base punch-ups. Some of the figures were his own, the result of monitoring stations up north. He had slipped into other data with a hacker's zeal and a submarine commander's nerve. Numbers, graphic translations, quadrant marginalia pertaining to a species of atmospheric chemistry Willard had been following, laboriously recalculating.

For over a year now, Willard had been out there alone, tracking something that few of his colleagues were focusing on any longer, and based upon connections Willard had made years before in the sorry look of an Adelie penguin. But such research was not easy for Willard. Because of the so-called "achievement" of the Montreal Protocol—the united decision to curb ozone depletion—all the pertinent science grants officers had concluded that the problem was going away, and that Willard's research was thus superfluous. Or at least that was always the excuse given.

"You ever been to Canada, Stan?" Willard said, posing the query almost in the abstract.

"Nope. Haven't had the time," he replied with great industry. "Anyway, missus ain't much on travel neither. But what say you, Capt'n?"

"Map. I need a map." Willard saved his screen, saved it again, transferred data from one disc to another, then rolled out into the corridor. "I'll be back," he said to Burt, heading for the elevator.

"No need for ya' to busy yourself. I'll get it," Stan offered.

"I'll get it," Willard cut back emphatically. They'd been through this solicitous business before. Willard, once capable of climbing glaciers, could get his own map, thank you.

Stan smiled graciously and returned to his "office" in time for the beginning of "Colombo."

Willard had his own key to the department library, situated down a long corridor two floors below his computer lab. The stale, spartan room was comprised mostly of atmospheric arcana—hundreds of volumes of transactions, missives from the annals of meteorology, a labyrinth of barometric readings, high-altitude particle physics; tropomass and stratosphere; highs and lows. And there was an atlas—a big one—1 to 25,000. It should do, Willard thought. Beneath the lonely, ugly fluorescence, Willard examined a small locale in northern Canada on the map. Outside in the hallway, a janitor mopped to a dull radio tune. And further down toward the far end of the building a night class concluded. Grad students, voices from Willard's past, were heading out into Seattle's unseasonably muggy night. The weather had been hot for weeks. It was unprecedented.

Sitting alone in the library, Willard pinpointed an approximate. Up in the Northwest Territories. 69.27N by 133.00W. Tuktoyaktuk. He was tracing a mere instinct of his, goaded by co-efficients off the computer. He called the operator, got a 403 area code, 999-2351. Royal Mounted Police. He used his office code to get out. He was calling cold.

No one was exactly racing to pick up, but he held on. It kept ringing. With no answer he finally hung up. He tried the police in Herschel, another Canadian town. The results were the same. Nobody picked up.

Willard wheeled himself back down into the computer room and conferred with the day's weather cumulatives from the whole Arctic Circle periphery. Beauford and Chuckchi Seas, Severnaya Zemlya, Zemlya Frantsa Josifa, the Wandels and Lincoln Seas, the Laurentian Basin. But it was Tuktoyaktuk and the MacKenzie Bay area that held his interest. He tried other numbers at random: 999-2352, 999-2447. Dozens of numbers. Lines were dead or busy in an ill-sounding way, or simply rang off in the late night. Something was not right.

Further south, at Fort MacPherson, however, he reached a voice, faintly disembodied but normal.

"Everybody's sick," she said. "We need more doctors."

"And the weather? What about the weather?"

"Horrible. Can't go outside. Can't even look outside. Too hot. To be honest with you, mister, I miss the old Canada."

"You mean shit weather?"

The voice chuckled, somewhere between incredulity and worried impatience.

Willard consulted the Suitland, Maryland, National Weather Service data, which he had at his fingertips in an adjoining room. A series of mathematical models transformed continually into national and international weather maps—wind speed, temperature, moisture content, and pressure at varying altitudes. He recognized a colossal confrontation of arctic and subtropical air, moving quickly southwestward—a Pacific high pressure system or anticyclone that posed no obvious threat.

But he also had other data, unrelated to the vagaries of weather. He'd been following it for months. It's what took him to the Antarctic years before.

Willard was not finished with his phone calls. He called Mayo, Little Salmon, Tungsten and Dawson, Whitehorse, Skagway. He rang up Sitka and Ketchikan, towns up and down the 1500-mile stretch of the Yukon, British Columbia, and Alaskan outback separating the Bering Sea, where he obtained his last finding, and the Pacific Northwest. He was looking for clues, a pattern, the size of it. The thing was moving, he was sure of it; moving elusively, perhaps, like a tornado high above everything. But Fort MacPherson was the only town to give any sign, albeit an interpretive one. Could it have stopped there? Willard asked. He had his doubts, rapidly figuring the logistics, geography, and the freakish itinerary. Too many unknowns.

Eighteen months he'd been in this chair, working the programs, obsessed with no other cause. Home alone at night, home alone in the morning. Cold sheets, a life bereft, save for the thin line of numbers. This was all he had.

Canadian officials were hard to locate on a Friday night anywhere, whether in Ottawa or Vancouver. Nobody knew anything. There had been no reports, no confirmations, except for that lone voice in the wilderness. Canada was fine.

Willard returned to the computer room. Stan was watching the news. As Willard swung around from the down ramp to his computer table, he heard something about whales. "Turn it up," he shouted.

CHAPTER 3

That same Friday night as Willard tried to reach phone numbers in Canada, twenty minutes away from the college on Seattle's Capitol Hill, overlooking a side yard adrift in dripping ferns, drooping blue spruce, riots of floribunda, and edging lobelia, in the downstairs study of a Cape house firmly built for $4,500 after World War II, John Gage worked at his computer. He was not happy about the way things were going, sweating with disinterest, with little time left to make something of the bland, obsolete copy that he was going to tape Monday afternoon atop the Space Needle.

Gage was, ironically, a video addict despite his venom on the subject. With a twelve-inch square-mounted dish outside, Gage had an avalanche of programming selections and his six-tiered television set continually played six different shows on six miniature screens. Whatever he was doing, this background accompanied him, particularly when his wife was away as she was this weekend. It also helped to cut down the persistent ringing in his ears, a malady he'd endured for ten years.

Gage had first noticed it when he was on a beach in southern California—the pounding of the surf when there was no surf. It happened just like that. Three different opinions, each prescribing different antidotes to suicide, which they assured him would seem desirable at times. They were right. The ringing constituted a silent war that he waged unmercifully alone, somewhere behind the inner ears, sometimes on the right, sometimes the left, occasionally in both. Then it was a murmurous annoyance; now it was an outright roar in the temples. It martyred him without consideration—no pride or accolades, only the constant fraying of a life. Tinnitus.

Gage was now at that point of impasse where he actively sought distraction. "Boom Town" on the lower left screen launched its familiar faces drenched in black gold, arms raised in rejoicing. Above it, a Japanese documentary on the Silk Route or some such; above that, adult entertainment, subjects looking less and less like adults, mostly Thai girls. To the right, on top, CNN—something about a flood in Siberia; lower down, a music video review. And below that, KCBD's Charles Fields was finishing up his nightly anchoring. Everything about Fields recommended his becoming a national anchorman, thought Gage. The asshole commandeered, executed all the right moves, walked over the next guy; he smiled with the easy flourish of a Miss America aspirant, shit jasmine, had been seen to use lipstick and powder his cheeks. Gage couldn't stand him. It's not that Fields was necessarily stupid. He graduated in economics from the University of Florida, produced for public television there, hosted a local news show, then got hired on in Seattle—the big time. Fields was going places and Gage was not.

At age thirty-eight, Gage was nervous. He hated TV, even though he'd been glued to it—producing it, thinking it, speaking it for over a decade. Like doctors' talk on a cruise, computer hackers to each other across electronic billboards, or lawyers' chatter over lunch, TV people wielded a language that was habit-forming. Gage was two people: his former, academic long-winded intellect and the new one-liner man. He had slid into a world in which he had virtually no one to talk to. His profession was about familiarity with highlights, punching up contraries, hitting upon opposition, reducing issues and complexity to rote aphorism and the quickest, nightly matriculation. If you could say it in ten seconds, you were welcome in their homes. Little words, little people, small ideas, two or three max in a newscast.

Keep to the picture, never stray. What you shoot is what you've got. In a crunch there's always the graphics department. Animate a map. Show some statistics. But try to avoid them. That's "Sunday Business Week" stuff. Not nightly news. Not the big eleven o'clock wrap-ups. Every argument in the world against television cannot change the fact that it works—it opens up the world—it showered the blessings of revolution on the Romanian people, provided access to the moon, and gave John Gage's aunt, a totally paralyzed victim of MS living out her life in a reclining bed atop Pittsburgh's Squirrel Hill, something to do all day long—British slapstick, biodegradable soap operas. But Gage was beset by larger doubts that had no business mingling with his manner of earning an income. He was thinking "art." He knew in his gut, as critic George Jean Nathan years before pointed out, that there could be no "authentic" art form that depends for its sole existence on the vagaries of ratings and of popularity.

Gage was stuck in that inner cogitation, seized by its punitive repercussions. He wanted out. He hated himself for knowing these people, struggling to get ahead in their world, for having, on this night, thrown a good life away in pursuit of an electronic split-second chimera. He couldn't elicit support from others in this. He had plenty of friends who had never watched Gage on TV because they hated TV. But that didn't help him. And he felt additionally stupid for imposing his ill-humor on his wife. Elizabeth thought TV was swell and felt great about her husband's involvement in real issues of public importance. John was out there and it made her and the kids rather proud.

Tonight Elizabeth was somewhere in British Columbia with a remote crew from the station covering something about whales. Elizabeth worked for the National Oceanic Bureau's Marine Fisheries Agency as a public information officer, in charge of the Seattle district. Gage called the station and was put through to Fields, who had just come off his nightly *high*. Mr. Self-Important.

"What's going on? Liz hasn't called," Gage asked, hoping Fields knew something. Usually the crew called in regularly.

"So? Hey, bud, that's between your wife and you, isn't it?"

"Just tell her I'm working at home if she should ring up."

"I certainly hope you've refined that blown-out script on the drug wars. The man's got his eye on you." Fields hung up.

"Screw you," Gage said. The man. Screw the man.

Gage stared at his six television screens. In another minute his phone rang, startling him. It was Elizabeth. Gage was kicking himself for having called Fields. "Where are you?" He knew that Fields's sexual ribbing was for real. Fields had been trying to impress John's wife for months. Gage was upset enough to encourage the affair; elicit the moment of rage, in between a righteous indignation and his own yearning to have an affair. He wanted to somehow tip the balance to manipulate her to such an extent that she, in her own way, would give him cause to stray. Not unlike his adversary Fields, Gage also had an ego problem and he knew it. His life was running out of time. He needed an excuse, and maybe Fields—Puke Head himself—was what it would take.

This night, John would turn her over to him. Only to taste a sweet revenge. He was just in one of those moods that people have been trained since childhood not to vent.

"The town's called Queen Charlotte. Dundas Lodge. There's only one phone. John, there's something wrong," she said.

She then paused, hoping he heard between her lines.

"What? Liz?"

"We were at a place called Kunghit Island. Check it out on the map. Tomorrow we're taking a helicopter a little farther south, to Cape St. James. It was horrible."

"What was horrible?"

"Three dead whales. Their odor. The look in their eyes." She paused, then spoke softly. "There's something totally off here, John. Maybe you should come up?" Her voice sounded tentative to Gage. "There's a story here," she said with more certainty.

"When are you gonna be back?"

"Are you even listening to me?"

"I can't focus on that right now." He hurt inside. Thirty-eight years old and still doing the local news. It was degrading. Like undergraduate school fazing. He should have grown out of it by now.

"Liz, I really am behind on this. You know that. Don't sabotage me with another one of your smoking guns."

"Okay. Fine. I'll be home Sunday."

He was silent.

"Did you hear me?"

"Yeah. Sunday night. I'll pick you up."

"One of the staff will bring me home. You could always call me tomorrow."

He didn't answer.

"John?"

"I'll try."

"Right."

Elizabeth lingered on the phone. "How are the kids?"

"Both of 'em still out. They're fine."

Elizabeth looked at her watch. It was too late for them to be out. She gave John the number at the Dundas Lodge, said goodnight and hung up. She was curt about it because she knew that John probably wouldn't call. He never did, when she was in the field. He missed her and he didn't miss her.

Elizabeth knew her husband's emotional turns only too well. It was just that time in his life. But it had been that time in his life for two years. Elizabeth was bored by his stupid melodramas, tired of his moodiness, the self-obsessions. She was a full woman, with little patience left to endure his so-called transitional period.

John had a Ph.D. in comparative literature but couldn't stomach the prospect of teaching remedial freshman English—after an erstwhile dissertation on "nothingness" in Sartre's and Beckett's fiction—and at Kalamazoo or Lincoln, no less. Those were his two choices. *Worse than nothingness,* he'd tell friends later on, while excoriating the new fork in his road. John had excelled before a classroom of eighteen-year-old poets whose buzzword was *semiotics.* But to his chagrin he was even better at the 6:00 A.M. "Farm News." And then at the evening weather. That's how he broke into television—pork futures and unseasonable frosts.

Elizabeth had none of John's bathos. She never shared in his frustrations. Not that he didn't try to persuade her. Her religion forbade self-absorption and its associated other taboos, like melancholy. Elizabeth had the ups, perpetually. Lucent, whitewashed, she was always the chirpiest mum to Jennifer—up front with her tampax, her politics, or her displeasures.

"I just don't get despair!" she politely affirmed once, after reading three pages of John's as yet unfinished thesis. "I mean, who cares?"

"I like that about you," John said, flexing muscles that didn't actually exist. What he liked, exactly, was her tongue —the way it hung out catlike when she effected her goofy "get serious" challenge. Elizabeth's skepticism, John thought, was a tonic, fresh, uncluttered, of the eighties. Much like Puget Sound—in its wild west blueness, that is. He liked her iconoclasm.

"You like my iconoclasm?" she'd remark. "That's bull shit. I can accept that maybe you like my ass. Or my boobs. Or my eyes. But you can dump this 'iconoclasm.' It's me you're planning to marry, mister. Me, my body. Not my mind. Got it?"

And he married her body, still suspicious of the inevitable combats in store for them. The loner, misanthrope, misplaced alien, pseudointellect, California State University doctorate turned TV hack and his upwardly mobile wife, messenger of quasiscience, harbinger of important marine world goings-on, the latest breakthroughs in dolphin communications or offshore oil regulations, salmon fry statistics, oyster harvests, whale watch trivia for tourists in January and October, new Law of the Sea treaty revisions relevant to the Northwest, or the most recent bans on

Korean gill netting. Her turf was the place in which she'd grown up. Elizabeth loved Seattle. She had those roots. John came from the Santa Clara Valley. John came from nowhere.

John stood before a mirror. Looking at himself, he caught a gray hair and expurgated it with a pair of small German thirty-dollar scissors. He and Elizabeth had had their battles before, moments where the desire for divorce after nineteen years of marriage burst forth with a ravenous sense of deliverance. A day, even two hours later, the radiance, logic and thrust of their break-up had faded. So that the same old syndrome of uncertainty, its foibles, behind-the-back baiting, and not infrequent shouting matches would continue. They had a superb marriage, actually, illuminated by two wonderful kids. John was simply going through a "routine late-thirtyish oh-my-god-there's-the-second-third-and-fourth-gray-sideburn yuppie kind of private hell," according to his fifteen-year-old boy, Evans.

Evans was a gentle, rather gifted child who'd rejected the so-called *gifted program* at school with an offhanded caustic "Forget it" that made the *Post-Intelligencer*. "I'm no hothouse orchid," he was quoted as saying in an article about kids reclaiming their own destinies from runaway ego projection on the part of their parents. Tonight he was at scuba practice. His fantasy was to start a new civilization thirty thousand leagues down.

John's thirteen-year-old daughter, Jennifer, was down the block at the house of her telepathic friend Gretchen, a schoolmate whose mother—Marion Matthiess—had inculcated the values and practice of bat worship in her little girl. The father, Leni, was a junior executive at a local aerospace corporation.

The Matthiesses had their own bat house in the back, and according to Evans's intelligence gathering, they left them live hamsters to feed on whenever they were away checking up on possible illegal laundering operations among the company's subcontractors. That was Leni's calling in life, according to his wife. It just sort of happened, like a religious revelation. "Illegal laundering operations—you know, the way some people become brain surgeons? Or bartenders?"

"They're ideal pets, you realize," Mrs. Matthiess had explained one evening to John and Elizabeth about the bats. "Whenever we go away, they seem to like to gather and feed on the hamsters and cockroaches, even piña colada mix left in a bowl. They sense when Leni has a job out of town. When we come back, they seem to want nonfat milk, half-used lemons, and rotting taco sauce. They also go after microwaved pea soup, toasted french bread with black, bitter papaya seeds—whatever's around. Very agreeable creatures," she alleged.

John realized that he and Elizabeth hadn't made love in weeks. He hadn't wanted to. He'd wanted to make love with twenty other women but not Elizabeth. Maybe he was just panicking about the goddamned "Drug Wars" story. His beat was due in and 700,000 viewers were going to tune in if the numbers could be trusted. And he still had no legitimate hook to the thing. His bottom-line thinking was unacceptable to the station manager. John wanted to legalize drugs. But the station group had a different philosophy, which reflected the attitude of the bank's board members: there was no way they were going to air a piece advocating the legalization of drugs.

The picture was there—they'd shot most of it—but John was still trying to twist those pictures to meet his eye. He was trying to write, as in real writing, unaware, still, that this was TV. Big mistake. Fields was right about that. Anyway, his heart was never in a drug story. He was on the verge of giving in to the easy way out. Don't mess with it. Do the basics. Get it done and move on.

John was avoiding the story and he knew it. He got up and guzzled two large mugs of fresh-squeezed lemonade purchased at the neighborhood health food store. Seattle had many more such stores per acre than any other community in the United States. It was one of the reasons the polls consistently picked Seattle before Cincinnati, Colorado Springs, or Orlando as the best all-around place to raise a child in the United States. It was Charles Fields who pointed that out just the other night on the five o'clock. One of these days Fields would make the six o'clock, speaking from New York or Los Angeles—while John Gage wrestled with demons in a darkroom, going nowhere. Around midnight, his kids still out, Gage swallowed a half tab of Valium in two robust shots of ouzo and headed to bed.

CHAPTER 4

SATURDAY MORNING
Queen Charlotte Islands

Local Joe, an Indian shaman, stepped out of the low-lying morning mist and prepared to make a ritual offering of an inlaid sheep horn that was carved into the legendary Thunderbird. The winged creature was said to have once inhabited the coastal range of British Columbia, swooping down from the glaciers to kill whales for its food. Somewhere out in the distance, the Indian heard a far-off approaching noise, what could be a small plane, probably taking tourists up the inland passage to some hunting and fishing camp or other.

Scattering prayer with one hand, the Indian presented his personal potlatch to the stricken mammals that lay writhing up ahead of him on the beach. Earlier in the morning he'd left an abalone shell filled with ripe salmonberry and blueberry, said his prayers, and returned to his campsite back in the forest. The berries were gone, most certainly squandered by squirrels or the ever-present gray jays. He left the sheep horn on the edge of the clearing, where two rotted totems leaned into the morning's mottled light, their once yellow and blue colors and gyrating faces faintly outlined in the red cedar. Walking out of the mist that had enveloped the forest of firs and spruce, Local Joe moved agilely for his age—almost in a trance—onto the black beach, as the airplane sound got nearer.

There was a time when both the Indians and the white

man approached the whales differently. Over one thousand of the leviathans were processed for their blubber every year on the British Columbia mainland and reformulated into oils, cat food, even braces for Victorian corsets. Out at sea, the females had always been killed first, to enrage the bull—ten times the size of an African elephant—who could then be counted on to charge at thirty knots, right into the waiting maw of harpoons, which would pierce and eviscerate the creature. More recently, his insides would be ignited with a charge. The rest of the pod was this way left without guidance and thus easy prey.

First the Basques hunted them, eleven hundred years ago. Then the Dutch and British. Local Joe's ancestors had invented their own ingenious harpoons. And when the Russians came, they adopted the local customs of marine massacre. By a century ago there were as few whales in these parts as there were Haida Indians.

The chanting shaman understood the folly of those times and stared directly at the whales. Their plight was not unlike that of Joe's now largely assimilated tribe. But whatever sorrows and psalms of the spirit might have conjoined in the past, or in the afterlife, such dirges were not then audible above the loud sucking of air overhead as three large helicopters suddenly punched through a low band of sea mist and set down on the sand fifty meters away from the whales. Local Joe stood watching them.

"Walk that way, don't stop. We're on a rise," the co-pilot shouted above the din of the rotors quickly winding down. All three of the Canadian mounted police on board scrambled to help the pretty blonde out of the large and powerful Sikorsky. In their rigid postures and shiny get-up they resembled the silly pomp of nineteenth-century Prussian officers, Elizabeth observed as she cleared the danger zone, then doffed her pumps for tennies, slinging her tote bag over her shoulder. As she and the others moved toward the sea, they were assailed by the odor.

Elizabeth winced, squinting, holding her nose, and gasping for air. Stumbling over the kelp-strewn beach, she joined a marine biologist who was ahead of her, quickly undoing his field kit, preparing to take tissue samples from the liver and stomach. Eight whales lay dead or stranded.

"Two are still alive," the scientist said. The accompanying two-person camera crew from KCBD was already at work shooting, moving a hand-held connected by a thirty-foot AC cord between the Betacam and the audio record. They'd seen other such sites from the air, circling at dawn, catching the rays on the massive flanks of washed-up cetaceans.

Elizabeth knew the animals well enough to have no fear. She moved past the kneeling scientist and came up to the face of the humpback. Its eyes were cloudy, Antwerp blue, enormous. The same look in the survivors yesterday. The mammals had all of a few hours left. The power in its tail, which has been likened to the force inherent in a 500-horsepower engine, was useless now. Elizabeth stroked the flesh, divining some meaning. The animal breathed with a forced respiratory inflection, mucilaginous air grating through its blowhole. It was struggling against the gravity that was causing its asphyxiation. The creature's tens of thousands of pounds were not meant to languish on a rocky beach, crushing its internal organs. Elizabeth stood before the mute and winsome eye—the size of her hand—trembling for lack of any remedies.

"Isn't there *anything* we can do?" she asked, as a second marine biologist joined her.

"Not likely," the voice behind her said. It was Wick Hallipeg. He'd been totally silent on the journey out. He was a cetaceologist from the University of Vancouver with a patch over one eye and—Elizabeth couldn't help but notice —an instant affinity with the whale. The man put his body against the expiring behemoth, stroked it lovingly, and whispered a prayer. "Just maybe . . ." The voice trailed off.

"Sweetheart . . . I'm so sorry . . ." Elizabeth mumbled, straining for contact, touching the whale beneath his eye. She was trembling, in a frenzy of instant pain. She emptied out her tote bag, got to the tide pools, filled the bag with water and rushed back to the first of the two whales still breathing. She poured the remaining two quarts-worth of ocean over the landward-side of its face. The eye responded, closing, then reopening.

"I can't stand it," she said, sitting down before the creature, openly in tears.

The news crew came in for a close-up. The cameraman wanted it on sticks. He unshouldered his camera a few feet away from the stricken Elizabeth and set up his tripod.

"Do you mind!" she shouted. "Get your shot at a distance. Have a little respect for chrissakes."

"Hey, just doing a job," Alex MacIntyre said brazenly. He and his audio engineer, Price, moved back.

"You're really . . ." But she refrained and moved over to the other beached whale.

This one had been there most of the night. It was going fast. The breathing was faint. Its ribcage pressed against the flesh. Elizabeth stared at the forty-five-foot-long masterpiece. Suddenly Local Joe came up to her and stood in a vigil by her side, continuing to murmur his old Haida chant.

"What does it mean?"

He continued for a few more lines, then stopped, looking at the tears streaking her face. He sized her up, took her hand and squeezed it hard. "It's the blessing way," he said in a broken English. "The whale is hungry."

His comments didn't register with her. The first scientist, Bulrich, joined them with his field kit and test tubes, tweezers and scalpels. "We won't know for twenty-four hours."

"What about this business of brevetoxin?" Elizabeth asked.

"There were other symptoms with the bottlenose dolphins that died by the hundreds back in the late eighties along the East Coast," he said matter-of-factly. "Although this is a peak stranding period. Rather predictable, in fact. What with the calving going on and all."

"The whales, they're hungry," Joe said.

"Well, that's one opinion," Bulrich countered politely. "But until these samples are processed, I wouldn't jump to any conclusions." He knew that Elizabeth Gage was there to

37

file a report with NOB. Whales were news in Seattle and in Vancouver—big news—at least, for a few days. "To be honest with you? I hope it is brevetoxin."

"Why?" she said.

"'Cause it's natural. Enough corpses should give a valid analysis, something other than mystery."

The choppers were leaving those on the beach behind. "Hey, Bulrich? What's going on?" Elizabeth shouted, sheltering the whale's landward eye from the pick-up debris. Bulrich was on his squawky.

"What's the plan, Wick?"

She could hear over the static and blade noise. "Give us an hour. We'll be back with padded steel cables. It's worth a shot."

Eight whales and seven humans, two totem poles, and a shaman were there for three hours, twenty minutes. The mist closed in. There was a slight drizzle. Local Joe escorted Bulrich, MacIntyre, Price, and the three policemen into a large, sixty-foot shelter—the remains of an old Haida long house—a Canadian archaeological monument. Enormous carved-out cedar trees formed its posterior. The remains of a dugout canoe, used in the old days for trading forays south along Vancouver Island, were stashed to the side. But Elizabeth preferred to remain out among the whales, speaking to them all the while. Eventually, Joe returned to the beach.

"You're too late," Elizabeth said. The female had died. Its eyes remained open. It was Elizabeth's first time.

In the distance, the choppers could be heard. They hung in the air over the site. The others returned from the shelter. Now all attention was focused on the barely breathing male. The three choppers hovered twenty feet above the animal; cables were lashed beneath its head and around its tail. Everyone worked, everyone save MacIntyre and Price, who had their priorities. The only thing they did was get close-up pictures.

The choppers coordinated their lift-off in a delicate rise, the blurring circles of the rotars kept thirty feet apart. It was a tricky maneuver. The weight of the animals, the wind of the three adjacent vehicles, placed a strain laced with cold sweat upon the pilots.

"Come on, sweetheart. Move!" There was a unanimous appeal as the choppers rose, sluggishly straining to haul the unknowable force a few feet above the beach and several hundred feet out beyond the surf. The choppers were distanced at an awkward angle from one another. But the doubts had already been lodged and discounted. It was the whale's only chance.

"Go, go!" Bulrich shouted.

Elizabeth's fists were clenched, her arms outstretched. The whale was slipping. The choppers speeded up.

"They're going to drop him," a policeman said.

"Keep going!" Bulrich shouted into his squawky. With those words the whale fell, slipping from the cable noose on its tail side. The head came next, slipping through the massive hank, crashing back into the waves. The choppers lurched, swinging in a circle to avoid one another, then flew clear.

There was jubilation on the beach. There was no sign of the whale. The water was deep enough for it to have gotten free.

Everyone collected themselves for the journey back. The choppers regrouped on the beach. "If it's the toxin, it stands no chance," Wick said.

"Think positively," Elizabeth insisted, turning to say good-bye to her new friend, Local Joe. "Thank you, Joe." The old Indian nodded politely at her. His lips were pursed, his forehead furrowed. No doubt he's seen a lot, she thought.

As the chopper pulled away, Elizabeth saw the elderly Haida gentleman sit back down on the wet rocks, staring out to sea.

"There he is!" the pilot said, talking into his lavaliere.

"That's the one, all right," the pilot from an adjoining chopper replied. "Doesn't look to be moving, though."

Wick saw the whale floating on the surface.

"Take her low," he said. They descended to within twenty feet of the whitecaps. The chopper door swung open. Leaning out, tied to his chest belt, Wick signed off on the poor thing. "I think he's dead."

Bulrich studied it, then concurred. "Take her back up. Nothing more we can do here."

Elizabeth looked back. Joe was gone.

CHAPTER 5

SUNDAY

"Every stitch counts, young man," Thesika Aghiapolous said, from her old Cretan rocking chair, one of the few remnants she possessed of her life before coming to Seattle with her husband, Dino, and their son, Clark, after World War II.

Thesika was gaining inch by inch on the mohair arm of a sweater she was knitting for Clark's upcoming birthday, as Evans Gage and Thesika's granddaughter Sophie sat out front on the lawn beneath a large sycamore tree, going over their trigonometry. Sophie tutored Evans in Russian class, a Cyrillic language natural to Greeks, while he massaged her mental block about logarithms and mantissas. The two had grown up together.

"Time flies," Thesika said.

Sophie looked at Evans and grinned with a teenager's know-it-all satire. "Grandma, do you have any idea how many times you've said that?"

Evans had grown up as much in Dino and Thesika's home as in his own.

Sophie's grandfather Dino still went into the shop every day at seven in the morning to tinker with accounts receivable and speaker parts, then left for the YMCA by noon to do his laps. Dino was the chairman of the board at Radio

Save. His house was wired. There were more CD players, ghetto blasters, VCR's, and hanging circuit boards around that house than at KCBD.

Evans was a natural-born tinkerer himself, far more adept at the technology of these things than his big-shot producer father. He appreciated Dino's obsession while Thesika had tried to ignore it for forty-odd years. On Sundays, when Radio Save's acting president, Clark, would bring his daughter Sophie to grandma and grandpa's house, Evans was invariably to be found there. A love-smitten convenience. For over a year Evans had harbored a terrible crush on his childhood friend, was dying to get her in a scuba suit—was really dying to then get her out of the scuba suit. It was a ferocious predicament for a young man whose sense of decorum and finesse were highly developed. He was aswarm with lust and only Sophie could properly assuage his restive craze. He may have been the last virgin of his generation at school. That's what he recently discussed with his dad, adopting a serious and concerned attitude. He was waiting for Sophie, Evans told his father. She was his gut-given sacrament just as her grandmother, at a similar age, back at the unknowable dawn of history, had apparently fallen beneath the insatiable roar of that old minotaur, Dino, up on some mountain. Thesika was also on to the boy's dilemma.

"Better hurry up!" she advised him.

Sophie turned red in the unseasonably hot sun and flung a bug off her tight-fitting jeans. Evans noticed how fast the termite-like insect fled over her zipper and onto the grass.

Evans loved such Sundays. His block hosted an inordinate number of linden, hollyhock, fir—even Japanese oak and something like an ornamental rubber tree. Garish bougainvillea splashed across the mold-white garages, even for the Northwest a special profusion, with cooing doves and boisterous stellar jays. He felt at peace with the monarch butterflies alighting on every honeysuckle. There had been no break-ins on this block, no fires. Nobody had died, no cats had been flattened. Raccoons showed up now and then in the trees and—remarkably, given his zeal and curiosity—Evans's dog, Wallace, had had no run-in with them.

Next door, Evans's dad was making guacamole. His mother was expected home anytime now from her work weekend. It was a regular thing. Evans's mom was a distinct workaholic. He wasn't sure about Dad. Talking before a camera seemed to Evans to be more about fame and pleasure than real work. Whereas John saw in his son's increasing uneasiness the epitome of paradise rendered self-conscious. Everything was going the kid's way, due in part to the Gages' easygoing emancipation of their children. Or so they believed. It was a rare mix that seemed to work: not merely liberal, but free. The children were disciplined only to the extent of protection, a concept culled—mostly by John—from books by Bertrand Russell, essays by Percy Shelley and Bruno Bettleheim, stories by Bashevis Singer. Elizabeth found such painting by numbers a trifle absurd. As long as the family "worked," then she was okay about not laying down laws—as long as everyone did his or her share and exercised restraint. Their house was small for four people, so they had to work together.

Evans's fascination with the sea, Jules Verne, and vintage Mothers of Invention albums and his younger sister Jennifer's passion for makeup and clothes were sufficient-enough distraction to keep the kids drug free and out of trouble.

Elizabeth was dropped off by Hank, one of her two assistants from the office.

"Hi, Mom," Jennifer said when she walked in the door.

"You're in time for enchiladas. How did it go?" John inquired. He flipped open the flour tortillas to scoop in guacamole atop the melted cheese and sour cream and get the chunky sauce evenly dispersed. Then he sprinkled the sliced olives and scallions over them. The sour cream was a new fat-free substitute, as was the sharp cheddar, which was smoked and comprised largely of soy.

"You got the lowdown Friday night."

"I thought you were gonna call again."

"I thought you would call."

"I did," John said. "You'd checked out."

"Oh, right." She went upstairs, unpacked, sat down, and stared in the mirror. Elizabeth was on edge. She rubbed her eyes.

"Mom, the enchiladas are getting cold," Jennifer shouted.

"You got quite a tan," John said, noticing, when they'd sat down to lunch.

"It was hard to avoid. I've never seen British Columbia looking like that. One hour of drizzle. Otherwise sun."

"You look good."

"How's the piece coming?"

"It's written. We'll see if it cuts."

"What time do you have to leave tomorrow?"

"Not so early."

"That's good." She gave him that maybe-we-can-have-sex look.

John was usually gone by seven thirty in the morning whenever he had a stand-up to do. Elizabeth didn't leave for her office before nine twenty. Now she definitely had plans for them in the morning. Enough of this idiotic fighting. She'd always been the one to initiate peace. It took a real man to swallow that kind of pride. It came easy to Elizabeth.

Evans was at the computer in the living room. Aqualung, a game of deep-ocean discovery. He'd written the software. Elizabeth thought he was going to make a fortune with it. The kid had been at it for six months. He took one introductory computer course at school and immediately translated everything he'd learned into his own agenda. Now he taught himself whatever he needed to know, standing in bookstores skimming the books, taking notes when necessary. His father had gone through school that way. Evans planned to finish the cluster by three and then show it to Sophie.

The phone rang. "I'll get it." Jennifer grabbed it. "Yeah, sure, just a sec. . . . Mom, it's for you."

"Who is it?"

"Who is this?" Jennifer held the receiver down against her thigh. "Guy named Emmet Jones."

"Thanks, sweetheart. . . . Yes, Emmet?"

The sixty-year-old Emmet Jones headed up a marine laboratory under contract to Elizabeth's office and located on Harbor Island near the West Waterway. Tanned, weather-beaten, his fatherly face rimmed with an unkempt white bundle of beard, he'd spent half his life in the lab, the other half on his boat docked in Lake Union. A healthy combination. From his desk he looked out across Elliott Bay into the sound, across Duwamish Head, past piers and terminals. It was a crowded corner. His three rooms were filled with high wooden counters beneath a congestion of chemical tools of the trade and two other working scientists. There were centrifuges, several gas spectrometers, a laser device, endless vials and tubes and bubbling cauldrons; powders, samples, bags filled with flesh and exoskeletons, scales and eggs; jars larded with the remains of the ocean, from black bituminous asphalt to partially degraded plastics; polystyrene materials, ossified urchins, sickly corals, a tooth here, a cranium there. A poisonous *Holocanthus ciliarus*. A live baby sandshark washed up in the city's sewers. A slide earmarked for red tide analysis; another concerned with amino acids in chiton-loaded fecal pellets. He had oil-saturated invertebrates, dying eel grass, and a large vat of Seattle's sludge, a representative grouping of the hundreds of millions of pounds of heavy-ended suspended particles hemorrhaging into the sound every day.

But what was on Jones's mind at the moment was a spindly-looking image of blotches and slashes that he'd just identified in his microscope. "Their immune system is shot," he said to Elizabeth.

"What does that mean?"

"I'm not sure." Emmet fiddled with the slide, which had been stained with tissue microorganisms from the belly of one of the dead whales. The creatures were writhing in pink dye, expiring on the thin sliver of glass. "Lot of dead algae in their gut. Could have been a plankton kill."

"You're thinking maybe an unreported oil spill?"

"Doesn't look like it. I mean, there's always going to be benzene and ethylbenzene, xylene, and toluene—the usual residue."

"Emmett, let's cut through to the bone here. My lunch is getting cold."

"Liz, off the record?"

"Goddamnit Emmet. . . ."

"Well, frankly I'm going to need a second opinion."

"Your eyes going bad? You've never needed a 'second opinion.' Emmett, what is it?"

"Liz, I'd like to get a photobiologist in here to examine the odd plankton or two that Bulrich collected from those tide pools wherever the hell it was. I know someone at NOB."

"What's a photobiologist?"

"Someone who studies the effect of sunlight on plants and animals, Mom," Evans said from across the room.

"Your boy's pretty smart," Emmett continued, having heard the boy in the background. "It might have something to do with what killed those whales."

"I think they starved to death, Emmet."

"They may well have. One thing for sure—they were sick. Their systems were screwed up and they'd traveled a long way to die. Muscles were exhausted, and they were taking in food they normally wouldn't touch. I have to confess, I've never seen anything like it."

"You're scaring me."

John whispered to her, "What is it?" but she waved him off for now.

"I wouldn't be telling you this yet but I figured you'd best hold off speaking with the press tomorrow until we have a firmer sense of what's going on."

"What do I tell them? It's already news."

"Cause of death still being investigated. I should have something a little more definite for you by the end of the day. I tried to reach this fellow about an hour ago. Anyway, let me call you tomorrow."

"Thanks, Emmett." She hung up the phone.

"Mom? What's going on?"

"That's what I like about this family. You're all in on it."
She chomped down on her enchilada.

"Well?" Jennifer pressed.

"Come on, Mom, spit it out." Evans had a particular
investment in his mother's line of business.

"I think the whales starved to death. That's what I
observed. This scientist, Jones—we've used him before. He
seems to agree but wants to check it out more thoroughly."

"Why were you scared?" John asked.

"Yeah, and what about photobiology?" Evans furthered.

"I don't know, all right? Look, guys, it was awful, okay?"

"Sure, Mom."

A minute later, Evans's curiosity twitched again. "What
did he say about photobiology?"

"Honey, I just got home. I'm tired. I don't want to talk
about it now. Pass the guacamole."

CHAPTER 6

MONDAY AFTERNOON

John Gage and his two crew members left the station midmorning for the Space Needle. Wendy Fox sat in back, checking the audio equipment. Andy Otero, John's videographer, drove. The white van was emblazoned on the side door with large blue lettering that read: KCBD TV—NEWS WORTH WATCHING!

Three years before, Andy had thrown himself into film in New York with a scholarship to NYU and the firm intention of becoming the next David Lean, film director, of Lima, his home. His head was aswarm with untold epics. Unfortunately, Andy's *thing* was religious or dietary or, rather, some arcane fusion of the two. He was an adamant vegetarian and planned to structure his films around the vulnerability of puppies, cows, even rodents, which, he adamantly informed his colleagues, were not protected by the congressional Animal Welfare Act. As a man driven by his conscience to do something about the ongoing crisis, Andy set out to make a career for himself in film that would reach people's hearts. He scripted a soft-spoken Ralph Bellamy type who finally won his girl upon shutting down her father's deli and a Chuck Connors ("Rifleman") type who similarly captured his lady's affection by his valiant, nonviolent closure of a turkey farm that had been in her family for generations. The guy used rubber bullets to disarm her unfriendly older brothers out on the range.

Unfortunately for Andy, these noble projects never materialized. Instead, he ended up at KCBD-TV in Seattle as a cameraman shooting cheap Betacam video for news and documentaries. Frequently he drove the station van to the various remotes, as they were called. John Gage was his producer.

Both John and Andy were normally partnered with Wendy Fox, an audio engineer. Thirty-one years old, single, unpardonably beautiful for a lesbian, she was adept at holophonics 3-D, the various reel-to-reel nagras, the simpleminded, hygienic dat, or the older field-mixing style of laying down sound. After a year working together, the thirty-three-year-old Andy had still not given up. He believed that sooner or later Wendy was going to partake of triumphant heterosexual communion in his bed.

She wore tight black jeans and sloppy basketball Keds and smiled with an unmistakable sexual electricity. Her eyes were large and black, her hair long—a bit limp but given to a show of vulnerability, he thought. Pliable, asking to be fussed up. Andy never saw her with another woman. She hung around the guys at the station. "Most women bore me," she'd once told the Peruvian exile.

Wendy lived somewhere out near Schmitz Park, overlooking the sound. Her parents had money, obtained in Alabama. Wendy had a trust fund. Probably not enough money to be at total leisure, but she certainly didn't have to put up with all the garbage of a TV station if her heart hadn't been in it. She and Andy had often ruminated together about their lives, hopes, dreams. She was his closest friend in America.

They pulled up to the Needle and parked the van in a red zone. They had a permit to park anywhere, anytime.

"You know what you're gonna say?" Wendy asked John Gage as the three of them schlepped the gear up to the near top of the Seattle Needle and made their way through a crowd of tourists out of the elevator into one of two restaurants.

"Course."

The first thing John saw was a long willowy woman plucking the harp over in a corner, engendering the noontime atmosphere of nirvana. "Will we hear that in the background?" he asked Wendy.

"More than likely," she admitted.

"Then she's got to go," he said.

"How do you propose to do that?" asked Wendy. "She looks like she's into her music. I'm sure the management is as well."

"I'll deal with it."

"Where do you want me to set it up?" Andy asked.

"How's the light on that background? I like the full view of the city with the sound. I want it to look like the pretty Seattle everyone knows. A city without blemish."

"A little hot. I could gel it."

"How long will it take?"

"Order lunch. It'll be done. Get me one of those quiche specials. Lots of salt. Ranch dressing on the side. A couple dill pickles, nonalcoholic beer. Oh, barbecue chips—no, that's all right, potato chips are okay—and a brownie, the ones with the choco chips in 'em, not the other ones."

"Uh—"

Wendy was already putting her microphone together, testing the battery, the counter, laying out the mixer, checking things. "John, get me an egg salad sandwich and a root beer. Put avocado, onions, lettuce, mustard, mayonnaise, tomato, pepper, no celery, toasted whole wheat—seven grain if they've got it—also some—" They always did this to him. It was sort of a game.

"Excuse me, uh—excuse me? You're getting your own food."

"The memory! First to go. It's your age, John. You're getting old. But we still love you."

They spent ten minutes wolfing down their food. John went over to the rear office and obtained a location release from the manager of the restaurant and payed the harpist to take a lunch break, while Wendy affixed the lavaliere mic to his lapel. Meanwhile Andy snapped on the 2K of Omni lights, fired off a battery belt to avoid having to run AC through a swarm of lunching tourists. It would give them fifteen minutes worth of John's stand-up. More than enough, unless he needed a dozen takes, which was rare. The gel on the window behind which John would speak filtered out some of the intense glare so that the heat of the light outside was balanced against the much darker light of the interior. Two thousand watts of electricity would help equalize that contrast ratio, which film thrived on, but not video. In video, unbalanced exterior light turned flat, white, like a bald light bulb, while everything on the inside went black. Andy's job was to set a compromise between the lighting and his aperture, so that the viewer would see John Gage in perfect light while glimpsing some detail and color outside the windows. Normal stuff, except that for some reason this day, like the past three or four, was incredibly bright. Andy was having a hard time beating the contrast. Especially in a revolving restaurant. He had 360 degrees to contend with. "I'll need to throw another 2K at least and we're not carrying it. It's like summer out there."

"Well . . . can we do it?"

"It may look like shit. I could go down and bring up the monitor from the truck so you can look at it?"

"What about if I move my position?"

Around one o'clock everything was ready to go. John looked over his copy, committed it to memory—he was a quick study—had Wendy fix his hair, straighten his tie, brush off his jacket, and he was ready.

"You got speed," Andy said. The camera was rolling, the tape was locked in forward speed.

John spoke directly to camera, consummate, sure of himself, empathetic. He had the trip wired. Hit it hard at the top, be brief, be startling. Spare none of the grim stuff, but contextualize it fast. Give it edge, even grit, but be eloquent. Make sure the grammar's correct.

"Eighteen drug-related murders or suicides in one month. More than half of them among minors. Whites, blacks, Orientals. Such deaths have crossed over into every precinct of Seattle. One pretty thirteen-year-old girl, her veins dark and blotched like those of an eighty-year-old, found slumped over a toilet in her school bathroom on Clyde Hill, the victim of an overdose.

"And this youth, once a budding gymnast, discovered dead with a bullet in his head in his grandparents' backyard. He was in debt, needed drug money to pay off other kids his own age who were leaning on him. He couldn't find the money. He was afraid to steal it from his family.

"And then this scene of mayhem in Highland Park on April eleventh. Three teens killed in a shoot-out over heroin. And most recently, four days ago, a whole family murdered in Boulevark Park, smack related. Wake up, Seattle!"

"A little over the top, isn't it?" Wendy said with her usual candor. They knew each other well enough for that sort of real-time critique.

"I don't think so."

"I do."

"Ratings, Wendy dear," Andy reminded her.

"Bullshit."

"Come on, guys. We're not alone here."

John told them about his plans to intercut his stand-up with shots of the morgue and of the deceased. He'd already gotten the permission from two sets of parents who were as outraged as they were grief-stricken. The city—like every city—had not kept apace of the epidemic, they had told John on camera. "What's wrong with authorizing police sweeps of the schools? Why the hell won't teachers raise the subject of drugs in class more persuasively? They're afraid of reprisals from pushers. Pushers and dealers right in the classroom for godsakes!"

John had all the right bites. He was there. He knew the piece was going to work. And "the man" was going to love it. While neighborhood campaigns and watches had been mounted, drugs were on the rise, and John meant to alert the sluggish city to the problem. It was the culmination of three weeks of background work and location shoots all over Seattle.

"Let's take it again. I could have been less glib."

"You want a push-in?" Andy asked.

"Perfect. Slow and even."

"Naturally."

"Around the time 'grandparents' backyard.' Okay?"

Andy set his focus for the end of the zoom-in, then pulled it back. "And you got speed."

"Eighteen drug-related murders or suicides in one month. More than half—"

There was a scream from one of the tables fifty feet away. Then other shouts.

Andy, still rolling, turned his camera to the source of the fracas.

"What the hell?" John said. People were diving away from the windows. John covered his head instinctively, seeing no danger as yet, and skipped away from the windows. Waiters and other diners stared in confusion, getting up, the impulse, as yet checked in uncertainty, to flee.

Something was slamming into the glass windows that looked out over Seattle, the Olympic Peninsula, Puget Sound. Things. Shadows. Clunks.

"Birds!" a voice screamed wretchedly.

The glass was thick. People moved back. The smacking increased. A whole flock of them, gray or white, were moving twenty miles an hour into the tower. A long gaggle of the heavy-looking nuts. They were all mixed up, and they kept coming.

"You getting it?" John shouted above the din of the disturbed luncheongoers. Andy's camera was still rolling and as the birds' beaks broke and the birds themselves cascaded downward, Andy was shooting the whole saga.

Guests were standing back, watching the bizarre creatures careening into the glass. The spectacle escalated. Hundreds of birds—a migratory assault, suicidal, lemminglike. It was one of those crazy unexpected flukes in nature, John figured. Maybe the oddly summerish weather, ninety degrees in spring, veritable heat spell, that was breaking every record was causing this.

The glass cracked. "Stand back," another voice among many rang out. Dumb waiters, so to speak, standing with their trays, unable to do anything. The management flopped around. People tried to get to the elevators. From below came the first wail of a siren. The birds were falling onto the street and parking lot below. People were getting hit.

"They've gone berserk," Wendy cried.

Gage picked up a kind of commentary. "Keep rolling, keep rolling! It's weird, all right. Must be gulls, maybe puffins. Or geese. They're coming from the north, probably from the water. They're smashing into the glass. The wind is coming through. They're breaking through . . ."

Two of the birds had now come into the restaurant. A whole sheet of the glass, meant to withstand fierce winter storms, had shattered onto the white-linened tables. The beaks were enormous. Multiplied over hundreds of hits, the force against the glass had demolished its holding strength. Now the remaining flock was pouring through the shattered remains, skipping beak down into the main entranceway. They were unsteady, injured, wobbling about and shrieking in timbres that Wendy was picking up.

"Glass breaking, people fleeing, it's a bloody mess," Gage continued.

"Andy, you all right?" Wendy shouted, squirming to keep up with the figure shrouded in a rasping discordance and the flapping of frantic wings. They were connected by an AC cord, Wendy running shotgun mic, a long Sennheiser.

Andy was covering it all. He went in for the close-ups of the birds in the restaurant. He was recording them streaming in from afar, plummeting sixty stories down, squawking frantically in search of the way out—injured wings, injured heads. Horrible.

"Is everybody okay?" the cashier cried faintly. A hundred people had assembled in the front of the restaurant. Others had already gotten out in the overloaded elevators. Still others, knowing it was an emergency, had taken the endless stairs. One elderly gentleman, a kindly-looking bartender, kept cool, helping some of the birds. He brought Pellegrino water to an older woman who was crying. "On the house," he said. Some of the birds had been bundled up. The Wild Animal Rescue Fleet and SPCA were on their way.

And KCBD was there. John covered it all with the remaining few minutes of power left in their battery belt. A couple of interviews, a dead bird, the face of something crazy.

"Your first take'll work," Wendy consoled John, referring to the drug stand-up.

"It wasn't over the top?" he chided her.

"No," she conceded.

CHAPTER 7

MONDAY MORNING
Seattle

Her day started out just fine considering it was Monday. But the sun had given her a terrific headache within minutes of getting on the freeway, and her heart still stung from the recurring image of those whales. The first thing she had to do was write up the press release for Drake Manders, the big cheese. Drake was not easy to get along with. The heavy-shouldered, phlegmatic veteran of uncountable scrapes had a bad temper and breathed down everyone's neck. He was given to harsh turns, and harsher language.

His boot camp had been the environmental front lines. He'd spent years fighting for city ordinances that might curb the growth of dangerous algae in Lake Washington and nearly a decade lobbying for new sewage treatment facilities, of which Seattle boasted more than two dozen. He had that *Washington Post* manner of tilting his head, dipping his spectacles, proffering a look of "You better be damned straight about your sources" then returning to busy normality with an affirmative nod that said "Run it!" More recently Drake's daily cross to bear was Puget Sound, an industrial waste dump despite its picture postcard–perfect look.

"I'm just glad it happened in Canadian waters," he told Elizabeth.

By ten in the morning the release had gone to their office's public relations firm, which immediately got it out to their own list of press recipients. By eleven o'clock, the "mysterious whale death" was mentioned on a local radio show and Elizabeth was back at Drake's cross, continuing a master compilation of discharge sources, both point and area, in metropolitan Seattle. This was a depressing task to which she and her staff had been glued for months. Runoff included heavy metals flushed through storm sewers, mine tailings, nitrates, every known industrial sludge, acid drainage, and a dangerous array of chlorinated hydrocarbons sprayed in the form of pesticides and insecticides on nearly every farm surrounding the city. With the amount of rain normally inundating Seattle, such constant runoff was nearly impossible to curtail.

"Liz, I've got a policeman on the phone who wants to know what they should do with a bunch of dead birds downtown. He says they're weird."

"Lucky, what does he mean weird?"

"You wanna talk to him?"

"Hi, this is Elizabeth Gage. What have you got?"

"You folks deal in exotic ocean-faring wildlife."

"Is that a question or a statement?" She didn't like the man's tone.

"Look, a couple hundred birds are down here below the Needle. I don't recognize them. Some sort of strange pigeon or seagull."

"You don't know the difference?"

"Well, ma'am, usually I do. But not today."

"Are they hurt?"

"DOA. They fell, after running into the windows up top. I guess a few of 'em are still kickin' though. So does anyone from NOB want to take a look before we bag 'em?"

Early the next morning, in a suburb of Montreal, a scientist named Roald Shiftren was having a bad dream. He recognized a head that had been severed clean, though a sliver of white gold, twisted like a licorice stick, still jutted into the tissues and muscles of the inflamed throat. Blood-swept ganglia, the blue of anemone, dangled like the roots of ginseng or jellyfish, as his ex-wife Margo carried the fresh kill closer to the source, her hair matted in cloying blood, the eyes closed somberly. Then an explosion of first light as the phone jangled him to consciousness. He threw his hands up to his temples, jolted by sudden recognition.

"Good God," he mumbled, the afterimage of a recent rendition of Richard Strauss's *Salome* swaying oppressively in his head. Except the head was his, and Salome appeared as his ex-wife. "She really was a bitch!"

Dr. Donald Willard had burst the bubble on a nightmare, waking his old buddy Shiftren out of bed at six thirty Saturday morning. Roald, a researcher at the Cold Weather Hazards Institute in Montreal, had co-written the definitive book on the so-called "ozone wars" in the mid-1970s. Since then, Shiftren had continued to track the mounting evidence for an incontrovertible depletion taking place in the earth's ozone layer. At one time he'd been accused of "personal reasons and emotional involvement in the issue," words regurgitated by the press at the time of congressional hearings in Washington back in 1976—as if to say that any personal conviction about anything was suspect in science. Yet as events would turn out, Shiftren was to become something of a cult figure to younger scientists for his courage in pointing the finger at industry long before others were prepared unambiguously to do so. And by the time of the Montreal Protocol Agreement, the Danish chemist had enjoyed a total vindication.

Amid a welter of suggested culprits responsible for ozone depletion—among them, bromine, carbon tetrachloride, methylchloroform, halons, sewage chlorination, chemical fertilizers, car exhaust, alkali metals, and, of course, the sweeping arena of CFC's—Shiftren had focused on one of the more esoteric realms of ozone chemistry, namely solar flares. He had been instrumental in reexamining data first obtained from NSB's NIMBUS 4 weather satellite following a strange but inadequately analyzed ozone fluctuation over the North Pole in 1972. As seen through telescopes, a scalding hoop of magnetized gas on the stormy sun's surface had bolted out into space, licking 200,000 miles of darkness.

It was a spectacular eruption, though at the time it received far less comment than did the breakdown of the Paris peace talks, the arrival in Washington of two Panda bears from Beijing, and a vandal's attack on Michelangelo's *Pietà*.

Shiftren subsequently calculated a 16 percent decrease in ozone over the Arctic as a result of the solar turbulence and was thus the first to draw scientific attention to actual global depletions. He had gone on to suggest that the extinction of the dinosaurs may well have come about because of a massive hole in the ozone layer sixty million years ago, perhaps the result at that time of solar convulsions.

The theory was not lost on Donald Willard, nor was the later inconvenient discovery of ozone depletions over the Arctic. But most scientists were unwilling to deal with the Arctic. It was not the time to switch gears. Too many research grants had already been allocated to the study of ozone depletion over Antarctica. Investigators had converged on the Chilean town of Punta Arenas, built a costly airstrip, and sent an ER-2 and DC-8 aircraft on twenty-four flights into the heart of the ozone hole to monitor a host of chemicals in hopes of determining the true cause of the depletion. The Punta Arenas data was the focus of intense international excitement.

Exactly one year after Willard's ill-fated expedition to the Antarctic western peninsula, scientists met in Berlin to examine the ozone crisis. The hole was deeper than ever before and it was now clear that nature had no hand in it: human chemicals were the cause. Willard's team members had proffered few statements to the press about their own melancholy experience, largely on account of the lack of consensus among those party to the deaths on the glacier. No report had been officially filed, and Willard's sense of professional failure and later his personal tragedy precluded his ever coming out with what were, after all, hasty and inconclusive observations made in the middle of the night. Even the ship's captain finally decided not to file a formal report. There was too little information.

But Willard never forgot the bright light. The astonished,

gruesome look in the eyes of both the birds and the dead men. He was forced to put aside research for nearly a year while coping with his new life in a chair and the loss of his wife. When he returned to the world of the living, he'd found a more subdued climate. Ozone had been usurped in the news by other calamities—like the greenhouse effect, oil spills, and the increasing global build-up of heavy-ended aromatic hydrocarbons.

The Exxon *Valdez*, the *Kharg 5*, the *American Trader*, the *Arthur Kill* had burned their respective names and nightmares into the cursory attention span of the world's helpless bystanders. The Japanese had even asserted that the thin film of petroleum covering the oceans was altering the global atmosphere. But how the world forgets. In succession, other more newsworthy events had grabbed hold of the imagination—Arafat's seeming change of heart on Israel's long-disputed Right to Exist, new legislative initiatives by the Green parties in Eastern Europe, the rings of Neptune, an earthquake in San Francisco, Gorbachev's acid test in Lithuania, and Saddam Hussein's invasion of Kuwait. And so on and so on. In England, the ozone crisis had been miraculously resolved in as few as three months. All over London hair salons were advertising "ozone-friendly" products. The hype had succeeded in casting the whole issue to near oblivion.

Only Roald Shiftren, and a small group of associates at NSB, in Norway, and in the Soviet Union, continued to look at the Arctic. By late January of 1988, it was clear that elevated levels of chlorine were causing ozone to disappear in the northern polar vortex, as it's called. Another international expedition was launched, this time out of Stavanger, Norway. Planes were flown toward the North Pole with monitoring equipment on board. This time there was no freakish solar storm upon which to blame the devastating data. The Arctic stratosphere was losing one percent of its ozone every day throughout the winter months.

Nevertheless, the government and media paid little attention to these revelations, largely because the data was understood to be ephemeral, short term in nature. Shiftren himself downplayed the discoveries and moved on to other research. Arctic ozone anomalies were deemed a fluke without, apparently, the lasting significance of the Antarctic depletions. In the Norwegian and Soviet Arctic, the polar vortex dissipated within a matter of weeks and the ozone levels regained their normal plateau of nearly 400 Dobson units.

Something then happened that should also have stirred considerable interest but did not. Three separate incidents were reported. A research station in the mountains of Switzerland, two West German researchers monitoring the troposphere over a rain forest in central Africa, and a laboratory in southern Argentina each reported spontaneous ozone depletions in the column of air directly overhead. But they too were all designated as so-called "short-lived phenomena." News briefs appeared in a few papers and that was it. Remarkably, with the exception of Reuters, the news and wire services hardly nibbled at the stories.

Donald Willard didn't get it. From his work station at his college he had followed the various expeditions, assessed continuous satellite reconnaissance, registered all the different data bases, and made computerized comparisons. For over a month he'd been assessing one of those "short-lived phenomena." The data he'd gathered over the weekend had proven to be the culmination of all that he had suspected and feared.

"Donald, it's good to hear your voice," Roald said enthusiastically.

"Sorry for the wake-up call."

"You saved me from my ex-wife," Shiftren chuckled.

"I'll be brief. I know you were following ozone in the Arctic. What about recent findings?"

"What about them?"

"I calculate a resurgence."

"I don't think so. It happened once. There's been no evidence since that time."

"You've been following?"

"Not exactly. I switched. My grant ran out. I thought you knew. Two years ago. I'm looking at nitrogen these days. But seriously, what's up, my friend?"

"What's going on in the Northwest Territories, Roald? What are they saying on the Canadian news?"

"Saying? Saying about what? What are you talking about, Donald?"

It was no good. Shiftren didn't watch TV. He listened only to a classical music station on the radio of his BMW. Willard felt suddenly alone, isolated, ready to doubt his own findings.

"Wait a minute," Shiftren added. "There was something about the flu, or the trees. Just a second—"

Yes! he thought to himself. The flu, that was a beginning. It would confirm. . . . Willard held tight, thinking with a clenched fist as Roald came back to the phone. "What about the flu?" Donald repeated.

"Just a minute. I'm looking—here it is. In yesterday's local paper. I'd only glanced at ît."

"Read it to me."

"It's posted from a place called Fort Nelson."

"I know it."

"That's in the Stikines, very close to Churchill Peak. Very high mountain."

"I know. Go on."

"It says seven deaths and a host of reported illnesses are being attributed to an outbreak of a flu virus similar to the Hong Kong variety. Similar outbreaks have been reported at Norman Wells, Port Radium, Inuvik, and at several Eskimo communities throughout the Franklin Mountains and Melville Hills. It says a freakish heat spell, occasioned by temperatures soaring thirty degrees above the seasonal norm, may have triggered the sickness. That's interesting."

"How hot?"

"Eighty-eight degrees. That's got to be a misprint."

"That's all it says?"

"There's one more thing, Don. At least in Fort Nelson. The report says the trees have taken a beating. It also mentions hordes of mosquitoes. It's early for them."

There was a pause on either end. Neither of them wanted to be the first to offer the obvious conclusion. "You're not thinking—"

"I've been tracking it all along," Willard rushed to acknowledge. "A minihole."

"But that's not feasible."

"It's feasible. You know there was a precedent," Willard argued, firm in his data now. "Come on. You were the one."

"Yah, but, Donald, it was never confirmed. And furthermore the projections—"

"Screw the projections. No one projected any of this."

"Don, Don, I'd have to see it. I'd need air samples. It's too farfetched. Spring in the Arctic is—I know from my homeland—it is about weather, not chemistry. It happened in Thule, twenty days, that was all. And only once. I just—"

"You're crapping out on me. I need you, Roald."

"Look. Don't you think the media would have been up there, pouring over a story like that?"

"No, I don't."

"You can't expect to assess a proposed disequilibrium from Seattle. You've got to be there. And as you must know, you're not the only one who has continued to look north. Krutzen, Solons, McDover, any number of others. Here at the Institute—why, there's McByers. He's somewhere in Europe. A wedding, but you could probably track him down. Talk to him. He'll tell you. We're not seeing anything."

"How long has McByers been in Europe, away from his computer?"

"I don't know, I think ten days. . . . Look, Don, I don't know where you're getting your data but satellites are fairly unambiguous."

"Fairly's not good enough," Willard said with a deadpan annoyance.

Roald was sleepy. He didn't need this at six thirty on a Saturday. "There's depletion around the North Pole for a few weeks early each spring. But that's it. You know as well as I."

"I'm sorry I bothered you, Roald. Go back to sleep."

"Don, I hear your frustration. If it were a minihole, we'd know about it."

"Of course you would." Willard hung up.

For the next two days he was on the phone calling colleagues all over the world. Not one of them shared his doubts. Many, in fact, had already been warned by Roald. It was like some conspiracy, backbiting. Willard should never have called Shiftren. He clearly felt proprietary about the Arctic. No one was going to claim his turf. If there was something there, it had to be Shiftren's find.

By Monday afternoon Willard was certain. He could feel it in the air. The sun over Seattle was different—not just unseasonably sweltering, but *different*. Intense enough to keep him indoors. He did not have fair skin and was not obsessive about avoiding sunlight for fear of skin cancer, but this sun was . . . deviant.

He'd interviewed a number of residents in Fort Nelson, including a local M.D., and pieced together a picture of dire ecological disruption. People had died. Plant life was wilting. There were intense retinal disorders, over ninety known cases of blindness. Local authorities assumed it to be snow blindness—something that lasts for a week at the maximum. The sun was melting eight feet of winter snow. There were floods. Other people were sick. And to top it all, mosquito larvae were maturing early and swarming across a region stretching south in an erratic swathe from the Bering Strait to the Alaskan panhandle.

Willard rolled himself the thirty feet back through the magnetic discs and put up the tape marked COEFFICIENTS. Burt had taken the afternoon off. He said his apartment had been broken into.

Willard jostled his mouse, enlarged a sphere in full color, plotting his points and taking measurements. A hundred thirty miles from end to end. The shape varied, much like the kind of bubbles children blew at birthday parties, warped, wafting, changing dimensions. A thin, translucent blob, moving like a blimp.

Willard tried to imagine it. A cannibalized, arid void, drifting like an iceberg, caught in the currents of wind that carried but could not penetrate. The ozone molecule, O_3, by-product of chemistry four billion years old, precursor of all life on the planet, was being wiped out at the rate of over 100,000 ozone molecules for every alien chlorine molecule that got in; that rose from the surface of human activities five, six, seven miles below. Or was there something more? Some other scavenger that was opening the heavens above and admitting the deadly aboriginal sun?

Willard's fingers tensed on the keypad. Was it true? Did his computer really know? Were the faint chemical residues picked up at several monitoring stations hundreds of miles north, on remote islands, atop mountains, up the Inland Passage accurate? The system was not immune to problems. Now Willard had to believe in his own devices.

He turned on the little Sony TV beneath a row of books on his desk. He caught the crucial tail end of a local report on the whales. ". . . and the on-site NOB—the National Oceanic Bureau spokesperson in Seattle—Elizabeth Gage said earlier today that marine biologists are still conducting tests to determine whether it was in fact pollution in the northern Pacific. In other local news this evening, birds—Chinese ring-necked pheasants, to be precise—a whole flock of them, smacked into the Space Needle around lunchtime. Whether they were hungry or just plain lost is unclear. Most of them died. Rites are being conducted by the Chinese Catholic Mission here as well as by the Children's Fund for Animals and donations to the Ring-necked Pheasant Society of Seattle are being encouraged. We'll have more on this and other stories at five . . ." Willard could hear his heart palpitating as he quickly noted down the name of the said spokesperson for the whales. Elizabeth Gage. He picked up the phone. It was 4:00 P.M.

"Yes?"

"Elizabeth Gage?"

"That's right."

"My name is Donald Willard."

"Who?"

"You don't know me but we need to talk."

65

CHAPTER 8

John Gage usually edited his own pieces but there was little time left before the five o'clock news. He was working with Herb, the station's master ace of the off-line rooms. They were cutting in the stand-up material from the Needle and adding quick fixes to an otherwise completed piece. Despite his fervent complaints, John liked the editing process. It was the one technical universe in which he was marginally competent. Changing a tire, fixing the switches on their hot tub, installing a stereo stretched the philosophy grad's acumen from apoplexy to evacuation. But high-tech editing seemed to meld comfortably with his left brain. John could assemble a five-minute piece in an evening, enacting fifty, sixty edits with studied aplomb. When the picture lived, he got a charge.

John took important news events personally, and the craft of journalism was not going to intervene in his subjective style. A point-of-view made television interesting. However, it was rare that such perspectives got past the media standards of objectivity and scared programmers. But such perspectives were the basis of any dramatic payoff, even in nonfiction television. Unfortunately for John, most professionals with whom he came in contact believed in objectivity. John, on the other hand, thought there was no such thing.

In his own private world of aesthetic arbitration, John

Gage delved in heady intellectual realms, even in the mundane interests of getting an evening news story about cocaine out under pressure with the expected six rating and twelve share. Blow up the face, bring in the audio of the cuffing, fold over a synthesizer pad of strings. These details were John's compensation, drawing him ever closer to the existentialist meanderings of his doctoral dissertation and away from the everpresent banality at the effective heart of what paid off his triple mortgage.

"That's quite a jump cut," Herb said skeptically. Herb lived in these rooms and had the keystroke agility of a rodeo star or flame thrower. At the same time, Herb had suffered the ineptitude of managers for four years on the job. He was burned out and thinking about getting his own gig together, maybe in his house. He haunted the electronic meets on his off hours, the national conventions, searching for a product line, an angle that could steer him clear of the nightly news syndrome. Like John, Herb had raging dreams he intended to satisfy.

"We don't have time. Print it." John wanted it done. The deadline was implacable in his business. Jeremy Singer, his executive producer, was a tough black veteran of the Vietnamese New Year assault of 1968, of the battle of Hue. Singer also commanded grudging respect at KCBD. He earned his title, starting as a wouldn't-spit-upon intern, cutting out newspaper clippings for ungrateful associate producers ten years younger, and going on to being executive producer for current affairs, a job he now wore with the dignity of epaulets. His wounds were real.

He was one of those who had first stepped forward to implicate both Charlie and Bravo Companies for the My Lai 4 and My Khe 4 massacres. Singer was not part of the 11th Brigade or Task Force Barker, but a close friend was, who told Singer everything. Three hundred forty-seven innocent, unarmed civilians murdered. Many of the women were raped prior to being rounded up and blown away, while a lieutenant colonel, a colonel and a major general looked on from circling helicopters. Singer wrote a letter to the Army chief of staff that eventually found its way into a Pulitzer

Prize-winning exposé. Singer had a thing about John Gage. He thought he was good, but something of a pussy. "Your sweet white untrodden ass would have gone down in forty-eight hours in Nam," Singer would snap at him. The oppression of John Gage's job was the unforgiving beeline that shot directly from his editing console and its own time-consuming tyrannies to the hawk-eyed scrutinies of the boss man who could, at a whimsy, demand petty crap changes, and changes were technically more difficult for Gage.

And then there was Charles Fields, Gage's real nemesis. While Gage believed that the forty-five-year-old Singer actually liked him, harbored real hopes for his future at KCBD, John knew that he'd never work through his animosities with Fields. And yet he had to submit editorially to the surly creep in crucial areas of script and timing. Gage could labor for a month on a project only to have that prima donna pollute its polish with his on-air delivery. While they both commandeered the news, Fields was anchorman and it was his face people remembered and listened to, in the end. That he was younger than Gage, even forgetting the fact he was a jerk, added to John's humiliation.

The phone rang.

"Yeah?" Gage said impatiently.

It was Darla at the message center. "I'm putting your wife through."

"Hi?"

John had little time for his wife's lingering question mark. "I'm crazed. What's up?" he said abruptly.

"You were at the Needle today."

"Uh-huh. You've probably heard the weird thing about the birds by now." His voice was flushed with the annoying why-are-you-bothering-me-right-now tone that she had come to hate about her husband.

"John, honey, listen very carefully."

"Sweetheart, I have a deadline in less than a half hour. Let me listen carefully tonight, in bed, with my tongue lodged in your secret mailbox."

She was not tempted, not now. "I said listen—"

68

"Really, I just can't focus on it at the moment." He was irritated, truly under the gun, and she did this to him regularly.

"You don't even know what I'm going to tell you."

"No. I don't. You're absolutely right."

"How's that?" Herb said.

"Just a sec." John looked at the screen, saw the final cut, and nodded approvingly. "That's perfect. Let's go with it." Then he turned his arbitrary interest to his wife. "Fine. Why don't you tell me. Liz?"

Elizabeth was debating whether or not to pass on the whole idea. She knew he didn't deserve to have it. On the other hand, she saw no better way to mend their relationship. His rude impatience had been a knot of contention for over a year, in her mind. In fact, she couldn't even remember when the two of them began drifting, first in bed and then at the breakfast table. Later, at dinner. The kids noticed and were discreet, but the whole family languished under the pall of John and Elizabeth growing apart. This morning had seemed to be a start toward normality. But it was more than normality she craved. He rarely touched her anymore, although he talked constantly about sex. It was always tonight. In fact their lovemaking had all but ceased. John didn't know it, exactly, but Elizabeth was getting desperate.

"There's a connection between the death of those whales and the birds that flew into the Needle," she said finally.

"Like what?" he snapped, seizing upon the words as if they'd been clipped by some page boy.

"There's an ozone hole."

"Sure there is. What else is new?"

"You always talk about the Big Scoop. This is your Big Scoop."

"Sweetheart, I beg you, let's talk about it tonight, please?"

She persisted. It was for his own stupid good, she knew. "Did you film the birds?"

"Yes."

"Have you looked at the footage?"

"No."

"Well, why not?"

"Because it has nothing to do with cocaine on the streets of Seattle."

"Would you please look at the footage—I mean, in close-up. Blow it up, look at the eyes of the birds and the way they were flying."

"How do you know how they were flying or anything about their eyes?"

"I spoke with a chemist, or a physicist—I mean, he's sort of both—and he specializes in the atmosphere. He's over at the college. Donald Willard's his name, and he told me this whole business. John, it's unbelievable what's happening, and when I told him you were who you were and where you were today, etc., etc., he said you've *got* to study the footage. Look, I've got to go pick up Evans—I'll actually be glad when he gets his learner's permit. If I miss your piece at five, I'll see it at eleven, but promise you'll study that footage. Now. I mean immediately. John, I'll tell you more tonight, in bed."

"That's a promise?"

"Yep!"

"I'll wear the red thingless."

"The red thingless? Excellent." He couldn't honestly remember.

"I love you."

"Yeah. Okay. Me too."

She put down the phone. For all his efforts, she thought, her husband had the makings of a perpetual *schmuck!*

Herb looked at Gage. "We're done."

"Thanks, man. And Happy Birthday. What are you gonna do tonight?"

"Laura's taking me out."

"Right. Have a good one." Herb threw on his leather air force jacket and headed for his Harley-Davidson out in the parking lot.

John ejected the master tape and took it down the corridor to Singer's office. He poked his face in and left it on the desk.

Singer looked at his watch and shook his head. "That's cutting it close. How much is there I haven't seen?"

"It's cued up. Just the last four minutes."

"Is it good?"

"I think so."

"Come back in ten." Singer always liked to screen the tapes alone.

John went back to the editing room, slapped in the final field cassette, cued up the beginning of Andy's bird coverage, threw the player into two-thirds slow-mo and watched.

There was a scream, then the jerking camera. It all came back for the first time. He increased the volume and dimmed the lights in the room. The first bird hit the glass. The screams were rising, chairs falling over, a man backing up into a table, knocking it over, and there was the crashing of objects, none of which Gage remembered exactly. And there—a crack—then another as hundreds of the birds slammed into the revolving restaurant windows. Then it all shattered. The entire wallowing, unsteady flock had collided with furnishings and with people.

He paused, rewound twenty seconds, then blew up the body of a bird pummeling the face of an elderly woman. Her spectacles were thrown off as she fell. Slowly, ever so slowly, a tray of antipasto twirled batonlike into the outer reaches, more tables collapsing in the avalanche of bodies, their contents borne by centrifugal illogic across the room.

The eyes! There was a disintegration in the birds' eyes. Gage saw the ulcerated cornea and watched the birds' descent onto the granite floor, covered with food, behind the anguished sluggish screech of human voices, their eyes swollen to the point of blindness, purple, acned abcesses, with ooze trickling from the gutted remains, diseased faces, all at the speed of slurred and unintelligible pain. Behind this burned the noonday sun like an explosion of white. The lights conflagrated in the lens. . . . *Holy shit!* he muttered to himself. John replayed the scene, more slowly. Every bird had lost its vision. Every bird was dying. He went back to the first hit of video again and saw the skewed incoming trail of unnavigable motion, wings struggling in a flux of uncommand against a weather quickly deteriorating, blue skies of combustion. The birds were finished.

Now back up to full speed. The horror in full complicity sixty stories above the street. Sirens, screams, frenzy.

"It's good, John. Nice piece of work," Singer said, putting his head in the room.

"Thanks." John was totally off his guard.

"Five minutes to air time. I'm sending it down. Again, way to go." He started back out the door, then: "What do you have there?"

"The bird thing at the Needle."

"Yeah, I heard about that. You were there when it happened?"

"I was. You want to see it?"

"Nothing we can do with it now. Anything there for the eleven o'clock broadcast?"

"Yeah."

"Right. I'll be back up. Don't go away."

John called Donald Willard over at the College of Washington. He remembered the name.

"You spoke with my wife."

"You're the journalist. I'm watching you right now. Drugs. Forget drugs. They're not today's story."

"What is today's story, Mr. Willard?"

"Tell me what you saw in those birds."

"I think you know what I saw. What in God's name did that to them?"

"The sun, Mr. Gage. The sun."

"And the whales?"

"Same."

"Same what?"

"We've known about the ozone hole over the Antarctic for fifteen years. A hole that's bigger than the United States. It moves. Parts of it have covered the tip of South America. It spins off into little minibubbles."

"I never heard that—"

"Yeah, well, there's a lot you haven't heard. Like the fact a similar hole hovers over the Arctic, about the same size—

and it moves. It throws off smaller replicas of itself. Well, sir, we got a big problem here in Seattle. What we've got is a hole. I reckon ninety—maybe a hundred, hundred-fifty miles across, fifty, sixty thousand feet up. One of those minibubbles, those replicas. And it's moving this way. And it's coming in fast."

Gage wasn't actually following. He couldn't see it, couldn't envision it, but Willard's tone convinced him. The sound of the peril. The nonchalance behind the urgency, or the urgency behind the nonchalance. "Okay. Supposing you're right about this. And I say supposing because frankly I don't know who the hell you are or where you're coming from or even what it means that you're telling me—"

"Make no mistake. It's true, it's bad, it could be the worst-case scenario."

"Worst case for what?"

"Are you totally ignorant of ozone depletion and what it does?"

"Skin cancer."

"Try the equivalent, within ten minutes, of an all-out nuclear exchange—but without any of the noise or smoke, or obvious damage. Try overnight skin cancers, fatal melanomas, blindness, the destruction of all crops, the interruption of all animal and plant and insect behavior."

"I see. The real hell-and-brimstone stuff. . . . What church do you belong to, Willard?"

"Don't try my patience. There are other reporters in this town. Frankly, if your wife hadn't shown the level of interest and intelligence that she did, I'd hang up right now because you sound like a moron."

"Fuck you," Gage snickered.

"Fine. Good-bye."

"Wait—" John caught him just before he hung up. "Look, it's been one of those days, you know what I mean?"

There was silence. "I'm sorry. I'm all ears." John knew he couldn't afford to act this way. It just came naturally.

Willard was also stricken with a timing problem. Maybe he could find someone more reliable, maybe not. Elizabeth Gage was at NOB. The match would *seem* to work, if only her husband, this two-bit hack reporter, would calm down and listen. Willard tried again. "If I'm not mistaken—and I've been following ozone for twenty years—Seattle is the first city that's going to get it. The first big city. Towns in Canada are already devastated. They just don't understand what's hit 'em."

John reprised in his mind everything the scientist just told him. Now it hit home. "Are you there?" Willard finally said, frustrated.

"Jesus Christ, Willard. What you're saying is that we've got a major—I mean *major*—emergency!"

"Oooh—good! You *are* fast."

"When can we meet?"

"I'm here." After John got his location, they both hung up.

Singer returned to John's editing suite. "Your story looked great."

"Oh—it did?"

"You didn't watch it?"

"What time . . ." he mumbled in total distraction. Then he looked at his watch. "I got to go."

"I thought you were going to show me the bird story?"

John was afraid. He was thinking of his family. He wanted to get a crew over to interview Willard. He was overwrought with the inflammations of the bird faces. He'd jotted down the building and room number at the college and needed only Singer's permission.

"I just got off the phone with somebody. . . . Let me walk you through it."

Gage rewound to the spot close-up of the dying birds, slow-mo'ed the film and escorted the open-mouthed Vietnam vet through a new kind of horror.

"I'll be a sonofabitch. What do you suppose?"

"The guy's name I just spoke with is Donald Willard. He's at the college. He first contacted my wife when he heard the news about the dead whales. He says Seattle's about to get hit by an ozone hole, which also killed the whales."

Singer remembered other fantasies from Gage's past.

On-air flubs. Flagrant distortions, rash connections. "Now that worries me, John."

"Worries the hell out of me, I don't mind telling you. Y'ever seen birds like that?"

"Nope. And I've never seen an ozone hole either. And I don't plan to."

"What are you saying?"

"I'm saying you've gone over the top before and I'm not going to let you do it again."

"You just saw!"

"I just saw a bunch of crazy birds. I don't know what I saw. Sure they were sick. And they had cataracts or something. I'm no zoologist. But I sure as shit am not going after a paranoid ecology story."

"That's what it is to you?"

"You're serious? You're going to pursue an ozone hole that just happens to be coming in for a landing at Sea-Tac International? John, listen to me, I'm your friend."

"You owe me."

"I owe you?"

"I fucking risked my life for the drug story."

"Yeah, you silly bastard, you probably did risk your life, hangin' around with some of those street folk like that. And we appreciate a job well done. Now I told you that. But I sure the hell don't owe you, so don't go giving me that crap."

"I want to investigate this. First thing in the morning. I want Andy and Wendy, and I want to go out and interview this guy."

Singer always tested his field producers. It was a game. Why should his department risk $2,000 on an instinct? Which is what a crew for a day and gear cost the department. It wasn't like a newspaper. Furthermore, as Gage had discovered on previous assignments, the station group that owned KCBD was managed by a very conservative bank in Bremerton with investments in certain industries that had on past occasions frowned upon certain stories. Singer was the sorry recipient of this pressure. With a sick wife at home and little security in TV news, Singer would always give in.

Vietnam was a different kind of battlefield. But his career was not about such risks. Gage in turn got the hand-me-down fraught nerves and insecurity, the mock brashness, the tirades, for Singer was not above taking out his own frustrations on Gage. Today he was in a worse mood than most. And Singer wasn't alone in that. Gage had noticed a strange hyped irritability in the air, on the surface roads, among employees at the station since early morning. Earthquake weather.

Singer thought it over, standing in the heated limbo of power that he alone commanded. "Yeah. All right. You go check it out. You get anything, we'll incorporate it with those birds tomorrow at five. No other news group has 'em or is on to this guy I presume?"

"That's right. It's ours."

"Go on then. Get outa here. Bring your wife some flowers. And just watch your ass."

"Thanks, Jeremy."

"I said get!"

CHAPTER 9

Six months before, back in December, Haskel Murphy had been brought out of a month-long Montana getaway with his wife and kids by a helicopter, three days after Mt. Redoubt had erupted for its twenty-sixth consecutive time on the Cape Douglas Peninsula of Alaska. These events were not unrelated.

On that December day, the helicoptor's pilot handed Haskel a letter. What that letter, Haskel Murphy, and Mt. Redoubt had in common was the accumulation of several obscure pieces of data by a National Space Bureau research team that had worked out of Maryland. Haskel's longtime buddy Felix Girard was the NSB project manager. That data had set wheels in motion favoring a third Arctic expedition. This was the one thing that counted more to Murphy than his time in Montana.

Haskel had worked with the research team before but had gone on to other projects, like the space shuttle jet. The team of investigators had continued their work, however, combing the upper gray-blue stratosphere above Redoubt's steady gaseous stream, and calculating what turned out to be an unprecedented burden of chlorine compounds spreading out over the far north. To many atmospheric physicists, the high-altitude atom is the purest expression of the life force.

Coaxed into being by elemental processes forged during the Big Bang, brought to fruition in the thin cirrus surrounding earth, these uncountable trillions of particles existed in a realm akin to spirit. One species of particles was of special interest to the NSB team, because its collective weight and extent could be directly attributable to Mt. Redoubt's ash-ridden caldera. Chlorine.

Sixty, seventy, eighty thousand feet above the planet, chlorine attacked the ozone molecule. There was chemical lust at work in this reaction, which resulted in a so-called mating syndrome and the depletion of ozone. The volcano had thrown up a massive amount of chlorine. That could mean real trouble.

NSB's findings from the first two sorties in Antarctica and the Norwegian Arctic had been made public. The latter expedition was even conducted in open cooperation with the Soviets. Both Willard and Shiftren had seen all the findings. But this new foray—for which Murphy was solicited—was under national security guidelines. The legislation mandating such privacy fell within the Pentagon's aegis over NSB: military missions were given Top Secret priority status not only on the shuttle, but on any other NSB endeavor. That included the sleek, lightweight high-altitude jet called the ER-2, which resembled the older U-2 spy planes. In this instance, environmental collaboration was sublimated to Defense Department concerns. Outside researchers like Willard were no longer in the information loop.

Murphy had built the instruments sent on the earlier Deep Ozone Project flights. Now Felix Girard needed data that was new and intensified. NSB understood that the Arctic regions were covered by cold clouds at eighty thousand feet high and that with the coming of spring those clouds might possibly break up, serving to randomly diffuse the winter ozone hole. In theory, that diffusion meant that the hole could fracture and potentially spin off in bubbles. The NSB Cray and Fujitsu supercomputers plotted the initial breakup using TOMS and NIMBUS satellites to track the hole's movement. But there were lag times and measure-

to be easier. Temperatures would be much warmer, winds less violent. Any rescue in the Northwest Territories had a better than fifty–fifty chance of succeeding. Not so in the infinite whiteout of Antarctica. Early this morning, in his shiny pressurized suit, Jake had boarded his plane with an easygoing stride. He was not worried.

The route would take Jake over Regina, Fort McMurray, Great Slave Lake, Great Bear Lake, and finally the Amundsen Gulf at the Beaufort Sea, the last point of contact with the hole. From there he'd turn right around and come back via Norman Wells, the Nahanni National Park, the Spatsizi Plateau Wilderness, Prince George, Kamloops, and Glacier National Park.

Less than two hours after takeoff, Jake found himself in deep cloud cover, the aircraft plowing through a continuing veil of ice crystals.

Murphy instructed Jake to activate a timing device on the left-wing pod. This would switch the measuring instrument into a mode that sampled ozone counts every ten minutes. The vectors were plotted and the data fed simultaneously into the computer routers in Maryland, where the satellite numbers were crunched. A slew of concentrations were tallied under the right-wing pod but Murphy's left-wing black box contented itself with other diffusion coefficients. He'd figured out how to measure molecular density at 500 knots in real time for a number of heretofore puzzling chemicals, including bromine monoxide, nitric acid, and chlorine. Murphy could even detect the elusive methyl chloride, a chemical resulting from the burning of rain forest, as well as from slash-and-burn agriculture. Methyl-chloride, which, like the other chemicals in question, rose up from a myriad of local sources around the planet and then apparently concentrated in the polar regions, was also known to cannibalize the ozone layer.

For Murphy, there was less suspense in this mission because he knew the pilot was not at risk. In Antarctica, when his devices had failed to record chlorine monoxide on the first two flights out, and only an all-night desperate computer search for the broken part kept the $20-million-dollar expedition alive, he was a nervous wreck. Men were risking their lives for nothing and he was to blame. Now the situation was more relaxed.

The blip on the monitor was still recording in the parts-per-trillion category, a relatively normal reading. Thirty minutes later, however, there was a surge.

"There we go!" Murphy announced. "We're on-line."

There was applause from the other team members present, as if a child had been born—perverse in the mind of Felix, who watched the readout beside Murphy expectantly. The levels were four hundred times higher than had ever been recorded, all in the space of an aerial edge. A cut-off point with no known circumference as yet.

"Look at this just in over the fax," said flight controller Winston Himes, seated at the computer array. "It's from Maryland. A still frame of TOMS eight minutes ago. Nothing!" The satellite image of the plane's coordinates showed no indication of substantial depletion. "Figure six minutes, minus the two for print and faxing. At five hundred ten knots that's, let's see—"

"Sixty miles," Felix stated matter-of-factly.

"Right. Sixty miles south by southeast. We're talking clear as of Darnley Bay."

"Get Maryland on the line. I need faxes every four minutes," Murphy said.

"Wish I could see the view, over!" Jake the Racer said into his mouth set. "We gettin' anything up here?"

"Nothing to worry about," Himes replied. "You just fly that baby, over."

"Yep. Over."

Five minutes later the quicksilvered aircraft headed back on its intended flight line.

"Another fax, Haskel." Faye Johnston, Himes's traveling secretary, pulled it off hurriedly, ripping it in two. "Whoops!"

"Give it here." Felix grabbed it and saw more of the same. Nothing. "What do you read, Haskel?"

"It's coming through now. Okay." Murphy studied the printout. The stylus had made erratic quivers on the graph.

Then it took a plunge. "We're back to parts per trillion. Have the Racer circle back around. Can you?"

"One time. That's it. We're cutting it very close as it is on the return fuel," Himes reminded everyone present. "Take her in a three-minute broad sweep back around toward the west. Do a full circle, Jake."

"You got it," the voice read back as if it were next door.

"Put Maryland back on the line," Felix said, anticipating Murphy's own needs.

"Felix, we're seeing a lag time of no more than a minute, ten miles of airspace, between what I'm reading and what the satellite is reading, is that correct?"

"Uh-huh."

"Now look—"

The graph jerked—lows, highs, parts per trillion, sudden parts per billion, back again—all in the space of a few minutes, while the satellite continued to picture a benign haze, scattered around the fringes of the North Pole.

"It's like the Swiss cheese of the McMurdo experiments," Felix acknowledged, remembering back to the late 1980s when physicists set off a number of balloons from the Antarctic McMurdo station and saw within a given column of air a patchwork puzzle of differing ozone densities that they merely summarized by month, height, and mean depletion.

"Precisely," Murphy said. "There's not enough to give the satellite a proper read. Tell the Racer to start home. I want to see a pattern here."

"Jake, you read me, over?"

"Loud and clear, Winse. What's the game plan?"

"Keep your helmet on and bring her on down, over."

"I'm there, over."

For the next hour Felix and Murphy charted a quilt of chlorine surges and dips that was as fragmentary and myriad as the thousands of lakes dotting the Northwest Territories. In one vector, thirty miles long, there was an enormous opening. The sky had been denuded. It was over a fibrovascular-looking scrawl of glaciers somewhere near the Montana border.

There was static interfering with Jake's radio transmission, proceeded by a shaky-sounding pilot. "Whoa!"

"What is it, Jake? Jake?" Felix was right there.

"Sunshine! Fuckin-A. Sorry. Be a minute—"

"Jake?"

"Good God!" Felix uttered. "Is that for real?" He was looking at the printout of data before him.

"Levels are all over the place," Murphy stated. "I read no ozone. Felix I also read a wavelength of 250 nanometers. We're into the UV-C band."

"But that's not possible," Felix said, clearing his throat of fear.

"Right. Tell him not to look at the sun," Murphy said. There was a second's pause in transmissions. Felix was bewildered. "Tell him now, Felix!"

"Jake—"

"I heard him," Jake said over the open channel. "Hey, folks, am I okay, over?"

Murphy spoke to him. "If you can, close your eyes until you're back in cloud."

"Yeah. Right."

It was the scenario they'd been looking for. Here was proof of the theorized breakup, an innocuous pattern of dissolution with its so-called local perturbations. As the plane moved farther south, the dissolution became complete. What Felix's team hadn't counted on, and this was not the time to prove it, was the magnitude of ozone depletion in any one bubble, not to mention the unprecedented, damaging wavelength. Both Felix and Murphy had known since Physics 101 that biologically active ultraviolet radiation reached earth in the 290-to-320-nanometer band. It was called UV-B and it could cause extreme damage if unmitigated. That is to say, if people didn't wear protective sun creams and visors. To most people, UV-B was simply UV, ultraviolet radiation. The B part was an esoteric add-on bandied about by experts. But that B part was what actually counted. It was the reason for controversy, laws, conferences, scientific expeditions. The fact that UV was biologically active, harmful, was what made for an alleged ozone crisis from the very beginning of its discovery.

There were wavelengths shorter than the 290-nanometer band but scientists never talked about them because such wavelengths were known to be totally neutralized in the stratosphere by protective chemical reactions that were inherent to life on earth. UV-B was bad. It could induce skin cancers, eye cataracts, and other ills. And Felix and his colleagues knew that nucleic acids—the basic material not only of the human gene, but of the genes of all living organisms—had no chance whatsoever against ultraviolet radiation in wavelengths even lower than UV-B, against the sun's intensity as it would have shone on the earth's surface four billion years ago, before the evolution of an ozone layer to block it out.

"Anybody live near there?" Murphy asked.

"Nah," Himes said blandly, staring at the USGS maps that had been stretched out before him, and getting up to move the operation outside. "Glaciers."

Himes knew nothing about genes or wavelengths. He had one thing on his mind. The plane would be arriving in forty minutes and there was much to be done in preparation. The ER-2's wings had to be supported by rolling stanchions as it slowed to a halt on the tarmac, or they would collapse, even in the slightest wind.

"He can tell that from the map?" Murphy asked Felix with more than a hint of skepticism.

"No. I'm gonna call and find out."

"Who ya gonna call?" Murphy pressed.

"Ghostbusters!" Johnston said with an idiot's smile.

As Felix went for the phone, Murphy looked at him and raised another point. "And what do we do if there *is* a town there? I mean, the depletion could hang around for ten minutes or ten *hours* for all we know. Those bubbles are moving."

Felix stopped short. "Now let's talk about that. We don't really know, do we?"

"No. We don't really know."

Felix turned and looked over at the flight controller. "Is Buddy prepared?"

"He's just finishing his oxygen rinse."

"Go tell Himes that Buddy's up next. Same route exactly."

Jake the Racer landed safely and went immediately to sick bay. His face was badly sunburned and he was in need of fluids. A doctor applied baby lotions and Jake consumed six large glasses of Gatorade, then fell asleep in his bed.

In the meantime, the second pilot, Buddy, had taken off and was re-covering Jake's same route.

Three hours later, Murphy noted a completely different configuration at around the 68th parallel. The numbers had no resemblance to the first flight. The dip in chlorine concentration at the 124th longitude by 64 degrees looked as if the plane had plunged off a Great Barrier Reef of chemistry. Still, Maryland showed no hole outside the Arctic Circle. At 6:00 P.M. the ER-2 was sailing toward Kamloops when the chlorine level surged again.

"Folks, we're on again," he said, looking at the wavelength.

At that moment, higher-ups from the space center at Maryland were on the phone as well. For the first time the satellite was picking up the reemergence of what looked like an ozone hole. Scientists there saw a concentrated smudge, something that only a trained eye could pick out from among darker shades and cloud formations. But the detected smudge was small, they said—barely an ascertainable image.

Felix and Murphy had on-the-scene equipment far more sensitive and callibrated than the satellites hundreds of miles above the earth's surface. The two men saw something else—a dramatic swirl, up around twenty parts per billion, a phenomenal, in fact, unprecedented amount of chlorine monoxide and chlorine nitrate—and again in the lower, unthinkable wavelength range.

"We got a problem here," Murphy said. He was dumbfounded. He'd never seen anything like it. But before he could classify the experience, the ER-2 had passed through the problem. Thirty miles away the ER-2 now passed along readings that indicated that things were clear as a whistle, a moderately healthy ozone level.

"I have no explanation," Murphy said to Felix sometime later that evening. "I have to presume that what we witnessed was simply the sporadic dissolution of ozone you set out to prove. Nothing more, nothing less."

Both Felix and Murphy cleared their heads. They each wanted to believe that things would go on, business as usual, that the sudden surges on the printout had merely reflected a freakish one-time event in nature—dramatic, to be sure, but irrelevant, an anomaly.

The two men eyed one another as they packed up their briefcases and prepared to close the file on the whole event. Felix was relieved not to have to deal with the press this time. He remembered only too well how the aftermath of the first ozone expedition years before had been mired in confusing signals from the media.

Felix and Murphy felt like they understood what had happened earlier this day, as they philosophically goaded one another over anesthetizing mugs of hot chocolate. Such atmospheric disarray as had shown up on their computer monitors was nature's way of combating imbalance. The earth's chemistry—guided by living organisms from day one—needed an ozone layer and was not about to see a single member of the species called man skew that all-crucial balance.

Comfortable with their shared wisdom, Murphy and Felix hit the sack. They had decided to repeat the mission with an altered flight plan the next day. It might be overkill, but the Defense Department was paying the bill and they could afford it. After all, Felix reasoned, the total annual budget for NSB's stratospheric research program was one-twentieth the cost of a single B-2 Stealth Bomber. And that made him mad.

CHAPTER 10

TUESDAY

It was another rare spring morning in Seattle as Charles Fields drove across Interstate 90 from his home on the east side of Mercer Island. Mt. Rainier boasted of magic, its ivory-white glaciers cresting into an azure sky. It was a *National Geographic* day. The air was clear enough to deceive the eye into believing that the mountain hovered directly over the city.

Coming home from the college at six in the morning, Stan the security guard had watched an amazing sunrise. The whole city seemed to be framed beneath a sparkling patina, as if the sky were dimly on fire, between stars and sunlight. It was exquisite.

Thesika Aghiapolous might also have welcomed the Grecian sun from her back garden on Capitol Hill. For her lavender-colored Bourbon roses—*Commandant Beaurepaires*—had come into majestic bloom early on account of the extraordinary spell of heat. But the heat was even beyond the roses' normal appetites. By seven thirty this morning they were dying. Thesika set up a canopy of towels to protect them, but the sparrows and robins kept exposing the flowers. She called Dino on his car phone to get him home to help her with the roses, which were rare.

At school, Evans and Jennifer Gage and the rest of the students were already stricken with the summer itch. This weather was two months early and quite strange for the city of mythic drizzles and athlete's foot.

"It's the Greenhouse Effect," Evans's friend Eric said. "My dad says it'll be great for the price of houses here." Evans could grasp that Eric didn't exactly understand the connection.

"What time are you interviewing Willard?" Elizabeth asked John, popping four English muffins in the toaster.

"At eleven," he replied, propping his legs up on the breakfast table, glancing at the *Post-Intelligencer* and the *Wall Street Journal.* The French doors were open to the side yard, where John normally left himself five minutes to do his fifty sit-ups and thirty push-ups. Later, after he'd gone to the office, Elizabeth would work out to an aerobics tape on her own little mat.

The phone rang. Elizabeth picked it up, then handed the receiver over with an exaggerated and amused grimace, whispering "It's him!"

"We did great in the ratings, John, old boy. Seems everyone and his sister watched the drug piece." It was Charles Fields.

"We?" Rage started to boil all over again in Gage.

"News is teamwork. Never forget it."

John controlled himself for the sake of curiosity. He wanted to know. "So what were the numbers?"

"A nine and a sixteen. Over the top. But Singer tells me you're off on a tangent this morning. I guess that's what life is all about. High ratings followed by fiascos. Just make sure I have something to look at by three thirty. No more of this five-minutes-to-air-time crap. Okay, Johnny boy?"

"Fuck you." John hung up.

"He's not that bad," Elizabeth said, trying to reinstate the mood of moments before.

"He's worse," John reminded her.

The phone rang again. "If it's him, tell him I already left."

"Hi, Mom. What's wrong? Uh-huh . . ."

John tuned out as his wife discussed various homeopathic miracle cures with her mother.

"She's so stubborn," Elizabeth said, having put down the receiver.

"What's up?" John said.

"Oh, they both woke up with the flu or something. Mom was up all night with a headache. We were supposed to have lunch. I'm going to bring her my bag of treats."

"I'm sorry about your folks. When are you gonna hear the final verdict from that Emmet Jones fellow?"

"Maybe today. But I know what I saw."

"Hypothetically speaking, I mean, I was thinking about it last night. What if—"

"What if what?"

"What if those birds were really telling us something, like the proverbial canary in the mine shaft?"

"You'll find out from Willard."

"Again. What if Willard's right?"

"I don't know. I'd say let's use that opportunity to take the romantic trip we've been talking about for two years."

"What about the kids?"

"I'm certainly not going to leave them at my parents', not if what Willard says is half true."

"So much for romance."

Elizabeth grinned. "They've seen us do it."

"Like hell?"

"You just don't remember."

"Yeah, well, hopefully they don't either."

She laughed.

"And what about your folks?" he went on. "We'd have to get them out also. And you can be sure that Evans is going to take a very sentimental attitude toward Sophie. And then there're her grandparents next door. You get my meaning."

"John, just do your interview."

"Sweetheart, do know what necrosis is?"

She squirmed. Elizabeth hated not to know something. "Maybe."

"If you'd seen those birds you'd recognize it. I was very upset by what I experienced."

"I know." She stroked his face. "I gotta go to work."

By the time John, Andy, and Wendy reached the college in

their press van, Willard had been at it for five days straight. His fatigue gave him the countenance and tired speech of a drunkard.

Unintroduced, Willard's slave, Burt, hung annoyingly around until Willard curtly dispatched him to the tape room.

"What happened to you?" Gage asked unpatronizingly.

"Car accident a few years ago."

"I'm sorry."

"You and me both. Now how do we do this?"

"What do you think about these overheads, Andy?"

The fluorescent lights tended to render a disconcerting moiré effect on video. "We'll be all right. I'll keep it angled low. Anyway, that'll give a neat high-tech look."

"Neat?" Willard repeated out loud. "Right." Turning to Gage: "And I look at you?"

"That's correct. We'll want to get some cover of you doing your thing—you know—at the computer, maybe wheeling yourself to some other computer to check things out. Then we'll do the interview and you'll just talk looking at me, not at the camera."

Burt came back out. "What do you want I should do?"

"He's not part of this," Willard said flatly.

"But it might be a good idea to have a busy look."

"A busy look?"

"Yeah, I mean to give the feeling of something important happening here, people at work and all. One lone scientist speaking out in a stuffy computer room—I mean, it lacks. I don't know, there's credibility in numbers I suppose."

Willard was too tired to argue. He just wanted to tell viewers on the five o'clock news what he knew and what was about to happen. That's all.

Andy adjusted his camera to the "9db" position, which enabled the inner electronics to operate in low-light levels. He used a sun gun off his battery belt for what are called "separates," shots of particular cutaways in shadow. Time would be saved by his not having to put up light stands. Wendy miked Willard while Gage carried a hand mic.

"Just do your thing," Gage encouraged the scientist.

"Burt, please put up reel nineteen," Willard said. "Thank you, Burt." Gage couldn't help but detect the sudden politeness in Willard's voice sawing through the hostility that separated the two men.

Willard punched up a baseline on his computer, wheeled himself over to another table, pulled out a disc from a file, came back, and reinserted it in an adjoining PC. He deftly struck a few keys and a three-dimensional graphic image blossomed on the screen. Willard brought up an x-y graph of longitudes and latitudes, as well as an underlay shadow approximating the Pacific Northwest. "This is crude but you get the point," Willard said.

"I'm standing at the College of Washington with Dr. Donald Willard, who has just called up on his computer an image of something strange and terrifying. What are we seeing, Dr. Willard?"

"Something strange and terrifying."

"Right. Why don't you tell us what it is about it that should make people . . . that is . . . oh, shit." Gage was fumbling. Something about Willard. "I mean, why should viewers care about you. I don't mean the wheelchair. Just give us your credentials. Wait a minute, guys. Cut tape. Roll back to the beginning. I gotta start over. Erase everything so far."

John was feeling slightly elated over the morning. In an unforced turn, he and his wife had mended months of ill-feeling. Nothing was particularly said. It was all in the doing. He loved the way she had sucked him off right on the floor just minutes after finishing her English muffins. She still had peanut butter and jam in her mouth.

They used to tie one another down on a big brass bed, heat chocolate syrup on the stove, then smear it all over one another, prior to the licking ritual. He'd paste it all over her cunt, in her soft forest of golden pubic hair—syrup warm and thick. He'd stir it up like an omelet, then sup the fudgelike cream until she'd come with her own cream. She'd then take his cock, dip it in a saucepan of chocolate— sometimes too hot, which was bizarre—and engulf him with her mouth for an hour. He'd come two and three times down her throat. It felt good to be in touch with those days. Though according to Elizabeth peanut butter didn't quite compare with hot chocolate sauce for enhancing the taste of sperm.

That was this morning. He shook it out of his head. Something was impeding his normal golden flow, bugging him, and he couldn't reach the source of it. He was just not hitting it, or thinking straight. The story wasn't coming as easily as he'd thought. Willard was clearly unamused by it all. He intimidated the crew.

"Something on your mind?" Willard asked.

At the KCBD offices, scanning the morning's outlook, anchorman Charles Fields had just seen the first footage off a syndicated satellite report of a strange flu epidemic in northern Canada. A minor footnote in the telecast worth 18 seconds. He moved on searching for something useful. He had two jazzed coed interns cutting newspaper clippings for him while he reclined on the talent couch in a closed room, nursing his own cold, issuing a hypochondriac's barrage of demands for Kleenex, tea, and fresh lemon. "Skip the lemon," he ordered. He was worried about the acid eroding the enamel on his teeth. And then, with sleazoid supplications he enlisted his pretty underlings' assistance in tracking down throat lozenges. He could get away with such weaseling, one, because the girls were naive opportunists and believed that they were competing for his favors, and two, because Fields brought in a noticeable eighty thousand dollars a year as the station's number-one anchorman. And that gave him the right to be a spoiled prick. If his throat were to go, Percival would step in and that would lower ratings within ten seconds. Folks would turn the channel. But more to the point, Fields was shooting for the moon. He was a control freak and didn't want to miss a thing.

Across town, Emmet Jones and a local NOB photobiologist, Spengler, had one more bioassay to run in order to fully determine what it was that killed those whales. The biologist had a sophisticated smog chamber in which they had placed some normal test samples for comparison with the tide pool samples taken from the Queen Charlottes. Plankton and algaes, water and whale tissues. Jones had already calculated the presence of mutase—a catalyzing enzyme capable of rearranging a molecule. What they wanted to know now was to what extent the DNA and RNA of the genes in the dead whales had been injured. Jones knew that the animals were sick and hungry. He just couldn't figure what made them so vulnerable.

Spengler was now looking for lesions in the genetic strands brought on by light. He had a hunch.

Standing at the computer-controlled console, Spengler activated the apparatus. "We'll just create a little ultraviolet —say, in the point two nine wavelength range."

Twenty-five thousand watts of artificial sunlight flooded the copper- and quartz-lined chamber. It was the same amount of energy found at the equator in summer. They exposed the samples for five minutes, removed them to a field of view beneath the lab's electron microscope, and compared notes with the Queen Charlotte material. "There's dimerization of one of the bases," Spengler said calmly. "The thymine. That's normal, harmful UV. Your samples are totally different."

"What do you mean?" Jones said.

"I mean there was more damage. It's right here."

"This is out of my league," Jones admitted.

"Join the club. There's not a whole lot that's been done on whales and light. We mostly stick to worms and fungi, an occasional crab and stomatopod. Point is—here—you see that?"

Jones studied the high-resolution image. "That's what's called a Langerhans cell," Spengler continued. "They're the skin cells that harbor immune responses in mammals. Looks to me like your whales might have had herpes."

Jones suppressed a chortle. "Come on."

Spengler found it amusing as well. "No shit. Too much ultraviolet causes the little Langerhans to hold back its natural immune-protective responses. And when that happens, the sun can cause any number of epidemics, including herpes."

94

Spengler proceeded to try a more intense UV exposure on a normal sample in the chamber. With the microscope hooked up outside in real time, the two men watched the disintegration of the cells. They turned brown and literally started to fry like nuggets of chicken fat rendered in a skillet. "That's UV-C range, point two six five. Now compare it with the cells from this odd bit of plankton recovered from the male humpback's stomach up there on the beach." He replaced one sample with another. A few of his lab assistants had wandered over to listen in.

"Looks damn near the same to me."

"But that's impossible," said Jones, playing out the logic. "We're talking the north country here. Winter."

"I'm not telling you that that's what it was. And I don't want to be quoted as saying that this whale and his mate succumbed to herpes. That would get a laugh. But it *was* infectious. And it was powerful enough to suppress the immune system the way ultraviolet would. Nobody's ever actually had the opportunity to test UV on whales—or, not that I know of. But every sample you've shown me reads the same. What's got me ragged is the fact that the bugs *inside* the whales were suffering from the same problem."

"What do I tell your gal over at the Marine Fisheries Division? They're waiting to release a more definitive statement to the press."

"It was some kind of infectious disease that killed them. Was it natural, unnatural? We'll never know. By the way, anybody check their eyes?"

"Don't think so, why?"

"Too bad. That might have given us another clue."

CHAPTER 11

TUESDAY EVENING

Elizabeth walked in the door and set down the groceries. "Wallace, will you shut up!" she screamed at the family dog. It was whining with a loud insistence. "Kids, just put the dog outside," she ordered. Elizabeth was in no mood, having fought her way across bridges and sat endlessly behind streams of traffic, first to pick up her kids at school, then to get home. She didn't remember ever having seen such traffic in Seattle.

"Can't you even see there's something wrong with the dog? Are you blind?" Evans snapped back, equally irritable. There was no air conditioning at school, none had ever been needed, certainly not in April. But the last two days had been unbearable.

Elizabeth didn't answer him.

Jennifer, sensing the rift and wanting to stay out of it, obeyed Elizabeth. "Come on, Wallace."

Once outside, Wallace scratched frantically. He had been doing this for days. This was just the first time anybody noticed. His whining increased.

"Gretchen's grandma died yesterday," Jennifer said, relaxing back on the couch in the living room across from the six-tiered TV. She deactivated the chip-controlled grazing box. This little Japanese leisure-tech device took family preference input and selected from the more than a hundred existing channels.

"Oh, dear. Bitten by one of their bats I presume?"

"Mommmm! It was pneumonia."

"I'll have to take a fruitcake over to Marion."

"She is a fruitcake," Evans said. Then, considering it: "You want to know my theory about euthanasia? We discussed it in school."

"No," mother and daughter applied in unison. Then: "What's youth-in-Asia?" Jennifer followed up.

"It's putting old and sick people out to pasture, dumbwit," her older brother clarified.

"Cut!"

"I'm just trying to compensate for her incompetent brain—"

"I said enough!" Elizabeth rapped the slate countertop with a cutting knife.

Evans offered a downbeat coda to a familiar routine. "I'll bet every family for centuries has argued before dinner. I'll bet it's in our genes. Maybe evolution programmed in a good fight or two to aid one's digestive enzymes."

Jennifer flipped through the monthly cable guide, then turned her eyes toward her brother. "Dad'll be on in two minutes. What's for dinner?" She thought the better of that, knowing when to lay off. "Never mind."

Elizabeth went upstairs and changed into an "I Love Kyoto" T-shirt and shorts and went up into the attic and brought down a fan for the kitchen. It hadn't been used in years.

"I bet you wouldn't let me wear something like that at school," Jennifer concluded. She could see the concentrated knots of her mom's nipples through the flimsy cotton.

"Would you let me wear it to the office?"

"If Dad didn't mind."

"When your nipples are as big as mine we'll talk again, young lady."

Evans sat down at the dinner table, adjacent to the TV room. He couldn't believe what his mother had just said, though he coyly spied her chest.

Elizabeth took out a ready-made lasagna casserole and put it in the microwave. She'd unwind while chopping up vegetables for a salad. Then she took a can of chilled beer from the refrigerator, dispensing with a glass.

"Beer causes cancer," Evans said.

"So does chocolate," his mother retorted, knowing how to hurt her son where it counted.

"Our teacher said in class today that President Roosevelt died of syphilis," Jennifer announced.

"Who said that?" Elizabeth started with a cockeyed frown.

"Sally Kirkhanger, in social studies group."

"Why that's the most appalling bad taste. . . . Jennifer, dear, what else did Ms. Kirkhanger say?"

"She told us what it was. I can't see why people would wanna make love if you can go blind."

"I am going to call her right now. I don't believe she's telling you kids this stuff."

"Better syphilis than cancer of the penis, or AIDS in the brain," Evans added, determined to fuel his sister's paranoia.

"He used the word again, Mom. *Penis.*"

"I heard. It's not the word that's bad, dear, but the filthy little minds attached to the word. And furthermore, you two, President Roosevelt died of a heart attack. What is with that snot-faced shrew!"

"Snot-faced shrew! That's a good one, Mom."

"Go wash up, guys."

The phone rang. "I'll get it," Evans said with his hand on the receiver. "Hi, Dad. Yeah, it's turned on." Evans motioned to Jennifer to turn it up and then said, "Okay. I got homework anyway. No, we practice Monday/Wednesday/Friday nights. You know that." He untangled the cord. "Here's Mom."

"How's it going?"

"Don't go out."

"I wasn't planning to. What's wrong?"

"Watch the five o'clock news."

"I'm fixing the kids' dinner. What is it, John?"

98

"You were right."

"About what?"

"The birds. The whales. It's a scoop. I'll be home as soon as I can."

"I love you." She smiled, kissing the receiver almost audibly. She knew it. They were definitely striking warmer water.

She unwrapped the casserole and dished it out onto plates. They ate silently as they watched the sweeping KCBD animated logos flying low across Seattle's high-tech skyline at twilight to computer thriller music. The station had spent three hundred thousand dollars on those twenty-eight seconds.

"This is Tuesday, April tenth. I'm Charles Fields. Top of the News tonight, collapsing food harvests and outbreaks of influenza throughout northern Canada. Some Eskimos have died and whole towns have been quarantined. What's it all about? A local scientist says ozone. Is Seattle next? Reporter John Gage filed this report earlier today."

Evans perked up. "Cool."

John was staying by his phone at the station, watching from an overhead monitor with a few of Fields's fair-haired groupies. John's gut told him there was going to be trouble soon enough. Singer hadn't been around earlier to screen the piece, but no doubt he was watching at home.

John looked back to the images on the screen: a dismal-looking stretch of tundra, an "Acquired Footage" marque in the upper left corner. Wind. Sloppy cornices of snow. Rivulets coursed the mud flats running past the camera. In the distance, beneath a pall of storm clouds, a small town. The voice of John Gage, as the picture cut to within the town perimeter, where we saw a dead horse being loaded into the back of an open truck by two uniformed officers and a number of Inuit helpers. Others watched from beside one of many wood and corrugated aluminum dwellings. Not much went on in this town. Save for the mosquitoes and horseflies that swarmed visibly around the locals.

Fields's voice continued as the tape rolled. "Manitu Flats, one of nearly two dozen Indian communities in the Northwest Territories known to have been hit by bad news during the last ten days. What kind of bad news?"

One of the grizzled locals, white man, volunteer with the sheriff's office, right out of the woods, not happy about much, spoke through a muffled cough to the camera. The interviewer had used a hand-held Camcorder. The footage was grainy and distorted—lots of white lines and speculai, dropout, for having suffered numerous generation losses in the dubbing process. It added to the sordidness of the image, Gage thought, haunted by ghosts that now insinuated something of an aesthetic. For the first time in his so-called career, Gage was feeling rather optimistic.

"You see this horse good enough. Dead as run-over skunk puke. I wasn't here personally but they tell me three days ago it was damn near Miami Beach in this town. Sunnier than a Miss Universe contest. That's what did it. Snow blinded the horse and half the Inuit here and in surroundin' villages. Lot a flu virus, some dead, mostly among the old ones. Winter crops gone to hell. Other dead animals. And these friggin' mosquitoes. What with the floodin' an' road mudded out an' snow too wet to three-wheelie—why, it's a mess. We're sendin' up food and drugs by heelicopter from Dawson. But I, I do think the problem's prob'ly bigger than you'r me."

Cutaways of townsfolk, mostly clustered indoors, many with eye patches. A local infirmary, each bed taken, even those in the hallways. For acquired stock footage, it was the best reality stuff Gage had ever gotten.

"Reports are just now starting to come in from other, similarly afflicted towns and villages across the northernmost parts of western Canada," Gage's commentary continued, over high meaningless aerials. "Best guess as to what it is? Ozone depletion."

The camera shot dissolved into another aerial, this time coming into a beach from out at sea on the Queen Charlottes, followed by the heart-wrenching close-ups from Local Joe to the final breaths of the two expiring whales. And finally there was footage of Elizabeth crying.

"Mom!"

"Sixty-five whales dead thus far, some of them seen here on a remote part of the Queen Charlotte Islands in British Columbia. Another eighty known dolphins dead up and down the Inland Passage. The investigating marine laboratory contracted by NOB, the National Oceanic Bureau, is attributing the deaths to a virulent infection relating to a strange breakdown in the marine mammals' immune system, not unlike an overnight onslaught of AIDS."

"That's like Roosevelt!" Jennifer commented.

"No it isn't!" her mother insisted, exasperated. "Your dinner's getting cold. Eat."

At a laboratory across town, Emmet Jones was also watching the news. He shook his head incredulously. "Jesus, John, where the hell did you pick that up from?" he said angrily to nobody in particular. "AIDS? That's a crock a shit."

A lot of people were watching John Gage's newscast. From an office in downtown Seattle a call was placed to Olympia, the capital of Washington State. "Buck? Bill Rodgers here. . . . Fine, fine. Listen, we, uh, may have a bit of a problem. I'm looking at our local evening news, an independent station I don't think you pick up there. Is the governor aware of what's going in in Canada?"

John Gage's story cut to a number of fast-spinning magnetic tapes, then pulled back to reveal hands busily at a keyboard. Pulling back even further, an image appeared of the continental United States, and the animated graphic representation of a descending shadow that had crossed diagonally from the Bering Strait to the Fairweather Range in Alaska, then straight down the northern Pacific, missing Vancouver altogether and heading in a beeline for Seattle. Pulling back further still, the camera revealed a man in a wheelchair.

"Dr. Donald Willard is an atmospheric chemist at the College of Washington in Seattle. We spoke with him earlier today."

Willard shook his head, considering his every word.

"Well, I've been tracking this thing for twenty years. No one ever believed me. It moves, you see. It breathes. It's some kind of monster and we created it. With our stubborn aerosols, refrigerator and air conditioner coolants, electronic solvents—chemicals known as chlorofluorocarbons, CFC's for short. I've got here a list of corporations, both in Seattle and all over the world, that are the primary abusers. They caused this. It's big, big money. Congress isn't doing squat because they know there's this military side to it— products they haven't figured out how to reproduce with other chemicals. So the world's churning the stuff out faster than you'd believe. Oh, there were treaties, well-meaning efforts to mitigate the escalating problem, but it's been window dressing to date."

Gage, now on camera sitting directly opposite Willard, questioned the chemist. "There was an ozone hole over the Antarctic continent some years ago and nobody was hurt. It was largely an intellectual problem, no?"

"No. Animals *were* killed. I would guess tens of thousands, maybe millions, though I'm sure members in good standing of the National Academy of Sciences would vehemently argue that point. I don't care to speculate on human mortality at the South Pole because, for the most part, there hasn't been any—or none that I can verify. What I can verify is the fact that we have an ozone hole coming down from the North Pole, coming fast, and if it continues, it's going to mean big trouble."

"Pass the low-cal dressing," Evans said, glued to his dad's broadcast.

"Any more spinach?" Jennifer asked Elizabeth.

"In the oven. Help yourself."

The camera jerked to the interior of a restaurant as the glass windows shattered and the birds came flopping in. Gage's commentary continued over the avian and human pandemonium, with a concluding series of close-ups of the birds' faces and of several plunging to their deaths outside the Needle. "As such footage suggests, these migrating birds may well have been exposed to the alleged ozone hole. Their eyes were burned by the intense sunlight.

"According to one published study, tens of thousands of people will develop cataracts for every percentage point of ozone that is depleted. And that's just the beginning. Cancer rates will soar. The Environmental Protection Agency has indicated that a one percent decrease in ozone can result in twenty thousand new cancers. Now most of those cancers are presumably nonmalignant skin cancers. But these flooded fields in Canada, this swarm of unseasonable horse-flies, these dead whales, this dead bird, this grieving family of Eskimos, and this freakish heat spell throughout the Northwest are only too real."

Gage had crafted his commentary knowing that it would enrage some and terrorize others. There was deliberate naïveté here because he himself had been convinced and wanted his viewers to be provoked. John was scared and he felt that Willard was on top of it. The camera returned to Willard.

"I estimate that the hole is somewhere in the neighborhood of a hundred fifty miles across. It's broken off from the existing larger hole over the Arctic and it's moving by the forces of internal chemistry and external weather. My sense is the thing's out at sea still. If we're lucky, it will dissipate. That could happen overnight. If we're unlucky—well, don't ask me to speculate."

From his anchorman's chair, Charles Fields looked at the marque and addressed his field reporter. "Thanks, John." He then turned back to face the key camera in the studio. "In other news tonight," he began, "Tacoma superintendent Mace Mecklenbaum hammers hard at the governor for money to buy dictionaries."

Evans's mouth hung open. He was staring at his mother in disbelief.

"I've got to go," Jennifer said. "It's girls' free bowling night. My class is doing its birthday party for Melinda." Prepared for whatever objections: "I told you. Bye."

"Uh—honey? I really don't think—"

The phone jangled. "Get the phone!" Elizabeth shouted. Evans jumped to grab the receiver before it rang again.

"John? Oh, Mom." Evans handed his mother the phone.

It was grandma. "Yes, we saw it. No. I don't know. No, he's not home yet. I will. How's Dad? We will. Just don't go out, you hear me? Don't let Dad out!" They had caught Alzheimer's early in her father. He'd been lost, walking around the block. Now he walked incessantly. Most of the time he was okay. But it only took one wrong neighborhood, sudden confusion, and he could be a goner.

Jennifer was out the door. "You can't stop her on bowling night—no sir, Mom. Not even the end of the world could do that," Evans said sarcastically. Then he settled back down, contemplating, stilled, like a parrot that had just had its first birdie pedicure, shampoo, and blow-drier treatment. He was figuring in his head how many oxygen tanks the family would need. His plan? To ride the crisis out underwater. He wandered upstairs as Charles Fields continued with other news on KCBD.

The phone rang again. Elizabeth picked it up. It was Jeremy Singer. "No, not yet." Elizabeth could hear that Singer was upset. He was trying hard not to let on about it. She knew nothing about his disguise. "I will. Absolutely. Bye now," she said, with the same escapist inflection as that of her daughter.

She'd have liked to go bowling herself. Maybe she just would.

CHAPTER 12

Chief of staff Frank Radino dimmed the lights of the meeting room and played KCBD's news piece on the White House three-quarter-inch playback for a gathered assemblage of three other key officials. The tape had been hand-carried on a red-eye out of Sea-Tac arriving at National at 6:00 A.M. Radino had reviewed the tape, consulted with NSB chief Admiral Brewster, who happened to be on board the *Arizona* in the mid-Atlantic; mentioned it along with everything else to the President, who was finishing a luncheon with his supreme NATO commander in Brussels; and then called his most trusted associates with news of the sudden get-together. Radino was known for such get-togethers, and since he controlled all access to the President, invited guests tended to show up. The last time he had called such a meeting was five days before, following the defection of a top-ranking Chinese military officer who was then found to be carrying AIDS. Radino's simple solution: keep it from Immigration, provide asylum, interrogate very carefully, and then give him the best available treatment. Keep it out of the press. Humane, clean, simple. Obvious.

Now Radino had a similarly clearheaded approach to things, which came to him within minutes of seeing the KCBD material. "Forget solutions. There's no such thing as

105

environmental solutions. I called you here this morning to talk about mitigation," Radino began, turning the lights back on.

"Then this stuff is for real?" asked Brian Sullivan, national security adviser to the President, a recipient of the Medal of Honor for action in Korea, former ambassador to Switzerland. He had served a single term as the U.S. Senator from Illinois, then became a partner in a prestigious D.C. law firm specializing in illegal foreign money. He had a working knowledge of four languages. No dummy. "I presume you've spoken with NSB?"

"An hour ago. Brewster's bunch is looking into it. You all know that they've been following this ozone muddle for twenty years. I guess the stuff fluctuates over the Arctic this time of year. It's a normal syndrome. According to Brewster there was some concern that the hole itself might reform south of the polar regions and that could be a problem. NSB had its top people out in force this past week examining the air over northern Canada. Just yesterday, according to Brewster, they concluded that there was no cause for alarm. In fact, they found nothing. Walter—"

"Well, naturally we've been apprehensive about this thing and, given the human component, we felt it best to run the operation ourselves, which would guarantee security until we knew what we were really dealing with." Walter Cummings was Army chief of staff, Radino's old boss. A fatherly figure, you couldn't help but like him and trust him.

"And what are we dealing with?" Sullivan said, working out an annoying seed from a chunk of salsa from between his lower molars with a toothpick.

"As we had hoped. Nothing. No problem whatsoever as far as I understand."

"You're sure?"

"There were some quivers. The satellites were not up to the equipment on board the aircraft, but then that's to be expected. And from what I gather the principal researcher assigned to the monitoring devices attached to the plane's wings saw a few unexplainable surges of ozone depletion—levels bounced around a bit. But they certainly found no hole and felt confident in shutting down the mission after just two days of flights."

"Then this Willard fellow has simply got religion?"

"Brewster already got back to me on that. NSB's top dog in this arena, and the coordinator of this mission in question, is one Felix Girard, and he says that Donald Willard's actually done some good science in the past but has had his share of problems. Described him as a sort of tragic figure. Heavy drinker. Prone to depression. Tried to kill himself once or twice. He'd be easy to publicly string up in a pinch."

"How'd he end up in the wheelchair?" Sullivan asked.

"Head-on collision. His fault," Walter said. "He'd been drinking."

"Look, guys," Radino concluded, eager to get on with his day. "NSB says things are okay. So the point here is very clear: I'd like to propose that each of you watch this situation. Hopefully, the news story will die a quiet death. Like the supposed measles disaster last year. Maybe it's already dead."

"And if the story picks up?" Jerry said.

Cummings knotted his brow nervously, showing off a preponderance of wrinkles accented by too many years in the sun. "I see certain potential problems with that. First off, I know at least seven major defense contractors in the Seattle area. It's more than likely that they manufacture these damn chemicals one way or another. I'd hate like hell to see them come under fire or, worse yet, shut down in order to revamp for any significant length of time. You understand what I'm saying."

"In that event, why limit it to Seattle?" Brian Sullivan aired with a polite yawn. "The twenty-five biggest contractors for defense in this country are in that category, Walter. And you know as well as I do we're talking in excess of two hundred fifty billion dollars a year, a couple million jobs, tens of millions of votes." It was a tired formula. Sullivan had volunteered similar equations, heard similar worries professed a dozen times during his three years in the White House. In Cambodia. In Nicaragua and Panama. In the

Baltic States. He was basically bored. Sullivan had looked at his watch four times by Frank Radino's count. That meant four times now that he considered this meeting over.

Radino was not happy with the changes in this conversation. Brian sensed that.

"Okay, so? Jerry, how legitimate is disinformation in a case like this?" Sullivan said.

"You don't mean disinformation. You mean setting the record straight," Jerry Jacobian insisted, with a bright sweep of logic. The President's press secretary-inquisitor, Jerry was the White House moderator of public response. He had the good humor and clout to correct the national security adviser without so much as a tremor. Jerry Jacobian had made commercials for right-wing political campaigns—including Sullivan's—before ghostwriting two congressional autobiographies. Forty-eight years old, with six screaming children, Jerry had a firm handle on what Americans watch on TV and on what they believed from TV. He wrote and spoke with the easy-to-grasp nuggets of a political Omar Khayyám and could wield the low, seasoned voice of a news anchor. The press corps had always liked Jerry. So had the President. Jerry liked himself. Radino, while necessarily confiding everything in Jacobian, was still not sure about the man's goals. And that suspicion was mutual.

"Why doesn't NSB make its findings public? Counter this tripe," Jerry went on. "What I observe is amateur night in Dixie. You've got a lone firecracker looking for ratings. No network picked up on it. And why not? And look at this"—he pulled out the morning's *Post, Times,* and *Journal*—"front page, page two, page three, page four, page five . . . zilch. Why's that, you may wonder, if in fact Seattle is soon to be history? I recommend killing this business with the truth."

"I don't want to see us serve the cause of a couple of jerks jockeying for the headlights," said Walter, with a look toward Frank he knew would be understood. "It could backfire."

"Well, you could be right," Radino said.

Sullivan had picked up a foul scent. "Frank? What is it?"

"Walter?" Radino passed the ball to Cummings.

"Twenty-five major defense contractors is about right, Brian. As well as a couple of million jobs. That's what's got me worried. You all probably don't remember this, but several years ago NSB failed to pick up the early warning signs of an ozone hole over Antarctica. The British beat us to it and that was one hell of an embarrassment. We took a lot of flack. And worse."

"So you're not sure after all!" Frank said sternly, trying to stay in charge. "Then have Willard talk to your people. Give him clearance. Let's get this done with. I don't need this crap. And the President sure as hell doesn't."

"Felix called him last night," Walter conceded, unhappy about the turn of the screw.

"That's good. And?"

"We missed bad."

"Oh, come on, folks!" Sullivan railed. He'd gone past his limits.

"There's still no confirmation on this," Walter went on. "Willard's lab has had balloons posted up and down the Pacific Northwest since that Alaskan volcano started making fireworks a few years ago. It's what tipped us off to a possible problem. Willard and Felix evidently spoke and Felix is looking into it. But his team had already packed up and left. The timing on this couldn't have been worse. It's not as if we haven't known about the potential. . . . We started building devices to monitor it six months ago."

"You're saying Felix is prepared to trust Willard above his own team?"

"I'm saying Felix has reason to be insecure. This ozone business is elusive stuff."

"Well, shit, call back the team. Run more flights. If you started it half a year ago, why give up now? Figure this thing out," Frank said, heating up. "What's the problem?"

"Time. You saw the video. My understanding from Felix is that Willard's already figured it out and there's no time."

"No time for what? Pardon me if I'm slow, but I'm not getting something here," Jerry interjected.

"They beat us to it, plain and simple," Walter admitted with the frustration of the losing team.

"Who is 'they,' Walter? Beat us to what?" Frank demanded. He was accustomed to Cummings's style, and he relished his connection to the old man, which he knew was utterly lost on the others in the room. He himself was still grasping after the reality. It was a military style filled with the sweet pleasures of one-upmanship.

Sullivan was less than amused. "This is a swell turn," he said with a razor-sharp inflection. "Walter, who are the jerks jockeying for the headlights? There's no hidden tape recorder in this room—is there, Frank?"

"Nope."

"And nobody's even bothered taking notes, so let's cut the mild-mannered politics here and get to the bottom of this. We're all on the same side. We all voted for the same President. It's nine sixteen and I have got a ballbuster day staring at me," Sullivan said, trying to retain the diplomat's imperviousness.

"There's no need to send another mission. Early this morning our satellites confirmed Willard's findings."

"Well, goddamnit, Walter, why didn't you just spit it out?" Sullivan shouted.

Frank now had the handle he needed. "All right. Let the thing blow over. No statements. None needed beyond what we've heard."

"And if it doesn't?" Jerry asked nervously. "Blow over, I mean."

"It will," Walter rallied. "That's one thing Felix is certain about. He and his team witnessed short bursts of ozone depletion, followed by normal measurements. That's why they didn't take their own findings seriously. It's a haphazard science. My impression of the situation, based on expert advice, is that this is one of nature's flukes, brought on by a volcano and posing little, if any, risk to anybody."

"And that flu epidemic in the news footage? The blindness? The dead horse? Birds and whales?" Jerry was trying to marshal thoroughness. He was always out to prove himself and had been since college entrance exams. He hadn't made the Ivy League. University of Arizona instead. It was his one real skeleton.

"No way. That was bogus stuff. Nothing unusual about a flu epidemic in northern Canada. Get serious."

"Let's leave it then. Walter, may I recommend an inconspicuous comment to the press from the Defense Department?"

"Absolutely!" Jerry said with a useless smile. "Hey, I've got an aunt in Bellingham, Washington. I happen to care what happens to her, even if she is a pain in the ass."

Somehow the men had come around. The mood had changed. "You're probably right. After all, we care too. Don't think we stand on ceremony just 'cause this thing was classified. I think it would serve everyone if we were to issue a statement to the effect that NSB and the military have once again confirmed minor fluctuations in the level of ozone depletion over Canada and the Northwest; that such fluctuations have come to be regarded by scientists as typical of this time of year; and that there is little or no risk to humans. Does that about capture things?"

Jacobian laughed. "You should have my job!"

"No thanks."

"Good. If that's it, I'll catch you all later," Sullivan said, smiling, to get up and be gone. He'd had his one shout for the morning and it felt good.

"There is one more thing," Frank said, contemplating aloud. "I'm just considering all the ins and outs here. Lest reality is not as it seems."

"What are you thinking, Frank?" Walter moved his chair an inch forward.

"You can figure it out easily enough. Supposing the press runs wild with this story."

"I thought what we'd just resolved here was to curb that kind of hysteria on the part of the American public?" Jerry reminded him.

"That's true. But there's never any way to totally control it. It is a free country, remember? What I mean is, the blame part of it. Someone always gets blamed. A company, a captain, a dictator. Who's our culprit here in the albeit unlikely event it's not just that volcano you mentioned?"

Walter was taken aback. "There's no culprit. Shit, China, Brazil, India, the Ruskies are manufacturing more of the stuff than we are. They're the ones that are wiping out the ozone."

"Tell that to Jerry's aunt. My point is simply that it would be nice to have a fall guy should we need one."

"Very decent of you, Frank." Walter understood at once. They had both been through the training, of dogs suffering fools in horse shit. His mind tabulated like a plodding, double-A-battery calculator, coming up with an inspired idea; and the paranoia of his preeminent military career began to surface the way a Venus flytrap might twist and strain to scratch its back. "We give out fifteen million defense contracts in this country every year, employing over thirty thousand persons whose sole function is processing all the paperwork. One more contract won't make much of a difference."

"Exactly," Radino said. "And it probably doesn't have to be a *new* contract—better that it isn't. No point initiating a new paper trail."

"You two have lost me," Sullivan said.

"Off the record, of course, I'll bet there's a local contractor busy manufacturing gobs of chemicals for some piddlyshit purpose that happened to play havoc with the ozone. Wouldn't you say? And I'll bet he's in Seattle. The point is to bring heat down on him. Make him sweat. Make him run for cover. He'll do what he has to. Probably hire outside consultants, so to speak. Professionals. That's his problem. We didn't say it. We don't know about it."

"Let him take the hit in other words?"

"That's right. Somebody's got to. I mean in the un-likely—"

"I understand. And I can appreciate Walter's concern. But it doesn't make sense to me. What's to prevent them all

112

from being implicated if this one you're setting up should go?"

"Stories die down, Brian. We'd need his contract complicity for a few days. Put him out of business, show the Defense Department's concern for public welfare, and let bygones be bygones. A major oil company doesn't go out of business because it has a major oil spill. But some of its *local* stations do go out of business. That's how it works, bud. The press won't let him get away. And having scored their victory, that'll be the end of it. It's all the other contractors I want to protect."

"Well, there's nothing particularly illegal about it," Sullivan added.

"Not from our end, anyway," Radino assured him.

"And you can be certain that reporter—what was his name?"

"Gage. John Gage."

"You can be sure he'd flush your so-called local station out as you say—with a little subtle encouragement from Washington, perhaps—an inside investigation to give him impetus, the air of real competition, things happening beyond his ken. He'll string it up on the five o'clock news and Seattle can go on with its supper, the weasel having been routed from its hole."

"In a manner of speaking."

"Right."

"Then we're covered here, gentlemen. Walter? Brian? Jerry?"

"Sounds good to me. Real clean," Walter concluded.

Jerry lingered with a doubt, scratching his scalp. "There's just one thing."

They all looked to Jerry. "What is it, Jerry?"

"What if the contractor doesn't go along with it? I mean, he could just as easily say, Screw it. Pass on the money. Let Defense work out their problems. He'd be a hero. Especially if his people sat down, and looked at the options, and figured it's a no-win situation."

"It's got to be the right company, this is true. A shell. A subsidiary that uses outside consultants, perhaps foreigners," Radino added. "Plenty of those. A manufacturer, maybe even one employing robots. Low overhead. Big profits. The lure of easy money, Jerry. It's a sure thing. Always has been. Always will be. And anyway, once the news picks up on them, it'll be too late for any heroism. They'll have to scramble just to cover their ass."

CHAPTER 13

Radino was back in his office, just a few feet west as the shit flies from the President's own suite. He called Governor Fred Stevens in Olympia and told him that the White House had met on the so-called "situation," that the President was aware of things, and that NSB's Office of Information would be making a brief statement to the press by early afternoon. "That statement should go a long way toward stifling any concern on the part of the good people in Washington State, Fred. We're just not going to buy the crap that local station doled out last night."

"I saw a tape of it."

"Can't you have their license revoked?"

"I think there's something called the First Amendment that might invalidate such action, Frank."

"Yes, indeed. Just to let you know, NSB's looked into this, and so has Defense. They had their own expedition out there in Canada checking up on things. And they give it a relatively clean slate." Radino, speaking on behalf of the federal government, had just signed off on the situation. He had an important golf game with the Japanese minister of finance to get to.

"I do appreciate the White House's concern," Stevens replied.

The two men were old cronies from Radino's governor days. Stevens didn't care for the pugnacious Republican, with whom he'd sparred publicly more than once at national governors' conventions. Stevens thought Radino about as environmentally savvy as Genghis Khan. Radino's moves were opportunistic and Stevens knew it. And whether the point at hand was an endangered species, wetlands policy, or the greenhouse effect, Radino used mob tactics, intimidated his underlings and critics into believing whatever crackpot notion he may have concocted—all for the President, of course.

Stevens listened politely. Animosities aside, he tended in this instance to believe what Radino told him. In fact, his office had already contacted the College of Washington and Willard had been encouraged to consider the public frame of mind before spouting off the next time. This inane and spineless reproach had made Willard all the more frantic.

Jeremy Singer was also frantic. The governor's office went directly to the chairman of the board of the bank that owned the station group that included KCBD. Consequently, Singer's boss was at the station before him, loaded with ammunition, ready to chew into him. Singer knew that something was going to go down. He'd watched his unguided missile, John Gage, skew and inflate the ozone story with the untempered flourish of a dice thrower in Las Vegas.

It wasn't what John had counted on. He'd dropped some medicine off at Elizabeth's parents' following a night of lovemaking with his wife. The story had pumped both of them. Kinky sex. That made a total of four ejaculations in one twenty-four-hour period for John. As for Elizabeth, she hadn't felt this good since John had bought her the Lalaounis 22-carat bracelet four years ago. The enormity of the news didn't phase them, because they somehow controlled it—or certainly John did. And that control made everything all right. His editing, the music, the whole video process commandeered the reality, though that was not Gage's intent. And vicariously Elizabeth felt the power herself.

In the excitement of the piece, the Gage family—perhaps

116

with the exception of a wary Evans—gave in to pride, uncorked a delicate Veuve Clicquot Ponsardin, their favorite champagne, and quietly celebrated John's personal triumph. It was no giddy outward show, to be sure, but rather a family reunion. Enough drug wars, Dalkon Shield exposés, police racketeering rings, public works bills. Good-bye to the days of low swipes and incest trials and the latest irrelevant closing down of a porno theater, stories about dispossessed Indians or marooned mountain climbers; so long to the dreary chasing of ambulances and the endlessly tragic AIDS twists. John had moved up, ascending to the heady realm of creative news documentary, of aesthetic clout.

"That's exactly what it is," he exclaimed. "A prelude to credibility. They'll say I'm the one who first broke the story."

"No, I'm the one smart ass, remember?"

"I'm sorry. You're the one." He paused, then said, "That's true, love."

They both smiled. He hadn't said the word to her in certainly a year. Forgetting the fifty-odd additional whales that had been discovered washed up, this time in U.S. waters, Elizabeth was on cloud nine.

Elizabeth's boss, Drake Manders, however was not. He had spoken at length with both Bulrich and Emmet Jones. Drake in turn had told others in NOB about the unprecedented numbers of dead whales, as well as the fact that other species of birds were flying into planes, windows, even drowning in Lake Washington. He was scared, especially after being filled in by Jones's friend Spengler about this alleged DNA business. Word got to the mayor's office, and then to the governor's office. But no word came back out again. Somehow the bureaucracy muffled the momentum of concerns. Drake and Jones both were astonished by the lack of official response or even of trust in the reports. But as of Wednesday morning, neither of them was prepared to fight city hall.

* * *

John Gage and Fields were sitting near one another in the open commons of the newsroom, working from their respective desks. Fields was schmoozing on the phone while Gage sampled the buzz around the station. People had begun to notice this and that out on the freeways, in their lawns. A unit manager's dinner table had been inundated with termite droppings. A girl in personnel saw a hit-and-run on her way in which she described not in any horrible terms but simply as the weirdest thing she'd ever seen. John's secretary, Lola, saw her dog Bobo throw up and die in her living room. It had eaten a plastic orange juice container —the whole thing—which was not at all like Bobo. John sensed that the world was going crazy.

Suddenly Singer walked by between John and Fields and said loudly, "I want to see your butts in my office. *Now!*"

Sidling up behind Gage, Fields pulled on John's coattails and said quietly, "You blew it this time, ace."

"Your mother's a dyke," John retorted. He was unnerved now. He was apprehensive about the confrontation with Singer, who was clearly upset. But John was also stoked, his feathers upright. No one could take away what he had achieved.

The glass door slammed behind them, though other employees close by would still be able to hear. As was customary in union shops where rancor transcended loyalties, several other producers and associate producers stood buoyantly by, discreetly watching the proceedings, stirred to contentment by the thought of trouble above them on the ladder to success.

Singer unleashed: "A dead horse, some groaning Indians and a dumbshit cowboy playing to camera."

"He was a volunteer state trooper," John declared.

"Auditioning for vaudeville."

"That was a first. The footage had never been used by CNN or anybody."

"'Cause no one else in this industry has the bad taste or ignorance to run it, you dumb fuck."

"Are you out of your mind! You heard Willard," John

said, raging. "Goddamnit, don't you know we just made history!"

"History shit," Fields said, picking up on the direction Singer was headed and taking the prudent side.

"Shut up, slob," John shouted.

Fields grabbed John's collar and yanked. The two men were inches apart, nose to nose.

"You're both bottom dredge as far as I'm concerned. Got it?" Singer yelled.

"Cunt fucker," Fields said, digging with an underhanded snarl.

"Piss brain," John retorted.

"Fuck you!" Fields countered.

"Fuck you!"

"No, fuck you!"

"Go on, you guys, just keep tossing your best English back and forth," Singer said, tired, sitting down. They joined him. The fumes dissipated.

"I heard a dissident. I heard one pissed-off, disenfranchised cripple with an ax to grind."

"That's bullshit," John rallied.

"John, did you ever stop and ask him how he knew so much? I mean, here's this one guy in a chair knowing more than a hundred people at NSB? How come he's so smart? No, the real question: How come *you're* so *dumb?*"

The NSB business had flown by him. He'd missed it. Stuttering, he stopped short. "W-Wait a minute? W-What about NSB?"

"They had their own expedition. They made their own press statement twenty minutes ago, or were you two too busy exchanging compliments to hear the news?"

Fields looked at John, who looked inside himself. Fields would not speak. He knew to wait. "I missed it," John said.

Fields played the other pole. "I caught it." He nodded knowingly. But he hadn't fooled Singer, who was in no mood to exploit the imbecile. He disliked Fields almost as much as John did.

"Well, the fact is, John, NSB ran its own tests up through

yesterday. There's no ozone hole. And they were up there, in one of the spy planes. Your Willard is merely looking to get tenure."

"I don't believe it."

"You were taken in, John. Oldest trick in the book. And you bought into it. Willard's not to blame. Your own greed did it, coming off the high of drug wars and all. Some high."

"What else did the NSB report say?" John pressed.

"You tell him, Charles."

Fields squirmed. "Oh, well, as you say, no ozone. That's what I got out of it. Makes sense. Frankly, John, you put us all in something of a bind, finishing the piece a few minutes before deadline—"

"Bullshit. It was a quarter to four."

"And making assertions that I had no way of checking. This is an organization of trust. I trust you, John, and when you tell me the sky's falling—well, I'm prone to believe you even if it goes against my better instincts, because I respect you."

"Shut the fuck up, Charles. Enough," Singer decreed.

Fields was silenced. "Right."

"They said that Willard has a history of drinking, since the tragic death of his wife."

"They said that? He didn't strike me—"

"They also said that his experiments in Canada were well run and yielded relevant data that could not be confirmed but contradicted more substantive analysis conducted by NSB satellites. They regretted his unwarranted candor and in so many words attributed it to confusion and an urge to be in the limelight. We—KCBD—are named as the unwitting accomplice."

"That's absurd," John protested.

"Isn't it! We, gentlemen, are a laughingstock."

"People are scared, Jeremy."

"Thanks to you, John."

"The birds thing doesn't strike you as a little odd?"

"It does. But it's no ozone hole. Nor are mosquitoes in Alberta or Eskimo babies coming down with the flu in a cold Canadian winter."

"It was hot—you saw the footage—just like it's hot outside at this moment. You're denying it. Did they get to you? Somebody got to you, didn't they!" John was burning up.

"Why the hell are we the only station in Seattle covering this?" Singer said, ripping into him.

"We're not. All three networks ran affiliate pieces this morning. Where were you?"

"Did you actually see those pieces, John?" Singer asked. "Because I saw the pieces. They were pieces about KCBD, John. They questioned the authenticity, the standards and practices. They nailed you, Mr. Gage. Your credibility—no, your career—is on the line, fella!"

Fields was gloating.

"I don't believe this," John said, hurt.

"Well, you better start believing, because as of now you are off this thing. We are not indulging any more fantasy. I just hope to God I can repair the damage. Now get out of my office!"

"Jeremy, I want a straight answer from you. Now I know you're looking for a promotion into upper management. We all know. And I saw the station group manager nail you to the wall for this."

"He didn't nail me—"

"Read my lips: he nailed you. And you're feeling the heat and I'm your Judas. Fine. Let me be your Judas. Look at me, Jeremy. I know you're under fire. And I also know that what I did could be construed as flagrant, in a certain sense. Jeremy, it wasn't. You've got to trust me."

"Jesus, Gage, don't you know when to stop?"

"Whatever you say, boss. Lord knows I've got better things to do with my time."

"Like dragging us all down with him," Fields preached.

"Fuck you." John hurtled a finger at his throat.

"Fuck you!"

"You two are the original odd couple," Singer said, unburdening himself, loosening his tie.

"Now what kind of heat, Jeremy?" John pressed the obligation that comes with censure.

"I don't have to tell you who owns the station group."

"Ah-ha. So that's it."

"John, the government says these events are unrelated, that you're majoring in fiction. We don't do fiction here. You're going too fast."

"What's too fast? Jesus, Jeremy, Willard gives us a matter of days."

"That's not an unbiased judgment. Just listen to yourself. You're over the top." He leaned forward and whispered, "The governor himself called the CEO, the mayor, I don't know who else. John, you have pissed off a lot of people in this town—and at the White House! That may have seemed like a feather in one's cap in journalism school. Well, forget it. This station is a business—"

"Did you catch the overnights?"

"That I didn't."

"Jeremy, you want to talk business, fine. Let's talk business. The story got a nine rating. When did we last get a nine? People turned on their sets because they know something's out there. Something's wrong. The ratings are going to get higher. The phones haven't stopped ringing."

"They're only scared because you're telling them they should be scared." Singer paused. He had been up all night with his wife who'd become ill. "All I'm telling you is, I was ordered—ordered, mind you—to cease all further activities on the alleged ozone business."

"Why are you whispering?"

"Am I whispering?"

"Yeah. You were whispering."

"I don't think there's anything more to discuss, do you?" He was already shaking his head. "Yeah. There is."

"Goddamnit, John. Am I going to have to fire your butt?"

"Jeremy, you just laid your finger on the nozzle."

"What are you talking about?"

"Give me a crew, Jeremy."

"Didn't you just hear what I told you?"

"I heard you say that this is a business. If this is a business, why the hell would the station manager have ignored the highest ratings in nearly two decades?"

Jeremy felt like an idiot for having missed it. He too began to nod, slowly, fighting against it but seeing undeniably a light that John had shone. "Yeah."

"Yeah!"

Singer hated himself for falling into a trap—an undeniable trap. But there was a door and it smelled fishy. Singer was a pushover for foul-smelling ruses. "Just cover yourself, goddamnit. Get *official* confirmation. Will you do that much for me? . . . I can't believe I'm listening to you."

"Thanks, man."

John went back to his desk, took some notes, and called Willard.

Willard answered and was quick to enlighten John. "Because they're controlled by the military. Don't you understand? Where have you been all your life? It was a military mission. They missed and they're embarrassed. And they know that Seattle—like L.A.—is the seat of the military-industrial complex, though you're too young to know that phrase."

"You're saying the defense contractors may be involved?"

"Certainly indirectly. Why else was it a top secret mission? You think they told me anything? But more than that, I'm saying that the military isn't going to sanction mass evacuation. It's an admission of weakness. But, look, I'm no political or military analyst. There are probably many sides to it. I'm just a chemist. I've been doing my job for many years. I know my computers. I know my balloon monitors."

"Evacuation?"

"Probably."

"But where to?"

"That's a good question."

"Look, Willard, are you telling me this straight?"

"What do you think?"

"Willard, I'm not playing games with you."

"Good. Then do me a favor. About three hundred fifty miles northwest of the Olympic Peninsula, in the middle of the ocean, my computers read 97 percent ozone depletion. If I'm right about this, then it's coming in fast. It's off the airline route—I've called. Korean is the closest—their Tokyo shuttle coming about eighty miles south."

"All right. So? What am I supposed to do?"

"Find a way to go out there. Doesn't your station have a helicopter for reporting on traffic? Go check out the ocean in that area. The damage I suspect is there won't show up on any National Weather Service maps. And NSB is not looking out there. They may—*may*, mind you—send another flight up into Canada now that the heat is on. But whatever they do is too late."

"What am I supposed to look for? And how do I protect myself?" John said.

"Spend no more than three minutes directly exposed, wear snow goggles and don't look up for anything."

"Three minutes? Is someone safe riding inside a helicopter?"

"I don't know. Normally the glass offers some protection. But we're dealing with a new situation here."

"Well, if you don't know for sure, does anyone?"

Willard was silent. He felt at a disadvantage, wanting himself to be the one, but trapped in a legless body. He saw the crevasse and the two men frozen in the ice, their eyes burned to the bone. "I'm just asking you to check it out. Go to the fringe."

"Three hundred fifty miles you say?"

"Wait a minute." Willard did some fast computer calculations—wind speed, approaching front, high pressure, abscissa, and ordinant. "Three hundred twenty miles, assuming you're out there by noon. Give or take a few."

"I'll try."

"It's all that's left," Willard said. "I don't know what else to tell you."

CHAPTER 14

"Two cameras, a shotgun—hell, what else I don't know, Andy? But let's go!" yelled John.

"Two minutes—the batteries are nearly charged," Wendy shouted above the noise of the overpass. The station ironically sat beneath a junction—ironic because the noise and vibrations played a number on the semi-insulated interior of what should have been a monastic silence. Instead, it was loud and shaky, particularly in the station garage, where batteries were charged and crews assembled for remotes. The three of them were loading the van. They had a chopper to catch and little time. The freeways were jammed. Sea-Tac International was forty minutes away.

"I hate helicopters," Andy Otero said anxiously. Nobody was listening.

Wendy was driving and as she pulled away from KCBD she happened to notice in her rearview mirror a large black sedan pulling out in tandem.

Their radio was tuned to the sig-alert emergency network. For a workday, the roadways were larded. But the freeway was their only sensible route, so they had no choice but to slug it out.

Wendy liked to drive fast. She swerved in and out of traffic, maneuvering around innumerable impasses. "Ms. Andretti here," Andy said, humoring her.

"We're late," John reminded them. "My wife'll be waiting to get us on board. It's an NOB chopper and they're not gonna hang around if we're late."

"Hey, guys, do we have company or what?" Wendy asked them. The sedan raced around traffic, caught up, and the driver, in a suit and sunglasses, motioned for Wendy to pull over.

"Lose them!" John said.

Wendy used to do obstacle car races in large Cow Palace and sports arena parking lots on Sundays, a sport with its own devotees, among them hundreds of Grateful Dead fans. It led her into the higher stakes world of dune cycling and then stock car races. Wendy knew her stuff. She lost them. They reappeared. She lost them again.

Suddenly a car in the right lane plowed into a vehicle two lanes over. John watched the driver, who seemed to have lost control of the vehicle, smash into three other cars. Metal, glass, flames jettisoned across four lanes. "Keep going, don't look, don't stop—keep driving, Wendy!" John bellowed, watching the aftermath.

"Holy shit. There's got to be bodies . . ."

"I don't know. Keep driving." John sensed that this was no ordinary accident. They had extricated themselves. Within minutes choppers and sirens were converging from the Tacoma direction over the freeway as the KCBD van sped toward the airport exit.

As they skidded on time into the private airstrip behind the main commercial terminal region, the chopper was there waiting, its rotor blades already starting to turn. They were just in time. Elizabeth was there, getting out of her car and rushing up to join her husband.

"Freeway was a bear."

"Yeah. Listen, there's not much time, but something's going on. The people who control the station have been censored—I mean, they don't want to run the story. And we were just tailed."

"I know," Elizabeth said, slightly panicked. "They've already been to the house."

"What?"

"Some government agency."

"Wait a minute—what government agency?"

"Let's go, you guys!" the chopper copilot shouted over the increasing din of the engine.

"John, we're ready," Andy added, locking the van and shouldering the gear toward the stepladder.

"Call Singer," John told his wife. "Stay in touch with him. He's on our side on this."

"The two men said this was a national security issue. They flashed ID's. They looked official. I haven't had time to check 'em out."

"They don't want us to report what's happening."

"But why?"

"They're afraid."

"You better go."

"Listen, follow up on these guys and tell Singer about them. You got it?" John lowered his head and started for the chopper. Andy and Wendy had already boarded through the hatch. John looked back as Elizabeth blew him a kiss and mouthed the words *Be careful.*

John was pulled in through the hatch and the craft swung free of the tarmac. The copilot instructed the three occupants on safety measures, showed them how to snap in their safety belts over the shoulder, what to do in the event of an ocean landing, and how to speak using the headsets. The noise was deafening.

Andy had brought a monopole along, a simple tripod that stood alone and could be hand assembled rapidly. With its gyroscopic fluid head the chopper vibrations were totally absorbed. Wendy miked John, who intended to do a stand-up from within the chopper. Their plan was to rendezvous with a large NOB research ship that was out there in the approximate zone Willard had recommended and to land on the back deck. A Coast Guard cutter was supposed to be on hand as well.

Everyone on board wore Annapurna glacier goggles. John passed around thick zinc-based cream which they applied to all exposed parts of the face, hands, and throat. They had a fifty-minute ride to the ship.

Elizabeth watched the chopper disappear, then turned to get back in her car. As she shut the door, the sedan that had tailed John and the crew pulled up to block her exit. One of the sunglassed men got out and started walking toward her car. "Oh, fuck," she said, locking the doors and rolling up the windows and sitting still.

The man stood beside her window looking in. He was over six feet tall, had a nasty-looking scar over his left eye and a particularly ugly square jaw. Elizabeth thought that he looked like a mobster. The man knocked at the window.

"Leave me alone!" Elizabeth screamed.

"We just want to talk," he said. Elizabeth saw a second man getting out of the vehicle. Now she applied her hand to the horn and stayed on it.

"You got speed," Andy said to John. Their chopper had been over water for half an hour.

John began his to-camera stand-up. "It could start to happen at any moment," he shouted, as much to warn the pilots as to inform the viewer. "We're approaching the area now. As you can see, the chopper's exterior offers no clues. A gorgeous day. And yet, there is the feeling of apprehension, of fear mingled with curiosity, and the sense that all is not right. I can feel it in my head, which happens to be throbbing." He looked to Andy. "Here, give me the camera," John requested. He wanted to document his two crew members, who looked dizzy and pale.

They exchanged positions. "Can you feel it?"

Andy answered, holding on to the overhead cords beside the open door. "Yeah, I feel something."

"Wendy?" John panned slowly. Camerawork wasn't his thing, but this had the touch of reality to it and it was not very different from home video.

"I don't know."

"You two—ohh!"

There was a sudden, violent lurch. The chopper plunged hundreds of feet, then righted itself.

"Wind," the copilot shouted. "You okay? Better stay low.

Take your seats, all right? Stay away from the door just now. We got some turbulence."

There was a loud patch of static up front in the cockpit. "What is it?" John shouted.

"Don't know yet," the copilot said over the melee, still calm, speaking into the mouthpiece. Out in the distance the *Glomar Challenger*'s successor ship floundered in brilliant sunlight. For two hours no message had reached the ship or been transmitted from its silent bridge. "There's no channel open on the ship," the copilot continued. "We got a beacon though."

"It's an emergency signal," the pilot said. "I think we're getting close."

John was acutely aware of more and more light pouring in. Brighter, brighter still. He lowered his sunglasses, told Andy and Wendy to do the same. "I can't shoot with 'em on," Andy advised, obstinately playing the video hero now. He pulled a raw carrot from his pocket-lunch—and took a bite, a premeditated form of obeisance to the gods of eyesight, he thought.

"Want some?" he said.

Wendy took the offered carrot and chomped down on it.

"Here." He offered one to John.

"No thanks," said John. "I'd like to roll intermittently—you know, depress speed every three minutes, conserve tape but be ready. Get an accurate depiction of things as we proceed."

"Right." Andy mounted his monopole and moved to the hatch. The turbulence had abated. The chopper was going down in altitude, crossing the choppy Pacific at 300 knots and an elevation of two thousand feet. His camera was backed up with a sling that attached to a running cord above the hatch. He hand-held the twenty-five-pound camera, which was tied to the same running piece of steel cable above as Wendy was. In addition, a bungee cord connected him by carabiner to Wendy's belt. He knelt down, placing one foot on a metal chopper strut, a bar several feet below the exterior of the hatch. The wind was hot. Wendy hovered close to him, her shotgun mic jutting out into the open ambience. Andy turned the camera to the interior, giving the frame of the hatch door to emphasize internal geography. Wendy remained totally covered up. Only Andy's eyes were exposed.

John rehearsed over the din and rattling. He didn't know what he was going to say but he wanted the tone to be right, taking his cue from the rapid accumulation of warnings and suspicions triggered that morning. "Okay, you got speed?" he asked.

Andy nodded.

"It's bright. Very bright! No cut. I want to start differently," John began.

The security police crossed the tarmac in a range rover at fifty miles an hour, lights flashing, skirting dozens of private planes. A Cessna 286 and a twin-engine Beaver crossed paths, halted in confusion, their pilots' heads shaking, but security moved on right-of-way protocol. Behind them, three large jets were coming in on separate runways. The siren from the rover was inaudible. Someone from a quarter mile away scoping out the back lot with binocs had recognized a problem. Elizabeth continued to lean on her horn. The man with what she perceived to be a fake badge continued to keep her in place. It was a standoff.

Security arrived, and to her horror, Elizabeth found she was actually the odd man out. They were in complicity with the goons. She didn't know how to interpret any of it. The officer helped her out, introducing her to the two gentlemen who'd scared the shit out of her. "We've met, thank you," she replied curtly to the assisting security guard.

"Well, Mrs. Gage, I've got your boss on the car phone. He'd like a word with you."

"Who's my boss?"

"That would be Drake Manders, m'am."

"Uh-huh." Still doubting this charade, she glared at the vehicle, left her own, and took up the receiver.

"Liz, who the hell gave you permission to put your

130

husband and crew on that chopper? That's government property and you were not authorized—"

"Drake, not now!"

"Hey, folks, dead ahead ten miles," the pilot said.

"You got speed, John."

"I'm speaking from a helicopter traveling some three hundred miles west of the Olympic Peninsula, two thousand feet above the ocean. For the record, it's early Wednesday afternoon. In the distance, less than ten miles away, our rendezvous point, a research vessel operated by NOB in conjunction with the Coast Guard."

"Something is out there. Something on the ocean," the copilot said, alerting all occupants.

"Get a shot, Andy. Use your twelve-hundred-millimeter lens. You brought it?" John asked.

The sea was clogged with coho, perch, largemouth bass, desiccated kelps, burned sea grasses, upended and lifeless squid. It was a trail of gangrene, rotting flesh for miles—in midday, a luminescence unlike any the sea had probably known for literally billions of years, a reflection like that off scintillating steel. Hell.

John stared in horror. Andy needed more room, greater slack. As the chopper swung down low, skimming a mere two hundred feet above the water, approaching the still distant vessel, he unsnapped himself from the guideline above and from Wendy's waist. He needed freedom to maneuver into his Velcro pack for a change of lens, cleaning off the filter with tissue, blowing air and carefully unscrewing and rescrewing square-mounted glass pieces. This was going to be video like nobody had ever seen. The light was infernal, even through John's goggles.

"How can you see?"

But Andy didn't hear John. Suddenly, two other choppers appeared from out of nowhere. No radio contact. The choppers approached on either side, unmarked, like escorts. A pilot waved them off.

"What's happening?" John shouted. "Andy, hurry up."

"You're on."

"I said, what's happening?"

"They evidently want us to leave."

"Hold your course. We're going down onto that ship."

The choppers came in closer. The pilot tried without success to contact someone. "This is weird, all right. Hey!"

Suddenly the choppers came within striking distance. The pilot screamed and threw the helicopter into a vertical rise. Andy, still unsnapped, was thrown out of the hatch. He clawed at the door, but the force was overwhelming, the light blinding.

"Oh, God, grab me!" Andy screamed.

"Andy!" Wendy cried, lurching toward him, clinging at the arm. "John, help me!"

John fell forward into Wendy, holding on to her waist with one hand, lunging for Andy with the other. The chopper was still soaring upward and slanting away. Wendy's grip was severed by sheer force of the chopper pulling around at such speeds. Andy was spit out. His body plunged, falling into the blur of rotors beneath him from one of the opposing choppers. The blur was at once punctuated by a hideous spray of particles, body parts, spread out into a fine splatter of blood that settled into oblivion below. His camera continued to dangle from the guideline above.

"Hold on!" John bellowed, clinging! to Wendy, gripping with an ironclad fear the metal stays along the hatch. "Jesus bloody Christ!"

Wendy turned her face. John continued to watch the remains of Andy careening far down into the sea of dead fish.

The chopper that had caught him was smoking, steel blades clanking, as it broke apart. There were screams from all sides now, picked up in the static, heard across the gulf of candescent light separating the three hell-bent flying machines. Veering off, it detonated, right after a pause that held it in some hiatus of impossible aeronautical stress—as if a charge had been set. John held the camera, capturing the black explosion, capturing everything. He spoke frantically now, trying to encompass the myriad horrors—the corpse-littered sea, the ghost ship, silent and alone, and now this.

The second attacking chopper charged away, while its companion sank in the pink ruin of flotsam and diseased tissue. "We're pulling out," the pilot announced, as his copilot slammed the hatch door.

"Help me with this," John said with a voice half breaking up. Wendy removed her fogged goggles. Tears had drenched the inside of the dark plastic. She tried to fiddle with it, but her hands shook. She was out of control. John smothered her with his weight, holding down the seizure of grief that had come over her. The chopper had gone to a high cruising position. The copilot sent emergency dispatches into the void, repeating a series of Mayday-like warnings and cries for help.

John had no knowledge of the Betacam. He set it aside and comforted Wendy, who within ten minutes had recovered and mustered the wherewithal to continue recording. She knew how to use the camera well enough. John spoke, rendering volatile commentary on the events of minutes before. When he stopped for a tape change, Wendy futzed with the apparatus. "It'll be twenty minutes."

"Whatever." John sat back against the leather reclining pads of his uncomfortable seat. His head throbbed. His skin was burned—he knew it.

"Who were they?" Wendy cried defiantly, shaking.

"I don't know," John said soberly.

"John, what's happening?"

"We'll know soon enough. Turn off the mic. Wendy, did we both see the same thing? I mean, there's gonna be questions, lots of questions. Are we together on this?"

"Of course we're together. What are you saying?" She started screaming and her screams broke down into a hysterical sob. "He was the first—I mean the first guy—"

"It was deliberate. Wendy, would you agree it was deliberate? They tried to kill us and they partially succeeded."

"I don't know."

"Wendy, you saw it."

"Yeah."

"Are you sure?"

"Everything is recorded."

"You're sure we got it?"

"Goddamnit, John, Andy's dead! Yes, the fucking camera got it! You can throw your bloody camera—" She fell apart again, holding on to John, her face pressed against his chest.

CHAPTER 15

John put the tape in his leather and canvas satchel bag, took a deep breath, and stepped out of the hatch. Three airport security vehicles and a contingent of stern-looking straights dressed in dark cotton suits were waiting for them. Low blue lights flashed in slow revolutions atop the vehicles.

"Where's the tape, Mr. Gage?" the lead man asked John, flashing a card with some meaningless acronym.

"Right, you sonofabitch." John knew what he was doing. He had the goods. "Wendy, take the camera and deck, put 'em in the van. I'll meet you in two minutes."

Four of the officers blocked Wendy's path. They stood firm and appeared slightly annoyed. Frustrated, Wendy looked toward her boss. "John, what do I do?"

The chopper pilots immediately got in one of the waiting vehicles. "Thanks for the ride, gentlemen," John said to them.

The oldest of the waiting party addressed John in a laid-back, conciliatory drawl. He looked less adversarial than the others, silver haired, but still in his late forties, perhaps early fifties. He was athletic, in spite of a slight paunch that suggested that office work had supplanted an earlier career out in the field, perhaps. He was trying to finesse the moment.

"Now we know what you've been through, what you've

seen. But it's out of your hands, kids. We'd like to spend a few minutes with you and tell you exactly what that means." Then, sarcastically: "By the way, you're one hell of a journalist."

John saw that the men were carrying guns and figured that at the very least, for them to have gotten through airport security and come so forwardly in emergency vehicles, they must have top-level security clearance. He allowed himself and Wendy to be corralled into the larger of the security trucks and driven a mile across the tarmac to one of many administration buildings behind the airport. There they were herded into a basement lounge, the institutional metal doors shut quietly, and the two of them were surrounded by interrogators.

"Who are you? What do you want?" John asked straight-away.

"Government. We're all on the same side here. Which is why I'm recommending you let us get you to a doctor. You look ragged. Too much sun. It can affect the mind." The man stared at John with all the patience in the world.

John stared back balefully, wavering. His skin was literally burning up. His eyes felt raw, blistered. "I'd like some water," he admitted.

The man with silver hair nodded to the associate closest to the door, who slipped out, then returned with two large plastic cups filled with water.

"What branch of government are you with?" John asked.

"Four agencies are currently in this room, John. I don't think the details are as important as impressing upon you one simple fact: you know and I know there's a problem. But neither of us can be certain what the scope of it is. Is that fair?"

"Go on."

"You were obviously taken with Dr. Donald Willard. Good man. But he's one man. What he didn't tell you— because he didn't know—is that NSB conducted its own series of tests on the ozone layer."

"I know. I heard about the press conference earlier today."

"And you'll be able to read all about it in this evening's paper. And we'd like viewers to hear about it on tonight's news."

"The gist of it?"

"A quirk. Meteorological. Short-lived. Benign. NSB and the surgeon general are recommending that residents throughout the Pacific Northwest wear visors and sunglasses if they have to be outside for the next forty-eight hours or so. You can never be sure with weather, but that's about the sum of it. I know you wanted an Armageddon to report on. You're relatively young. It's a competitive field you're in. I can understand that."

"John, it's a line. They're jerking us," Wendy said with resolve.

"Ms. Fox, isn't it?" the fellow said, shifting his style. "Audio engineer?"

She just glared at him, detecting a chorus of misogynistic impulses in the room.

The man picked up on her suspicions at once. "So how does the world sound to a dyke anyway?"

"Fuck you."

"Whenever you're free, sweetheart."

"We're out of here," John said, charging for the door with his weight. Two men grabbed him, held him back, and the silver-haired man pulled out a pair of cuffs. "Now I could send you to jail. And I don't even have to read you your rights. Because in security situations like this, you have no rights."

He looked at the two security guards who held him firmly at the door. "Let him go." Then, addressing John in a more affable manner, he said, "We'd like that tape, John."

John kept quiet.

"Give us the tape."

"I can't do that."

"We can make it easy or hard. Your choice, hotshot."

"No way."

The man unlocked his handcuffs and started toward John.

"Give him the goddamned tape, John. It's not worth it," Wendy shrieked. She'd reached her pressure point. Her nerves were frayed. She'd never seen someone die before. Andy continued to spin downward toward the water in her mind.

"A woman's voice of reason," the man's number two, some spastic-looking goon, spit out with a feeble grin.

"Andy paid for this tape with his life and I'm not handing it over to anyone. It's our responsibility to him, to the public," John said with enough patriotic vigor to enervate the room.

"Will you listen to that!" The man looked to the others and almost as an afterthought said, "Now who's Andy?"

"Don't give me that crap. You bastards killed him."

The silver-haired man pulled out a pocket tape recorder. "I think we ought to tape this, don't you, Clive?" he said, speaking to the second goon. "Because I don't know what Mr. Gage is referring to and I'm sure others would like to know." He pushed the record button. "Now why don't you tell us about this Andy?"

John was dizzy. It was over his head. They were pulling a fast one—he could smell it but didn't know what to do about it.

"I'm not answering any questions without a lawyer present. You have no right to be questioning us. We didn't do anything wrong."

"And we're not saying you did. We simply must have that tape, John. Now I'm going to ask you one more time nicely."

"I want your name—all of your names—and titles."

"That's no problem. Greg, give him your card."

"Here you go, Mr. Gage. Call any time."

John studied it. GAO. General Accounting Office. Greg Morton, assistant director for inter-agency intelligence gathering. "What does GAO have to do with it?"

Wendy looked pleadingly. "John, this is not the time. Just give it to them. It'll be okay."

"You really have no choice, John," the silver-haired man reminded him.

"Fine. Fine. You got it." He relinquished his treasure. There was such a thing as fatalistic wisdom and John was banking on it. "I didn't catch your name?" he said to the silver-haired man.

"I didn't give it. That's Rick. Rick Caldihamp. DIA. Look it up, wiseass." He looked around the room at his cronies and then back at John and Wendy. "Now why don't we escort these well-meaning citizens back to where they came from."

Wendy and John were driven by the security guards back across the airport tarmac to their van, Wendy clinging to the gear.

John was utterly dejected. He was not thinking fast enough and he knew it. There was a connection—or series of connections—he was unable to draw.

"Did they seem for real?" he asked Wendy, as she turned on the ignition of the KCBD van.

"Andy's dead. I can't believe it," she muttered, steering the vehicle toward the on ramp. "His parents are in Peru. Who's going to tell them? A helicopter accident? Murder? Jesus, John, what did happen?"

"I can't believe I gave them the tape. Our only evidence."

"I made a copy."

"You what?"

"I did."

"Wendy, you're beautiful. How?"

"I made a dub of that tape during the flight back. The deck recorded off the camera. We're able to do that. That's what took twenty minutes."

"Okay. It's three twenty. Drive, baby, drive like the wind! We've got a deadline to meet."

"I've got a better idea!" Wendy swerved the van across an oncoming lane, forcing a police car to swerve to miss her.

"Are you out of your mind!" She slammed on the breaks, dove out, and ran toward the officer screaming. He and his partner, guns raised, were taking aim. "Put your hands up and spread those fucking legs. Now!"

"We're press! KCBD TV. We need your help. It's an emergency!" she screamed, reaching for her wallet.

"I said, don't move!" one of the cops shouted back, as

derailed traffic to either side slowed to a crawl and the crowd of onlookers converged upon the scene. The sun was pouring down. There was, observed John, a total unreality about it. A hundred yards away, the freeway vented a halting flow of what was probably impossible delays. They'd never make it, unless . . .

The two cops saw the TV logos on the side of the van and approached warily. They'd been through too many crazy scenarios already today—untold accidents, drivers flipping out, missing lights, plowing into one another, blinded by the summery mirages.

Wendy and John both extended their ID's slowly. "We have got a crisis to report. You've got to help us get back to the station for the five o'clock. Please."

The lead cop, the driver, stalked closer, then recognized John. "You're that reporter who did the drug wars, Gage. John Gage. Right?"

John smiled.

"Hey, you're famous," Wendy said with a smirk.

The cop got on his radio and confirmed Wendy's ID. "Okay. You got it. But that was real dumb."

"I had to."

They moved the vehicle off the road, locked the van, making a mental note of its location, and threw their things in the back of the squad car. The squad car pulled back onto the highway, burning rubber, lights flashing, siren wailing.

"This is good," John said to Wendy, touching her thigh. "Just maybe."

"That's near the stadium, right?" asked the driver.

"Yeah. Eighth Street near South Charles."

"That was a good story," the rookie cop in the passenger seat said, looking at John.

"Thanks."

"Except for that abuse business."

"You did the dental fraud story, didn't you?" the driver remarked.

"You have a good memory."

"My sister spent fifteen hundred dollars on a root canal she didn't need. I told her, Florence, you jerk. She turned around and blew a thousand on cavities she didn't have. For cosmetic purposes, she tells me. Then there was this bogus hysterectomy. I tell you, my sister. She needs reporters like you. Except Florence never watches the news."

The older cop at the steering wheel was traveling in and out of traffic, gunning at eighty miles an hour, even ninety when he could, diving down side roads, bus routes, keeping to the underpasses, a maniac, talking about Florence, retirement, and finally, as if by least curiosity, this ozone business. "We got fifty times more traffic accidents than usual. They're sayin' it's ozone. What do you think?" He looked at John.

His rookie partner added to the older man's concerns. "Yeah. They say the dogs at the kennels are going crazy and something about the monkeys at the Woodland Park Zoo, the little gold ones that come out at night—they're dying."

The patrol car squealed around South Charles Street and plowed into the one empty space in front of the station garage. John and Wendy thanked the cops, got out, and headed inside with all their gear.

"Wendy, we better talk," John said quietly, holding tightly to the crucial tape.

It was 4:45. Flying past Security, ferrying the small Beta cartridge, they charged down two corridors to the stairs, knocking into Louis, the FM classical music jockey who worked downstairs, colliding with Mason, an associate producer balancing tapes and pizza on the stairwell. John was howling, "Out of my way, out of my way!" as he made for the off-line rooms shouting, "Herb! Where's Herb? Jennie?"

Jennie, his assistant, ran up to meet him, and together they skidded into Singer's office, but he was gone.

"Where's Singer?" John demanded.

"He must be downstairs, in the loft," Jennie said, keeping up with her boss. "Calls are coming in from every fisherman in the Northwest. What's going on?"

The loft overlooked the studio where Fields would be doing makeup about now.

John ran across to Studio B, up the stairs. "Jeremy!"

He sat within an all-glass high-tech control room. Fields could be seen down below in his anchor chair directly before the teleprompter.

Looking to the loft, Fields saw Singer and John arguing. He knew something was up.

Singer sat back down. He was stunned by what John had just told him. There was no time to consider consequences.

"There's no time for next-of-kin calls. They're in Lima, for chrissakes," said John.

"I can't let you run any of it, John. I'm sorry."

"You gave me permission to pursue the story. It's a big story, Jeremy. Bigger than either of us imagined."

"I told you. I never imagined anything. I only do what the network says I can do."

"Bullshit. You stayed alive in Nam and spoke the truth!"

"NOB. The Coast Guard. The governor. The station manager. Even the goddamned White House has called me in the last five hours. And they all said to cool it. Not one other station has covered this thing, John."

"They killed Andy. Do you understand that? He didn't just accidentally fall out of a helicopter. He was maneuvered out. They saw he had the camera."

"Who are 'they,' John? The White House? The Coast Guard?"

"I don't know. I'm going to find out. You've got to let me run this."

"If I do, I'm out of here."

"If you don't, we may *all* be history."

"That's your drama, Gage. Big words. You're feeling real important. Who's gonna believe you?" Jeremy's voice was angry. His heart was pounding, though Gage had no idea of it.

John was feverish, desperate. Desperate to get to his family. Already seized by the dilemma: follow this crusade or start the exodus from Seattle?

An awkward pause seemed to stand rigidly, irrevocably between the two men. One with the simple power of saying yea or nay. Perhaps John could get it on the air in spite of his boss. The power of his fomentation was beyond any chain of command. He was inspired. But the power was also contagious. Singer was no dummy. He knew something was coming down and it was heavy.

"Go. Do it. Do what you think is right."

Jeremy was out of breath, laboring under the foreknowledge of his own personal doom. Fields saw that he had caved in. Now he had his own dilemma.

Wendy met John in the engineering room, where the tape was inserted into a wall of switchers, routers, and players. This was the brain unit for on-air. Leaving for downstairs, John asked Wendy to call Elizabeth to make sure she watched it and to tell her that he was safe—so far.

John polished himself in the mirror, straightening his tie. He ran his fingers through his hair, wiped a smudge of helicopter grease off his ear lobe, then walked, steadied and controlled, into the studio. It was not his normal bailiwick —until now. As he passed the chyron operator on the fringe of the studio, he told him to type in the title of his piece for cueing-up purposes, utilizing a font that was sedate with a seraphic filmy look: "Ozone Crisis."

"What are you doing?" Fields demanded, as John sat down beside him.

"I'm the story tonight. You got a problem, talk to the Man."

Cagily: "I have no problem, John."

"Two minutes!" shouted the assistant director on the floor.

Fields threw an indignant look upstairs into the glass tech room, where Singer stared back sullenly and resolutely. "This is your moment, John. I guess I always underestimated you."

"Just do your job. Introduce the fact that I've got an exclusive eyewitness report on the fisheries disaster and the encroaching ozone hole."

"That is total bullshit."

"Look, fuckface—you don't like it, remove your hairy ass *now!* I'll introduce myself. Decide, prick."

Very coolly, Fields stepped away, unbuttoned his mic, and walked over to a mic that could punch in to the upstairs.

"It's down," the assistant director said.

"Shit," Fields barked. He then ran upstairs to confront Singer.

"What is this?" he said angrily, arriving in the viewing gallery.

"It's whatever John has to tell. He was out there. Now get back into your chair, Fields, and sit down."

Fields was furious. "I don't believe this ad hoc protocol shit. I mean come on, Jeremy!"

"Charles," Singer began. "This has not been a good day. So don't say another word. Understand? Now move your ass!"

Fields muttered, left the room, and returned to the studio, adjusting his "presence." He sat down without looking at Gage and awaited the countdown, reading through the notes, the habitual "we're *always* busy in this newsroom" look. Teletype background audio, the sound of a computer printer muted in the rear set, mirrors, lights, monitors reading the day's lineup.

"One minute," said the associate director.

Upstairs in the tape room, Wendy sat glumly watching the goings-on, mulling over everything. The Beta tape rolled into preview mode on the sixth VTR. The others were all covered with the coming KCBD logos. "Oh, no!" she groaned, then looked to the engineer. "Fast forward, fast!"

The operator did so and saw, as Wendy did, a fuzzy, scratch-consumed roll of black. "What did you shoot, or what didn't you shoot?"

"God, it can't be. Put it on pause, now roll back, in real time."

"Zilch."

"But that's—" She lost her breath. "Danny, that can't be."

"Sorry, babe. She's blank."

"Pull it out, reverse it. I mean, look and see what's wrong."

He did. "Tape's loaded all right. Nothing jammed." He checked it in the scope, using the various broadcast specs, all in the space of fifteen seconds. "She's defective. This tape should've been scrapped. Where'd you get it?"

Defeated and helpless, she turned to Singer, who sat through an open door thirty feet away. He was self-possessed, somewhere else. She looked to John, put on the headset, and spoke. "John, John, the tape is blank. Someone gave us a defective tape. Do you hear me?"

"He doesn't," the tape op said. "Headsets are down today."

"Why in hell doesn't this place work! Oh, shit!"

John looked confident and gave her a determined thumbs-up signal, as she ran in to tell Singer. John followed the action. So did Fields. Now Singer lowered his head and rubbed his eyes.

Wendy ran downstairs but it was too late. The logos had already run and Fields had started his introduction. "Good evening, I'm Charles Fields. Top of the news, the National Space Bureau earlier today released a report stating that the recent weather disturbances over Canada that caused widespread flu and unseasonable heat, as well as the death of some fish in the Northern Pacific, were relatively inconsequential. NSB spokesmen concluded that while there were apparent fluctuations in the ozone layer, they were not significant. In terms of the Vancouver and Seattle areas, scientists with the space agency have put out an advisory recommending that people wear visors and sunglasses if they are going to be in direct sunlight for more than ten minutes. All of this is good news. But there may be the proverbial fly in the ointment—namely, our reporter John Gage, who is here with me in the studio. John has a live report on what he alone is calling, 'the Ozone Crisis.' John—"

The over-the-shoulder monitor to camera cued up the "Ozone Crisis" title as the lead camera held on the two-shot and the technical floor director cut to camera two, a medium tight shot of a very nervous John Gage, whose children happened to be glued to the TV, munching anxiously on pretzels and carob chips.

Evans ran upstairs. "Mom, Dad's on," he said gently, touching his mother's hair. She lay in bed pondering the day's events.

"Okay," she sighed, breathing a trail of mixed motives and infuriation as she went downstairs to watch in the living room.

Early in the afternoon she'd been fired from her job, allegedly for providing her husband and crew a ride on the chopper. She knew it was more than that. Drake Manders had been essentially her friend and supporter. They'd been through worse, it seemed. Someone had gotten to him. But she had no obvious recall. Her position carried with it sufficient clout to fight it out in personnel, perhaps. But the "insubordination" clause would probably defeat her in court. This was no job discrimination or unlawful firing—not in theory. Only in practice.

Along with KCBD, they had every other evening news channel up on the six monitors at home.

Whatever happened, Elizabeth knew she had done the right thing.

Wendy had tears in her eyes as she entered the studio and whispered something to the floor director. He in turn directed the teleprompt operator.

"At noon today," John began, "I flew in a helicopter operated by the National Oceanic Bureau . . ."

As he continued, Singer called down to the switchboard to have them put all incoming calls through to the voice mail. He was preparing for the worst. He also instructed night security, which came on at five and consisted of two armed guards, to patrol the periphery very carefully.

"Please roll the tape," John said. At that moment, as he looked toward the over-the-shoulder monitor, he caught the teleprompter and the technical director's frantic waving of arms, which, being unaccustomed to live studio action, he had not observed. The teleprompter read: TAPE IS BLANK. WHAT DO YOU WANT TO DO? SORRY.

John took a beat, saw a devastated Wendy drowning in the moment, and decided not to follow her.

"Something's wrong," Evans said, picking up at once on his father's pause.

Elizabeth turned up the volume. "Come on, sweetheart." She too sensed something was wrong.

John had pulled it together before on camera, in the field, where life was actually happening. Here, amid props and an obvious adversary sitting beside him, John mastered the full conflict of his situation and turned it around, making a point of the conspicuous absence of any video.

He pushed on after a ten-second abortive pause. "You're not seeing anything on your television because the videotape we were about to show you was in fact confiscated by the government on the grounds that the disaster posed a national security risk. That's right. Earlier today, I witnessed history three hundred miles off the Olympic Peninsula. The ocean was thick with dead fish. What's-killing the fish also killed the whales last weekend and has been devastating whole towns in the Northwest Territories as we reported here last night. It is an ozone hole. It caused birds to crash into the Space Needle and has resulted in the hottest April in Seattle's history.

"Two nights ago Dr. Donald Willard, an atmospheric chemist at the College of Washington, indicated that the ozone hole was moving in a direct line toward Seattle. At that time he was not altogether certain whether it would avoid Vancouver or not. Apparently it has, having moved southwest from Canada into the Pacific and down the coast. At this hour the hole seems to be hovering just off the Olympic Peninsula."

"That's powerful stuff, John," Fields declared affably, one anchor to another. "How come you and NSB are telling opposite stories?"

"The government's running scared. And they should be."

"You're accusing the U.S. government of something pretty serious, John. Complicity to cover up the full scope of a possible environmental disaster."

The technical director was giving a gesture of a slit throat while the teleprompter display read: STOP BICKERING.

"I don't believe this schmuck," Elizabeth said, broiling with pointed fury.

"Nobody wants people to panic," John said, attempting to cut Fields's inane backfire.

"And should they?" Fields expressed. He didn't believe John's point-of-view, exactly, and was more concerned about making him look like a jerk. But he could also see the avalanche coming down. He wanted a winning ticket. If there was truth to all of this, he wanted it to make *him* look good.

"Seattle has a big problem, Charles. As of this hour, I, for one, would like to know where the guidance is going to come from to see us through it."

The technical director cut to a commercial break.

"See us through what, exactly?" Fields continued off camera.

"You guys are the two biggest fuckups in the history of broadcasting!" Singer screamed, stampeding across the studio, throwing a file of papers in both their faces. "What do you think this is!"

"We can hear you, Jeremy," John said, holding tough.

"No. You don't hear a thing! And you—you stupid sonofabitch—we are dead. *Dead!* This is the end. You two have dug a grave so deep you have no idea!"

"You're full of shit," John shouted. "Wake up man!"

"I was awake while you were still crapping in your pants, you white piece o' shit!"

"Andy's dead, you dumb sucker. You know why he's dead?" People on the studio floor were staring at them.

"Ten seconds," shouted the floor director. "What do you want to do?"

148

"The both of you get back up there and finish the newscast. Do it right. Get off this story!" He turned, then turned back. "Just get off it!"

"In other news tonight, animal rights activists have called for a ballot outlawing all furs in the State of Washington. Perry Salich filed this report." Fields smiled, turning to the over-the-shoulder monitor.

There was a moribund energy in the Gage family living room. Jennifer stood up restlessly, saying, "Mom, this is totally weird."

"Not really," Elizabeth replied. "They've always hated each other."

"That Fields is a jerk," Evans added. "And these environmental disasters happen all the time. Valdez, Bhopal, Chernobyl. But you're too young and too dumb to know about these things."

"Shut up, you two, I can't take this!" Elizabeth screamed.

"He started it!" Jennifer protested.

"Just be still, please."

The three of them watched as the other evening news stations erupted with "This just in—" reports on the "extraordinary developments" occurring offshore in the Pacific.

She smiled faintly, for the vindication of it, looked at her children, around the living room. "Where's Wallace?"

"Outside," Evans said.

Elizabeth was beginning to see beyond the news story to the essential fact that something—like a tidal wave of light—was heading toward Seattle. A wave of light on top of light, for the days had been especially bright, fatiguing, penetrating. She felt the first urge to get out. "You two," she said quietly, parting her little girl's hair.

The phone rang. Elizabeth jumped for it. It was Sophie for Evans.

"I'll take it upstairs," he said, running for the phone, the universe of doom usurped by the flash and premonition of loin magic.

* * *

149

Evans spoke softly. "Do you believe what's going on?"

Sophie was confused. "I don't get it. Was your dad serious?"

"What do you think?"

Sophie then confessed the bad news. "My dad is taking me and Grandma and Grandpa to New York."

"What? When?" Evans said with manly unconcern.

"In about a half hour. Evans, I'm really worried about you and your family."

"Don't you think your dad's maybe being an alarmist?" Evans asked her.

"He's only responding to your dad, Evans. We watched the news."

Thanks, Dad, Evans thought to himself.

"Are you gonna get out?" Sophie continued.

"And go where? The sun's everywhere." He was feeling rejected. Scared for the first time that Sophie's dad, Mr. Straight, *would* leave town because of this. It didn't square with Evans's plans. He was hoping to take Sophie out Saturday night. "That's too bad," he said solemnly.

"Yeah. Grandpa's been sick the last two days. And Dad's really not himself at all. I'll call you when we get there," she said.

"I probably won't be home," Mr. Macho informed her.

"Yeah? Where you gonna be?"

"I don't know. Scuba practice."

"Mr. Practice makes Mr. Perfect."

"I don't know."

"Well, I'll try to call you at least. Listen, I better pack."

"Yeah. See ya."

They both paused, knowing or hoping that there was more to this conversation than seemed apparent.

Sophie took a deep breath so that he could hear it. "Listen, Evans. You know I really have strong feelings for you. More than just us being friends."

Evans was afraid to say anything. "Uh-huh."

"Did you hear what I just said?"

"Yeah."

"Do you have feelings about me?"

"I guess so."

"You do, don't you?"

"At my age guys don't have feelings, Sophie. They have hard-ons they're afraid to talk about."

She mushroomed with a smile he couldn't see, or know. He was dying for having said the words. Relief came like a gusher.

"I was hoping you'd say that one of these days."

He opened, complying with the tone of her invitation. What did he have to lose? She was going to New York and he was probably going to die.

"It doesn't scare the traditional Greek girl in you?"

Boldly, dramatically, giving in: "No, 'cause I love you, Evans. I think we're going to get married someday."

Evans was blown away. "When you come back from New York we're gonna go scuba diving."

"I look forward to that. And to touching your hard-on . . Say good-bye to Jennifer for me." She kissed the phone.

"She really said those words!" he screamed out loud.

A very agitated production assistant walked into the line of fire to whisper something to Jeremy Singer.

"What?" he railed angrily.

The production assistant tried again. "Your phone, sir. The one in your office. It's important I think."

Singer stormed out of the studio, leaving the fray to the twenty or so who had congregated at their peril over the news of Andy's death. He walked into his office and picked up the phone. It was his manager calling on the direct line that circumvented the switchboard.

"No, I'm not going to fire you," the voice said calmly. "Or not yet. What you're going to do is reverse the damage. You're going to have your Laurel and Hardy get up there at eleven o'clock and tell the public that all signs indicate that the alleged ozone hole has blown out to sea, where it has evaporated."

"Where, in hell's name, did you come up with that one?"

"I don't like your tone, Jeremy. You've got one shot to keep your job and this is it."

"Just tell me something, why are you guys so scared of telling the truth?"

"Ordinarily I wouldn't dignify that kind of question. But recognizing the unusual situation, let me just say that we're in the business of abiding by the law. And the law came down earlier today from the governor's office. Now the governor doesn't usually dictate nightly news policy, does he?"

Singer was silent.

"No, he doesn't," the voice continued. "But when he does, we figure there's a good reason. And for you to encourage two crackpot squirrel brains on air to argue and report the most outrageous garbage—well, it's a shame, Jeremy. I thought you had more sense."

"I didn't encourage that. I expect an honest day's work from the staff."

"I'm not interested in your Deep South morality play. Just do as you're told. If this blows over, you have maybe half a chance of getting another paycheck in life." The line went dead.

Jeremy sat in the mottled light of his penned-in office. All around him it was empty. The whole staff had now amassed in Studio B. The station had come to a virtual standstill.

At the Gage home, the phone rang again. Evans lurched for it.

"It's Dad!" he hollered.

"Put your mother on," John said.

"Jesus," she groaned.

"I know. Lock all doors. I'm on my way home. Don't answer the phone. Don't answer the door."

"What are we gonna do?"

"I don't know. Just wait there. Don't leave the house. I'm on my way."

"John."

"Yeah?"

"I got fired over this." She was dreading saying it.

"That probably makes two of us." He chuckled, unburdening her. "See you in a bit."

CHAPTER 16

Donald Willard had watched John Gage's report with a drunken man's sense of melancholy and self-pity. He knew that he'd done everything humanly possible to anticipate the crisis. Still, he felt vaguely responsible. His expertise implicated him. There was no escaping that association in his mind.

The crisis loomed in a most personal way for Donald Willard. He could only imagine the sunset from Tatoosh Island off Cape Flattery, on the northern tip of the Olympic Peninsula, where his laboratory's closest monitoring device was stationed. He'd been to the more southerly town of La Push years before, prior to the accident, and had camped on the hard cold beach of strewn driftwood. He remembered the fanfare of colors—pink and magenta, a sea smitten with foaming gold turning taffeta green in the aftershocks of a long day's settled sun, the never-never light of a glacial dawn the next day and the ensuing rain-sodden mystique of a storm out in the wild ocean.

He was seated in his laboratory before a 3-D graphics display on the computer that simulated the ellipsoid formation of the ozone hole atop a rather precise outline of the Pacific Northwest—a computer image signaling a world of unchecked chemical waves and eddies, gigantic trenches of heterogeneous gas. He had written a program to define instability in the upper atmosphere, a tsunami of turbulence around which swirled a shadow of numeric coefficients. Would the shadow come inland toward Victoria and Seattle? he wondered, waiting, watching. Such pure mathematics had its own willpower, or fickleness, and Willard knew that the fate of several million people and hundreds of millions of animals might hang in the balance. It was a thought as monumental as it was random. The computer was, after all, a machine, given to guesswork and miscellany.

Willard worked alone. For the past week he had shared none of his findings with any other colleagues at the college. He'd made only a few phone calls far away, like the one to Roald Shiftren. Even Burt had no idea what Willard was up to, Willard assumed. Burt was gone again tonight. This time he had not bothered to tell anybody. Willard could only hope it was a permanent dereliction.

The scientist's brief conversations with Roald Shiftren a few days before and Felix Girard more recently had served to isolate his findings even more, rendering them suspect. He had never been given the security clearance that might have enabled him to work with NSB and upgrade their own inadvertent omissions. NSB had simply missed the boat. Girard's instincts were off and he was not about to have Willard claim any victory. Girard had, in fact, projected a southward drift and could claim credit for the fact. But that was merely a supposition. And clearly, in Willard's perception of it, NSB's so-called expedition the other day had lent little clarity to the alleged "southward drift," or none they were talking about. Willard was frustrated. How could military secrecy stand in the way of important scientific collaboration? He just didn't get it.

Now he had reason to suspect circumpolar transport. This routine meteorological syndrome meant that the mass of cold polar clouds and associated ozone-depleted bubbles would descend south by southwest, not merely south. Had the NSB mission accounted for that? Willard had calculated the mean average of possible drifts and seized upon an itinerary, which he had then programmed into his computer software system of analysis. There was no confirmation of his findings from any other lab, because Willard had not only devised his own monitoring equipment, but written his own programs for interpreting that data. A simple conversation to compare data with Girard's people was all that would be necessary. But Girard—with bountiful excuses—said no dice.

Now, examining data just in from the station at Tatoosh Island, Willard saw that his calculations had proved to be correct. What he could not know for certain was the actual size of the spherule, or oval, or bubble, or the consistency of its flow. Two hundred miles across? Three hundred miles? Twenty miles? To speculate about the consistency of snow crystals on the eve of an avalanche or the salinity of a coming tidal wave made little sense to Willard—like trying to pacify a mass murderer by browbeating him. But his tools were limited, it was the best he could do, and only two people seemed willing to listen to him—John and Elizabeth Gage.

What had totally surprised Donald Willard was the relatively benign itinerary, up until now, of the hole. Somehow, providentially, the yawning gulf had missed every major town, sticking, by and large, to high mountains, which happened to connect like a Canadian cordillera all the way into southern Alaska, out to sea, and back again, to where the nearly eight-thousand-foot-high Mount Olympus jutted out from the center of the peninsula.

Willard's monitoring of chlorine monoxide and dioxide registered so mammoth a molecular cannibalism taking place as to wipe any existing ozone off the map. Moreoever, the depletion was occurring in both the troposphere and stratosphere. In every previous instance, ozone depletion was restricted to the higher stratosphere, not the troposphere. Willard knew the data was correct. He realized, though could not quite imagine, what it meant: catastrophic ultraviolet, fatal exposure.

And it was this unimaginability, this featureless enigma without precedent, that had sapped Girard's willingness to stick with it. He had given up too easily, like those in the municipality who'd voted against bomb shelters because they were convinced that there was no defense whatsoever against nuclear attack. Maybe they were right, maybe not. But Willard had not given up, not in twenty years. And he'd succeeded in getting that fix on a monster. Girard wasn't interested. His career, his ego was at stake.

"Evenin', Capt'n," the night watchman, Stan, hailed, as Willard rolled down the ramp toward the corridor elevator that would take him into the below-ground parking lot where his Datsun was parked.

"You're leaving early tonight?"

"Tired," Willard said.

"You do work like an engine, I'll give you that much."

Stan was not wearing his normal uniform this evening, but regular duds and a Pendleton shirt. His two blue overalls were at the cleaners. His portable hand phone, clipboard, a small handgun, and dozens of keys attached to a small brass bangle lay on his desk. Usually he wore such paraphernalia. But tonight he'd started drinking early and without his normal outfit—with its belt that held the gun and keys and phone. He even had left his metal security badge in the drawer.

Stan and Dapple were on Willard's mind. "You know, Stanley, I've been thinking. You've got relatives down in Portland, don't you?"

"Why, that's right. Though they're Dapple's really. First cousin. Henry and Louise. Good people, all right."

"Well, with all that's goin' on, you ought to take a few days off. Get out o' town. Go stay with them. I'll be fine."

"Oh, I wish, Capt'n. But Dapple's—she been sick o' late. Yessir, bad colon. That's what the doctor says. She don't even wanna leave her bed."

"Well, then, here's what you do: take the rest o' the week off, stay inside with her."

Stan protested with a flimsy gesture.

"No. I'll lock up for you," Willard said. "No clock to punch. You've earned it. But you promise me one thing— you stay inside during the day. I've been studying the sun, you know that. And the next few days are gonna cause a real bad sunburn if you go out. Skin cancer."

"You ain't jokin'. I knows when you mean it," Stan said with an earnest smile. "And I sure appreciate the good thoughts. But the missus—she be real pissed if I stay home. After all this time I think that woman likes her privacy."

"Oh, don't you be too sure. Take a break, Stan. Surprise her. I'll see you Monday. What do you say?"

"You are somethin', Capt'n. And I sure do thank you. I'll just finish up tonight and take Thursday and Friday off as you say." He paused, embarrassed, doubting it all, then: "Excuse me, Capt'n—that's with pay then?"

"Stanley, of course it is."

Stan smiled and settled in to his nightly TV chair. An old rerun of "MacGyver," one of his favorites.

As Willard drove out of the parking lot onto the first level, a slow-moving van entered. The driver wore a white smock and sunglasses. The van, the color of buckskin, had no writing on it.

That was odd, Willard reflected. Ordinarily he wouldn't think twice about it. Except that it was nearly 9:00 P.M. Deliveries were never made after five. Willard usually was the one who requisitioned supplies for the lab and was familiar with nearly all the venders.

Willard drove slowly around the underground, following the one-way arrows and keeping his eye on the van. It had parked and the driver and passenger got out. Both men were massively built, dressed in the attire of lab technicians. One of them carried a large metal case; the other slung a hefty rucksack over his shoulder. Both men moved hurriedly to the elevator, looking around with a singleness of purpose. Willard waited. One of the two inserted a security card enabling them to operate the lift. Obscured from view by rows of other vehicles, Willard was unable to see either man's face but now reckoned that they must be okay if they had a security card.

As Willard drove forward, reaching in his attaché case for his logbook, he realized that he must have left it in the office.

Willard never left the book around. It contained a daily diary of all that had preoccupied the scientist since the accident. He had planned to write in it tonight.

Willard drove up to the van, got out of his car, and wheeled himself to the passenger side adjoining the elevators. The motor had been left idling in its double-parked position. No one was around. The doors were locked. He activated a switch on his wheelchair that enabled him to rise three feet higher than the usual rolling position. At this height he could see inside the vehicle. It was empty, the vinyl seats torn. On the dashboard, however, there was a book of matches that read THE GRAINERY. Willard knew The Grainery, a small café half a mile from campus.

Shifting his focus, he lowered himself back down and wheeled around to the elevator, inserted his card, and waited. The elevator was delayed. Three minutes passed. The elevator was jammed, he realized. It was not coming down. For Willard to go an alternative route was a major hassle. He'd have to drive out and around and wheel himself a few hundred yards to a steep ramp he had rarely used, then hope a night guard would be at his station on the first floor to let him in. It was not worth it. Willard went home. For one night he could do without his diary.

Stan had come back from the john and ventured into the lab to make his routine check of lights. It was a large area, with dozens of big machines spanning nearly the length of two driveways in four different walkways, each hidden from the other by the nine-foot array of computer gadgetry. Tens of millions of dollars' worth of stuff.

Stan saw Willard's little book, stuffed with chits, bound by a leather snap and toggle. He knew what it was and secured it in Willard's desk, lest someone during the day shift get too nosy. Stan sat in Willard's chair, a second wheelchair, more comfortable than the one he used to travel around in. Just to feel what it must be like to be him.

Stan, who had known Donald since long before the accident, felt an enormous empathy with the scientist, though had never managed to do more than be his friend on the job. He contemplated the kindness of Willard's insistence that he take a few days off. He knew it was awkward for Willard to suggest it. Maybe it was time to invite him home for dinner one of these days.

The two men from the van had already checked both ends of the corridor, and compared the walkways with their diagram. They knew that Willard was just a touch hard of hearing in the right ear. They also knew that Willard's access code could be read off the log-on position of any tape master, which could be put up independent of the chemist's PC. The PC would be locked, if it was there at all.

Approaching easily from the rear, one of the men sized up the weight of their only other company in the lab—a big man, bigger than he was supposed to be—and proceeded to silently unravel a dozen coils of special magnetic tape he'd brought with him. A very strong tape, as strong as a rope. He took the wide concentric hanks in one hand, holding the guide end that connected with the heavy two-inch metal reel, and without pausing stepped up to Willard and encircled his throat with the loose web. He pulled on the circles, snapping the half dozen layers in a vicious, inextricable gridlock. They had never told him that Willard was black.

He held tight as Willard writhed in a half-twist to catch his assailant, sliding out of his chair and flopping desperately. The gloved figure held firmly, reeling the older man in like a marlin. In an instant it was done. The figure replaced the reel of tape onto the nearest metal drum, activated the machine, and towed the excess tape until it was taut against the black man, whose legs suddenly jerked in the afterlife.

"They didn't tell me he was a black man," one of them said nonchalantly.

"They're all equal under my law," the other remarked.

The men got down to business. The murder had not been "ordered." It was a last option, if they felt it would simplify matters or expedite the real task at hand, which it did.

As one of them checked the hallway, the other opened the case, withdrew from it a computer, got power, then read off one of the reels in storage as he'd been instructed to do.

There was Willard's access—MARDI.GRA. The man smiled.

The program was alive and the man—using his own computer to supersede Willard's—proceeded to delete everything, tape after tape. And since he was accomplishing the task from another computer, he knew that there'd be no record whatsoever of the deletion; no automatic notation in the computer's inherent clock. Zero. As if it had never been.

It took the men a good hour to move through the two dozen reels. The phone rang twice during this period, though neither of the men had any intention of answering it. When they were done, they found the surge protector box at the mainframe, played with its circuitry, and managed to trigger exactly what the safeguard was supposed to prevent.

One of them put the computer back in its case, while the other removed from his rucksack several bottles of 100-proof tequila and three prescriptions for downers, Willard's name still legible on one of the vials, even though the rest of the prescription, its number, and the name of the doctor and location of pharmacy had been soiled and watered off.

He forced some tequila down the victim's uncooperative throat, along with dozens of anti-depressant pills, then diluted the lethal concoction in the cheap liquor of mescal, flooded the nose, the mouth with as much as could be insinuated, looked around, fussed with this and that, then departed, walking calmly to the elevator with his partner.

Real clean. They were not particularly worried. This was not their country. Where they hung out, this was normal.

CHAPTER 17

John Gage made his way home from the station along East Madison, turning off on Nineteenth Street. It was a sweltering night and there was a low ground cover of mist, no more than thirty feet high.

The night was also alive with a mass of flying insects. At first John thought they were cotton balls, or gossamer cobwebs drifting in the breeze, but then he recognized in his headlights the migratory flurry of wax wings and hairy tibia, a grotesque multidiversity of claws, antennae, and the telltale mosaic of spattered parts against his windshield. For Gage, who was not fond of insects, this was a bad dream.

Whole houses were faint and mussy behind the locustlike swarms. As the result of a news piece he'd researched and produced a year or so before on soft wheat in the Palouse area, he knew of such eruptions, remembered the signs, and now inadvertently slipped into playback mode. There was tar spot and cytospora canker, dieback and gall, felt fungus and sunscald. Anthracnose, wilt, girdle, bunch and soak. He knew the jargon of plant illness. And he easily connected such diseases with this sudden explosion of insects—weevils and stinkbugs, vinegar flies, no-see-ums, pismires, vespids, assassin bugs and spittlebugs, treehoppers, scarabs, dung rollers, and fireflies. Four thousand-eyed adults, spasmodically flashing sphingid adolescents; potter wasps and aphids. Termite soldiers and mormon crickets. Diving beetles, killer bees.

Along China's Hawang-Ho River, perhaps, or among the *Dociostaurus maroccanus* or *Chortoicetes terminifera*—feared locust swarms in Morocco and Australia. But Seattle? Were they locust? Or Rocky Mountain bloodsucking tick? Gage had no idea. He drove on, nearly amused by the carnage. It took his mind off the pain around his eyes and the last forty-eight hours.

John had stormed out of Studio B following his disastrous encounter with Fields's treachery. An associate producer remembered seeing the anchorman switching tapes on the remote crew, when the batteries were being charged in the garage. At the time, she didn't think anything of it. Only later, when it was too late, did Wendy, the tape operator, and John learn that Fields had by design given them faulty stock.

After the newscast Gage exposed Fields's subterfuge to Singer in hopes of having the bastard fired. But Singer had other things on his mind by that time. Thirteen hundred frantic callers had been metered on the station's phone-answering device by five fifteen. The number was escalating by the second. John was asked by his boss to stick around and make amends on the eleven o'clock. John refused, reminding Singer that he'd agreed as executive producer to go forward with the story and Gage was not about to lie about what was going on just so Singer could placate some fearful bureaucrat who sat on the board of the station group.

The exchange left Gage's own job—and certainly that of Singer's—in jeopardy. And this contagion of lost jobs, considering in addition the plight of his wife, slightly bemused John, as he parked the Saab in the driveway and headed toward the kitchen. On the way, he bent over and tried to stir some life into a moribund Wallace, who sat persistently scratching himself, whining in the grass on a thirty-foot leash that attached him to his little dog cottage. There was an odd odor in the air, John noticed. A hospitallike odor, of an antiseptic. The air was thick with the continuing flight of organisms. And, John thought, the whole neighborhood sounded different.

"Liz," he said, taking his wife in his arms when he got inside. "Where are the kids?"

"In their rooms. Wendy told me about Andy."

"It was horrible."

"I can't believe it! I'm so sorry, John."

"He was an awfully sweet young guy."

"Do his parents know yet?"

"No. Hardly anybody knows. The killers know."

"Killers?"

John recounted his day for Elizabeth. The accidents on the freeway, the death, Fields's sabotage of crucial evidence.

As he spoke, John connected things. He grabbed the phone and called Singer's direct line. Finally, a Fields groupie picked up.

"Get me Karfman," John said. "Quick."

"She's gone home."

John put down the phone, reached under a bookcase for the phone book, and flipped through its pages. There was no L. Karfman.

"Maybe she lives with her folks," Elizabeth suggested.

There were dozens of Karfmans. On the eleventh listing John reached the mark. "Laura, how many tapes did Fields switch?"

"All three, I think," she said.

"You're sure?"

"Yes. It's what made me assume that there was something special about the batch, like you were supposed to be using those tapes specifically. I feel terrible about everything, John."

"It's not your fault."

"So what does that mean?" Elizabeth said, applying a damp cool wash towel to John's face when he hung up. Blisters had started to form around his eyes. Red welts, pus.

"It means there's no record, no proof."

"There's a helicopter down in the ocean and bodies. That's proof," Elizabeth reasoned.

"Maybe," he said.

John's thoughts were racing now. *GAO. GAO.* "Why GAO? What kind of investigation," he conjectured out loud.

"What are you talking about?" Elizabeth butted in.

John kept on thinking out loud. "And DIA? I don't even know what that stands for."

"Defense Intelligence Agency," Elizabeth surmised.

"Okay. Good," John acknowledged. "But why are they trying to suppress everything?"

Elizabeth was boiling from her rude dismissal earlier in the day. She was thinking that she had just spent five years in government for nothing. And she was seeing logically to the core of bureaucratic ineptitude. John couldn't quite appreciate the extent to which an agency was willing to go to conceal the rotten layers underneath, the mismanagement and waste. It wasn't the same in television.

"They obviously think that they need time to see if what Willard's saying is right. Everyone covers their ass. Drake Manders covered his ass. It's the oldest gag in politics," she reminded her husband.

"And the General Accounting Office? What are they covering up?" John fired back.

"Somebody's wasting money somewhere in the chain of command," she posited. "Maybe NSB had a contractor studying ozone and they screwed up."

"It was military, we know that. Willard was barred from the inner circle. They weren't even interested in what he was up to."

"So first they miss the crucial piece of data. Then they try to prevent the story from leaking and issue their own version of what's happening. But they're too late and now they're scurrying for cover. You put a death on top of that and there's going to be real fallout in some personnel department. It'll go to the courts, and for everyone who goes to jail, five others are going to lose their jobs. These are desperate men. It was the same scenario of cover-up at Hanford with the revelations of iodine poisoning during World War Two, remember?"

John was deep in a flurry of speculation. "Who came to the house?" he asked.

"They were with NSB, I assumed. They wanted to talk to you. They can't afford to mess up twice. The story's out there. Every other affiliate picked up on it. You're the rage around town, Mr. Hotshot. And you're my husband." She gently put her lips to his, then drew away with a pained expression. "John, this is more than a sunburn. Come upstairs. I want you to lie down. I'm going to pour you a cool bath and call Dr. Steinhaltz."

John followed her to the bathroom. He was hyper—too many things were rattling in his brain. He had a schizoid temperament to begin with. And there was so much unfinished business with Liz. Maybe that had all changed now. Maybe they'd begin to appreciate what they had. To get out of Seattle.

He was secretly glad her job was gone. Though he wouldn't say so. There were so many things her freedom from work might mean to him. She'd have more time for him. He computed it all in one sensation. He knew that there was a strong likelihood his own job had come to an end as a result of his division with Singer and Singer's own abysmal situation with his employer. John and Elizabeth would either have to hustle for new work or sell the house and start over, perhaps in northern California. A small town. He could teach at a university. But this was crazy. A depressing scenario. It wouldn't happen.

"Have you seen what's going on outside?" he asked, lying down on the bed.

"What's going on outside?"

"Insects. Lots of 'em. You haven't seen it? Stand at the window. Look."

She had been preoccupied for hours. She walked to the bedroom window, opened the drapes, and saw what he was talking about.

"Good God!"

She stared briefly, then closed up the drapes, making sure the window was shut tight. She returned to her husband.

"Evans says he's seen three families on the block, including Dino and Thesika, leaving town," she said, touching John's cheekbones with moistened fingertips. "You didn't hear what I said," she repeated.

"Sure I did. Maybe the insects are also leaving town."

She put a topical antibiotic cream on John's face, trying everything to ease the pain. His eyes were half open, angry lesions suppurating around the swollen fringes.

Elizabeth called the doctor's service, left a message, then tried his home. A maid answered who informed her that the doctor and his wife were at their condo on Longboat Key. It was after midnight in Florida, but Elizabeth called their old friend nevertheless. He recommended another doctor.

"What's that?" Elizabeth whispered with a motion of stealth, putting down the phone.

"What?"

"Wait!" she listened. "I don't know. It sounded like Wallace."

Down the block, Gretchen Mathiess was watching the TV and painting her toenails black, while speaking with Jennifer on the phone. Gretchen's mom had gone out back to start spreading bat guano in the garden. She preferred to work the mass of high-nitrogen pellets into the rose beds during the evening, when the hundreds of Big Browns who hung from the rafters of the family garage during the day were out foraging for fruit and rodents. But tonight did not feel right. The instant she opened the screen door from the kitchen, something stung her, then another. She swatted at herself, reentered the kitchen, and slammed the door. The bite was still working itself in. Frantic, she pulled down a shoulder strap on her halter, searching out the noxious digger, but found nothing. The pain didn't go away. "Gretchen, honey?" she shouted. Then, suddenly, there was a horrible slapping noise, high squeaks, slap upon slap into the back of the house. "Honey?"

Jennifer had the receiver cradled between her shoulder and neck and sat up on the bed in her panties, legs akimbo, filing down her fingernails, shooting the bull about this and that fox at school with Gretchen, and listening to an old Beatles tune on the CD player. She suddenly saw a large pair of eyes staring at her from the edge of the bed. Fascination and horror choked her reaction and she simply watched it, eye against eye, as it slowly approached her. "Gretchen, I don't believe this."

"What? My mom's screaming about something. I can't hear you."

"There's a black widow—I mean, like, the most humongous thing I've ever seen—crawling up my bed. Oh, my God, what do I do?"

"Kill it. That's so gross!"

"I'll call you back."

Jennifer was now glued to the thing's advance and slowly returned the phone to the receiver. Just as her hand stayed on the receiver for an added second of determining time, she felt something, flung her hand away, jettisoning the phone, only to see her hand covered in minute bugs she'd never seen before. They stung.

Screaming, shaking in paroxysms, Jennifer hurled herself toward the door.

Elizabeth was just reaching down to start the bathwater for John when they heard their daughter down the hall. John lunged from the bedroom, racing toward the screams.

He carried Jennifer into their bedroom, yelling for his son and wife. Elizabeth was there, but Evans—who was messing around in his own bedroom across from Jennifer's—heard nothing above the din in his headset of heavy metal music.

John placed Jennifer on the bed. Her face and arms were red and peppered with sudden blisters. Then he noticed hundreds, thousands of little midgelike creatures swarming over the floor. John stomped the floor in a futile rampage. Tears welled in his eyes where the creatures were sucking him dry.

Attracted to the vibrations, a flood of organisms, each harboring a stinging proboscis, attacked Evans. The boy threw off the yoke of his headset, drowning in pain, crashed into the door, and escaped to the hall, where he collided with his family in their desperate hurdles down the stairs. He was breathing rapidly, clung to the banister, clawing at himself, then tumbled downward in panic.

Four doors away, a similar scene was playing itself out, with the additional frenzy of Brown bats pummeling through the darkness into the car, the garage, trees, searching for their bat tower, which Marian had erected out back.

The bugs were storming, biting at everything in sight. Marian and her daughter fled the stinging midges only to be struck headlong by the wave of hysterical furry bats. Their house was under siege.

"The faucet. She needs water!" Elizabeth screamed.

John reached for it, turned it on only to see a river of worms, ants, roaches, and other creatures pouring into the sink. "My God!" John said.

The family ran into the yard, whose grassy surface was a wave in motion, an imperceptible spleen, in the form of things swarming with an equal fervor through the soily darkness. The air was as it had been when John came home: fulminant with insects. Wallace lay face down at the extremity of his leash. He was no longer moving or whining.

CHAPTER 18

WEDNESDAY, 11:30 P.M.

Willard lay on his bed unable to sleep. He put on a CD of an orchestration by the European composer René Clemencic and drank ice tea. Willard had confronted an onslaught of bugs getting out of his garage. His gardener had not been to the house in weeks and the yard was proliferating with sprawling hedges and weeds and thickets, overgrown breeding grounds for the winged creatures. He could read into the situation and divined, in one scientific stroke of intuition, what was happening out in the wilderness all over the state of Washington. Willard sensed preternatural frenzy in the air, in the soil, in the ocean. He could imagine out among the atoms hundreds of elements stricken with a chemical tickling—an atmospheric imbalance tugging at the genetic machinery of everything from dust mites to human hemoglobin.

He suspected that the glaciers outside of town, two-mile-deep remnants of the Pleistocene, on Rainier, on Baker, across the whole touristy uplift of the North Cascades, were probably responding to the heat and the chemical assault; they were probably melting. There'd be floods for sure. And that melting was likely to release other chemical gases locked away in the ice, greenhouse gases. Below the glaciers, farmlands of wheat, apples, potatoes, hops, and grapes would turn yellow and rot. And in the ocean, the plankton would be so disoriented by the sudden onslaught of ultraviolet as to go belly up. And when they died, everything else would die. Willard saw it all. He sat up in bed, slid into his wheelchair, and rolled himself into the kitchen to get a beer. He couldn't sleep.

As midnight approached, the Gage family checked into two rooms atop a ten-story downtown hotel. Nobody on the inside seemed to care one iota, because everything was presumed to be basically normal.

"You mean you don't know what's going on out there?" John heated up before a soporific bellboy.

"Is there something wrong, sir?" the head man asked sleepily.

"Wrong?" He looked around. "What isn't wrong! Why is it that this place resembles a morgue!"

"John, Jennifer is in pain," Elizabeth said. "We're all very tired. Cut the crap. Let's check in and get to our rooms. Okay?"

"Family's very tired," he said to the check-in clerk, coming around.

The hotel was shiny and smooth, hermetically sealed. A tower of icy-blue glass and steel. The clerk at the front desk had all the humor and warmth of a refrigerator. Here no bugs would get to them, no news would reach the guests or staff, unless they wanted it to. No phones would ring. The TV could be kept off and the hotel staff would never utter a word about it, because they knew nothing. The night shift hanging around the front desk of the Parallax Room & View Hotel did not watch TV or listen to the radio. They listened to ambience music, New Age whales and wolves, electronic sax, Indian sirangi, Green Party melodies, the anesthetizing Muzak for the new millennium. There had been no report of bugs in the kitchen.

"Excuse me, sir, but we at the Parallax Room & View pride ourselves on running one of the best Four Stars in the city," the cashier said, stamping John's credit card and responding to John's sudden allegations that the hotel looked sleazy. "Great food, peace and quiet for our guests. A real home away from home."

"Your name's David?" John snapped.

"That's right, sir."

"Listen, David, do you live somewhere, outside of work I mean? Yeah? Do you have a dog?"

"No, sir."

"How 'bout a cat!"

"I have a cat."

"How sweet. What's the cat's name, David?"

"Limerick."

"His cat's name is Limerick. Isn't that funny! David, call your roommate, ask him how Limerick's doing. I'm serious. Do it for me. You deserve to know."

Did these employees ever go home? Had they been outside in the last seventy-two hours? Who knows. If so, they didn't seem to notice anything peculiar. Some people were naturally good-natured. Others were not. And what about the morning paper, politely slipped under the door of every guest in the hotel. What about it? As of Wednesday night, no print journalist had yet written about the crisis. John wondered aloud who really owned the local dailies. Probably the same kind of money that owned KCBD.

John turned over their three frantically stuffed suitcases to the concierge, examined the hotel menu that lay atop the concierge's desk, and used the lobby white phone to call the cook. "You still serving dinner?"

"Everything on the menu," a mellow female voice responded, sounding more like a madame in a massage parlor than one accustomed to sending up hot-fudge sundaes at three in the morning.

John felt compelled to break through the bizarre unreality enshrouding the hotel. It was driving him bonkers. "What's your fish of the day?" he asked, ready to pounce on the answer.

"The chef says we're out of fish today."

"Yeah, well, that's a good sign," John remonstrated, hanging up. "Evans, Jennifer—let's go, guys. To the elevator."

Once safely secured in their respective rooms, the Gage family took stock. John turned on the news, grazing through the dozens of available channels, while Elizabeth put Neosporin on her children's welts. Remarkably, at midnight, there was not a single piece of relevant news. No special news breaks, nothing. What had been a story on the five and six o'clock was no more. John had no way of knowing what KCBD had run at eleven.

Elizabeth went into the bathroom, pausing before the bath faucet.

"Go ahead, turn it on," John said.

"I don't know if I can deal with this," she cautioned.

"Do it!" he said.

He waited on the defensive, at a distance, hands extended in a gesture calculated to ward off any avalanche of insects.

Elizabeth grabbed hold of it. It was one of those awkward, indecipherable bath fixtures. Suddenly the shower jettisoned a clean spray.

Breathing in a sigh of relief, she detoured the shower spurt into steamy hot bathwater by depressing a little metal dowel over the fixture.

"The water's probably from the hotel's own supply," John surmised. "The management must have auxiliary pumps and storage tanks."

John got undressed and sprawled onto the bed. "I don't believe what's happening."

"Call Willard," Elizabeth suggested, taking off her clothes in the open doorway to the bathroom. She wore black lace, ready for action. John couldn't believe the woman beneath the disaster.

"I tried him earlier from the station. No one answered at his office." He looked her up and down. "I can't tell whether you want to get laid or photographed."

"Call him at home. Why should he be at the office on a Wednesday night?"

"He's got nothing else. What—a chair? The guy's work is everything."

"John—"

"It's after midnight. . . . Right." He queried his computer watch—which he constantly updated according to his current projects—and got Willard's home phone number. He placed the call, letting it ring ten times.

"No go," John said.

"What does he do in a wheelchair after midnight?" she wondered. "Call his office again."

He tried it. "Nothing."

John and Elizabeth got in the bath together, Elizabeth applying a delicate curettage to John's angry inflammations around the eyes. He put his fingers between her legs. She licked his tongue. John nibbled on her ear. They felt embarrassed by such intimacies, face to face, after many years of marriage. Kinky, fast, rapelike was different. But this, quiet, overtly made them aware of the wrinkles, the time, so much time together. Whatever they felt, it was released in the trustworthy waters of the Parallax Room & View.

John's eyes were getting worse.

At the station, Wendy and others were staying over all night, sleeping in the lounges. There were insects in the halls, on the walls, in the studio. Nowhere near the density as could be found outside, but KCBD was not as tightly protected from the night air as certain hotels downtown.

Wendy had cold compresses on her burned eyes. She listened, incredulous, as Charles Fields tried to downplay the whole ozone story at the eleven o'clock news. She knew that Singer had left the station shortly after the newscast without speaking to anyone.

Felix Girard was on a flight into Seattle from Washington. His wife thought he must be a fool for going, but Admiral Brewster had made the request. NSB needed presence, and while there were plenty of public information officers at local military installations—from the Umatilla Ordnance

Depot to the Boardman Bombing Range—Girard needed to be there to certify, on behalf of this country's system of defense satellites and military expertise, that things were okay. And to counter any "irresponsible statements to the press" by Dr. Willard.

On the same night, the governor from Olympia had dinner with the mayors of Seattle, Spokane, Tacoma, and Bellingham. They ordered a Thai smorgasbord at the Lonely Siam Cottage. The subject of conversation was the governor's powers of prescribing a State of Emergency if necessary.

The governor was no dummy. He noticed the insects; he'd watched the news, taped it, studied it; he'd conferred with his own team of experts—all in the past twenty-four hours. These were men whose normal idea of an emergency up in these parts was running out of beer in the middle of Lake Union on a Sunday.

The mayor of Seattle would meet with the press in the morning, following Girard's assessment. "He's to be picked up at the airport around seven A.M.," the mayor stated, adding, "Girard's got one scientist to meet with at the college—Dr. Willard—and then he plans to issue a statement."

"What's the statement?" the governor wanted to know.

"A basic reiteration of what was said earlier today from Washington."

"I wouldn't be too hasty in all this. Lives and property—"

"Governor, I understand. Let's not beat around the bush. How much money might we be entitled to were you to declare a State of Emergency?"

"There are assessors and assessors. I can't predict what the President will make of this. It doesn't duplicate the glamour of toxic crude or the lyrical catchiness of a Love Canal, but it's a good one nevertheless."

"A guess, governor?"

"I'd be prepared to request a minimum of five percent of total annual shipping transactions in the ports, what with anticipated agricultural and fisheries losses, timber destruction, metal and paint fatigue, insurance premiums. Figure two to three billion dollars. Plenty to go around, gentlemen."

John Gage fell asleep in the bathtub. Elizabeth, meanwhile, sat on the faucet side, a bunched-up towel protecting the small of her back, periodically replenishing the bath with additional hot water, letting out the cool.

"What are we going to do?" she voiced out loud to the clicking of the automatic timer and the sizzle of outgoing steam. She didn't even realize John was asleep. And then, seized with panic, she realized they'd forgotten all about her parents.

She lunged from the bath, waking up John, threw a towel around her waist, and called her mother.

"John, there's no answer. Did we leave the machine on? Shit. They're out there. Are you listening to me?"

John curled up in bed.

"Do we take the kids to school in the morning?" she went on.

"Yes," he mumbled. "'O' course." Then, thinking the better of it: "Maybe."

"You need to see a doctor," she said.

"Nabokov used to live out of hotels, writing from a chair in the middle of the room. Nothing on the walls. Imagine living in hotels all your life," he said, carrying on, half here, half there.

She felt his forehead. "You have a fever. I want to find Mom and Dad and get us all out of Seattle. We need air."

"You ever try to read *Ada?*" he started. "I loved Nabokov's writing but *Ada* always baffled me. You hungry? You want to make love? I feel strangely good about everything."

Elizabeth started to giggle, and John joined in. Goosing and tumbling, doing everything in their power to violate the absurd solemnity of the Parallax Room & View.

"This bed is hard," he complained.

"You're hard," she advised with a look. "Now close the drapes."

* * *

Across town, Donald Willard sat drinking coffee at The Grainery. The claustrophobia of his own home had gotten to him. He had again braved his driveway, managed with mosquito netting to keep off the insects, got in and started his car, and pulled out onto the street. As he drove, he could hear and feel thousands of crickets on the roads being smashed under the tires until the roadways were slimy with the death toll—not just crickets but frogs, salamanders, snakes, and other things that moved in the dark.

Willard used a pay phone adjoining the restrooms at the rear of the restaurant. Three unanswered calls to the lab set him to worrying. Dapple never picked up at Stan's home. He called the University's all-night emergency line and to his surprise found it busy. He called the operator, who put in a repair order. The line was down.

He headed back to the lab, parked underneath, and took the elevator up to the fifth floor. It was no longer jammed.

"Stan?" he called, rolling himself down the lit corridor he knew so well. He heard a television but saw no guard. "Stan?" He entered past the glass room into the main chamber.

"Oh, Lord." Willard waited, craning his neck behind him. His temptation was to flee. Then to stay. Before him was Stan, hung by tape, flopped low in Willard's other wheelchair. The bottles, the strewn tapes, an empty prescription jar, chaos. He rolled beside Stan and noticed his logbook was gone. He could hardly bare to look at his friend, whose body was not yet stiff but whose eyes bulged black and blue with the lifeless incredulity of their final testimony.

Willard closed Stan's eyes, unlashed the tape around his neck, and sat him up in a dignified way. Without thinking, Willard picked up the vial that had contained pills and saw his own name. The confusion left him weak. Now he panicked. He addressed his keyboard, whose power was on and whose heat-safety screen was blank, and punched in:
MARDI.GRA

CHKDSK
= = = 184,000,000 BYTES TOTAL DISC SPACE

```
= = = 4096 BYTES IN 4 DIRECTORIES
= = = 0 BYTES IN 30 USER FILES
= = = 183,995,894 BYTES AVAILABLE ON DISK
= = = 2,800,000 BYTES TOTAL MEMORY
= = = 2,712,079 BYTES FREE
```

"No!" He stumbled, forging clarity out of ruins. He opened his desk, found scattered microdiscs and inserted the first. They'd also been touched—his only back-ups. He tried: ***Mardi.Gra***

The same. He rolled through the maze of strewn magnetic discs on the floor and activated the two-inch tape machine. The data spun, lines of fire throbbing in a whiteout of cueing up, and then zero. Black.

"I'm dead," he said.

Willard struggled with a second computer, righted Stan, threw out the tequila bottles, and put his PC in its case. There were shards of glass sticking to his chair's rubber wheels. He couldn't do anything about it but endure the crunch as he rolled himself to a telephone.

The line was dead. He twisted around and exited the lab floor to the outside wall. There was a fire alarm. Willard breathed deeply, then smashed the glass. It was only afterward, waiting for the sirens to punctuate the silent night, that it dawned deceptively upon him: he had destroyed evidence. His fingerprints were on everything. Everything!

CHAPTER 19

THURSDAY MORNING

Getting back to their home at around seven thirty proved to be difficult. The streets were mobbed with insomniacs, night stalkers, restless souls. Families that had freaked out and had driven around all night, finding their automobiles to be the only safe haven. The long night's insect attack had had no obvious provocation, making the morning's relative calm all the more suspicious. Only the blood-red streets of the suburbs evidenced the onslaught. The glass and steel and concrete of downtown had remained relatively immune.

Every radio station signaled the disaster. "The highway patrol strongly urges all you commuters to bag it for the day. Though the state health board and pest control agency are asking children, the elderly, and anyone with heart, EMF, or chest ailments to stay away from their homes. They're recommending doing as little exercise as possible. Don't know if that includes yoga and sex. We here at KRMZ one-oh-nine point three on your dial sure hope not! Seems old Mother Earth's gone a little daffy the last few days. Feels more like the Sahara than Seattle. Anyway, we're gonna take a short break, then I'll be back with a whole slew of callers on the line. Hang in there!"

An ambulance sat in front of a house at the far end of the street. Distracted observers came and went. Others returned to their homes, like survivors of the fire in 1906. John had reason to recall Clark Gable's impudent, stubborn persistence in the thirties film *San Francisco,* as he stopped the car and stared, stunned by the gutted remains of his yard. The grass looked like sauerkraut, dark and scavenged, beds of flowers charred and denuded, whole stalks frayed and consumed. The leaves on the trees as well were devastated, gobbled up, withered. Ferns were reduced to wiry shadows, bark like impetigo. The whole block, and those for miles around, read a little like "Ozymandias," with more than a touch of feeding frenzy in the becalmed air—and yet also the promise of aftermath and quiescence.

"I'll bury him, kids. Don't look," John said, stepping up to the worst of it, untying the leash from the mangled stew of bones that was Wallace.

"I don't believe this!" Evans winced stoically, turning his head away from what had been a dog, pausing, then entering the front door as if he were defusing dynamite. "Okay, we're cool."

Jennifer crumpled on the front porch. She would gladly have sacrificed herself instead of the dog. Wallace had been her private eye, her love-listener and hope. Wallace had been her friend.

"Nothing to eat for them inside," Evans said, checking it out. The wave of insects had washed back out to sea, so to speak. Or at least it seemed so for now.

"How brief the moments of artistic fantasy," John mused.

"What's that supposed to mean?" his wife rejoined with annoyance.

"The love of nature business."

"I don't think this is the time to be philosophical, sweetheart."

"No?"

"Albert Schweitzer said we should love all insects as much as ourselves," Evans stated. "We read it in school. Even though the African army ants ate whole villages, including all the girls," he said pointedly.

"Just shut up!" Jennifer screamed.

"Evans, honey, sometimes you can be an insensitive prick!" Elizabeth added.

Her son was in some neutral, unreal void.

The moment was unreal for all of them. As a family, they could sense the violation all around them, an intangible aftertaste of penicillin or uric acid, perhaps sulphur, a wash of cannibalistic pheromones that had scoured the carpets and moved like the wind in previous hours. All was eerily still now, save for the jagged edges in the trees and schizophrenia in the air. What questions to ask? Who to call? What to do?

"Get what you need for school, you two, then we're outta here."

"What about tonight?"

"No. We're staying in the hotel," John answered, all manliness aside.

"You bet we are," Elizabeth threw in. She was thinking about her parents, and how best to deal with that situation.

The kids went to a private middle school, Mallory's, named of course after the ill-fated Brit who either had made it or hadn't made it to the top of Everest. The school's founding fathers preferred to believe that he and his partner, Irvine, had made it and had strived to inculcate that same courage and tenacity in two generations of privileged snot-nosed scions of bird-watcher types. John and Elizabeth had to spend $15,000 each year to keep Jennifer and Evans in school. Next fall, Evans would be off to prep school, a floating campus program out of La Jolla.

There was a contingent of Lazarus Pesticide Cooperative trucks in front of the school. Men in white-hooded space suits were busy spraying down the already ravaged lawns as well as the perimeters of the building, where its walls met the soil.

"Must be insecticides. Don't breathe. We'll pick you up at four," Elizabeth said.

"But I have bowling!" Jennifer protested.

"Not tonight you don't," Jennifer's mother informed her.

"That's brilliant. How are we supposed to not breathe?" Evans said, aping the absurdity of school on such a day.

"Ask your teachers. That's what we pay them for," his father advised, stretching for a weak and meaningless grin.

Later, Evans listened to the general ignorance of his peers at an all-school assembly.

"It comes down to nuking the bugs or breathing in the chemicals," the first kid reasoned with a little man's put-on, standing in one of many cliques in the gymnasium, where all the students had been assembled.

"I say kill every last one," Evans's second cronie recommended.

"We've already heard that brilliant suggestion, stupid," Evans said with dispatch, never one for subtlety.

"Screw you."

A third kid passed along his pop's suggestion that everyone skip town "like immediately."

"It's probably just as bad in Snoqualmie," another said.

"Try the whole planet, jerkos," Evans informed them. "In case you dodos haven't heard, it's an ozone hole."

"Now listen up, children!" the schoolmaster began. Evans rolled his eyes. He was pissed his parents had left them at school. He thought it was a really stupid idea.

Elizabeth took John to KCBD. It was nearly 9:00 A.M. The sun was unbearably bright. Both of them felt queasy, bound by headaches. John's eyes looked better for the five hours of sleep he'd managed.

"What are you going to do?" he asked his wife.

"I'll go back to the house and clean up."

"Stay inside. Keep the drapes closed."

"Yes."

Apprehensive about showing up for work, John aired his uneasiness. "I don't know what to do. I don't know if I have a job. How are we going to pay the mortgages next month?"

"We'll just take a penalty on the mutual fund. There's twenty-two thousand dollars plus some change. I got a statement last week. That's definitely a couple of months' stay of execution. Just don't worry. We'll be fine."

"Even if I have a job, I'm a witness to a murder. There's a story. I don't know where to begin. I don't know who is on my side."

"I'm on your side."

"You know what I mean."

"John, this is what you always do. Overintellectualizing, worrying the subject to death. You know you do. And every time—"

"Goddamnit, it's not what I do and this is different."

"I can't handle a fight. Not this morning."

"I'm not fighting," he shouted.

"Just see what happens. Play it out. Now good-bye!" she said emphatically, appealing for peace, and dropped him at the front door of the station.

A news van was on its way out in a hurry. There was a slight commotion at the entrance—Hare Krishna types demonstrating or chanting. They were wearing sunglasses, dancing under umbrellas, their faces plastered in sun lotion.

"End of the world. Renounce your car and VCR's. Give in to God consciousness!" John was assailed as he passed security inside.

"You all right?" said a production assistant, passing Gage in the hall.

"No, I'm not."

"Quite a night. Listen, they're looking for you."

"Who's they?"

"Everybody."

John's heart pounded. He walked into Singer's office. An armed station guard stood talking to the executive producer. They'd be beefing up security round the clock. "Here," Singer said matter-of-factly, handing John a message.

It was from Willard. "You talk to him?" John asked.

Singer nodded with an unyielding smirk. "He's been taken down for questioning on suspicion of first-degree murder. Down at the third precinct."

John didn't react at first. Then: "Bullshit. Who'd they say he murdered?"

"They didn't. And he's not under arrest from what I could make out, though the guy was badly shaken. They're just taking a statement. I guess there was no probable cause to book him."

Pointing to the mad gab of assistants staffing the phones and computers out in the main newsroom, Singer said, "I had one of them make a few calls. Seems there were only three murders committed by people in wheelchairs last year in the whole country, and two of those were acquitted in court. Your boy might be something else." Singer was also testing John.

"No way. Who's his lawyer?"

"Don't know. Just call him. Sort of sounded to me like you were his only dime."

John bolted toward his desk.

"Hold it. Before you do. There's something else."

"Something else. Right. Shoot," John said.

He sat down, Singer motioned the security guard outside, and John prepared for the worst. He wouldn't even allow himself to think about Willard—not yet.

Singer turned, thinking over his oration, took up a slip of paper off the front of his teeming mahogany desk, then spoke quietly. "I don't know whether to applaud you or bemoan the day I didn't fire you." They stared questioningly at one another.

"Go on."

Singer gave John the slip of paper. There was a name and a number written on it. "Peter Mather? What does he want?" John said, hungry with curiosity. Mather had just recently beaten out his six network rivals and had captured the indisputable lion's share of the evening news ratings game nationwide. He had become the Walter Cronkite of the nineties. KCBD, though independent, now acquired the bulk of its syndicated programming—Movies-of-the-Week, sit-coms, game shows, daytime soaps, nightly miniseries— from Mather's Dutch-owned network in New York.

"They want to borrow you."

"You're kidding?"

"Nope. They figure you've got it—you've got the lead, the edge, whatever you want to call it. Nobody else has Willard. Of course I don't know if we've got Willard."

"How would this work?"

"What we air, they air. And they're ready to bankroll an exclusive live telecast."

"How long a piece?"

"As long as it lasts."

John was breathless. This was exactly what he'd always dreamed of—or something like it. "What of their own local affiliate?"

"I guess you haven't seen this morning's paper?"

"We stayed in a hotel last night. Insects." John had glanced at the morning's paper slid under his door and had been amazed to see nothing about insects. There had been a recap of John's five o'clock news piece, but in the TV section of all places, adjoining a critic's list of the ten worst new video releases of the spring. A few years back at this time of year, on Earth Day, the insects, the sun, the impending "situation" would have commanded an unrelenting front page.

"I know about the insects," Singer said, exhaling with a show of exhaustion, holding back his own night's saga. "Channel Nine lost its transformer. They're down, maybe all week."

"That's fantastic. I suppose you mentioned it to the goons who own the joint?"

"No. Not yet."

"You going to?"

"I don't know. That depends."

"On what?"

"On Willard. We spoke all of two minutes. He says he's been framed professionally, John."

"Obviously."

"You have a lot of faith in a man you spent all of what—an hour?—with."

"Get serious. Everything he said is happening."

"I know. That's why we're having this conversation."

"And furthermore, that's the biggest money-making coup this station group could ever hope for."

"Maybe."

"What about Andy's family?"

"They're steaming. They don't know who to sue first. And that includes you, by the way."

"Me?"

"Let the lawyers deal with it."

John's whole being was trembling. "You were the one to tell them?"

"Me and a translator."

"Where's Wendy?"

"In the garage, checking out your remote gear. She slept on a couch in the talent lounge last night. Her eyes are pretty messed up. Yours don't look too good, either. You all right?"

"Yeah. I better call Willard."

"I told Mather you'd call him by ten o'clock. They want a transmission to start by four thirty eastern time. And I want our own local introduction to start up no later than four o'clock our time. And by the way, ease your mind on one other score. Fields is history."

John was awash in dual glints. "You know what he did?"

"I was just looking for a legitimate reason to fire that arrogant prick. You and Andy gave it to me."

"Who's going to anchor?"

"I guess I am, for now. I don't mind sitting up there. I may not have the chiseled California look of a mannequin or illiterate gay Ninja surfer from hell, but at least people will believe it when one former drill sergeant tells it to them straight. You get out there and figure what the hell's goin' on. I'll back you up in the hot seat. Now make your calls, because I want you down at the mayor's office at noon. There's a press conference and I suspect there'll be sparks. Oh, and talk to your associate producer, Loder. There's some head guy named Decker at the city hospital. Seems they have more work than they can handle this morning. Check it out. And don't worry about Andy's family. You were in a government chopper. They're totally liable. Now get—I've got work to do."

"Thanks, man."

"Piss off. And make sure you take a spare pair of sunglasses. I'm serious, you look like shit."

John called the police station. Willard had been there and

had left. John decided to try him at home. Willard answered, slightly broken up but calm.

"He was my friend of twenty years. They killed him thinking it was me. It's me they want. To shut me up," Willard expounded with a deflated sense of finality.

"Hold it, hold it. Take me through it. What happened? Who got killed? And how are you involved?" John was taking it all down on a notepad.

Willard spoke slowly, conveying a feeling to John of the end. There was no immunity, no chance. They'd finished him.

"Somehow some connection to the government. Those two men entering the facility," Willard said, his thoughts and words continuing to rise with disjointed ponderousness.

"You told this to the police?"

"Of course. I told them everything. I just hope to God they believe me. I mean it's obvious. The set of matches from The Grainery I saw in their van. The fake vial of pills with my name on it. The bottles of tequila. Shit, who drinks tequila? The cops will figure it out soon enough. They're taking a laser scan of Stan's neck and all the equipment. They've got my computer, the whole lab sewn up. Not that it matters now."

"What do you mean?"

"Whoever did it was real smooth. They erased all my data and all the backup data."

"You don't keep copies at home?"

"I keep copies on my PC. And it was in the lab last night. They got everything. There's no trace, John. A year of research."

"It's got to be in RAM memory. No?"

"You're dealing with professionals. They wiped the slate clean. The data may be gone, but not the reality of it."

"So let's say the chances of a state's attorney indictment against you are nil. One way or the other, they get a lead, they find whoever did it. And I'm real sorry about your friend. Now what else? The insects? The sun? What's our reality this morning?"

"Did you happen to catch a glimpse of the sun?" Willard

asked, coming back to the world of galling and distorted chemistry.

"I'm trying not to look at it."

"Very wise. I'd have to guess that the bubble, the hole—it's probably more like an ellipsis—has moved inland from where you approached it out at sea. It's got to be close."

"How do you know it's not already here?"

"I don't, for sure. But everything I know about it theoretically indicates you couldn't go outside, you couldn't drive. People would die. Everything would die."

"How fast?"

"I don't know. Ten minutes. An hour. A day. You gotta understand, I've been working on a computer, not in the street."

"Look, the mayor's giving a press conference at noon. I need you with me. The story I'm now doing is running with Peter Mather tonight. They plan nonstop coverage."

"That's good," Willard said, almost flippantly.

"You don't sound too happy about it?"

"Happy? Don't be stupid."

John paused, thinking that perhaps the journalist in him had overstepped some private boundary, a link between Willard and his dead friend. "I understand."

"I know you do. You're the only one I figured I could trust. That's why I called you from the police station. You need to know that I'm something of a loner, John. I'm outside the academic community."

"You teach?"

"No. I'm on the faculty as a researcher. I gave up teaching. All I'm saying is, this could get even dirtier. They're trying to save their own asses."

"Who is?"

"I'm not sure, but whoever it is, they sure don't like my data. I can't believe Felix Girard had anything to do with it. It's someone, somewhere, in a high office, at the top of a hierarchy. Couldn't be government, even though it's government that really screwed up."

"What should they have done?"

"Told the public weeks ago. That's when the bubble

started drifting south into populated areas. I just don't believe that I'm the only guy alive who knows what's coming down."

"You're not—anymore. Look, Dr. Willard—"

"Donald."

"Listen, Donald. I've been on this all week. I trusted you and you trusted me. Neither of us has time for semantics or recriminations. You're the scientist. I'm just a journalist trying to do a competent job. How about I pick you up at eleven?"

"Okay. Make sure you and your crew are totally covered. And John?"

"What?"

"You have a family?"

"Yes. My kids are at school. They should be all right. At night we're all staying in a hotel."

"Don't you understand? You've got to stay in the dark."

"The kids are all in the basement at school. And we've got the draperies closed in our hotel room. I don't know what else we can do."

John got his address, then called Elizabeth and told her what Willard had said. Then he called Peter Mather in New York.

"Your two reports were incredible, Gage. Rather hard to believe."

"That's what my boss says. And call me John."

"What's really happening, John?"

"The sun is brighter—much brighter—than anything I've ever seen. This morning people are getting sick. Hospitals are already overcrowded. The insects went crazy last night. My own family was attacked. I don't know what to predict."

"Will you be able to get us a fifteen-minute story by four thirty? Twenty minutes of picture, several stand-ups, explanatory copy—it doesn't have to be polished. We'll do that. In fact, it should play rough, verité-style, scared, almost as if on the run. Get in fast, get answers fast, then get out. We want to see it."

John curbed his excitement. "We'll need to use very dark

filters just to make the video broadcastable, but, yes, you'll have what you need. Frankly, I'm surprised you don't come out and do the live stand-ups yourself. You did it several years ago in front of the Nimitz Freeway collapse in Oakland."

"No thank you. Anyway, it's more dramatic from New York. Keeps Seattle trapped, isolated, at peril. We want the seriousness of the situation undiluted with props or hype or personality. To be honest, you wouldn't catch me dead in your town—not this week."

"Leave it for the dogs in other words?" John chuckled. He felt himself playing up to Mather, trying to impress him somehow, and immediately checked the impulse.

"You understand."

"Peter, on a different but related note, you should know that there may be a government cover-up aspect to this whole thing, as well as two murders."

"This is not an investigation, John. I heard what you said about the tape being confiscated a couple nights ago. Just tell us what's happening. Any cover-up will come out soon enough. That's not really at issue here. This is not Watergate."

"You're right. It's ozonegate."

"John, get off it."

"Yeah. Sure. I'm off it." John fumed silently.

"Do we have Dr. Willard?" Mather asked.

"He'll be with me at the mayor's press conference at noon. It was a friend of Willard's who was strangled in his laboratory. They thought they were getting Willard. And they did get his computers. All his data was erased."

"If he feels compelled to talk about it, fine. Just make sure he tells it, not you," Mather warned him.

John hung up, then skipped momentarily in the air. He was—for all of his weariness and upset—quite elated.

John attached his associate producer, Garrison Loder, to the crew, picked up MacIntyre as the cameraman, then headed down to the garage for Wendy.

"Hey." He put his arm around her. "How you doing?"

"Bad."

"Can you handle another day out there?"

"I don't want to, but I will. I heard it's gonna be played out of New York."

"Word travels fast."

"Singer already secured me and MacIntyre. Nobody knew where you were."

"The family stayed at a hotel. Parallax Room and View. I guess we'll be there tonight as well."

"I slept on the couch. My roommate split when the bugs started getting in."

"Singer told Andy's parents."

"Yeah. I just—"

"We'll catch who did it."

"Who cares who did it. Andy's out there."

"Andy's parents care. I care. You care," John assured her quietly.

"What's the plan?" she asked.

"I'll tell you as we drive. You got sunglasses? A hat? I've got the zinc oxide. Button up your blouse all the way. Smear this on your throat"—he handed her para-aminobenzoic acid, with a deceptive 100 SPF rating—"and bring a bunch o' towels. Find some white umbrellas. They must have them with the lighting kits in the shop. Let's move."

They all piled into the station van. John took the wheel.

As the vehicle moved up the on ramp, a car slammed on its breaks to avoid being hit in the far right lane. "Watch out!" Wendy screamed. John pulled away from the car in front of them, skidding in and out of a rising embankment. He pushed all the way down on the gas pedal, erupting into the mad rush of traffic.

John brushed back his hair. It was already drenched in sweat. A small Toyota spilled off the far right lane into the side of a U-Haul. John veered left watching a chain reaction in his mirror. The Toyota's side was bashed in by a car that shot out of nowhere, yet the driver kept pushing onward, not even acknowledging the collision. The U-Haul had buckled and slid off its rear wheels. But the truck kept moving, dragging the ludicrous hulk of bent steel through the spillway. Clothes, an ironing board, and kitchen utensils bounced between bumpers.

It made no sense at all, John thought. Old women were out drag racing—or so it seemed. But not in haste, rather in oblivion. As if beneath the chaos there was an eerie cloud of unknowing. John had a bad headache and drove on between lightninglike impressions of the sun on rush-hour metal. Blinding moments, distant buildings whose shadows and edges had been distilled. Motorists veered in and out of their lanes, and a few even crossed the median strip. Others actually tried driving into oncoming traffic. Three million commuters straggled up and down the many festering lanes, sirens hailing from throughout the city continuously. Everything was out of control.

A cobalt blue Bentley convertible, scarred with fresh dents, rocketed out from an entry ramp and was sideswiped. Its hoary occupant, a sporty fellow perhaps in his seventies, someone who looked as if he'd lived in the fast lane all of his life, let out a frantic cry. Other cars were drawn into the scuttle. Within seconds a chopper passed overhead. It was no ordinary helicopter: it carried a dangling stretcher by a cable.

Hearing a Chuck Mangione tape blaring away in concert with the queasy din, John looked out on the Seattle skyline. He saw a sickly-looking sun that was impaled in a mirage of fumes engulfing the horizon. The city seemed to be disappearing beneath a cavity of light, light permeated with pall, smog, a new darkness at noon.

CHAPTER 20

Seattle Mayor Charlie Higgins's executive administrative assistant, Buck Martin, pulled out the fax just in from the airport. It was the routine twelve-hour forecast that had arrived by teletype from the National Weather Service. The forecast itself meant very little to Buck. It was the commentary he was concerned with and that his office had requested.

```
SEA-TAC FP3 4/12 GMT1710
SYNOPSIS
RAPIDLY ESCALATING HEAT PHASE IN TROPOPAUSE
AMPLITUDE HIGH AND VERIFIED FOR PACIFIC NORTHWEST
NO MIXING HEIGHT ASCERTAINED
REFER TO ZROSE INVERSION CHARTS FOR BLOCKING OMEGA
```

Dear Mayor, we've never seen anything like it. 500 millibar, wind shear factor, Goes-West satellite summaries of gradient levels, everything's berserk. Next thing you know, it will be raining toads. Wish I knew what to recommend. No joke. Half our staff down. Sorry. Call if you have any questions. Stop.

These people were nameless, faceless, thought Buck. Weather people, civil servants, bureaucrats who labored for thirty, forty, even fifty years behind closed doors, within offices, behind other closed doors. Buck was tired. A civil servant himself. Now all he saw was the blur of paperwork, suffused in eight to five psyches, time clocks, ways of doing things, rolled-up J. C. Penney's sleeves. There were no ties in here, but rather sack lunches, mimeograph machines, plastic pine, plain metal chairs, orange shag carpets in the commissary. One office looked like another. The nerve center for the city was nowhere, its chain of command lost in a labyrinth of deferrals, excuses, insufficient data, coffee machines on the mend, phone lists yet to be acted upon. Here and there a momentary hero appointed himself, going beyond the motions, perfuse with a theory, weighing administrative universes, spilled some red ink, stirred up some down-home outrage, pointed out a glaring omission in a key document that no one had read or would ever read, then faded away toward his lunch. The pleasures here were those of cynicism. Someone was reminded that the last Earth Day assemblage in Central Park had resulted in 153.4 tons of unmitigated garbage. That was 153.4 tons of fodder for cynicism in departments like these of Mayor Charlie Higgins.

Buck was stewing in his own sense of mutilation and ill-humor at six thirty this morning, after a ruinous night with a girl he'd been angling to lay for weeks. By morning, anything but exalted, scabies-molested, running like a samaurai parrot, having sought safe haven in a Denny's, smothering his perverse luck in a bowl of green chile and three gluttonous rounds of mustard-smothered pancakes for breakfast, he made his way into work. Only to be engulfed in the bedlam of bumper cars careening like acidic bees without their queen. There was a swarming huddle of exploding shrapnel, he remembered, as he escaped from the firing line of a bad pileup. He remained unscathed and out of breath. But barely.

And now this cockamamy report just in from the National Weather Service. What did it mean? Buck had hoped for answers. He was the man charged with assimilating all incoming data and recommendations for his boss, Higgins.

Buck was not amused. He had to help prep Higgins's staff—folks who were down to earth and bought their socks at Montgomery Ward.

Buck was having a hard time keeping his mind on all of this. Certain personal matters weighed more heavily than another disaster. Buck had been in high school when Mt. St. Helens had erupted. He was not into disaster then either. He was into girls.

Of course, he also sensed an opportunity here. He hoped certain obstacles to his professional upward mobility might be eliminated by the crisis. Disaster socialized the beast out there. Shrews scampered out of dark nooks and rose to preeminence as dinosaurs collapsed to their knees. This was not Darwin but original Buck.

Buck knew that Felix Girard from NSB would be at the noon press conference to help defuse the expected melee. Higgins was not noted for his tact. He'd cagily postponed a meeting with a Pacific Rim delegation whose corporate clients represented $60 billion in annual trade through the port of Seattle. He was not happy about rocking the boat with these Oriental heavies.

If the federal government declared Seattle a disaster area, an idea at first welcomed by the governor, it could mean revenue in the hundreds of millions, possibly a few billion for the state. Even so, such money was child's play, nickels and dimes by contrast to the incoming Southeast Asian dollars, Higgins had reminded him. Soaring interest rates had long induced Japanese and Taiwanese investors to keep their money at home. Shipping, however, remained the one solid medium of domestic profit and Seattle was the queen of such trade. But if this ozone business got out of hand, the smart money might just as easily move to Vancouver. It was Buck's job, along with his buddy Bill Rodgers, lieutenant governor, to work a PR miracle.

Buck walked into the conference room. It was 8:00 A.M. sharp. Around him sat half a dozen city, state, and federal experts from as many sectors of government, each looking through documents that sat before them on the large oblong

table. They had four hours to prepare for the press conference. Meanwhile, the mayor was at home, preparing his
speech. He wasn't expected to show until 11:55 that morning.

Within minutes, Bill Rodgers joined the group. Rodgers
was a balding anal-retentive statistician who had every
reason to be a politician and had participated in a feasibility
study for large-scale disaster evacuations in the state of
Washington some years before. Moving briskly into the
inner sanctum of the mayor's downtown compound, he
greeted Buck and the others, then pinned up a series of
diagrams on the closest wall, laid out a dossier of arcana on
the table beneath the compacted fluorescent bulbs, and
proceeded to explain why martial law was crucial. Rodgers
spoke with a self-possessed grin, making a furrow between
his two large eyes. The effect was unpleasant, his rather
hypercephalic forehead rising and falling as if squatting to
defecate.

Buck had left the agenda open.

"Disasters do not stand on ceremony or protocol," he
said, opening the meeting. "I see many of us aren't here.
Melissa, call Gary, Owens, Fraser, and I don't see, uh,
what's her name?"

"Ellen Parler," someone reminded him.

"Right. Call them."

Buck brooded in some unconnected dreamland. Today's
agenda was annoying. It was his lady friend Nestra that kept
his mind attuned, not an ozone disaster. He thought suddenly of the moment with her, how he'd gotten to within a
fond tease, a word, a zipper length of Nestra's crotch, had
smelled the proverbial honey drops, nearly tasted the heavenly victuals, only to be checked by a tentacle-laden assault
right out of the Illinois or Texas backroads of a bad fifties
horror movie. Bugs that spoiled their near tumble of
intimacy in bed. The insects seemed to have emanated with
intent to kill from the recycler garbage bins right outside her
door. One of them bit him on his dick. The ultimate insult.
Buck took today's disaster very personally.

"And I say martial law is a very bad idea!" Madeline Thomas shouted in a forceful rebuff to Bill Rodgers, displaying five pages of slightly dated material, which she considered firm enough evidence, between wheezes. She was coughing badly, like a mule. "In practice runs," she exploded, forcing a hankerchief to her mouth, bringing up a wad of sputum. "I'm sorry. In theory an entire six-story building was evacuated in my district within four minutes. There are nineteen traffic lanes egressing from the so-called Puget metroplex region. In twenty-four hours we could easily see a million and a half vehicles out of here. Safely. Soundly. Without risking the problems associated with what you're suggesting. Martial law might work in the Philippines. Panama City. Not in Seattle."

"Excuse me! Are you on drugs or what?" Rodgers said sternly.

"I beg your pardon?"

"Well, you're dead wrong, babe, that's all."

"I am not babe, prick!" Madeline shouted.

"Folks?" Buck said, hitting the table. "We don't need this. Just calm down, okay?"

Buck looked to Rodgers.

Rodgers pulled out more data and spoke with authority, directing his words at Madeline. "Maybe you're forgetting all the coefficients? Mountains. Accidents. Shock. Panic. Stalled vehicles. To cite the nineteen eighty-three draft submitted and approved by the Department of Emergency Services, and I quote, 'the problems are so great, the planning would have to be divided into subcompartments just to permit minds to cope with them.' We estimated back then that one point two million vehicles might—might— get out of town within a week's time. That's taking into account all the obstacles. The traveling speed—about four miles per hour. Hell, you can walk faster than that. Problem is, we don't have the time."

"I'm afraid he's right, Madeline," the elder statesman for Seattle's transportation board, Loewi, admitted. He had walked the freeways, lived with the computer printouts analyzing rush-hour trivia. He loved the freeway system and looked upon the asphalt clarity of a straight new road stretching like a necklace through the city of freedom with the blushing pride of a young man at the beginning of creation. To him it was alive, seething with a design, a tapestry of transcendental ebb and flow.

Loewi spoke calmly. "We maintain some twenty-five hundred maps of the freeway system in town. Density analysis of contra-traffic flow, etcetera. Seattle's got five people per acre off the freeways, eight hundred per acre on them. At ninety-eight percent usage, we're looking at two point three accidents per million vehicle miles."

"You mind translating?" Madeline said.

"Road jams, in other words. We'd need at least a week to get people out. The 'eighty-three report was overly optimistic."

Buck was not concentrating because the noon press conference was a foregone conclusion. Higgins had already figured out the basic tenor of his declaration. It was Buck's job to provide him with any last-minute tidbits of information that might be useful—like the fact that the National Weather Service was totally baffled by certain meteorological conditions perhaps responsible for the situation.

Pieces of the ongoing table chatter ran up and down Buck's spine, certain facts lodging in the dull zone of his left brain, others fizzling in the horse latitudes of an ear or puzzling into fidgity distraction. Even as the talk was heating up, turning toward estimates on damages, deaths, past precedents from other cities—as if the whole thing had been worked through and understood—Buck was fading out, leaving for a fishing trip in the Bugaboos, or dipping his tongue into vaginal brooks and labial pools of the auburn bombshell, Nestra.

Rodgers was holding forth, expounding on a litany of previous catastrophes all justifying martial law. "Hurricane Alicia, remember? Tsunami evacuation in Sitka, July tenth, nineteen seventy-two. Quasi-random study, Hilo, May nineteen sixty. And that delineation of hazard zones surrounding St. Helens. We all remember that one: seventeen dead, five hundred injured, sixteen hundred homeless, a hundred million dollars in damages. And here, a file on Topeka, seven twelve P.M., a four-block-wide by eight-mile-long swath. This document takes the psychosociological approach. And here's one—a train derailment, high-impact ratio."

"You're forgetting that nearly three million got out of London in time, before all the bombs started falling, in nineteen thirty-nine, mostly by their own devices," Madeline stated emphatically. She gained support from Loewi, who nodded in reaffirmation.

"And I quote from the Federal Emergency Management Agency, Vogt and Sorensen, TM-one-oh-two-seven-seven," Madeline continued. " 'The more specific the warning message, the higher the level of perceived personal risk. The higher the level of belief the greater the probability of evacuation.' "

She went on to quote from Perry and Mushkatel, 1984, "Disaster Management," and so on.

"Best argument for keeping it a secret!" Bill Rodgers said. "The minute we scare people, we'll have mass pandemonium. That's exactly what the mayor does *not* want in this city. Understood?"

Buck snapped back from his muse, earnestly above the boredom eating at his throat.

"Are you all crazy? Am I the only one who drove to work this morning? Or who happened to look around? You're talking as if people don't *know* what's happening. They do. See this?" He put his finger to his forehead, taking off his sunglasses. Everyone in the room coincidentally felt the need to wear sunglasses. "Wearin' shades 'cause the future's so bright? Right, Jack. It's called eyestrain. Am I right? You? How many Tylenol did you take this morning? Three, or was it six? With codeine? You bet. Extreme anxiety. Frontal lobe irritation. Migraine. Got it? No tsunami's headed toward Seattle, folks. No train wrecks either. We got a different sort of problem and Charlie needs your help, not your academic unction.

"Now Bill has this plan, and I think it's a hell of a good one. Evacuation's simply out of the question, with all due respect to Madeline and those others among you who might be tempted to agree with her. The real problem, as I understand it, is the sun. We have got to get people out of the direct sunlight. That's what NSB's saying. And I figure since they know how to protect their boys on the moon, they sure as hell know what they're doin' in a place like Seattle. Bill, why don't you explain the plan. And let me just preface it by saying that the governor and mayor have already made their decision. You all have got to make it happen, stand behind it."

Rodgers took over, pointing his pencil around like a swagger stick, full of a Patton's brio.

"The buzzword is bomb shelter," Rodgers began. Hands went up in protest. "I know, I know. They're a mess. But we're only talking about a few days here," he ventured, clearing his throat of a placid dismay, linguistically indescribable, unique to residents of eastern Oregon, where Rodgers had originated.

"Who told you that?" Loewi broke in, cocked and reproachful.

"Felix Girard of NSB spoke with me at the crack of dawn today. He'll have more on that at noon," Rodgers reassured him.

Loewi saw his beloved city hurtling toward paralysis while these so-called experts tossed their dwarfed and confused estimations back and forth. He hadn't had this queasy a feeling since Hungary in 'fifty-six. A superstitious man, he was an avid user of the *I Ching* and kept his own yarrow sticks wrapped in a teak and velvet container atop the toilet bowl beneath a framed poster of Moses Maimonides guiding the perplexed.

Loewi held on to his line of attack. He was not ordinarily given to argument, keeping his own counsel by inclination. But this business of evacuation didn't sit well with him. He'd never gotten the Soviet invasion of his homeland out of his system. The crying children. The lines of refugees. Army tanks tearing up the streets.

He also had information enough to know that Bill Rodgers was speculating for the sake of firmness and resolution, even if what he was saying was dead wrong. "Your own study reported that there's only enough shelter space to hold roughly twenty-five percent of the city's population," Loewi stated. "They're rat-infested, no food, no drinking water. There are no chemicals for sanitation, no medical provisions. The intake valves haven't been checked in twenty years. People would suffocate down there in this heat. That's assuming they can even find out where the shelters are."

Rodgers held his ground. "Some will. And some is enough. The rest will divine other means, stay at home, or head for Red Cross stations in the schools and post offices. But, you see, the shelters are blastproof, more or less, which means they were designed to withstand radiation. That's what we're talking about here. Ultraviolet. It may not have the mass of an explosion, but it certainly has the same energy. And from what I've heard, the results are also similar. It's as if the nuclear reactors over at Hanford melted down."

Rodgers hadn't known he was going to say that. There was a sudden quiet in the room. "I mean, of course, it's fundamentally different—"

"What he means, of course, is that the shelters could offer some protection to some of the population," Buck said, breaking the thin line of nerves. "We estimate that as many as twenty percent of the populace will try to find shelter space spontaneously. Once martial law is decreed, most people will voluntarily stay indoors, down in their basements, where it's cool and dark and safe. We have a unique problem and a logical solution."

"I'm still waiting for the solution," Madeline said, grasping to understand how the square fit the circle. "What you're telling us is fine, for a day or two. But it doesn't address the problem of an ozone hole. How do we explain to John Q. Public when he asks why this wasn't planned for, publicized, scientifically addressed?"

"It was, it has been, it will be. For chrissakes, Madeline! This is a freak thing, all right? I mean, shit, how do you plan for a tornado in Denver or a hurricane in Palm Springs?"

Rodgers broke in. "And pointing the finger at the mayor

or the governor is certainly not going to expedite the public good. We need a unified thrust here, firm backing for a policy decision that's already been made. Everybody understand that?"

"By martial law I presume you and the governor mean the National Guard?" Loewi said, downcast and resolved.

"Yes."

"Army tanks?"

"I don't see why they'd be necessary," Buck volunteered, not really knowing one way or the other but anxious to get out of this spat.

"Army tanks really chew up the streets," Loewi added, worried stiff about the road surfaces. They were his baby after all.

CHAPTER 21

By eleven o'clock Thursday morning the Seattle Police Department found itself preoccupied with more pressing business than murder or possible suicide over at the college. Nevertheless, encouraged by Willard's own insistence, one persistent detective had bagged several dozen cigarette butts on the top layer of the garbage bin out in the alleyway behind The Grainery. They'd be checked for fingerprints on the FBI's national computer file, which compared and contrasted millions of sets, including those of all government employees. In addition, an all-points bulletin was put out for Burt. Someone had turned over an elevator card and an access routing to the computer data to those guys in white coverlets. Burt had disappeared. The detective was not overly optimistic.

Elsewhere in Seattle there were other reasons not to be optimistic. At Harbor Island on Elliott Bay, Emmet Jones and the photobiologist Spengler had been at it all night, examining cultures under an electron microscope. The fish and birds were dying of an oncogenic (tumor-causing) viral infection, triggered in whole populations of cells by the ultraviolet light. Genetic recombination was occurring at a massive and rapid rate.

Out along the wood and tarmac quay adjoining Emmet's

laboratory, a horrifying struggle, or migration, was taking place. Thousands of fish—bream, salmon, halibut, snapper—were vying to get out of the sea, throwing themselves onto docks from wind-swept waters. Emmet had heard of this happening two other times— once a century before off Long Island, when nearly a billion tilefish perished, and once in the early sixties, one winter south of Sydney, Australia, along two hundred miles of beaches.

It was still dark, no sign of the dawn. Driving a pickup truck through a maze of the still-quivering heaps of expiring flesh, silver and gold bodies illuminated in the headlights, Emmet and Spengler came upon one enormous mass of snakes and tentacles. They got out of their vehicle and approached the bizarre thing with their flashlights extended. Walking slowly around it, Emmet had moved in when suddenly the stuff erupted in a frantic spasm. A sucker smashed into the scientist, throwing him against the vehicle. Emmet was shaken but unharmed.

By the time Emmet and Spengler gained safe distance, they were just able to make out what was in fact two creatures wrapped around each other—a giant squid and the rare oarfish, each forty feet long. By the force of their respective death throes, the animals plunged off the dock, back into the benthic depths from whence they had mysteriously come.

Meanwhile, overhead, a continuing glut of bewildered birds sought refuge. Sooty shearings, petrels, gulls and grebes and lesser terns, pelicans and puffins, Chinese ringed pheasants and eagles could be seen by the scientists crashing into buildings, into the sea, flying straight up into the air and disappearing in the dark, hitting everything in sight. The whole night was filled with restive odyssey, from the cellular surface of a frantic specimen on the slide beneath a microscope to the eerie evacuation of birds outlined against a full moon.

Early in the morning Emmet had called Drake Manders at NOB as well as the Coast Guard, most of whose contingents were farther out at sea coping with lost ships and stranded fishermen. Ship-to-shore transmissions were congested and incoherent. A chopper set down on the drifting NOB research vessel only to find it engulfed in gray mold, surrounded by dead fish, and the twelve crew members looking the worse for wear.

By 8:30 A.M. a frog team had been assembled at Harbor Island. Emmet and Spengler wanted the two creatures. A giant squid was a rare thing these days, its nervous system quite advanced. As for the oarfish, Emmet had only seen one other before this time, frozen in a museum. The two animals inhabited the dark cold arid sea bottoms, hundreds of fathoms beneath the surface. How could ultraviolet stress have brought them—along with all the fish—to the mundane shores of a Seattle dock? the two scientists wondered. Unfortunately, the giant squid and oarfish would not provide the answers. The two Navy Seals who went down after the beasts never resurfaced. And when a second, larger rescue team also failed to reemerge, the whole operation was put on hold, pending the requisition of a robot submersible, which could not be obtained on this day. Five men were declared missing in action.

On Capitol Hill near Nineteenth and Aloha, several hundred of the seabirds suddenly alighted, attracted perhaps by the distressed flood of sonar generated by Marion Mathiess's bats, which had been on the rampage all night, biting into trees, doors, people, and pets. The incoming seabirds now joined in this Hitchcockian orgy, even turning upon one another.

Though she could distantly hear the squawking amid the general ambience of wailing sirens and helicopters, Elizabeth was spared this particular freak show as she concentrated on her family's belongings up the street, rifling through the bedrooms in search of any necessary items. She was taking every precaution. The Parallax Room & View might be home for quite a while. She just didn't know.

The carpets were peppered with black specks. She carefully picked one up, using her thumb and index finger like a tweezer. She brought the minute creature close in, examining the source of her agonies the night before, thinking it a mere flea at first. For it was approximately the same size. Suddenly she felt a sting on her thumb, like a pinprick or the juice of annoying electricity. It was alive! She squashed it, rubbing the remains on the mirror before her. Sitting on the bed, focusing on the smear marks, she breathed in very slowly, noting that all around her there were thousands of the little not-quite-dead things resting in the rug, on the bed, everywhere. Waiting. The wave had totally thinned out, gone underground, or into the trees to avoid the sun. But they were there, gaining strength for the coming night. She could feel it. A sickly revulsion lingered in her throat and for a brief moment Elizabeth looked toward the toilet, holding her stomach.

The sensation passed as she stared at herself in the mirror.

"Okay, kids. On the floor!" the teacher commanded.

The bug spraying was still going on around the outer walls of Mallory's. In the meantime, following a mandate issued early in the morning by the superintendent in Olympia, an ozone alert was to be conducted, as in all schools throughout the state of Washington.

Preparations for the alert were now in effect. In the headmaster's office, Ralph Potash, assistant headmaster, sat before his boss digging something out of his hair with his fingernails, while headmaster Mordant Jonesly concluded a choleric phone conversation with the insurers regarding compensation for the cost of bug spraying. The insurance company was calling it an act of God. As far as Jonesly was concerned, God had nothing to do with biting insects. He slammed down the phone and looked at Potash.

"Well?"

"We've never had an alert before," Potash said anxiously.

"I know that. But there's got to be a handbook!" Jonesly demanded with vexed impatience. He didn't like exceptions to the rule, nor disruptions of any kind.

"I don't think so, Mr. Jonesly, sir." The two had worked

together for seven years but it was still "Mr. Jonesly" to the assistant. "The last handbook for this sort of thing was distributed by the school board back in the early seventies, and that was for nuclear war. Basically, it says to dig a hole."

"This is not a joke, Mr. Potash," Jonesly stammered contemptuously. "What, precisely, were we instructed to do with the children?"

"It's part of what the state is terming 'Personal Protection Plan,'" Potash went on.

In the gymnasium, there were conspicuously fewer students than in previous days. Nobody was happy about the proposed exercise. They were scared and they wanted to go home. A few had already skipped out altogether, against the better advice of their peerage. One ten-year-old wiseacre, a younger friend of Jennifer's, went out onto the playground, where he remained. Several kids saw him out there, sitting oddly against the rear fence, which he had tried to ascend, only to climb back down. There was something wrong with the boy, who was separated from his classmates indoors by a miragelike sea of undulating candescent light. Those few who saw him through the window said nothing. They were afraid. Afraid of what might happen to them.

Evans was unhappy about the charade being perpetrated here today. He sniffed the teachers' fear and held in the firmest disrespect the underlying presumption at work in the minds of the authorities. Furthermore, Evans, a senior in his middle school, felt certain proprietary responsibilities, not least of which to his younger sister. "It's just crap!" he blurted out, when told, along with the others, that they'd be asked to crawl under the chairs and hold their hands to their mouths and eyes for thirty seconds. "I mean, give us a break!"

"Evans, young man, this is no joke. You will do as you're told!" Mr. Potash said.

Potash was not a bad man, Evans thought, just stupid—at least, compared with all the other adults he knew. Potash had never learned to get along with young people. He had no kids of his own. Evans and his cronies knew that Potash was always on the lookout for secret, conspiratorial slangs, inner whispers from clique to clique. To pique his paranoia, they'd exaggerate their communications, and this open stealth tended to augment Potash's unfortunate sweat gland condition, his dandruff, his itchy scalp, making him easy prey for the snideness of youth.

"And you will watch that mouth of yours, young man!" Potash said, igniting at hearing a four-letter word under Evan's breath.

"Fuck you!" Evans repeated.

"I'm calling your parents!"

"Go for it!" he retorted. "*Fuck* happens to be one of their favorite words. That's why my sister and I exist. In fact, that's why you guys are raking in thousands of dollars each year in tuition."

"You incorrigible mouth-spewing little punk. I will not—"

"Nice!" Evans said with the smile of cool disarmament.

"This is not the time or place, Mr. Gage, thank you!"

A school fire alarm signaled the moment at last, sirens blazing from centrally mounted metal megaphones. For Jonesly and Potash, it hinted at their domestic Cold War reminiscences, Bay of Pig red alerts, routinely scheduled bomb shelter crazes, "Better Dead Than Red" bravura, and sandbags—mental baggage of which these kids, with their kayaks and mountain bikes and simple innocence, grocery bagging jobs four hours a week, fixation on the here and now, could have no idea. The children threw themselves under their chairs, covering their faces with portions of their shirts, blouses, dresses, and hands.

"This is really incredibly stupid," Evans grumbled to his nearest chum.

John was at the wheel amid stifling congestion on the surface roads, forcing his way across town to the mayor's offices. They had all of twenty minutes to get there and get set up. Wendy and MacIntyre sat behind John in the first of three tiers of vinyl seats, preparing the directional

Sennheiser microphone, marking tapes, checking camera and battery belts. Garrison Loder, John's twenty-three-year-old associate producer, a TV ingenue quickly working his way up the KCBD ladder, rode in the passenger seat taking notes.

John was thinking out loud, rummaging through a tentative plan of attack. Maneuvering through traffic heightened his aggression. He drove angrily, hyped and insistent. In the rear of the truck Willard reclined, his wheelchair collapsed with the other equipment behind him. In the last three hours everything had changed. "It's coming," Willard remarked from the back, almost offhandedly, as if this day's sun burst were merely one more telling piece of evidence to confirm a private and dearly held theory he'd worked out long before.

"As soon as we get in there and set up, find a phone," John told Loder. "I gave you the station credit card number. I want you to call those two names in Washington, play them off each other. You know. You're a mole processing paperwork. You need verification of an unassuming detail. Government business. You're with one department or the other, DIA or GAO. A secretary to an assistant. You're putting stuff through the shredder, on orders. But before you do . . . you understand?"

"Not exactly."

"Loder, I need to know what stake those two men have in this."

Willard was listening to their conversation. "Try military contracts. It was a military mission that NSB messed up. I'd be willing to bet my chair and my catheter that somewhere a military contractor was involved. Has to be chemicals."

John, intently: "CFC's?"

"Probably not. There's hundreds of millions of pounds of CFC's consumed every year. They're in everything. The genii's out on that one. Something more esoteric. Methylchloroform or carbon tetrachloride, perhaps. F twenty-two, maybe F one hundred thirteen. Thing is, it could be any number of weird products. Maybe a very potent microchip solvent, or coolant used on the shuttle. I don't know."

"I don't follow," John said, making his way through an intersection whose lights were down. "Why jump through hoops?"

"Could be a company in Seattle the military's not exactly anxious for the public to know about," Wendy suddenly flashed. "I mean, it's logical."

"Of course it is. That's good," John pressed. "Let's say there's this company that's producing tons of this stuff and it simply got out of hand."

John saw Willard shaking his head no in his rearview mirror. "What?" John asked.

"There's no such chemical. This thing descended from the Arctic. You all know that."

"But what about the chemicals you just mentioned?" John said, doubly confused.

"I was just speculating. The fact of the matter is, I don't see how any one company could have triggered what's happening. This is a catastrophe that's been building for years. Hundreds of companies, chemicals, and chemical reactions." He paused, thinking. "I just don't quite get who the bad guys are."

"What if they *all* fucked up," Loder reasoned. "What if they've been getting away with murder for years as a group—you know, the military-industrial complex—and they're not about to admit it because they need to continue producing this stuff for the military." Loder looked around. "No?"

"Perhaps," said Willard. "That's certainly more plausible. I'm sure that's how Hollywood would interpret it." But Willard was still unhappy with the train of thought. He was playing tennis with amateurs here. They were all anxious, irritable, suffering with migraines. It was hard to think. And John was driving like a madman.

"You're the one who suggested chemicals," John incited, catching Willard's tone.

But Willard knew when he was merely spinning ideas.

"They were desperate enough to kill for it. They wanted my information, or they wanted it destroyed. But I had no evidence, or none that could be used against any particular company."

"Could you have given anybody reason to believe that you did?"

"I don't know."

"Think. Who have you talked to about this?" John prodded.

"Nobody. I mean, Burt, who has vanished."

"What did you tell him?"

"Shit, I don't know—nothing. The guy was an irredeemable schmuck. And then there was—but no."

"Who?"

"He's a scientist. It's not possible. This guy's a hero."

"Who, damnit?"

"A Dane, in Canada. Roald Shiftren. He was the first to spill the beans on the chemical industry's assault on ozone nearly twenty years ago."

"Could he have sold out?"

"Never. You're talking about the Rachel Carson of ozone depletion."

"Could they be tapping his phone?"

"You're reaching."

"I'm reaching? I'm reaching? You're nearly killed and I'm reaching? Whoa! Donald, hold it: we're both missing it. My interview with you. Christ, of course. When was it, Tuesday? So much shit's gone down since then I can't even remember. Didn't you come out and say you had a list of corporations? Yeah, you did. And you also implicated the military. And we ran it just as you said it. I didn't change a thing."

"Okay. So who are they protecting? The whole god-damned lot of them, that's who. And where does it leave us? Nowhere."

"Do you remember the list?"

"Everybody knows who's making what—it's no secret."

"Is there one particular company?"

A buzzer was ringing in Willard's head. He remembered

an incident three, maybe four, years ago. "There was a certain company—what was it called?"

"What about?" John pushed.

"I'd gotten a memo from Shiftren, as a matter of fact. This was a military contractor, part of a large foreign company, I believe. And they were to produce some extremely volatile halon. Yes. That's what it was. An ingredient to be used for putting out fires on board the shuttle. The thing was unbelievably expensive. I mean it totally dignified the fifteen-thousand-dollar military toilet seats. But this was small potatoes."

"The name, Willard?"

"I can't think of it."

"Donald, your colleagues say you've got a one ninety IQ. Think, goddamnit."

"Yes! Happy Valley Chemicals. That's it."

"You're kidding?"

"I have no idea if they still exist. I never heard anything more about them."

"That's what life's all about," MacIntyre said, encapsulating the irony of it, having pretended to have paid little attention to the discussion up until then.

"It's a lead, at least," John said, exasperated. He turned to instruct Loder on the fine art of turning crap, useless leads, into gold. A basic technique of all good investigative journalism.

When they arrived outside the press conference, they encountered a few hundred religious zealots who stood weaving in and out of the entranceway, mostly clad in cotton dhotis or saffron robes, their joined hands forming a chain, chanting "We Shall Overcome," or "Namu Amida Butsu," or "Om Mani Padmi Hum." Others with placards painted in blood prepared for His arrival, for the apocalypse, the end of the millennium. And still others were protesting the city's lack of preparedness, lack of response. But they were in a small minority, beleaguered by observable coughing fits, various degrees of heat stroke, beneath the scorching rays of the sun. The air was white, smoky with the apparitions.

John and the others unloaded Willard. John noticed that the bulk of Willard's weight was in his waist and stomach, and it was an enormous balloon of life. Willard handled his transfer gracefully, like a pro, even producing a sympathetic grin for the inconvenience of his useless legs.

Once inside, having laid two full reels of AC cord to the truck, MacIntyre and Wendy needed only three minutes to get the camera on its tripod and ready to roll. They had to stay within eye contact of the van to utilize the vehicle's portable microwave, which would uplink the transmission to the KCBD tower.

MacIntyre got his focus, dusted his fingers, and nodded to John. He had a very different shooting style than Andy, who thought about the aesthetics of filming. MacIntyre was a TV mercenary. He did news.

The room overflowed with the press, police, and officials John had never seen. The eyestrain was evident everywhere. People could not stop rubbing, squinting, putting contacts in, taking them out, complaining, seeking wet towels, eyedroppers. Incessant wheezing was equally manifest. There was a medical problem here, in this microcosm of a city whose populace, John noted, had gotten out of control.

"We rolling?" John asked MacIntyre.

"You're on," MacIntyre replied.

The signal was to go out live. At KCBD, Singer and crew were standing by. From there it would be retransmitted to New York. John looked at himself in Wendy's pearl-studded compact, brushed back his hair, wiped off a smudge or two, and began.

"It's about noon, April fourteenth, and any minute now the mayor of Seattle, Charlie Higgins, is going to address a large gathering of press and other officials on the unfolding crisis here in Seattle . . ."

Higgins arrived flushed and disoriented, having just gotten his own family out. He came by chopper from the house at Ferncliff on Bainbridge Island, fully apprised of the conditions on the freeways. His plan for martial law had already been usurped, at least in part, by spontaneous panic. He'd call it a voluntary evacuation.

Introduced by Buck Martin, Higgins started by committing his first feeble reassurance to the press. "Everything is going to be fine. I just want you to know that. We're on top of it. The federal government is going to help. We're going to pull through this. So hang tough."

He introduced Dr. Felix Girard. Willard rolled into striking position. Girard had planned to call on Willard, then received orders from above not to. They hadn't spoken.

"We believe that ozone is a contributing factor to this—ozone depletion, that is," Girard said nervously, eyeing Willard. "Chemicals play a minor part—chlorine to be precise. We've all known about that chemical reaction for nearly a decade. But Mount Redoubt—the active Alaskan volcano—has complicated the situation at sixty thousand feet. I won't bore you with the details, but we do believe nature has run amok here."

"Is there an ozone hole over Seattle at this time?" a local print reporter shouted. John could read the assemblage. Many of them no doubt debated whether to show up here or get the hell out of the Pacific Northwest altogether. Career moves, the possibility of a scoop must have motivated most of those who were here.

Girard responded. "A hole, a minibubble, whatever it is. There is certainly significant ozone depletion in the upper atmospheres of the region."

"What's the story, NSB? How long? How serious? Will it get worse? Where will it go?" The questions were fired in a chorus of anger and disapproval.

Which a now pressured and stumbling Girard further aggravated. "A day, maybe two. Then we expect it to dissipate. This has been the pattern for months."

"Why hasn't the public known about it for months?"

"It's been confined to the Arctic until this week."

"Bullshit!" Donald Willard called out with a rapier voice. The audience turned toward Willard.

"Full shot," John directed MacIntyre. "Wendy, get in close."

Willard continued, "I sent memos six weeks ago to you folks in Washington. We've been tracking it at the college for months. You wouldn't listen."

"This is not at issue here!" Buck Martin broke in, protecting the mayor. "We're here to assure you that city officials are aware of the situation, we're monitoring it, and we're going to conduct an orderly response. We're not here to facilitate shouting matches or unsubstantiated and useless accusations. Okay? On that note, the mayor has an important decision to announce."

"I have decided under the circumstances to call in the National Guard for as long as it takes to work through this. Eight hundred troops are, at this time, moving into the city's financial district, as well as numerous residential areas, to protect against looting and assist those in search of shelters or in need of medical care. In addition, they'll be protecting vital city utilities in keeping with a declaration of martial law to take effect at eight o'clock this evening. That should give parents enough time to get their kids home from school after the sun has gone down. This is not a curfew I'm talking about, however—this is martial law. You all know the difference. I want people off the streets, in their homes until such time as the experts deem it safe to venture back out. Part of the city's Personal Protection Plan. We've had the schools conduct ozone alerts this morning. I want everyone to stay indoors. Put that message out. It's for all our safety. Ultraviolet radiation is no laughing matter."

There was an adamant show of alarmism and dissent among many of the press. "What about the insects?" someone shouted. "Damned if I'm gonna condemn my family to that again!" There was other insurrection in the room.

The mayor staved off total mutiny with a gesture of warm and knowing sympathy. "Yeah, we had insects too. Not much we can do about them. They'll go away. Nuke 'em with everything you've got. Hell, there's going to be all kinds of inconveniences, I know that. But this is not a unique situation. I repeat. Governors and mayors have frequently had to declare martial law during violent labor disputes or other disasters—floods, hurricanes, you name it. The writ of habeas corpus, you should note, is no longer in effect as of this minute in the city of Seattle. So no funny business. Set an example. Watch your butts."

"And if the ozone hole lingers for weeks?" Donald Willard declared, looking at Girard.

"NSB has a plan, Dr. Willard."

"You mind telling the world what you've got in mind?"

"I wish I could. I can't."

"Another military secret, is it?"

"As Mayor Higgins just said, we know that the pattern has been for the miniholes to last for a few days, sometimes merging together before dissipating out. We suspect several have come together here in the Seattle area and that it's only a matter of days before they're history. Our plan is to help expedite the process."

"And then what?" some other reporter demanded. "Portland? San Francisco?" A second voice erupted. "Or is it north to Vancouver? Or east to Boise?"

"Look, I can tell you that it involves seeding the hole, much like farmers looking to extract rain from a cloud. Our plan is to neutralize the chlorine."

This one was new to Willard. He didn't believe it, he didn't even buy the concept. He shook his head cynically. "I've been a chemist half my life. I've never heard of what you're describing."

"You're not the last word, Dr. Willard."

With supplicating hands, he answered, "I'll be the first to admit it. Good luck, Felix."

As Higgins and other officials spelled out the terms of the city's response, conveying medical recommendations, specifying those bomb shelters that could receive people stranded on the streets, and as John continued to cover and lend commentary to the event, Loder was in another room down the hall on the phone testing his wings, lowering his boyish voice to impersonate a newly hired assistant in the accounting department at Happy Valley Chemicals. He had gotten Greg Morton's number two on the line. "We're trying to track down the original purchase order on our last defense contract," he explained, playing the one gross trump card he could think of. As he spoke he knew he was blowing it.

"I have no idea," the woman said, slightly annoyed. She was just a normal person with a slow Virginia drawl. "Just a minute."

Loder worried that she was going to record the conversation. He was thinking about hanging up when she returned.

It sounded to Loder as if she were reading from some document. "It says here that all such orders went through your mother company at Offshore Industries in Mexico. A Mr. Mantoya in Purchasing."

"Do you happen to have any purchase order numbers or dollar amounts? I'd like to check them against our records."

"I see only two purchases in the past year, both in the amounts of three and a half million dollars. According to this, payment was made last November and December on goods delivered last spring."

"Which goods?" Loder asked. She was being so cooperative, he'd push for as much as he could get.

"It just says 'Batch,' but I'm sure Mr. Montoya will be able to tell you exactly."

"You probably know that both Rick Caldihamp over at DIA and Greg were here in Seattle the other day on this terrible ozone business and the figures they were using for chemical production here at Happy Valley didn't correspond in any way with what my records show on the computer. I see an overpayment by the government of nearly ten thousand dollars per batch."

"While I'm sure Mr. Morton will be delighted to hear that and I expect he'll be checking in by the end of the day. I'll be sure to pass along the fact that you called. What was your name?"

Loder winged it, called Montoya only to learn that he was out of the country, got Montoya's assistant, who knew nothing about any such batch. Loder then called Happy Valley Chemicals directly, got accounting, feigned his purest Spanish accent, claimed to be from the equivalent mother company accounting section in Montoya's department, described the batch numbers and purchase price. What he found was a very paranoid individual who clammed up and refused to give out any information.

Loder tried Caldihamp's number, pretending to be Morton's assistant, but got nowhere. Caldihamp was out of the office and would be calling in. Loder persisted. He was enjoying the process, playing at it now, way over his head and not even aware of it, feeling high and immune. It was his first sense of being a part of a news team and it was a good feeling.

He now called Caldihamp's boss and got through when he mentioned a live national broadcast on CB-9 network tonight involving the alleged DIA/GAO involvement with Offshore Industries in Mexico.

The fellow on the other end was not easily amused, listened silently, gauged Loder's inexperience, then politely confirmed—"It's no secret"—that the two agencies had been cooperating in a number of ongoing investigations meant to reduce the level of paperwork, inefficiency, and waste amongst defense contractors. "We've modeled our efforts after those of the IRS," the man said. "Anything else I can help you with?"

The guy was real smooth, Loder thought. He heard subterfuge. It was written all over the man's voice. But Loder was also completely out of his league. There was nowhere to take this. His whole motive was lost, forgotten. It was simply too complicated for him on the phone like this. He was a fine arts major at Evergreen and had virtually no real journalistic experience. Loder pursued it no farther.

Background noise was now competing with his conversation. The press conference was adjourning amid what sounded like the brandishing of swords. He tried one last angle, hoping for gold. "You've been very cooperative and I appreciate it. Let me just say that we understand one of the companies you're investigating produces ozone-depleting chemicals and that the recent murder at a chemical laboratory in Seattle may be connected. Would you care to comment?"

"I have no information on that."

"You were aware of the murder?"

There was a pause. Loder's fingers were crossed and pressing tight. "Off the record, this agency is conducting its own investigation into the matter. Is there anything else?"

"No. Look, I really appreciate your time. We may need to call you again as the story develops if that's all right? What was your name again?"

But the man had already hung up.

CHAPTER 22

THURSDAY AFTERNOON

Elizabeth pulled the drapes over the window and picked up the phone.

"I'm all right. We're all all right. I've loaded the car. I took out the garbage. I cleaned out the fridge. There're still bugs all over the floor. Live ones. I'll get the kids and meet you at the station around five. We may be there before you. Are you okay, Johnny?"

His wife was breathing hard. He didn't recognize certain irregularities in her voice. She hadn't called him Johnny in months, maybe a year. Their conversation was suspended, somewhere outside time, outside this, the hallway from where he was speaking, the bald lime-green overheads, the surreal crowds out beyond. He suddenly regretted his involvement in the story, as if it was *his* doing, his zeal to get a story which had somehow *created* the whole disaster.

"I'm having a hard time connecting," he mumbled like a boy, his throat laboring to vibrate between mucousy ills and implacable laws. "I feel old, I'm churning inside. Like I could puke."

"We've got to fight it," she said.

"I'm fighting," he conceded passively.

"Johnny, you've got to win this."

"What? What does *that* even mean?" he said aggressively. "I can't even remember."

It was getting to him, Elizabeth feared. "Remember what?" she pressed impatiently. "John?"

"Well, what it used to be like." He was stalling, wanting the comfort of her hand and the remedy of her words.

"What are you talking about?" She had far more punch in her tone now than mere comforting, anxious to get their kids out of school, inclined to escape, not to whine.

"I don't know." He meant their relationship. He meant the carefree days of age fifteen. He saw the period before his four grandparents died, when his own parents still gave him an allowance, when he used to hitchhike, or spend whole days "messing around." When the most serious thing in the universe hinged upon a girl's yes or no. The pressing logic of adult life, its countless responsibilities, had abolished all that, left him plagued by doubts. He did not feel up to the task of an investigation, an exposé. He did not believe in the facts and numbers anymore. He was not James Bond, never had believed in a James Bond. Any more than he believed in himself.

"Goddamnit," she screamed, coming from an instant before that he had missed. "I don't want to hear this now. It's plain pitiful and stupid. Do you understand? Snap out of it, John."

He lurched back, stamping out the creeping poisons of fear. "I didn't even tell you, I'll be on CB-9 tonight with Peter Mather. And tomorrow."

"You see!" she said, more reasonable now. "You can do it."

"Yeah. We did it," he said matter-of-factly. *I'm scared.* He repeated it to himself, as if to firm up his intention. And then he said it out loud.

"Me too. Now I got to get the kids. I'll see you shortly?"

He didn't answer. He would have given anything for a week on a beach reading something light, a novel by Lem, or snorkeling with his son, nothing else on his mind. To have Seattle back the way it had been, blurred, pastoral, simple.

"John?" Elizabeth said again, beckoning with a time-to-go curtness. She wanted another baby. The reasoning blossomed in her mind with vivid candle power. Her queasiness this morning was not easily defined, a province of fear, confused with the hope that their lovemaking this past week had paid off.

"Yeah. Right. Promise me you'll drive carefully."

"That's funny," she said.

At school, Elizabeth found dozens of other mothers and a few fathers there to collect their children. They all resembled Tuareg converts—North African nomads burdened beneath so many space age goggles, fighter pilot goggles, chic downhill racer sunglasses—whatever was around. Faces gobbed in zinc and lotion, and concealed behind head coverings. They had it all, this wealthy congeries—mantillas, purdahs, silk scarves from Paris. The scent of methyl azinphos, a sickly sweet-smelling pesticide that had been sprayed all over the school's ivy-covered brick walls, the grass, the trees, filled the air. The streets were bare. People huddled in shadows, or waited in their cars. Golf ball-sized hail could not have produced so fearful an avoidance mechanism.

"Go, go go!" shouted one teacher, as two kids ran out the school's front door to their mother who waited in a loaded-down four-door Mercedes on the street. The kids ran through the afternoon heat mirage as if it were a downpour.

"Good luck, Liz," Janis Marley said to Elizabeth, as she pulled her car alongside her friend's. Janis's daughter was in Jennifer's class.

"You too, Janis. Where are you going?" Elizabeth asked.

"Reno. Bob's parents are there."

Reno. It sounded like paradise to Elizabeth.

"Okay, you kids, run! Run like the dickens!" another army cry hailed from the school entrance. This time it was Jennifer and Evans. Like paratroopers, one after the other they raced into the chaos. Jennifer tripped in the grass beneath the wild blue yonder. A bird dive-bombed her from out of the adjoining mountain cottonwoods. Suddenly, the whole flock went crazy, shrieking in aerial displays of no direction. The birds were tired, many of them blind.

221

"Get up!" Evans screamed, helping his terrified sister to her feet.

Elizabeth ran out to meet them. "Baby . . ."

"Mom!" she cried. The bird had whacked her hard but caused no apparent injury. It flopped, seeming to expire in the desiccated grass.

"Don't touch it, Evans! In the car. Hurry up."

Trying the backroads in an effort to get downtown, Elizabeth noted that there was smoke billowing from that direction. It was just after 1:00 P.M. The sky was a hazy pink, burned over. Elizabeth was driving scared. The kids were strapped in. Evans was thinking of Sophie. In his mind, he was making love to her, groping slowly through a terrain of unknowns, an Eden supposed to have materialized this weekend. She really loves me, he thought. Jennifer was shaking, afraid her mother wouldn't be able to handle things.

John and crew dropped Willard off at the station. He was afraid to go home. He decided to live in the lounge at KCBD, foraging among vending machines like the rest of them until the immediate world realigned itself. Willard had lost his appetite for combat, acquiescing to what he perceived to be an utter travesty in terms of the city's and NSB's responses. He was totally benumbed by the death of his friend, and now he called Dapple, Stan's widow, at the hospital, to tell her of this unspeakable sorrow, which she knew all too well, stoically working this day to avoid confronting it.

John and crew found the All City Hospital surrounded by a phalanx of the National Guard. Up the block a fire raged out of control, black smoke pouring upward and spreading throughout the downtown area. A bevy of fire trucks were there fighting it. Two military tanks could be seen rolling toward the scene. The pitch of battle had escalated. The sound of gunfire exploded in more than a few zones. Looters.

"Sure. Get it," John said.

MacIntyre panned the block, pulling focus from a tight

shot of a trooper's rifle, past the oncoming tanks, to a slow zoom into the smoke. "Beirut," the shooter remarked without conviction, as they lugged the gear inside, Loder running ahead to "fix" things, since John was supposed to hook up with Dr. Ralph Decker, head of Infectious Diseases for the state of Washington and former chief of internal medicine at the hospital.

"We've got speed," Wendy announced to the others.

John began. "Okay. Dr. Decker, tell me, what's happening here?" They walked with him along a refugee corridor of sick and dying. Loder now kept the cord that attached Wendy and MacIntyre from getting in the way as the whole group moved in one tracking momentum down the endless emergency area.

"Speak louder," John told the doctor, fighting the background din for clear audio.

The late-middle-aged Decker appeared ragged. "As you can see, we're too few in number. All City can't accommodate the incoming patients. It really jumped yesterday afternoon, along with the temperature. We can't cool it down in here. Must be nearly one hundred degrees. That's spreading disease. We're in trouble. All the city hospitals are experiencing the same thing."

"What diseases? What's happening? How contagious?" John wanted answers.

Wendy looked at Loder. Loder eyed John. *Oh, great!* Loder said to himself, shrinking with the fear of suddenly imagined diseases.

"We've seen every kind of optic ulcer, ophthalmia, keratitis, massive, overnight pinguecula, destroyed conjunctiva, excruciating corneal ulcers that are blinding the patients."

"In English," John waged, combating the harried informant.

"I'm sorry. The eyes are burning up. And that's only the beginning. There are new viruses showing up, perhaps spread by the dead animals all over town. We've got systemic lupus erythematosus, skin eruptions and renal failure; rampant herpes on the genitals, face, tongue, and in the throat. We're having to contend with infectious hepatitis, more parasites than we can analyze, serious skin cancers, throat cancer, nasty bacterialike meningococcus and streptococcus."

"I'm afraid I have to ask you again. In layman's terms."

"I mean stuff we've never even seen in this hospital. Here, look at this." The doctor led them up to one patient's miserable stash of a bed. "Tabes dorsalis," Dr. Decker stated.

"What is it?" John inquired.

"Syphilis of the nervous system. Destroys the whole person. Why, I ask, are we seeing dozens of such cases today, when we haven't seen one in this hospital in the past five years?" The doctor took them farther down the corridor. "We've had to amputate bloated limbs. We're recording internal body temperatures of a hundred five. It's not an epidemic—it's multiple epidemics. Immune systems seem to be cracking. And then there's the rash of other emergencies—victims of car accidents—more than I've ever seen."

An internist came flying past the cameraman accompanied by two medics who had rushed a dying patient in.

"What's happening to him? What's he got?" John asked.

But no one was listening to a journalist with his own "yellow" fever. The boy was hyperventilating.

"Oh-two tension?" the medic requested.

"Hypocarpnia, thirty."

"Okay. Same routine. Skip the ABG's. Kid's clammy. Let's go six liters nasal cannula."

The nurse hovered over the suffering child, attempting to restore normal breathing reflexes, while the medic inserted the cannula and a therapist took a PO_2 reading.

"Acute respiratory distress," the internist snapped for the benefit of the camera team.

"That's the eighth such case today," Decker said angrily.

The internist witnessed the boy turning blue. "We're losing him."

The kid jerked one last time and went lifeless. The defeated troupe of specialists took off their masks. The nurse slumped against the arterial blood gas machine, a Venturi apparatus, and removed the piggyback IV tubes that dangled over the tiny corpse.

The internist was baffled and protested out loud, hostile and incredulous with fatigue. "Goddamnit! He was fine. Clear lungs. Good heart. Normal. Just a kid. Nothing was wrong with him until this morning."

"Did you get that, MacIntyre?" John asked.

"Got it."

Decker filled John in on the grimy particulars, highlighting the myriad symptoms of a killer syndrome that had appeared in the last 48 hours: central nervous system enfeeblement, an overnight aging process that had left victims looking twenty, thirty years older than their years; sunburns equivalent to third degree, with malignant blisters approaching the level of abscess and decay more normally associated with leprosy. The doctors had noted a bizarre impairment of the body's time sense, accompanying hallucinations, cardiac and pulmonary breakdowns resulting first in headaches, dizziness, vomiting, skin eruptions, eventual coma, and respiratory failure.

"How many dead so far, Dr. Decker?"

The doctor looked at his clipboard. "As of eight o'clock this morning, over two hundred. I don't see how any of the hospitals are going to be able to cope much longer with this. We need help."

"What kind of help?" John was feeling mired and smothered. He couldn't stand the heat. He had always sweated a great deal and now was drenched. It was pouring off his forehead. It was pouring off everyone's forehead. If Seattle's utilities went down, and the power overloaded, it would be catastrophic, John reckoned. He wanted out. As Decker continued to rant, John had Loder call for the station's chopper. He wanted to cover the fringe of the city and marshal some sort of context for the story. Glaciers. The surrounding farmland. Swollen rivers. It was also an excuse: he had to get out. Willard had connected the ozone depletion with the Greenhouse Effect. John didn't exactly understand the link except that both situations were unleashing higher and higher temperatures. The glaciers could melt, Willard had suggested.

The answer to his question swung John back into reality. "We need more helicopters. More doctors. More beds. More blood for transfusions. More money. More microscopes. More nurses. How's that for a starter?" Dr. Decker said forcefully.

The crew gathered its gear and headed for the hospital exit. There was no relief outside. The fires down the street had spread. KCBD was less than a mile away. John's crew could see a wall of flames building and hear intermittent explosions as walls and windows and gas lines detonated. Machine-gun fire punctuated the deafening inferno. As they loaded into the truck, they saw members of a SWAT team in military garb pursuing a gang of long-haired punks who were fleeing with ghetto blasters and VCR's in their arms.

At KCBD Singer was watching the footage, which was being bounced off a building to the station tower from the satellite dish atop the van. From the tower, it was transmitted via satellite to New York. The goons that had ridden Singer's ass had vanished. There had been no call from the station group that day. No friendly advice from the governor's office. Silence from Washington, D.C. He couldn't help but wonder whether the deaths of Andy and Stan might have had something to do with the unimpeded silence that had replaced the threats—that and the fact that most networks were now covering Seattle round the clock. KCBD's honeymoon of exclusivity was over. Singer could breathe more easily. He had room to focus.

Dust and smoke were blown in all directions as a chopper from the station—coming in amid other helicopters in the immediate vicinity—landed on the street. John locked up the van as he and the others leaped aboard. "How long to the nearest glacier we can get on to?" John shouted to Harry, a pilot with whom he'd frequently worked in the past. John had to be back at KCBD no later than four o'clock to get his report out.

"Twenty minutes," Harry replied.

"Good. Get us there."

Thirty miles to the north, a second chopper was bringing Felix Girard to a military airstrip. There an ER-2 was being readied for flight. A team had been assembled that included the major players from earlier in the week—Haskel Murphy, Winston Himes, Jake the Racer, and Buddy. Felix had orders from on high. This time their mission had a new element: not only was Murphy to quantify the ozone depletion, amount and rate, but Jake was then to jettison a kind of cloud-seeding missile into the center of the hole, loaded with oxides of nitrogen. The idea was to disperse large masses of the stuff in concentrated gaseous form at both low and high altitudes so as to trigger a conversion of the ozone-depleting chlorine monoxide into the relatively benign chlorine nitrate molecule.

Girard was nervous. He knew it was an untested chemical ploy. Willard had called it "science fiction" and he might be right. But Girard was trying to save himself as well as his colleagues. It was just bad luck that things had gone this way, he thought, feeding his remote and private persecution complex. He was rather desperate. But theoretically, anyway, it *could* work.

Within minutes of their lift-off, en route to Mt. Rainier's Russell glacier, flying low over the crammed, insane interstate traffic, John made out a horrible sight. A dog was trapped along the inside median, swaggering in the heat and soot, moving south in an effort to find a way out, off the freeway. It had no chance. Traffic was bumper to bumper as far as the eye could see.

The dog kept peering back, veering off into the closest lane. John knew he was going to be creamed any minute. The dog could have been on the freeways for days, desperate for water, its eyes probably burned to a crisp. It looked like Wallace.

"We've got to go down!" John hollered, swept with remorse. "The dog. We've got to save it."

"Can't do it," Harry shouted into the headset.

"For my little girl, goddamnit. Her dog just died. We've got to do something! There's a cable!"

"Shit. All right. Get in the harness."

Harry didn't usually do this sort of thing. He was no hotshot. It was difficult to see. The reflected light from the cars blinded him. That coupled with the weird haze of car exhaust enfeebled his line of sight like ectoplasm in the ether. There was a wall, four feet high, separating the inbound traffic from the outbound traffic. The chopper hovered thirty feet above truck height.

"I'm snapped in. Let me out," John ordered.

"What if he bites you?" Wendy said.

"One minute. You got one minute," Harry yelled. "You two get ready!"

MacIntyre and Loder lowered him down over a fixed anchor. The cable ran smoothly. The sound of horns and skidding tires engulfed the operation from below. The chopper moved at the speed of the animal, which Harry had already figured. Wendy and the rest of the crew remained speechless, urging John on in their thoughts.

John knew he had to get that dog. "Five more feet!" he screamed. "Hold me," he repeated, twisting in the air on his cable at eight knots. The dog was out of its mind, deranged, dying.

It can't see me, John thought. Suddenly, a wretched odor, hot and unassimilable, swept into John's lungs.

He swung toward the dog, hanging low, nearly brushing the ground. He touched and then grabbed hold of its leg.

"A truck!" Wendy screamed.

Harry maneuvered fast. The truck was higher than they'd anticipated. The chopper could virtually turn on a dime. Harry shot upward, dragging John with him. John was yanked like a weightless marionette high into the air over the freeway.

"Fuck!" he hollered with a convulsive squirm.

The dog looked backward at John and yelped. It had the bewildered look of the nonseeing. And then, frantic, it fled into the middle of traffic as John came hurtling back down at the end of his cable.

The enormous truck swerved in an effort to avoid the ascending chopper. It sideswiped a landrover, careening back toward John, who pirouetted in a pendulum across eight lanes, thirty-five feet up in the air, suspended from his cable.

The dog disappeared beneath the barreling wheels of the truck.

"No!" John screamed, holding on for dear life and watching the canine muddle beneath the body of the huge vehicle. Vermilion spread over the concrete as the dog's final howls outlasted the flood of ruptured organs being sprayed from one vehicle to another, under pipes, iron bellies, radial tires, axles, and shock absorbers.

Wendy and the others dragged John inside the helicopter. His clothes had ripped on the metal edge of the pulley system, but he was now safely inside, cowering by the door. Seeing him safe, Harry flew out of the fray.

MacIntyre looked at the freeway below through his camera lens. It was a vision of exploding glass. A car shaking violently from impact with another vehicle moments before, the driver crumpled forward into an airbag, while whorls of shattered steel involuted around him, around the others. Down the road, a six-ton two-linker vehicle jackknifed, smashing into the concrete retainer of an underpass. The flames, the alloys scattered. Debris, chemical fires were everywhere.

Harry flew John and his crew south at breakneck speed to avoid this crowded moment. Wendy felt sick and powerless. Loder was frozen, MacIntyre glued to the lens. He couldn't leave it now. He was capturing everything on film. John vomited, the dog rebounding in his brain.

"Use a towel," Harry yelled to John. It stank.

"What do you want to do?" he continued to shout at John, as they approached the moraines beyond the forest on Rainier. John wiped himself off and sat upright with Wendy's mothering.

"A stand-up, on the ice. Put us down on the ice," John shouted.

"You sure you feel up to it?"

"Just do it."

They swung in above the terminus, where misshapen seracs reared up in disarray. The chopper cleared the ice by fifty feet, entering the world of the glacial plateau, leaving behind a view of metropolitan haze down in the western distance, where forests of the Puget Sound gave way to the mountain.

"There, if you can!" John directed, pointing to the spot.

Harry was not sure that he could land on the spot John selected, but he was literally too tired to fight it. The sun had given him extreme eye fatigue. His forehead was burning. If the skids crumbled through a crevasse, so be it. They'd be dead. But it was unlikely and he decided to take the chance, wanting to get it over with. Eight of Harry's friends had died in the last ten years flying choppers. Every rating in the world was useless against the vagaries of machine and circumstance.

The chopper set down, tentatively at first, then with a final settling determination. They'd made it.

The team stepped outside into the blistering heat, swathed in headdresses and other protective garments, ointments, and goggles. MacIntyre set up the tripod, Wendy hooked up John's mic and called, "Speed."

John spoke into the camera. ". . . In addition, an unprecedented heat spell with temperatures soaring to a hundred ten degrees. Croplands have been wiped out, water reserves contaminated. And the ice is melting. The ozone hole and the Greenhouse Effect would seem to be triggering one another."

He knew he was just speculating with a rampant disregard. He suddenly grew dizzy and sat down. "Stop camera a minute," he said wearily.

"You want to dip your hands in the water there," MacIntyre said. "While I grab some cutaways."

"Yeah, good."

The sun was scorching the glacial basin where the group worked.

"All right. You guys go up and get a shot of me on the ice from high up, dramatic angle-type stuff. Loder, am I okay here?"

Loder had climbed the mountain before. He knew crevasse country but he had never felt such heat. The snow atop the ice was wet, running off rapidly, glacial rivulets out of control. Crevasses in spring were normally risky business because you couldn't see them. They were there, the springtime temperatures had opened them up all right, but fresh blankets of snow could easily conceal them at the top. They were perfect death traps. And today such traps were everywhere, Loder detected in a glance. It was a literal spider's web of perilous lines and gaps, some exposed, more hidden. "I don't know."

"I thought you climbed."

"I would need to check it out, John. With a long ice ax."

"Well, shit, we obviously aren't doin' that. Look, just a few paces. No big deal. You guys swing around once. Get me walking. I'll be fine."

Harry and the team took off, disappearing momentarily over a side canyon. There was silence. Maybe they wouldn't ever come back, John thought, whistling the first introspective dixie of freedom in weeks. The oppressive glare of the overhead sun did not diminish his sudden sense of exquisite emancipation.

The sound of rotor blades returned, this time, to John's surprise, from the opposite direction. The chopper was there all at once, descending over the granite ridge, emblazoned against the churned up effluvia of earlier eons. John squinted inside his glacier goggles. Something was different. He moved back slightly as the vehicle hovered, then descended lower and lower, fixing a landing position.

"That's him," a voice inside the approaching chopper said.

"Where're the others?" a second man asked.

"Let's just get in there."

"Could be a setup," the pilot risked.

"Are you kidding? Just do it."

John was confused. He took off his goggles, rubbed his eyes. The trochlear nerve quivered violently, rousing the visual motor fibers. There was pain, in other words.

John stepped back as the helicopter landed. He had a suspicion in his gut. He moved back five more feet. He saw that it was a different helicopter.

The chopper set down twenty feet before him, its rotors at full throttle. Now John recognized the helicopter. A large man in jeans and a T-shirt stepped out. He was bald. John remembered him. There had been a bald man in the chopper that killed Andy.

"Hello, John. How you been? We'd like to talk to you for a minute."

John was on the edge of soft rim snow—up to his knees in it. He fell backward into the wet blanket of glacial thicket. He was stuck, his butt and hands inextricable. He squirmed around to regain a stance but found himself free-swimming in the hot arena of blinding white powder. Every bodily movement sent him deeper into the belly-encompassing mire. The heat was infernal, the brightness of the sky as brilliant as the white of the glacier.

"Who are you?"

The man looked around. He didn't understand why John was alone on the snow, or where the chopper they'd followed had suddenly disappeared to. He approached with a hand in his right pocket. John struggled, falling backward. He was on an invisible lip.

The man inched his way toward him, slogging through the snow.

"I said, who are you?"

John thought he heard something. He turned urgently. There, a thousand or so feet directly before him, having given no advance warning, was Harry and his team's helicopter, rising vertically from down below, where the glacier must have formed a deep valley against the canyon walls. It had flown through muted shadows, across five-hundred-foot-high dips, hidden by seracs and the overhanging terminus of ice.

Wendy saw the scene before her and screamed. "Harry!"

"Who are they?" the unsuspecting pilot said.

"Just go! Go, Harry! They'll kill him!" Wendy shouted.

Loder immediately hung out of the chopper, holding on to a steel cable, while MacIntyre, who was already positioned to pick up the shot, gave him a hand. Harry approached fast.

The bald man, deep in snow as he approached John, turned, raising his gun. The other pilot, who was hovering directly over the bald man, added additional thrust to his rotors, preparing to take off. The chopper inched upward off the ice. John could see the second man inside shout something to the bald man. He was inaudible over the noise of two helicopters.

"Intercept him!" Wendy screamed.

Harry's chopper swooped in. John, seeing it and calculating his two seconds of grace, threw himself flat against the snow as the corner of a strut slammed through the space separating predator and prey. A bullet penetrated the helicopter's underbelly, just missing Wendy as the bald man was hit on the side of his head and thrown face down in a pool of blood.

John crashed through the fragile bridge of snow on which he stood, falling into the concealed crevasse. The whole rim collapsed, opening up a sudden world of darkness beneath him. He plummeted, but was suddenly snared on a buttress twelve feet down. John knew that the whole thing would break off any minute. Wedged against the ice, he tried to scream out.

He was pushing out with his arms and legs to keep from slipping deeper. The cold air underneath rushed up from unknown blue-blackness, countervailing the surge of heat from above. It was all blinding. He was trapped. His legs were jammed. The air above was rushing into his brain, the altitude filled with unbearable light of snow blown by the chopper blades. He was dulling fast. Below the waist, he was frozen, numb.

"Hold on!" a voice bellowed above the roar of the two helicopters, both hovering now, the one overhead and the second moving away in a breakneck curve. Loder spit out the cable—"Grab it!"—as MacIntyre threw himself to the other side and got a shot of the escaping chopper through the dull plastic window. He didn't see the pilot from his angle. He set down the camera to assist Wendy and Loder pull Gage out of the crevasse.

The other chopper was gone. Harry set his bird down, rotors at full revolution. They lifted off the hood and goggles of the dead man. His head was dented in. Blood oozed from his nose. He was unrecognizable. His hand still gripped his gun.

"Let's get him in," MacIntyre said. "Hurry."

CHAPTER 23

"Get down!" Elizabeth cried. The machine-gun fire smashed through the rear window behind Jennifer, missing her by inches and fragmentizing the adjacent pane of glass.

"Oh, God, oh God!" Evans said, with none of his normal cool, deploring everything about their situation. Jennifer shrieked and her mom swerved under an overpass, screeching to a stop at the entranceway to a barren alley. In the distance they saw troops, backstretch bravos with official sanction, running after final vestiges of a mob, rifles loaded, importunate, smoky discharges clouding the street. Overhead, the roar of traffic had the aural timbre of a mighty wind tunnel or of ball lightning scraping clean the earth's surface.

"We gotta keep going, Mom! I can drive," Evans volunteered, between wracking bursts of a congested lung. He gagged, held himself, then jettisoned an inadvertent wad of gluey phlegm, like a small cannonball. His eyes and throat were burning.

"No, you cannot drive! Honey—"

Jennifer was sobbing, afraid to move, to touch herself. Her cheek was bleeding. There were needle-sharp fragments embedded in her forearm. "I can't feel my fingers!" she muttered pitifully. Her eyes were glazing, her whole face badly burned and swollen.

Evans ripped off his shirt, dove into the backseat, and feebly ministered to his sister as Elizabeth shot out into the roadway—a mile to go to KCBD. She was losing her mind.

At the TV station the editor, Herb, MacIntyre, and John were putting the final touches to the material that would go up on the satellite in twenty minutes.

"Jesus, look at this!" Herb groaned. He saw his neighborhood off in the distance.

"You believe that?" MacIntyre said with the selfless edge of heroism. "I flew over it!"

In the meantime Loder had had a discussion with Mather. The mundane details of the live broadcast had been worked out. Both Singer and John would host the in-studio wraparounds. The matte window behind the anchors would read: OZONE CRISIS. The same wording and font style would coincide with that of Mather's background window.

Willard reclined nervously in the lounge, anxious and exhausted. He was prepared for whatever might come. Antarctica had come back to haunt him. He sought recognition now, sweet vindication beyond the face-saving gambits of nameless bureaucrats, all the malevolent babble and churlish lies launched venally to conceal the simple fact of chemical imbalance.

Willard was watching news coverage that Singer had been anchoring since midafternoon. Singer was marshaling his own commentary with the force of vengeance aimed at the goons, the station manager and every sleazy member of the director's board that feared to confront the truth. Willard almost enjoyed Singer's piss and vinegar, as he spouted acerbic lessons and hard-won evidence.

More footage came in from Canada. There were comments from officials in Vancouver, a city that miraculously had been spared the bulk of the problem. It was hot, all right. But nobody was losing his eyesight, insects hadn't gone on the rampage. The whole city was on a kind of useless alert. Officials were carefully studying the situation down in Seattle but Vancouver city life was continuing normally. The provincial lieutenant governor had invited

U.S. refugees across the border in a show of friendly support. Plenty of hotels. Restaurants. Doors always open.

None of it surprised Willard. He had known a week ago that Vancouver was not in the swath of things to come.

There was a call to the station from a policeman out on the road. Charles Fields had killed himself while driving north, probably to Canada, his new Porsche wrapped around a tree. Fields's neck had snapped, exposing his face directly to the sun. His eyes had melted. KCBD employees were not particularly grievous over the news.

John had his leg wrapped in gauze. When he fell in the crevasse he'd ripped open his thigh.

"I never knew ice was so sharp," he said, wincing, speaking with one dogged detective in Singer's office. The cop was perhaps in his late thirties, had an auburn ponytail and was clad in tight-fitting jeans bearing a Santa Fe-style silver belt buckle. This was no Colombo. John kept trying to avoid eyeing a mean-looking scar over the cop's right eye. Finally, Rubin—that was his name—remarked that he'd been hit with an iron by his ex.

"Ah-ha," John said, nodding agreeably.

The body of John's assailant was still in the back of the chopper. The detective had shown Willard the body, thinking that he might know him. Maybe there was a connection. Burt, or a jealous colleague, or some skeleton from his past?

No such luck. Willard had never seen the man.

Rubin looked down at his cowboy boots and spoke to John while trying to get a wad of chewing gum off his sole. "Yeah, if that creep had gotten his way, you'd have been in that ice for thousands and thousands of years." He frowned. "Does it hurt?"

John acknowledged that it did, then wondered aloud, "Who is he?"

"No idea," detective Rubin avowed.

"Then you have discounted Willard as a suspect?" John declared, less by way of a question than an exclamation of relief.

"More than likely," the detective concurred. He was a rational man. John seized upon that at once.

"Then shouldn't he have police protection? They must know that they took out the wrong man. They're bound to try it again."

"You got three armed guards here," the detective said calmly. "Lot of people milling around. He should be okay. Just make sure he stays here until it all blows over."

"Bland assurances," John stated.

"It's you I'm worried about." The detective looked John directly in the eye.

It never dawned upon John until this moment that the silly little news pieces he concocted for a living had the power to trigger the desire for lethal revenge on the part of strangers. It added to his sickness, the ill-begotten jazz in his stomach and brain this day.

"We're still running fingerprints on cigarette butts," the detective continued. "It was Willard's idea. The two jokers are either the same slob or kissing cousins, I would guess. It shouldn't take much longer, if we've got anything at all. Did that guy on the glacier say anything else?"

John paused, thinking back. Then, "No."

"And you say the gun was pointed at you—in a threatening manner, I mean?"

"Yes." It wasn't, exactly, but John was not about to dicker.

"Um. And you say your assistant heard from this fellow in Washington that they're conducting their own investigation into the alleged murder?"

"Murders," he said adamantly. John hadn't known Stan, except for a momentary exchange at the lab when he'd first interviewed Willard. But the searing loss of Andy into that broiling sea had tormented him for two days now. He had the nagging concern that somehow the young man's life had not only been lost but forgotten.

"You'll want to speak with Garrison Loder about the conversation," John indicated. "I was doing something else at the time. Interviewing doctors." He stopped, weighing his anger, considering a target. Then, decisively, he asked, "What do you have on Andy Otero's death?"

"We don't know it was murder," detective Rubin said in an exploring, almost apologetic frame of mind.

"It *was* murder!"

"A cameraman fell out of a chopper," Rubin charged, reciting facts known to him. "He wasn't clipped in properly. You said so yourself. This can happen I suppose."

John pelted the detective's supposition, enraged. "Jesus, you're in on it too."

"In on it?" the detective repeated, annoyed. "Are we a little paranoid, Mr. Gage?"

"I don't believe this." John sat down.

"I can understand your frustration. These are hard times for all of us. You see, police work is about patience. We do know it was the same helicopter. We're still tracing it. If it's any consolation, the helicopter is definitely guilty as hell. It's the occupants that are troubling me."

"It's time," Loder said, having rushed in on the conversation.

"This is the guy you want to talk to about that conversation," John reminded the detective. "And you'll keep me informed?"

"Naturally. Just do me a favor—stay out of trouble."

John's family pulled into the parking lot of KCBD and raced past security. Down the hall, in engineering, the pretaped footage that MacIntyre had shot had already been sent out. The live in-studio wraparounds and local commentary, hosted by John and by Singer, followed up on the dedicated transponder, downlinking into the CB-9 studio in New York, then going back up, refashioned with Mather's own commentary, to the entire nation. It was a normal approach to disasters, habitual technology, the way wars became comfortable as viewed from the confines of home. Few in Seattle, however, were watching.

Elizabeth, Evans, and a disoriented Jennifer entered the unilluminated outer perimeters of the studio in the shadows of the lighting grid. John saw them and motioned his relief from his anchor post forty feet away.

"I love you," Elizabeth silently mouthed.

Five seconds on the countdown. John took a brisk swig of Evian from the bottle and then gestured for his assistant to help them.

"Good evening, I'm Peter Mather. Seattle, Washington, is under siege. Not since nineteen oh six, when a devastating earthquake destroyed much of San Francisco, has an American city been rendered so helpless. Authorities have confirmed the existence of a massive ozone hole—"

The technical director on the floor made his mark for the switcher upstairs to cut to satellite shots of the burning sun, a huge ring of vomitous coronalike substance fanning out over the Northwest, as seen in a matte window behind Mather.

"—seen hovering here twelve miles above the city. Believed to have drifted south from the Arctic, it has induced—"

A cutaway in the matte window of scientists in a lab covered in protective garb that in turn was swarmed over by ants and beetles.

"—massive behavioral changes in the insects, driven other animals mad and killed off thousands, perhaps millions, of fish and marine mammals. Multiple epidemics are engulfing the city, spread by plants, animals, and humans."

Another cutaway appeared in the matte window of wilted crops seen from low chopper aerials.

"In addition, the crisis has unleashed an unprecedented heat spell with temperatures exceeding—get this—110 degrees."

Mather emphatically and slowly enunciated the number, shaking his head in bewilderment from a rainy Manhattan studio. Outside, in New York, the streets were clean, fertile, washed in April showers. Darkness had set on the city, which seemed to slumber in the passive promise and glow of normality.

Mather continued. "Meanwhile, croplands have been wiped out, food is in short supply, water reserves are contaminated."

The screen then showed Mayor Charlie Higgins's press conference, as Mather lent commentary.

"At noon today Pacific Time Seattle Mayor Charles Higgins instituted martial law. Seen here responding to that declaration is local Seattle reporter John Gage, the man who first broke this story. The mayor has told Seattle residents to stay indoors, out of the sunlight, or to make their way to bomb shelters. Most experts in Seattle agree that evacuation is out of the question. It would take a minimum of ten days."

"Roll in mark five," the technical director said quietly in his headset. The screen showed shaky guerrilla video cover in the matte window of fighting between members of the SWAT team and looters. Four armored national guardsmen, looking like thugs in shining armor, the sun flaring off their steel chest protectors and hoods, were seen firing live ammo on an angry crowd of teenagers, while three other heavily armed policemen kicked and bludgeoned an unidentified victim, who squirmed on his back against the pavement.

"Violence and looting have erupted in parts of the city, which armed riot police and the national guard are attempting to combat. Other cities—Miami, Boston, L.A., New York—have witnessed such street fighting. But Seattle is a virgin in this department. Those in uniform are just now coming to grips with the scope of the problem. And it would appear from the footage that there's no obvious, nor effective, nor even humane approach by which to curb these outbreaks. John, it looks as if there's real irrationality on the streets. Am I correct in saying that most of those in apparent conflict are not actually involved in the looting of stores?"

"Seems to be the case, Peter. Many are simply running. They're not trying to steal anything."

"You and Jeremy Singer are there in the thick of it. Any insights into the behavior we're witnessing?"

Singer started. "I saw it in Vietnam. Folks are scared. They're sick. The police would rather shoot than wait. They're also scared, and probably going nuts under all those protective clothes. I pray that the police exercise restraint in this matter. You can't apply normal standards of culpability or punishment in a time like this. I repeat, people are sick. They're running for their lives. You can't expect them to abide by martial law."

Mather picked up easily on that. "Which brings us to the next major development. This just in from a radio broadcast in Seattle. Apparently, people are not abiding. And only minutes ago, the mayor's press secretary issued a statement suggesting that the earlier martial law proclamation was indeed failing to have its desired effect. We understand that an all-out spontaneous evacuation is taking place at this moment . . ."

Coverage continued behind the anchormen. A freeze-frame close-up of an army tank before a restaurant that was in flames, a sign in the front reading ALL THE LOBSTER YOU CAN EAT! There were no fire trucks anywhere to be seen. Too many larger fires elsewhere. The footage then reverted to the freeways, aerial tracking shots that John's crew had gotten prior to the incident with the dog.

"It's been this way for two days," said John. "There's no avoiding it. People don't know what's happening. And so far science is offering few solutions. Why, for example, has Vancouver, which is three hours to the north, been totally spared? And why didn't the government prepare the populace for this tragic eventuality? There is no indication as to when the ozone hole will lift or where it might go next. It seems to have a mind of its own. Where is the government in all of this?"

Mather responded. "Of course, the mayor did single out two particular chemicals earlier in his press conference, did he not? Methylchloroform and carbon tetrachloride. Both of them, he said, are as yet uncurtailed by any form of legislation."

"That's right, Peter," John continued. "And he also called for a Seattle Protocol Conference, in which world leaders—particularly those from India, China and the Soviet Union —would discuss banning any further production of chlorofluorocarbons."

Singer added a bit of his own homework, looking through a prepared set of notes before him. "There are, of course, dozens of unharmful alternatives to these chemicals. They're no secret. Industry has known about them for a decade." He lifted a sheet of paper from the anchor desk before him. "I've got this comprehensive list of alternatives here that Washington is simply going to have to take the lead in pushing through. Our government is, after all, a major consumer. It has the financial clout to trigger new markets, new products simply through its own massive purchasing power. Industry needs to be prodded toward these alternatives."

"Can you be specific? What sorts of alternatives?" Mather asked.

"New foams, air conditioners, solvents, sterilizers. The list is extensive. I mean, here, for example: a company apparently exploring a chemical found in orange peels that might replace CFC-one thirteen, one of the worst of the chlorofluorocarbons. It's the one used to clean electronic parts. Can you imagine? Orange peels!"

Mather's impatience was palpable. "Orange peels are a good idea. But for now they're not going to curb the mad exodus that's engulfing all roads leading out of the city." He paused, then: "For those of you just tuning in, this is Peter Mather. CB-Nine's ongoing live coverage of the crisis in Seattle. An ozone hole is now hovering over the city. Seattle's international airport is closed and at this time there are hospital estimates of several hundred, perhaps as many as a thousand people known or presumed to be dead. We're going to take a short station break."

As John started to leave the dais, the commercial break held him in thrall. He couldn't imagine what sort of company might expect mileage from Seattle's crisis. He wasn't all that surprised to see melancholy fire truck strobes, lightning, and a confidence-building narrator describing a friendly insurance company. "Had a hurricane? Roof cave in?" There was the sound of a screech preceding a hefty head-on. "Car problems?" Footage of a street opening up,

243

horrifying screams. "Fault line running through the front yard? Don't be shy. Be prepared. We've seen it all. And we're just a phone call away . . ."

John removed the microphone from his lapel, a bit baffled by what he'd just seen. He stepped down from the dais and went over to embrace his family. Jennifer's tears had dried. Elizabeth had gingerly scrubbed her wounds.

"We look like shit!" John said. Mother and daughter both managed a smile. Elizabeth embraced her husband. There was nothing to say.

"We're not leaving anymore," Evans tossed in.

"We'll figure out everything. Don't worry, son," John said. "I'm back up. Evans, get these two war veterans something to drink. In the kitchen. Honey, put her in the talent lounge. There's blankets, couches, pillows. We'll stay here tonight. There should be a medical kit somewhere if you need it."

North of Seattle, five stories belowground, in a high-security armory of steel, sealed by cool darkness and the warm glow of a hundred computers, Felix Girard and colleagues guided the jet pilot, Racer, into the heart of the ozone hole.

"We read you loud and clear, Racer," Girard's cohort, Winston Himes, said. "Get in, detonate, and get the hell out. We show your ambient temperature dropping rapidly. Over."

"How close am I, boys, over?" Racer requested.

"Four minutes, Racer," Winston Himes replied nervously, speaking through his headset.

A small group collected around the computer screens. The region to be seeded—the so-called "chemical containment vessel"—appeared to encompass a thirty-mile radius. It had shrunk down in size. That, coupled with a decreasing temperature, had given Felix and Murphy real cause for optimism. It was a shift, as yet unpredictable. There was wind sheer, the first hint of incoming storm clouds. Murphy's missile was calculated to escalate the transition to a stable state, if Felix had his way. His only doubt was

Willard, whose warnings resided in his mind like a dark force he couldn't shake. A pointed finger.

Others around them had picked up on a thin, as yet unspoken ray of hope. Clouds meant weather. And weather was what they'd been praying for. Most of the men in this flight control room were young, fresh out of military academies; they virtually lived here. These boys had all but forgotten the world outside. Most had not even stepped into the swirling shadows of dust and sun-crisp heat that had buffeted the earth upstairs for nearly a week.

The occupants of this military depot slept in steel cocoons along corridors that were hermetically air fortified. Most of them were navigators, land based. Others were pilots, trained on the military's secret high-altitude spy planes.

There was no war fever here. It was the technology that turned them on. The young men flew and charted these jets with consummate grace, and charted courses with the mathematical tyranny of a Bobby Fisher. Racer was the oldest, most experienced pilot among them. His joy in life was stoked at about 50,000 feet and then it just got better and better. Racer was up there now, ready to shit in his pants.

Girard and crew heard a strange croaking sound.

"Racer? Racer? Talk to me, goddamnit!" Felix couldn't stand the tension any longer.

Racer rapped his helmet, shook his head. "It's fogged up, I can't . . ." His voice stopped suddenly.

"What is it, Racer?"

"I don't . . . it's beautiful up here. You're not gonna believe this, but there's"—he ogled with a whine between pain and bewilderment—"this broad, outside—my God, she's bitchin'!"

"He's losing it," said Himes.

Felix's arms cloaked his face. This can't be happening, he thought.

"Racer, do not remove your helmet. Do you understand?" Haskel Murphy said adamantly, sitting beside the baleful Felix and Himes. Haskel read enormous chlorine levels and a depletion rate of almost 100 percent. The aircraft windows were not sufficiently multiplexed and tinted to deflect that level of nearly supernova-quality cosmic rays.

In the cockpit, Racer stared fixedly at the most attractive blond he'd seen in years. And damned if she wasn't naked! Standing atop thin puddles of stratospheric mist like a veritable angel in heat. She beckoned the aircraft to park beside her.

Racer should have known better, of course. He was a veteran of every species of hallucination and high-altitude hypoxia. But he'd had too much sun. And Murphy sensed it. Furthermore, the poor guy had a hard-on pressing insistently up against the silk and mylar undergarments of his flight suit. He squirmed in his seat, ready to eject.

"Racer! Listen to me!" Murphy said, striving for methodical calm.

But Racer was too distracted to respond. His eyes cleaved to the vision before him. He was traveling at 500 knots but was fully prepared to exit the aircraft, gamboling right out into the perceived zephyr of waiting arms, tits, and ass.

"He's there. He's got to detonate it—we can't do it from here," Murphy confided urgently in his two dour compatriots. The three men leaned against the radar screen.

"Talk him through it, for chrissakes," Felix rejoined, leaning on Himes.

"Now take note, Jack!" Himes began. He'd guided Racer through a good hundred missions in the past ten years. The two men trusted one another like father and son.

"Uh-huh—" Racer's voice quavered. Its presence was nonaligned, distant, purgatorial. Something had happened to him from which those in the control room were hopelessly blacked out.

"You're going to do exactly what I tell you, understand?" Himes continued. "And then you're going to make a sweep back to base at full throttle. There is no woman. You are suffering from ultraviolet. Ignore it, Racer, do you hear me? Is your helmet on?"

"Took it off." The voice was struggling. Racer sounded like a little boy.

Himes wiped the sweat off his face. "Jesus fucking . . ." He stopped himself and whispered to his cohorts, "I've never seen him lose it before."

"Get back to him," Girard ordered.

"Put your helmet back on, Jack," Himes resumed. "Okay? Is it on?"

"He's deviating from the course, sir," a young lieutenant navigator at the computer terminal noted. "Ten miles and still traveling."

Himes spoke firmly and quietly. "Racer, do you hear me?"

There was abysmal silence. All faces turned to the radar screen. Continued silence.

"Racer!!"

"Yeah . . ." Racer's response was clouded and scared.

"Put your helmet back on."

They waited. Nothing. Racer's eyes had been dulled, stung with the glass-sharp residuum of intangible light. He squeezed them like lemons only to suffer the burning beneath the dripping of tears. The burning went all the way up his optic nerves, touching the brain core, seizing everything. His voice was thick, garbled, salt-mouth. Then came a feeble "Okay."

Those in the control center gave a collective sigh.

"Now you're off course. We need you to break speed to three hundred knots and turn twenty-two degrees south by southwest. It's on your chart. Do it. Now!"

"He's hitting it," the navigator said anxiously.

Thank God, Felix thought, trembling.

Murphy reminded Himes of the little blue glowing button on Racer's most forward console. Hard to miss. His gloved hand had only to push the button. "Tell him!" Murphy said, frazzled. Six months of work went into that button. "Tell him right now!"

Himes took Racer through the steps. "Ground zero is coming up, Jack, T minus nine seconds, eight seconds, seven, six, five, four—"

"Another object!" the navigator shouted.

"Abort, abort. Hold on, Jack!"

"Huh?" Racer's startled half-reply sounded like pleading, enfeebled and confused. He didn't need yet another counterdirective. He was already straining his limit.

"You can't abort!" Murphy shouted. "Are you crazy?"

They didn't dare ask him what he saw. The screen showed a blip moving at nearly eight hundred knots. There was no communication with Sea-Tac. The tower was closed down. All flights had been detoured.

"I'll be a sonofabitch," Himes mumbled, waffling between cues and uncertainties.

The men eyed each other with no time to think.

Felix popped the obvious query. "Altitude?"

"Forty-eight thousand feet and descending fast," the lieutenant said, adroitly marking the direction in grease pencil on the monitor coverlet. "North by northeast across Canada, looks like. Could be a Concorde. I think she's preparing to land in Vancouver. Rapid descent. She's in trouble."

Himes got Vancouver's control tower on the phone. They had no such confirmation. They too were tracking the incoming plane but had had no success so far in communicating with the cabin. Furthermore, Vancouver had no suitable landing site, if indeed it was a Concorde.

The men looked at one another with shared horror. If it was what it appeared to be, the plane was on autopilot and she'd remain on autopilot until she crashed. There was nothing anybody could do.

"Swing back into position, Jack," Himes ordered.

There was a pause, infinitely long, and then a response. Racer was laboring hard, they had no idea how hard, down below. It was obvious that he could scarcely hear or understand.

"He's moving at ten, twenty G's," the young navigator stated for all present.

"That's gotta be tough," Felix Girard said.

Up above, Racer sped through a realm of staggering glare, heat, cancer-causing penetration. This man was the best. He could jump over the moon if given a chance. But now he had been reduced to hanging on for all he was worth.

"Got it," came the flexing mumble.

"He's there," cried Himes, seeing the turnaround on the radar.

"Okay. Bring him to T minus nine vector . . . south by southeast, Jack, five degrees . . . that's it . . . cool and easy, nice, we're showing T minus nine seconds, Racer, eight seconds, seven, six, five, four, three, two, hit it, Jack!"

"Missile jettisoned. Time to implosion four seconds, three, two—" The third radar blip vanished. "Done!"

"All right!"

There was applause all around. "Get him home, Wince," Girard said, blowing out air.

Murphy's job had just begun. He was following the black box instrument below the ER-2 jet's wing second by second. So far nothing had happened. There was no change in the ozone depletion rate. Once the instrument was returned to the military base, Murphy would expose the sensitive instruments to the ground level column of air directly above. He'd be able to measure the depletion differences between low and high altitude levels. It might take hours before they knew anything definitive. Felix sat down. His stomach couldn't handle this.

"How you feeling, Jack?" Himes said.

Jack was coming down, slowing into fifty thousand feet and circling at sixty miles from the base.

"I hurt bad. Can't see. I got to get out of my suit." He was doubling over inside with paresthesia—a thousand unreachable pinpricks, itches, like spiders crawling all over him.

At eight minutes before Racer's landing, men were already at the hangar doors, but this time there was no waiting outside. Once the jet touched down, they'd run out to support the wings. Murphy and Felix waited. It could be a long night. And it was their only chance.

The ER-2 landed safely—by Braille, Racer told them later. Murphy stayed at the computer while Felix and Himes went out to escort the pilot to sick bay. He looked like hell. There were third-degree burn blisters all over his face. His eyes were glazed, slow, unblinking. His lips had cracked and were oozing blood. Around his nose, angry lesions suppurated in a contagion of injury and pain.

"It's a miracle he got back here," the base surgeon told Girard and Himes outside the intensive care unit. "I'm going to be straight with you. I know he was your best pilot."

"Was?"

"I'm sorry, gentlemen, but this man will never see again."

"It was so beautiful!" he kept on muttering, falling in heavenly cartwheels down the windy shaft into the vortex of narcotic-induced sleep.

Down below, inside the command room where Himes had guided Racer home, the phone rang and the lieutenant base navigator picked up. Murphy saw the young man's face stiffen.

"There's been a terrible tragedy at Vancouver International," he said quietly. They'd all guessed correctly. It was a ghost ship, en route to London. Passengers and crew had perished while passing through the hole. They'd all fried inside. The captain had managed to execute autopilot but the equipment malfunctioned.

The insects were dead, burned and whittled into ash and carapace. Crops throughout the Seattle region, like those up and down British Columbia and the Yukon, were the color and consistency of dust. It meant relief for those sleeping at home tonight, this absence of midges and mites and ants and nameless grubs—relief for those caught up in the great migration, the tens of thousands of residents who by ten thirty this night were behind the wheel, slumped and twisted with fatigue along roadbeds, moving aimlessly at three, four, five miles an hour in the unrelenting streams of headlights, heading anywhere but back to Seattle.

John's reserves were finished. He lay against his wife on the floor, their heads together atop pillows from home. The kids shared the couch. A dozen other KCBD employees and their families sprawled across the uncomfortable semidarkness of the talent lounge.

Downstairs in the studio, Singer continued feeding coverage. Mather was still going strong in New York, where it was

1:30 A.M. What does he have to worry about, Singer thought, between live studio interviews with Willard, an Atlanta Disease Control specialist, and Emmet Jones. Mather and Singer had their own silent war going, a sort of marathon of who could remain lucid the longest throughout the night. John had already thrown in the towel. He was dead to the world.

There was a plan in place. The Needle. A safe haven overlooking the battleground. John and his crew had talked about it late in the afternoon, on their way out to the glacier. A place where John could continue to report the news in isolation, with hoped-for immunity.

While John and his family tried to get some shut-eye, MacIntyre and Wendy finished checking the gear down in the garage, preparing for the shoot atop the Needle. They hadn't slept. Charging batteries. Rolling seven hundred feet of coaxial cable onto reels. They knew they'd need it for the distance between the restaurant on top and the microwave unit on the van down at street level.

Upstairs in the lounge, John lay awake staring into space, hearing distant sirens out in the darkness. He turned to his wife. She was also awake. "Liz, I was just thinking." He paused, and put his fingers lightly to her cheek.

"About what?" she murmured, listening for the erratic breathing of her daughter, whose arm she gently held with one hand. The other hand rested upon her husband's cheek, lightly so as not to hurt the area around his eyes.

"We've been married a long time."

"Yes, we have."

"I've wanted us to—to do something significant, for ourselves."

"Significant?"

"I mean something great, a dream, what we've always prevented ourselves from doing. Break away, to do something different." He was speaking in rustles and sighs.

"Such as?"

"Move."

"Good. Where?"

"The Seychelles. Bora Bora."

"Um—I don't know."

"Kauai."

"What would we do all day?" She muttered, half teasing. A side of her thought they were all dying and she was happy they were dying together. She was tired, ready and willing to dream. Her eyes were burned. Her cheeks, like those of her children, showed the soldered red of solar molestation. Her headache had not gone away since the Queen Charlottes. She wondered what Local Joe was doing at this moment.

"Sleep on the beach under a colored parasol," John said, breaking in on her thoughts.

"Can we have room service?"

"Absolutely. Better yet, a Hawaiian villa in the hills. Grape arbors. Coconuts. Crumbling bricks. A barking dog, just like Wallace, tail wagging."

"Poor Wallace," she groaned.

"I know. I loved that little guy." His mind went to the incident on the freeway and he started to convey the horror to his wife. "I didn't tell you. There was a dog, on the freeway. I tried to save it . . ."

She grasped his look. "Don't—stop! I don't want to hear it!" She put her hands to her ears. John had a way of always sharing the worst with her. His way, she assumed, of ameliorating wounds—by spreading around the pain. It wasn't her style.

John thought better of divulging any more. He continued to dream. "Mellow scented air. The sound of crickets at night mingling with the waves, one upon the other. Do you see it? Hear it?"

"And those olives. Ohhh—"

"Oil, cold tomatoes."

"Yes. And the goat cheese. Don't forget—"

"Five kinds of cheeses, melted, Dijon mustard."

"A hammock."

"Fucking in the hammock! Eyeing lazily the four horizons."

"The kids are asleep."

"By that time they'll also be fucking."

"You're terrible," she giggled.

"Mom?" Jennifer said, waking from her own purgatory. She took a deep, labored breath, and then groaned dangerously.

Elizabeth stroked her head. "Go back to sleep, darling."

Evans got up suddenly.

"Where are you going?" John asked.

"Vending machine. I want a doughnut and apple juice. You got six quarters?"

Evans wandered downstairs through the emptied corridors of KCBD. He saw a stranger, a large man who looked lost. Evans thought to ask him where the vending machines were, then changed his mind. He walked all the way up to the front security desk and was led to the nearly empty machines. He found some stale chocolate-chip cookies and a mixed-fruit drink in a wax container. Dinner.

On his return, Evans ran into the detective, Rubin. It was after midnight.

"Who are you?" the detective asked.

Evans didn't know he was speaking with a cop. Rubin wore no badge. "Evans," he said, tired.

"Evans who?" the cop asked.

"My dad's the producer here. John Gage."

"He's the man I'm lookin' for. You want to take me to him?"

"What do you want him for?"

"I'm a cop."

"You got ID?" Evans couldn't be too careful.

Rubin was impressed. He took out his wallet and by the flashlight in his hand proved who he was to the young skeptic.

They went up the stairs together.

"Dad," Evans whispered.

"Mr. Gage, got a minute?"

John's hand had been on Elizabeth's belly. She had a hunch and wanted his psychic confirmation, which he'd given, as much from support as diagnosis. It left him utterly bewildered. There was no way he wanted his family with him up in the Needle. It could be dangerous. They had to get out of town. On the other hand, he wasn't sure how wise it was to send his possibly pregnant wife and very sick daughter off alone, though he had every confidence in Evans.

"We've got a match on the prints," detective Rubin said.

"D'you tell Willard?"

"I wanted to talk with you first."

Rubin and John stepped outside the door.

"Who was he?" John asked.

The detective handed him a fax containing copies of fingerprints, a photograph, and description of the mug. A strange cross between Lino Ventura and Tatsuya Nakadai. Tanned, brazen not-bad looks, thick neck, bald. A brutal-looking tough.

"Bray Morehall's the name. We think. Used to be an operative for the CIA in Central America. Shady doings. Knows a lot of people. Could probably call in any number of owed favors. Made professional drops, and probably a few hits, for the Colombian cartels. Showed up in Noriega's Panama. Lost his various clearances when he was convicted of raping a girl with cerebral palsy at a military hospital in Washington, where he himself was recovering from injuries allegedly received in the line of duty. Supposedly, Noriega's ouster. Only we found it wasn't that. No bullet wounds in this freak. But gerbils."

"I don't understand?"

"You'll excuse me, but I thought you'd like to know what sort of person or persons we're dealing with here. The guy got his sexual kicks from many sources, including stuffing baby gerbils in a condom, greasing it down, tying it off, and inserting it up his anus."

John couldn't even respond.

"As the poor gerbils struggled and died, his sphincter muscles essentially jacked off. His way of getting a buzz. Only *this* time he couldn't get the condom out and he found himself down there in Panama with dead gerbils up his ass. Two days later they pulled them out up north. And that same night he raped the girl. He was a real sex maniac. She was a virgin. Nineteen years old. Couldn't move, couldn't speak. He denied penetration. Said her legs were tightly locked and he couldn't find the hole to stick it in.

"He had one count of indecent exposure, which was then dropped because of his alleged longtime 'superior' record of government service and he being a first-time sexual offender. The gerbils business worked right into his court. His attorney attributed his client's behavior to the stress of undercover work. Morehall went to work for a company in Mexico. Offshore Chemicals. Ring a bell?"

"Yeah. Sure does." John was still stuck on the image of gerbils. "That's just the most disgusting thing I've ever heard. My little girl had a pet gerbil once. What kind of pervert?"

"Anyway, Mr. Gage, we may have our link to Washington. It seems Offshore Chemicals had hired this Morehall because of a continuing association with—get this—James Wenders."

"Wenders? Wenders?" A flashing light went off in John's head. "James Wenders, friend of Frank Radino? New Jersey gubernatorial campaign, election-rigging scandal, etcetera? That's the White House."

"You got it. Everyone was cleared. Radino, needless to say, went on to bigger and better things. Wenders went to the Defense Department. Some deep tunnel somewhere. Interagency work. They recycled him to Intelligence. The guy knows a lot of people. For the last three years his beat has been Latin America."

"And the pilot? The second mystery figure?"

"Vanished. I don't think he's coming back to Seattle in the very near future. We've got an all-points bulletin out for a stray chopper. We've already checked Happy Valley Chemicals to see if he'd parked it there. Haven't actually alerted the company to any investigation—just poked around. No such luck. Most had already split. But we'll catch him."

"You do good work, detective."

"You too, Mr. Gage."

CHAPTER 24

FRIDAY MORNING

KCBD and CB-9 stopped broadcasting at 2:00 A.M. By that time most of the daytime people had crashed. Late-night technicians continued to hold down the beleaguered fort and facilitate a transmission fraught with signal disorders.

Singer checked in on Willard, whom he found slumped over in his wheelchair, seated before a monitor still turned on in one of the outer lounges. A Coke bottle lay next to him, a bag of potato chips rested on his belly. He was sound asleep.

A good man, Singer thought.

Singer went upstairs and stepped between a dozen bedrolls sprawled out on the floor of the talent lounge. He found John and roused him from sleep. "If you're gonna make it to the Needle, I suggest you get your crew together before sunrise. You got my meaning?"

John had managed to catch some legitimate slumber for an hour or two. Now, awake again, it all came back. He moaned, overloaded. A week ago at this time he'd been trying to finish a drug story. He could hardly believe what had happened since.

John immediately looked over at his daughter. It wasn't the same Jennifer. Her face was horribly swollen, chicken pox-like welts all over her neck and arms. Her breathing was checked and raspy.

256

Singer paused, sharing John's dilemma. "We don't have enough food for everybody. Vending machine's dry. Can't drink the water here. Something's wrong with it. We got a problem," Singer said forthrightly.

Both men could faintly hear rumbles outside, distant gunfire, far-off sirens. But the din of freeway traffic had definitely died down. And so had the temperature.

"I don't believe it," John exhaled. "I'm not hot. You been outside?"

"Yep. Sixty degrees. Clouds to boot. I don't know what it means. Can't get a weather report."

"What time is it?"

"Three twenty."

"Honey?"

"What is it?" Elizabeth said, snapping into attention from out of sleep. She turned over, creases all over the left side of her face.

Evans, who'd slept between his mother and Jennifer, rubbed his eyes sleepily, waking up. "Jennifer's breathing funny, you guys," he said.

Elizabeth cradled her daughter. "Oh, boy . . ."

"You got to get her to a doctor," Singer exhorted.

"You saw All City Hospital. No way," John retorted.

"Then get 'em out! Traffic's diminished. I suggest Vancouver."

Now the family was up, whispering in fast attuned strategy. John held his wife as Elizabeth tried helplessly to comfort Jennifer, but she was sinking fast. And something else. Elizabeth controlled her urge to shriek: her little baby's hair was falling out! Even the color had changed. It was a gray, moldy color.

"Oh, my God, John!"

Elizabeth's thoughts were scattered. "Okay, okay, baby," she said. "Mommy's here." Elizabeth looked at her husband. "Here's what—uh—we're gonna get our things together. The car's windows are broken. John, is there another vehicle? Vancouver. We know people in Vancouver . . ."

"The Mochs," he said, standing up.

"They have a big house," Elizabeth affirmed, quickly

coming up with some kind of plan. Her daughter was aging rapidly right in front of them. "Vancouver, of course!" She pleaded with those around her, with John, with Evans, Jeremy Singer, with God.

John was stunned by his predicament. He looked first at Jennifer, then at his wife. Evans sat on the couch slowly futzing with his shoelaces, afraid to confront the situation.

Singer appreciated John's dilemma. "You got to give it up, John," he said.

John looked at him, ready to break open.

Elizabeth understood for the first time her husband's sense of commitment. It hadn't ever meant anything before, not in terms of the family.

She began to shake her head while thoughts traversed the distance between them, unspoken.

"We can do it," she said.

Finally, John avowed his duty as he perceived it. "I've got to finish here," he said painfully. "I mean, don't you think?" He looked at Elizabeth.

She tried to soften the decision for her husband. She knew that she was, after all, the one who had first forced his attention to the story, styled him a journalist with integrity. "Forget propriety. This is not about love or chivalry. You've got to do what's right."

"What's right?" he asked, pleading for a clear directive.

Elizabeth shook her head. She didn't know. She was holding back tears, thinking about Kauai, those dreams.

"We'll be okay, Dad," Evans said, breaking the hiatus.

"Okay. Ten seconds." John closed his eyes, tensed his open jaw, then made his decision. "It's not a choice," he deliberated out loud. "I'm taking the crew to the Needle. We'll continue reporting this thing. It'll be safe up there. Safe enough, I imagine. I know too much. This is too big." He knew that everything was going to work against him in this. And there was absolutely nothing he could do but see it through. The resolution came instantly, beyond impediment.

Singer looked at John's wife, but he wasn't about to throw in an opinion on either side.

"There's nothing private here," John declared, seeing the bind they'd put his boss in. "I guess that's my decision."

Elizabeth broke open and sobbed. John sat down and held her. She had no strength to fight the decision, caving in to the inevitable.

"Okay, then," Singer said. "Loder's in my office. He already called over there. Plenty of food and drink. One man, a bartender, stayed behind. Place has been closed ever since the bird incident. The windows up top are still broken out. Guy's name's Jason. He hasn't been down below all week. Assumes the guards will have stayed. Anyway, he knows the layout and told Loder enough to get you folks up there. You can either run cable through the elevator shaft or drop it out the window direct to the van. Whatever works. Up-link from the portable microwave. Basic configuration. Beam it up **anyw**here midwest and the station tower'll pick her up. We've done it before. I spoke with Mather's executive producer about a half hour ago. They want to start broadcasting at seven o'clock, about half-hour from now. I'd like you up and running if possible by eight their time. That gives you less than an hour. You're gonna have to move your ass. We've still got enough crew support here for at least another day. Can you do it?"

"What about the food and water business for all of you staying on here?" John asked.

"Don't worry about us. I'll send an assistant to loot and pillage if that's what it takes. Can you do it?"

"I'm here, aren't I?"

Elizabeth looked up at her husband. Suddenly, his show of professional valor made her crazy.

"You're really staying?" Elizabeth recoiled.

John hesitated.

"This is my fault!" she burst. "I got you hooked on this thing. John. This could be our only chance."

"I've got to—"

He considered his words. The frustration and the well-founded paranoia had been building for days. His leg hurt. His eyes and skin throbbed. He'd been penetrated by the sun. His insides were traumatized and he could feel it everywhere. Last night, he worried about the future. He knew they'd all taken intense amounts of ultraviolet radiation. But now, he was only worried about today. Making today right.

"What about our child!" Elizabeth said.

John shook his head. Closed his eyes.

Elizabeth was incensed now. "You're just like the rest of them. Stupid. Shit."

"I am not like anybody. Liz, calm down!" He tried fecklessly to touch her.

"Get away from me!" she cursed.

"Jesus, Liz—"

"Don't Jesus Liz me, goddamnit. You'd place your fucking career, this goddamned idiotic business of television before your family? Your little girl? At a time like this? Have you lost all sense of—of sanity! . . . John!"

John was wobbling, losing the confidence he'd only just mustered moments before.

"You know, John . . ." Singer started.

"No. Stop! Now you listen." He forced Elizabeth's hands into his own hands. He was thinking carefully, enunciating with the full measure of his beliefs, beliefs he'd never voiced before.

"You talk sanity? Was Andy Otero or Stan's death sanity? Or my nearly getting killed? Was that sane, huh? You weren't there. You don't know what it's like to have a man point a gun at your head. We've uncovered a story that nobody's admitting. People have been murdered. People, lots of people, have died and are dying. There's been a cover-up, sabotage.

"This is not a game. This is not about decency. This is not about ego, or about just another story. This is the rest of our lives we're talking about. I'm not passing the ball. We've all been through it. But someone's got to be accountable. The public deserves that at least. We all deserve it. Don't you see? Our daughter needs to get out of Seattle. She needs to get to a good doctor. The best. It's not going to happen at All City. We know that. It's not going to happen anywhere within a hundred miles. Vancouver. You go. I stay."

There was silence now. Elizabeth did not believe in her man. She believed in her family. John had become a traitor to that. A moment later she thought, he was no traitor. Slowly, her perception of his stupidity softened.

Finally, Evans spoke up. "Maybe you're right, Dad," he said, breaking the infernal conflict in a hushed demonstration of meager support for his father.

Singer, John, and Elizabeth stared at one another.

Elizabeth wanted to scream. Her little girl was dying. But now she knew what John had said was perhaps true.

"We're leaving!" she finally said hoarsely, unavailingly angered by the selfish hint of it but willing to concede. She brushed the hair out of her face, wiped the tears and now came back with a surge of strength. "It's best the three of us run for it. You do what you have to do. I understand . . . I do."

Others were now up in the lounge, family members of KCBD employees who'd spent the night there, near their loved ones, rather than face the insect hell of the neighborhoods. Pale beams from two flashlights grazed against various human clusters. "What is it, what's wrong?" a voice shouted out toward the chiaroscuro of movement.

"It's okay. Go back to sleep," Singer cautioned, still whispering.

John and his family moved downstairs. Loder, MacIntyre, and Wendy were there in the garage. The van was loaded. Singer volunteered his own Volvo for Elizabeth and the kids. It had a car phone, a loaded Beretta under the driver's seat, and a tank three-quarters full.

"The gun's really loaded?" Evans inquired.

"You know how to use it?" Singer asked, throwing caution to the wind.

"Yeah." Evans didn't flinch. He'd been skeet shooting once.

John carried Jennifer in his arms out into the night air. She was covered in a blanket. There was no bird, no insect, just the scintillating breeze against wounded faces and injured eyes. Above, on the freeway overpass, a continuous rush of traffic made its dire trail. John laid his little girl down on the backseat. Elizabeth handed him pillows for her head. One of the pillows had come from Jennifer's own bed, embroidered by her grandmother for her tenth birthday. It was the last thing Elizabeth had thought to retrieve from the house before they'd evacuated.

"Get on the freeway and just keep going until you're there," John said collectedly. His lips were pursed. The two parents stared at their child. She was only half awake. She mumbled facedown into the pillow. She'd wet herself. John took her hand and kissed it. There were impossible strikes against him, flashes of pain that showed all over his face. Yet he held firm.

Elizabeth caught John's dilemma. It was a moral dilemma and he was acting courageously. She didn't know if he was right, but she now came round toward grudging respect for what he was doing.

"Here's the telephone number of the bar in the Needle. This is where you can reach me."

"Don't pick up any stray women," she said, forcing the least spark from utter desolation. She was still crying.

"You take care of the two ladies, mister," he told Evans, hugging the boy. "Enough. Go. I'll see you in Vancouver."

John and Singer watched the Gage family disappear into the darkness down Sixth Street, heading toward the Dearborn on ramp to Route 5. Empty steam rose up from manholes in the road. A few lone flashing lights from an earlier fire cleanup pierced the sky. The streets were empty, save for an occasional corpse and multicar wrecks.

"I have no idea if I've done the right thing," he admitted to Singer.

The crew found it relatively easy to snake its way across downtown, past City Hall, the library, the statue of Chief Seattle, to the Needle. The city seemed to have changed. It was getting cold.

They parked, unloaded, and shouldered the gear, unraveling the eighth of an inch coaxial cable.

"We've got good videotape and enough batteries to last us a whole day," Wendy said. She breathed in the chilled air and smelled the sound. Her mind was fresh, despite no sleep. The Space Needle was dark.

"I say do it out the window," MacIntyre volunteered, looking up toward the cloudy darkness. The Needle was silhouetted against the overcast predawn.

Loder had been told where to find the emergency backup power box for the elevators and lights and telephones. The building was locked. He used a hatchet from the back of the van and smashed in the glass. Feeling for the doorknob and finding none, he knocked out the whole glass facade and they all walked through.

Carrying large L. L. Bean camping lights suspended from handles, a hatchet in one hand, and his hand-written notes in the other, Loder made his way to the first door headed down to the stairs, and began examining a causeway of power boxes. Far more than he had counted on.

He heard a noise somewhere behind him.

"John? That you?"

There was no response. Loder continued, flipping every switch in sight. He cursed himself for taking inadequate notes and not asking enough questions.

He continued down a long underground hallway, surrounded by pipes and hissing and dripping water. There had been a leak. Loder got good and lost in the darkness. He was starting to freak out. He retraced his steps, easy enough, along the corridor. All the way back. *There!* A door he'd missed. He entered. Bingo!

Loder proceeded to the large gray box Jason had described and opened it. It was like a telephone switchboard. There were more wires than in the engineering bay at the station. He zeroed in on the master switch—a big, stand-alone red lever—and flipped it up.

The light startled him, but more so the pain. It consumed his back, then his neck. He felt his eyes twist inward, twist all the way into darkness. The blood avalanched through his head until he felt his breath collect at the edge of a canyon. A canyon of darkness. In the stunted instant of unspeakable pressure and stinging pain, he closed his eyes and drifted out into space, falling over the canyon.

The hatchet fell from his hands. Loder collapsed against

the concrete, his hands blindly straining at his back, where the pain had penetrated.

"Let's get going," John said, anxious to be set up in time. "Loder'll follow." John was still benumbed by the image of Jennifer huddled facedown in the backseat, lying very still. Perhaps, mercifully, she was unaware of what was happening now. He begged for that.

Wendy and MacIntyre lugged the coaxial cable reel through the shattered glass facade, into the elevator, and up to the top of the Needle. John carried the mountain pack with the Betacam. Both Wendy and MacIntyre would go back down for the audio gear and assemble the microwave hookups.

Old man Jason was there to meet them at the restaurant. "How you all this mornin'? And you must be the Mr. Loder I spoke with?"

"He's on his way. I'm John Gage."

"Why you sure are! I recognize you. You're the ones had that run-in with the birds here last week. I see you all the time on the tube."

Jason had doffed his normal black tie and cummerbund, the elegant attire in which he'd volunteered to serve up mirth and spirits for the past forty of his years.

"No other view quite like it in the world," he said with the sonority of prayer. "Usually, that is."

Traffic on I-5 was bumper to bumper at four in the morning. After an hour of parlous maneuvering through traffic, Elizabeth had scarcely gotten them to Mountlake Terrace, ten miles north of the city. Evans saw black bears feeding on the devastated remains of a produce truck along the side of the freeway. Stranded motorists had left broken-down vehicles and wandered into oncoming traffic. Remains of pandemonium and guerrilla warfare tactics were visible everywhere. If he ever made it to driver education class at school, Evans would be amply prepared for the very worst, he figured.

Elizabeth knew they'd never get to Vancouver before sunrise. In fact, at this rate, they'd be on the road all day. The goggles, flimsily constructed, had ceased to counteract the sun's intense rays two days before. Elizabeth knew their only chance was the ferry. They could get a boat and head to Victoria.

Evans looked back and leaned over the seat. "Mom?"

"What?"

"I think we better stop."

Elizabeth followed Evans's eyes to the backseat.

"Oh, no . . . *No!*"

Jennifer was dead.

She pulled off onto a small forested road. Water was streaming everywhere. Up ahead, a river was flooding its banks. She took out a piece of paper from her purse on which she'd written her husband's barroom number atop the Needle. She tried to dial, using the push-button car phone, but her fingers were too unsteady just then. She gave the number to Evans. He called.

At the Needle restaurant, Jason answered the phone, then got John's attention. "Mr. Gage, got a woman here claimin' to be your wife."

He left MacIntyre, who was busy unraveling coaxial cable out the window. Wendy had gone back down to receive it.

"Where are you?" asked John.

The dam burst inside Elizabeth, as she tried to explain their situation to her husband—that they were now a family of three.

John tried to halt the convulsive flow of her sorrow as she graphically outlined their problem, the congestion, the impossibility of their ever getting anywhere near Vancouver, even of reaching the ferry for Victoria.

"Elizabeth, Elizabeth, listen to me. Is Evans with you? Okay. You're going to leave her covered. You're going to take back roads. It was a bad idea. Come back immediately. When you're at the front door of the building, ring up. You'll see the van parked out front and the plate-glass window shattered. Come through there. You got that? Put Evans on, sweetheart. I love you. Do you hear me?" He knew Elizabeth had stopped listening.

Evans was holding back. He knew he had to be the one to get them out of this. Somehow—and he didn't quite understand it himself yet—the dead body of his sister lying there on the backseat did not affect him in an overwhelming way. He sort of took it as a natural consequence of everything.

"Dad?" Evans was in control.

"Okay, son. I know, I know. Now listen to me. Do not touch your sister. Do you hear me? She could be, well, you know, contagious. You watch your mother's driving. You're going to drive back on side roads to the Needle. I'm up top. You're going to park at the bottom, before the front door. There's nobody guarding the place. The glass is shattered. You're going to call me on the mobile phone when you're there. I'll come down and meet you at the elevators. You got that?"

"Yeah, Dad."

"Put Mom back on. . . . Liz, Liz! I'm so sorry, sweetheart. We're going to have another. Yes. We are! Jennifer's happy now, Liz. We have to believe that."

John put down the phone and collapsed in a chair. His fingernails were digging into his thighs.

Jeremy Singer was sitting in the anchorman's chair on the dais in the studio at KCBD. The morning broadcast had begun. Over his shoulder, in the matte video window, the image from New York rolled. Singer stared directly at the camera. It would be his turn to speak any minute. First, his coanchor commenced the newscast.

"Good morning. I'm Peter Mather. The crisis in Seattle continues. Throughout the day we'll be bringing you live coverage of what is now being described as the worst natural disaster in U.S. history."

Mather's cohost this morning, the striking Diane Ludwig, countered with what was meant to be an optimistic twist on events. The affirmation was accented by her luscious tonality with which she had notably seduced presidents and dictators alike.

"It is worth remembering, I suppose, that there have been far worse catastrophes in recent years. In terms of keeping this in its proper perspective."

Mather maintained that odious good cheer of the veteran, an unimpeachable veteran, immune to emotion. "For instance?"

"I'm thinking of the devastating Chinese earthquake in nineteen seventy-six that leveled the industrial city of Tangshan and caused considerable damage in Beijing and Tientsin."

"That's right. And didn't nearly a million people die in that quake, Diane?"

"Sure did. And then let us not forget the horrible Armenian quakes . . ."

Singer listened to the bantering New York journalists with a mounting nausea. John Gage's story, the one he'd fought for, nearly died for, stayed behind for was the very story Peter Mather had, so far, refused to acknowledge. But not just Mather, Singer thought; the many two-bit whores and three-bit morons in management, in politics, God knows where else. Natural disaster? Try *unnatural* disaster, you fuckers, Singer resolved. Today, he declared to himself, the record needed to be set straight. He had learned something from John Gage.

He tested his connection with John through headsets. A phone patch had been implemented that connected the outside line to the live studio switcher. John could speak directly on-air with Singer.

"I hear you, Jeremy. Do you hear me?" John now utterly suppressed the realization that little Jennifer was gone. He was working somehow above the knowledge, around it. Stranded atop pain.

"Loud and clear," Singer said.

Jason sensed it, though. "You want somethin' to eat? Kitchen's right around back."

"Thanks. No." Then: "That where you've been sleeping?"

"Right next to the refrigerators. Only thing that put out any cold air this whole week," the old man admitted. "Got my cot all rolled out nice like. Feels like we won't be needin' air conditionin' any longer, though. Ain't that a kick! I guess that's how she works."

"How *who* works?" John asked.

"Earth, o' course."

John could see he'd been around.

He also noticed changes quickly taking place outside. The sun had been obscured earlier in the morning by the first heavy clouds in three weeks. By five o'clock the temperature was fifty-one degrees and dropping. Loder had mentioned it to John and the crew while driving over in the van. It was no small miracle.

North of Seattle, from their bunker, Haskel Murphy and Felix Girard conferred with the morning's National Weather Satellite data and compared notes with ozone-depletion measurements tallied throughout the night. At fifty thousand feet it was snowing hard. And the snow was already turning to drizzle over northern portions of the state. The hole had contracted to little more than a small anomaly, a minor gash in the sky. It barely registered.

Meanwhile, a second major storm front was moving rapidly to the south out of the Coast Range of British Columbia. The men were elated. Neither would ever truly know the real cause of this deliverance. Oxides of nitrogen? Or some unexplainable fluke? Nor would they be at liberty to divulge the particulars of Racer's final mission.

Surrounded by others who had been in on the navigation of Racer's craft and the maintenance throughout the night of the computer array, Felix popped the first cork on a surprisingly good bottle of French champagne. If nothing else, this bunker was excellent for preserving spirits. All present toasted to what Felix knew, but would never admit, was sheer luck. He okay'd a phone call from NSB's press secretary.

Admiral Brewster and then Peter Mather would be the first two to know out in the real world.

* * *

MacIntyre went down to street level to set up the microwave connection. Wendy was already down there getting the audio gear.

At KCBD, Singer had Mather's continuing video in his matte. The New York anchorman had summarized the leading developments, flushed with the news, just in from NSB—that a mission to seed the ozone hole performed late yesterday appeared to have been successful. The temperature was plummeting and all indications suggested that the levels of ozone depletion were almost normal. It was cause for jubilation. NSB had apparently saved the day. Felix would be a hero.

Those on the studio floor at KCBD looked at one another and began to shake with laughter. There seemed to be relief coming in from callers and well-wishers all over the country. The whole mood had changed. Singer, who found himself playing second fiddle to the smoothly orchestrated broadcast from distant New York, felt a wave of skepticism rising in his throat. He had the sense that all was not as it appeared—that TV itself, the whole operation of which he was so willing a participant, had managed unwittingly to commandeer the event, the perception of that event, for viewers all over the country.

Meanwhile, Mather went on to interview a top biochemist from Canada, aligned with the National Academy of Sciences, who urged caution, reminding Mather that predictions could be premature. A senator from the state of Washington, speaking from CB-9's affiliate studio in D.C., had no place for caution in his agenda and welcomed NSB's news with prose better suited to orgasm. Mather had now opened the show to live call-ins from all over the country.

A real estate broker from Palm Springs phoned up offering to buy whole neighborhoods, referring anyone who'd finally had it with Seattle to his company's eight hundred number.

A cheerful well-wisher from Idaho phoned in and prescribed useful, home-grown hints for curbing insects.

A Seattle teenager named Tammie, whose parents had been vacationing in the Carribean all week, called very confidently. She was a brave young woman, it seemed, who said that she had not been scared, stayed right at home the whole time, in her basement, liked insects, and thought that this whole ozone business was the best thing that ever happened to Seattle because maybe people would wake up and start treating nature with the respect it deserved.

A caller from somewhere in Canada attributed all the panic to the media and wondered how different things might have been had the press left it alone.

A scientologist from Omaha pointed the finger at big business. A Greenpeace volunteer from Arlington angrily singled out the Administration. "These are the same people who suggested that a visor and a shovel would curb a nuclear first strike, remember?"

Mather was not so inelegant or stupid to presume that things were instantly better in Seattle. In fact, he tended to side with the biochemist who had urged caution. The longer Seattle suffered, the more mileage CB-9 could continue to get out of it.

Mather broke for a commercial.

Singer had lost his connection with John. Engineering confirmed that the microwave on John's van below the Needle was not picking up the signal yet. The phone to the bar was dead. Finally, Singer sent a production assistant over to see what was happening.

Minutes before, at about five thirty, Elizabeth and Evans had arrived, just as the first wide aurora of light touched the top of the Needle. All around them, encompassing not only the eastern dawn but those silent shadowy recesses of the west, a broad golden hue, circuitous and animated, enlivened the darkness. It was spectacular to behold, Elizabeth realized, with its multiple folds of pink and soft orange, opening, reformulating like sensuous, stimulated lips. For her, they were the soft funereal colors of tribute to the little girl lying in the backseat. The pernicious blue sky had clouded over this morning, assisted by a chilling wind, and now an honest-to-God blizzard purified the air. It was all too bizarre. Weather. What Seattle was famous for.

John knew that MacIntyre and Wendy should have been at the van by now. He stepped toward the open window frames and screamed down to the street, "Wendy? MacIntyre? . . . Can you hear me?"

He heard nothing in response. He waited five minutes then shouted again. Nothing.

Suddenly, there was a noise out in the corridor. John shouted. "MacIntyre? Is that you?"

There was no reply.

Spooked, John went back to the window and started pulling on the six hundred fifty feet of coaxial cable. It had been mounted on a little plastic and steel mountaineering pulley. He eventually found the end. It had been severed.

The suspicion hit him like a thunderbolt.

"Not a word!" he said, silencing Jason the bartender. He stood half concealed behind a beam support, peering down. But he couldn't see the van. Loder had never come back, he realized. Both MacIntyre and Wendy had disappeared. He went to the phone only to discover it was now dead. Suddenly the video monitor went dead as well, its signal being replaced by black.

"Do you keep a gun?" John whispered to Jason.

Jason pulled out a sawed-off shotgun from under the sink, cocked the trigger with an unmistakable noise, and nodded. He was holding on to it without the slightest trepidation.

"How many bullets?"

"Stupid question. Enough to do the job right," Jason informed him.

"All right then. Just be ready."

"What's goin' on?" Jason asked.

"A real bad guy," John said in petrified quiet.

His chest was pounding. He moved rapidly to the entranceway of the restaurant, motioning to Jason to work with him. Jason laid down the gun on the long varnished bar. They locked the door, shoved furniture into it, then tightened the table and stacked chairs against the door by stringing multiple layers of the steel coaxial cable from opposite beams in the room. They turned off all the lights. Jason unsealed a fire extinguisher, handed it to John, and took a hidden strategic position behind the bar. John took an opposing position, squatting behind the maitre d's booth.

Down below, Elizabeth parked the Volvo near the KCBD van.

She looked at Evans and said, "Okay, go!"

They ran for the entrance, avoiding the increased glare occasioned by the change in weather. It was the unassimilable white glare of a desert. Perspective had vanished, save for the faint lumbering outlines of Seattle's skyline through the snow. Their eyes were brutally sensitive by now. Reflex prohibited looking down, looking up, looking across. They kept their goggles on, and groped through the broken-glass facade.

"I can't believe the snow," she said, shivering out the freeze.

Evans picked up the phone from inside the lobby. He heard no dial tone. The phone was dead. "Phone's not working, Mom."

"Try it from just outside," Elizabeth advised. "And hurry!"

He called the bar from the mobile phone as John had instructed. "Nope." Then: "I say let's just go up." He pushed the button. The elevator was not working either. "Oh, great!"

Evans went outside again and shouted up to his dad. "Dad? Can you hear me?"

With the windows broken and taped, the incoming snow carried Evans's voice several hundred feet up to the restaurant. John was cornered by indecisiveness. Jason sat on the floor tucked up, thoughts inward, just in the range of eye contact with John. Neither of them knew what was best now.

Outside the door to the restaurant, someone else also heard the boy. A man, who'd just jammed the elevator at the sixtieth floor, took off his sunglasses. He was large, wearing a face mask, sporting a well-kept crop of black hair styled back with gel. He was clad in an Italian nylon jumpsuit and tennis shoes.

Now that his partner, the bald man, was dead, he intended to finish the contract properly. He could easily have slipped out of town. But it was a small international community for whom he worked. He was a professional.

John was pumped with fear and the throw weight of sheer direness. Suddenly he let loose with a ferocious holler. "Evans, stay back! Do you hear me? Liz? Get the police, *go, now!*"

Quickly, the man outside the restaurant took a clean solid breath, then pulverized the center of the door with a lightning-quick bolt of his leg.

The door remained closed. He reached in, searching for the knob.

The gun! Elizabeth said to herself down below, panic rising in her legs. She ran for the car, throwing her hand under the driver's seat. A metal edge sliced her skin but she was oblivious to it. Holding the cold implement away from herself, she made for the building.

"Evans, darling, listen to me," she said. "You have to drive the car. It's a stick shift. Can you manage it?"

"I'm not leaving you."

"Evans, don't even think about it. Now, I want you to drive the car to the station. Can you do that? Tell Singer and find the detective. Get people over here. Do it fast!"

"I said I'm not leaving you."

"Honey, please don't fight me on this. You've got to get help, you've just got to!"

"No way, Mom! Dad needs our help now, not in an hour."

"Damn you!"

Evans rushed inside. He was fighting off the cold. He'd mustered every source of strength. With Jennifer in the car, his mom shaking violently in the lobby, and his dad in deep trouble up in the restaurant, he knew he was their only hope. He was aware of the murders, had heard his parents agonizing over alleged government involvement. He put his hand to his mother's arm.

"The stairs! Come on!" he said, hurrying her.

"Evans?" She was bewildered, then gave in.

It was sixty flights to the top and the stairs were usually

273

locked and off-limits to tourists, but this morning the metal door to the rear of the lobby was open. They headed up. Within minutes they were both out of breath.

"Keep going, Mom!" he insisted.

She fell, dropping the gun.

"No, Evans, give it to me!" she said. But he held on to it now.

"Keep going! We gotta hurry! I've got it, Mom."

"Hold it aimed down."

"I've done target practice. Don't worry."

"Who are you! What the fuck do you want!" John yelled from up above.

The man didn't answer. Seeing the way blocked, he took aim at the door handle and blew it away.

"We have a gun, you sonofabitch!"

Jason winced. This novice can't keep a poker face, he thought. He smashed open a bottle of whiskey.

The man outside pushed the table violently. It jammed against the cable. He crawled through the opening to circumvent the impasse before him.

John looked to Jason. "Do it! Do it!"

Jason lunged forward and discharged his weapon. The blast deafened them.

"Got him!" Jason shouted.

"My God!" Elizabeth cried, hearing the voluminous rebound down the shaft of the Needle. She threw her back against the side wall, clutching her head. "John!" she screamed.

"Don't give us away!" Evans hammered back in a frenzied, hushed tone.

The man slid away. His foot had only been grazed.

"I think I got him," Jason said coolly, moving out and closer to the door to check it out, a raised, ready-to-fire gun in one hand, bottle of Scotch in the other. John moved behind him, on his hands and knees, dragging along a useless chair.

The man was two feet to the side, feeling around his toes. A piece of the shotgun's spray had nibbled a small chunk from his heel. No big deal. One more scar. He was duty bound to make a clean sweep of things, but was tired of these creeps and was now starting to have second thoughts. He hadn't counted on their having a shotgun.

The whole week had gone wrong for him. It began as a simple computer break-in, a simulated suicide, and quickly deteriorated into one glaring mishap after another. Covering tracks, taking heat. It was not his fault things didn't work out as smoothly as planned. He felt—if not exactly badly about it, certainly annoyed—liking to do things neat and clean, the way he'd done so many times before. Clean slate, that was his motto all right. Professional, simple, no complications. He had to live with the consequences, no one else; always looking over his shoulder, in his rearview mirror, fake passport, hotel rooms. It could endow a weaker man with a veritable persecution complex. He had to learn Spanish—hated the food. He was the one who always had to explain to impatient contractors. And now this! These family affairs really turned him off. So he had every reason to be mad.

He put his sunglasses back on, steadied his .22 Walther PPK, moved slowly, surely into firing position. "It's a no-win situation, Mr. Gage."

"What do you want?" John shouted, bristling with the first real contact, horrified that the man actually spoke aloud his name. So it's true. It's me they're after! he thought.

Jason, agile despite his years, rolled back toward the bar, motioning John to resume a cloaked position. The man was going to burst through any second, and when he did, Jason intended to nail him. It had been over forty years since his stint in the Korean War, but like pouring a good, stiff drink, he never forgot tactics.

The pause was interminable. The man was giving them time to freak out, to make the first move.

Meanwhile, their pursuer was having thoughts of his own. Whoever had fired that gun knew a thing or two about depth and steadiness of hand. It couldn't have been Gage, he figured, given what he just detected in the TV producer's addled voice. You could rate all sorts of quavers under pressure and this, he reckoned, was a quaver called coward-ice.

"Okay, okay!" Elizabeth whispered, her index finger to her lips.

They'd reached the door at the top, totally out of breath, asthmatic, cut off. They were both seated on the top step. Evans had the gun aimed at the door.

"What are you gonna do!" she murmured inaudibly.

Her son caught his wind and exerted the barest pressure on the door. He had no idea, of course, upon what it would open. He hadn't been up in the Needle at the restaurant in over two years and there had been months of renovations. The whole place was apparently different now. He peered through the crack and saw a short, empty hallway that turned off to the left. It was dark, but not too dark to see. That must be the entrance, he reckoned.

Down below, a production assistant had arrived. Before opening up the van to find out what the trouble was, he saw the thin puddle of blood dripping beneath the door into the fresh snow. He opened the side doors.

"Wendy?" he questioned, seeing a figure.

Turning her around, he saw the hole in the back of her head. MacIntyre was facedown. The production assistant turned, looking up at the dark tower, the horror now drenching him. He was afraid to touch the doors of the station van. He ran to Singer's Volvo—he knew there was a phone in it—only to find those doors locked and a body in the back. His knees gave out. He fell to the ground, his spine suddenly jelly, got back up, walked to his car not looking to either side, got in, started the engine, and skidded away toward the station.

Jason reloaded his weapon. He took a bottle of Napoleon brandy, slid around through the pale light of the interior, coordinated his gestures with John's, and on the count of three hurled the bottle at the demolished door as John tossed the chair. It was certainly no hand grenade, but the smash seduced the visitor into the opening all the same. The

276

man's gun fired, passing through the chair, missing John by inches. John was flat on his stomach, exposed.

"Out of the way!" Jason screamed. He fired again, blasting the shotgun spray all through the opening in the door. He missed.

Outside, Evans made his move, dashing to the edge of the hall just in time to see the figure moving inside. He checked his own impulse to fire. Moving in closer, he kneeled low to the wall.

Jason hurled another bottle.

The man turned, shooting at the direction it had come from. Jason had rolled in closer to John. There was another shot. The force of it pushed him across the floor, numbing the area near his neck, shredding his shoulder, but not so heavily as to prevent his pulling around and blasting his assailant a third time. Again he missed. Out of bullets.

"Goddamn you, fuckin' pig!" Jason screamed.

"That's it, old man. Over there, Gage, move it!" The man stood well over six feet, apparently unaffected by the superficial wound to his foot. He had the menacing shoulders of a linebacker. John could not see the man behind the sunglasses and skintight mask.

"Who are you!" John implored.

The man chuckled at Gage's temerity.

"Shut the fuck up!" he said. "I don't give interviews to reporters."

With a sudden, paralyzing jujitsu kick to John's rib cage, using his workable foot, he corraled the two of them against the far wall, out along the broken glass where strands of tape had marked off the area. Jason's shoulder region was bleeding badly. John was doubled over.

The man took off his sunglasses. There was a glint in his eye.

"Now jump, both of you!" he ordered with a detached savagery, his gun leveled at John's face.

"Or we can do it with a bullet to the brain!" The man was feeling inspired now and thought that it was this sort of inspiration that truly set him apart in his profession from the average "outside consultant."

John didn't blink. Evans was right there, kneeling behind them, his two hands clasping the gun, shaking like a toy poodle after its bath. He extended the weapon clear of the obstacles of furniture at the door. His angle placed his father directly behind the man. There was no other angle.

Jason started, "All right. I got nothin' to lose. I'll jump. I'll be the first."

"Don't talk!" the man screamed.

Elizabeth couldn't stand it any longer. She opened the door to join her son and her husband.

The door creaked as she pushed on it. The man turned toward her.

"Now!" John roared.

Evans fired, holding the weapon with fierce and mindless exactitude.

The man got off two shots, into the ceiling. Evans fired again, hitting him a second time somewhere in the chest as he fell over backward toward John and Jason.

The boy stepped into the restaurant, followed by his mother.

"Kill him!" John demanded, eyes stretched to full fury, jaw stiff, seeing the gun still in the man's hand, pointing wild.

Evans ducked, John and Jason flinging themselves to either side. Then the man's arm went limp. Evans toyed with the trigger on his own gun, pausing.

"I think he's dead all right," Jason said, leaning forward, blood all over his fine white shirt.

John took a deep breath, free, unlabored.

The light of morning had filled the restaurant. It looked like Christmas outside, large snow flakes blowing in through the void where, less than a week ago, Chinese ring-necked pheasants careened.

Both hands still clutching the weapon, Evans stood over the masked figure who lay flat on his back. The man's gun, upon which Evans's eyes were frozen, had slid from the white-gloved grip of the assailant and lay separated a few feet away on the floor.

"He's still breathing, Dad."

Elizabeth stepped up from behind and carefully lifted the gun away from her boy, while John removed the killer's weapon from the floor. Evans turned to his mother. John rose painfully, a wince from his busted ribs, and gathered his remaining family.

Down below, they could hear an approaching siren.

EPILOGUE

In subsequent months Seattle—and the rest of the nation—put the weeklong incident far behind. There were magazine and newspaper stories, of course, implicating various government and corporate culprits in following the coverup that John Gage had exposed. CB-9 in New York managed to extract a few subsequent specials out of the affair. Homeowner policies became prohibitive in the Northwest. The United Nations convened a rather glamorous conference to address tougher global ozone laws.

John and Elizabeth discussed the notion of moving somewhere far away, starting whole new careers. Elizabeth was pregnant. Ultrasound showed it to be a girl.

John read about the physicist and his family from Wales who, fearing the outbreak of nuclear war some years back, had moved to what they considered the most isolated, risk-free island on the planet. The Falklands. A week after the family settled into a remote and private sanctuary, a little farmstead in the middle of nowhere, it was blown to smithereens, the first house hit in the Falklands War. It just went to show you, John remarked.

"I got it," Elizabeth had said.

They buried Jennifer atop Queen Anne's hill, in a shady plot beside her grandparents, who had been found dead in their car along the highway leading to Vancouver a few days after "the incident."

Evans took his long-awaited sophomore year abroad on a ship, happy to get the hell out of the Northwest.

Donald Willard testified before a high-ranking congressional committee in Washington. He informed them matter-of-factly that ozone depletion levels would get worse before they got better.

An impatient senator reminded Willard of the new laws, protocols, and agreements. "At the risk of sounding overly optimistic," the senator said, "may I remind you, doctor, that most of the civilized nations have agreed to curb production of CFC's by the year two thousand?"

Willard was not impressed, however. He articulated his belief that increasing damage had already been set in motion by a chemical chain reaction occurring all across the planet. Too many harmful chemicals were exempt from the new laws. There would be other incidents.

No one wanted to hear that.

For that matter, Willard was tired of hearing himself speak. He retired from the college and took up painting. For the first time since his wife's death Willard started dating again. Eventually he got married—to Stan's widow, Dapple.